Sanctuary

Seeking Asylum Book 1

S. M. Olivier

Independently Published

Copyright © 2020 S. M. Olivier

Cover By: Jenifer Knox
Editing By: Jenifer Knox

I was once an average college student with dreams of the Olympics. A better future had been within my grasp. I was weeks away from graduating from college, and I had just received my invitation to the National Team. Sure, I was still nursing a broken heart and coming to terms with the betrayal delivered to me at the hands of people I once trusted and loved dearly. However, things were finally looking up.

Or so I thought. The news began to report disturbing stories about a new virus. This virus was turning people. The infected became violent and attacking anybody and everybody.

My plans for a relaxing weekend with my friends and family turned into a nightmare. We were told to evacuate to Sanctuary. On our journey to safety, I run into old friends and find myself becoming attracted to them and their friends. I realized that even in the most harrowing of times, I could find solace and affection.

This may be a whole new world and life wasn't going to return to normal anytime soon, if ever, but at least I had five men at my side to face it with.

*** Sanctuary is a contemporary, post-apocalyptic reverse harem, why choose series. This book contains some triggering content that may be sensitive to some readers. ***

Prologue

Eight years ago...

The ice-cold water swirling around my feet was a stark contrast to the hot, humid air pressing down upon us. We sat on a floating dock that bobbed up and down gently in the middle of a large man-made lake. Surprisingly, Trevor and I were the only ones out here.

Almost everyone else was getting ready for the big Fourth of July bash that my grandparents threw every year at their campground. The Cavaliers, Edens, and Harris-Harrisons –my family– had been coming here since before I was born. It became our yearly tradition to visit the campground Nana and Pop-pop had bought after all their "children" had left.

Typically, the campgrounds were for groups. It was a place for church groups and other large groups to come during the offseason. During the summer months, campers started arriving in the second week of June until the end of August. Late fall into late winter, hunters rented out the cabins near the foot of the mountains. Pop-pop and Nana closed it down to the public the week of the 4th for their family.

Pop-pop and Nana Young had raised Scott Cavalier, Mitch Eden, and my Dad, Bryan Harris. Pop-pop and Nana, unable to have children themselves, began fostering children sometime in their late thirties, after having focused on their careers.

They'd had a lot of children come in and out of their home. The young ones seemed to get adopted relatively quickly, but Uncle Scott, Uncle Mitch, and Dad had been eleven and twelve when they were placed with them, almost being too old by many people's standards.

Eventually, Pop-pop and Nana decided to adopt them, and just like that, they were a family. Honestly, my uncles and Dad were more than family, though. They were so close, they even decided to join the military together. This vacation was one of the only times of year that Uncle Mitch and his family could spend time with the family he practically grew up with.

Uncle Scott, Trevor's dad, had been placed in a similar career field, so we were PCSed– Permanent Change of Station – together since my dad had joined. Sometimes the Cavaliers would get their orders first, and other times we did, but eventually we were reunited.

At the age of thirteen, I had lived in four different states and one other country. Granted, I only remembered two of those states, but still, that was an awful lot of moving and making new friends. I used to be able to rely on Emery, my twin sister, and my younger brother BJ– or Bryan Junior – as my friends, but honestly, we were growing apart. Trevor, though, he was my constant. Sadly, we were given orders once again. Uncle Scott, however, hadn't yet.

"I'm going to miss you," Trevor said, his voice softly cracking. I wasn't sure if it was his testosterone or his emotions that made his voice break.

My mom, Aunt Mary, and Aunt Pam became best friends through their husbands. Aunt Pam had been pregnant with Trevor when my mom was carrying me and Emery. And if that weren't enough, they had even gone into labor together as well. Trevor was born twelve minutes before I made my entrance into the world and nineteen minutes before Emery. Our parents called us the Deployment Triplets.

They embarrassed us by telling everyone we were conceived the nights our dads came back from their deployments. Our parents, and even Uncle Mitch and Aunt Carol, were way too affectionate with each other and loved to gross us kids out by all their sexual innuendo and openness.

"I'm gonna miss you, too," I said, trying to hold my tears back. "But at least we have the next three weeks together."

I tried to sound upbeat, even though my heart was breaking. The parents would be leaving by the end of the week, and we would be staying behind to spend some more time with my grandparents. We had been doing that since we were around five or so. However, this year had been more than stressful, and it was a heartbreaking one as well.

This year had been a year of changes. Tough changes. Changes I couldn't have gotten through without Trevor by my side.

It began with my dad and mom deciding to send BJ to a military boarding school. With Dad regularly deploying, he wasn't home often. BJ was three years younger than Emery and me, but four years behind us in school because last year he had gotten out of control and was failing his classes. He had been getting into fights, ditching school, and became a "troubled" child.

Mom tried her best, but BJ was strong-willed and just missed my dad. They put him in the military school thirty minutes from home. Even though he came home on most weekends and holidays, I still missed my basketball buddy.

The military academy was working wonders on him, even though he had only spent nine months there. I had to admit he was more responsible and disciplined, but that didn't mean I didn't miss him, especially now.

"I just wished Emery would hang out with us like old times," he grumbled.

We had been the three musketeers for such a long time that her choice to change had affected him too.

Emery and I had reached a crossroads in our lives, and at the beginning of last summer, it became evident that we were old enough to make our own decisions. Dad encouraged it. Mom hadn't liked it. She had hoped since we were identical twins, we would be like inseparable or something.

I secretly had, too. Mom dressed us identically until we could dress ourselves. After that, she just purchased us the same exact clothing until recently. Ever since we were six months old, though, it had been clear we had two distinct personalities. As we grew, it became apparent that we also had a lot of different interests.

"You know she doesn't think we're cool enough for her anymore." I frowned.

Emery was very much into Barbie and baby dolls. I liked balls, wrestling, and bicycles. Emery hated getting dirty, and I fought my mom over a bath.

Mom and Dad thought we needed to get involved in activities, so they compromised. We'd been modeling since we were born, and when we were three, Mom had us in gymnastics. But last summer, while I went away to gymnastics camp, Emery had gone to cheer camp. It was the beginning of our separation.

It shouldn't have been such a surprise to me that Emery became a cheerleader. As much as I loved her and craved closeness, I was unwilling to become a cheerleader to follow her, and she didn't want to continue doing gymnastics with me.

She also held a grudge against me ever since I'd decided I was done modeling. Dad had a rule in that area, an all or nothing approach. If we both didn't do it, neither one of us could do it. She knew why *I* was done with modeling, but she behaved as if I should just get over it. She was well aware of the circumstances surrounding the decision of why I chose to quit modeling, even if she lived in denial of it. There was a good reason why I chose to quit.

"Do you think it's because of your... mom?' he asked, knowing the subject was still sensitive for me.

It had been months, but I was still known to break down in tears over the topic. I bit the inside of my cheek to prevent the tears from falling.

Watching my brother getting shipped off was hard. Realizing my sister and I were taking different roads had been difficult. But losing my mother had devastated me.

Watching my beautiful mother die had rocked my world. I still felt lost and in a constant state of grief six months later. One day she was okay. The next day her head started hurting her. When she developed migraines, they became unbearable. I had to call the ambulance after a terrifying episode. She visited the doctors, and it was all downhill from there in a blink of an eye. She had an aggressive tumor that took her from us by winter break.

I felt Trevor lean in, and he linked his pinky with mine as if he knew I was wallowing in my grief. He seemed to always be intuitive like that.

"I think that has a lot to do with it," I admitted. "However, I also think she enjoys creating her own identity. I'm just thankful you were there for me. I don't know what I'm going to do without you."

And it was true. I didn't know what I would have done without Trevor. Emery had taken her solace with her new best friends on the cheerleading squad. BJ didn't want to be home; instead, he took comfort with his new friends at the military academy. Dad had come back early from his deployment and had only stuck around for a month after Mom died.

Dad tried to tell us that the military owned him. He had to go back. I knew it had been hard for him to lose his wife, his best friend so quickly. I knew it was hard to look at Emery and me and not see my mom. Everyone said we were the spitting image of her.

Eventually, Emery and I moved in with Aunt Pam. We had been living there for the last six months, and Trevor had been my only constant. Dad had just gotten back from his deployment three weeks ago and told us about the move. A move I had to make with just Dad and Emery, since BJ decided he wanted to stay in the academy.

While we stayed part of this summer with our grandparents, Dad would be packing the house up. When he picked us up, we would be moving into our new home. At least I would have BJ there in the new house until the end of the summer to help me adjust to my new life.

"We'll be joining you soon," Trevor spoke again.

I knew that was wishful thinking and not a guarantee.

I looked over at him. When had I developed a crush on my best friend? I mean, I knew he was always cute, with his ash-blond hair and soulful brown eyes, but he had always been so skinny and was just a few inches shorter than me. Emery and I had always been tall for our age, and although Uncle Scott was six-foot-two, Aunt Pam was only five-one. Up until a few months ago, everyone thought Trevor, the youngest Cavalier boy, wouldn't be as tall as his dad or brother. But then he'd hit a growth spurt.

He wrestled, and his coach encouraged his team to lift weights. It seemed like he had grown to my height and filled out into his lean frame overnight. Suddenly, his voice became deeper, and I wasn't the only one to notice the changes. The girls at school started to see it as well. I saw it in the way they were suddenly talking to him.

"I hope so." I sighed, brushing my tears away. "I don't want to lose you, too. Dad doesn't even think he'll be there long enough to settle in. He says he might have to deploy again. He's started to look for a live-in nanny for Emery and me."

"You'll never lose me," he promised fervently. "I promise I'll call you every day. I'm sure Dad will get his orders soon, too."

I tried to pretend I wasn't hyper-aware every time his feet brushed mine. After the fifth time, I looked over him. His soulful eyes were intent on my face. Why was he looking at me like that?

He reached over and cradled my face. His thumbs wiped my tears from my cheeks, as he had done several times since the loss of my mom. He had touched me in comfort, and he had helped me in the dark of the night when my nightmares plagued me. However, this touch was different. There was this hum of awareness crackling between us.

Where did that come from?

He leaned in, and I knew what was coming—my first kiss. I closed my eyes, as I had seen the girls do in the movies, and felt the gentle brush of his lips on mine. We kissed like that for several moments before I felt his tongue push against my lips. I opened my mouth, and my eyes widened as I felt his tongue enter my mouth. It was...different. It wasn't unpleasant, but I never really thought about what it would feel like to have a boy's tongue in my mouth. It was a little wet and sloppy, but it'd get better with practice. Right?

I mentally shrugged. That was okay. I knew Trevor had kissed Cathy Muster last summer, and it had been his first kiss and crush. They dated for a few months, but he was thirteen, what did he know about kissing?

I had seen our affectionate parents kiss. I also saw Corbin Cavalier sneak in a string of girls when his mother was working the night shift at the hospital since we moved in with them. He was five years older than us and was considered a player. In the six months that I had been living with the Cavaliers, I didn't think I'd ever seen the same girl twice. Corbin loved making out, and he didn't seem to care if

Trevor and I walked in on him and his girlfriends in the many scandalous positions that went passed kissing.

I had been beyond embarrassed numerous times, but Corbin didn't seem to care. He seemed to be overly confident that Trevor, Emery, and I would never say anything. We didn't, and we wouldn't, but he was braver than I could ever be.

Trevor reached out and I felt his warm hands caress my tanned hips and over my ribs. It felt really good to feel his fingers on my bare skin. I knew I made a sound of pleasure. Suddenly, I was thankful for Aunt Pam insisting that my dad allow us to wear bikinis. Up until this summer, we had always worn one-pieces.

Mom and Dad might have had zero compulsions with their public displays of affection and weren't shy in letting us know how they loved their "adult time," but they wanted us to dress modestly. When we modeled, they were strict with what shoots we were able to take. Secretly, I wished they had been just as severe with who they trusted to monitor us while we were on the job.

Mom and Dad had discussed a lot of the things they felt were age-appropriate for us as we grew up. However, Mom knew Dad was going to fight to keep us as his little girls as long as possible and had enlisted Aunt Pam's help with these matters. Mom had written letters and had given them to Aunt Pam in the event that he needed to be reminded of her wishes.

Mom had told Aunt Pam that she would allow us to wear makeup- in moderation- our freshman year of high school. She also said she would let us wear bikinis by that point. We were going to be freshmen this fall, and Pam had talked to my Dad in permitting us to wear them.

I had picked out a modest bikini, one you'd see on women volleyball players. It had a blue and black razorback top and a pair of matching boy-cut shorts. Emery had pushed her luck with a bright red, halter-top bikini with matching string bikini bottoms.

Dad had nearly flipped when he realized he no longer had little girls. This past year we had filled out quite a bit. Our breasts had developed more, and since we were both athletic, you couldn't miss the fact that we had long, lean legs and a great butt to go with them. Not that I cared. In fact, when my boobs filled out, I had been disgruntled. I had gotten unwanted attention, and I had to suddenly be conscious of what leotards I purchased so that my girls wouldn't flop out.

I was yanked back from my thoughts as Trevor laid back, pulling me towards him so that I was now draped halfway across him. I was surprised to find out that I liked lying on him like this. He pulled away from me for a moment before he latched onto my neck. The initial contact felt good, and I let out a breathy sigh.

He must have taken that as a sign to continue, because his hands were cupping my breast. He was a bit clumsy in his movements, and I tensed for a moment. He was fumbling with his hands, and although I was happy he was as inexperienced as I was, it felt uncomfortable.

"No finesse, baby bro," Corbin's deep voice said with humor.

I squeaked and hastily stood up. I covered my bared stomach and looked towards Corbin, suddenly very self-conscious about my near-naked condition.

I knew I must've been beet red, even underneath my tan. I nearly groaned aloud when I noticed he wasn't alone. Wyatt, Emery, Ashlynn, and Cara- or was it Cora?- was with them.

Wyatt Eden was almost five years older than us, like Corbin. When those two were together, they were trouble. They also were man whores. Wyatt's parents were more... open-minded, so they allowed Wyatt to bring his girlfriend, Cara, Cora- or was it Carey?- this summer.

I was utterly shocked when Aunt Pam and Uncle Scott had allowed Ashlynn, Emery's friend, to accompany us. They knew Corbin had expressed an interest in her. However, I was certain Aunt Pam didn't understand how her oldest son *was* with girls.

Emery had helped him with that conquest. Ashlynn was going to be a junior this year. She was also a popular cheerleader. Emery had just come home from cheer camp last week, and she and Ashlynn were like best friends now. Of course, Corbin had capitalized on their friendship, since he wanted to get in Ashlynn's pants.

I was just surprised that Emery was helping them out, since I knew she'd had a crush on Corbin for the last two years. Emery was a little more boy crazy then I was and had been all googly-eyed with guys for years now. I never really paid them much attention.

Especially after my experience, and I was too busy being a tomboy and playing with the boys. Boys my age had zero maturity level. They had belching contests. Laughed when they farted. Don't get me wrong, I laughed, but they were gross. Thus the reason why I hadn't looked at many boys or cared to get to know them.

"Shut up, Cor," Trevor mumbled as he stood up and placed his arms around my waist.

That was new. Sure, we had hugged and wrestled around before, and he comforted me a lot when I had cried over the loss of my mother and through those dark nights. However, there hadn't been this tension, this awareness before. I kind of liked it.

Wyatt and Corbin looked at each other and started to laugh. Corbin and Wyatt were the oldest out of the Young "grandchildren." They always had a penchant for mischief and always teased us younger kids when they were together.

Up until we had moved in with them, Corbin had teased

us mercilessly. Things had changed after we lost Mom, though. There were weeks after she passed that Corbin would hang around Emery and me, but he hadn't teased us. I think he didn't want to tease the girls that had just lost their mother and wanted to be there for us silently.

It wasn't until a few months ago that things changed between us. It was like Emery, Trevor, and I didn't exist to Corbin. He seemed too busy living up his senior year of high school. At the beginning of the summer, Emery had started Operation Get Corbin Cavalier. They became friends, but I don't think Corbin was aware of her flirting.

"Aren't you guys cousins?" Ashlynn asked with a disgusted look. "Isn't that what you told me and Cara, Em?"

"That's really gross," Cara added. I remembered now. It *was* Cara.

My embarrassment was soon replaced by indignation. How dare they make fun of us? I knew the only reason they were out here was because of Wyatt and Corbin, who must've wanted to take a swim. We had just arrived yesterday, and Ashlynn, Cara, and our other cousin Katie were still in the stage where their beauty outweighed their comfort. They didn't want to get wet and ruin their hair and makeup.

Emery was now permitted to wear makeup and was a follower when it came to the older girls, so she had decided to emulate them, refusing to swim, too, saying the water was gross, and she didn't want to ruin her hair and makeup. She had no such compunction last year. What had changed?

They had spent all day yesterday laying out on the shoreline in their bikinis, getting tan, and hoping to get the boys' attention. BJ and Mitch Junior, MJ, had been the only ones to join us. Dad, Uncle Mitch, and Uncle Scott had promised to take them fishing in the other lake today, so they weren't around.

Aunt Pam had excused me from cooking duty, so Trevor

and I had rushed down here to get cooled off. When I had left the cabin, the girls had been getting ready. When I asked them if they were swimming today, they had laughed at me—well, Katie and Emery hadn't, but they hadn't stopped the other two from teasing me either.

I was just trying to be kind, and I still didn't understand the concept of wearing a bikini if you had no plans on swimming. It was so oppressively hot. There was no way I was trading in my comfort for makeup and perfectly straightened or curled hair.

"We're not blood cousins," I scoffed out crossly. "And I hate to break it to you, but you look like raccoons with your make up running. Also, you wasted over two hours this morning getting ready for no reason, since your precious hair is all jacked up now."

I think I heard Wyatt and Corbin snort behind their hands, but I wasn't confident, since my eyes were glaring at the girls.

I looked over at Katie and Emery. Why weren't they defending us? I knew for a fact that they both had a crush on Corbin. I heard them talk about him while Ashlynn and Cara had been up to breakfast in the "big" cabin, AKA Nana and Pop-pop's house.

Corbin shrugged again and laughed. "Hey, Wy?" He gave Wyatt a wicked glance. "Wanna show this young pup how a girl should be handled?"

"I feel it's our duty," Wyatt said with an answering grin.

As if they had rehearsed it, they turned and grabbed Cara and Ashlynn, who tilted their heads backs to accept their passionate kisses. When the guys started caressing the girls from hips to breasts, I reluctantly had to admit the girls looked thoroughly pleased. The guys had a...delicate touch. I turned my head, embarrassed for watching with rapt attention.

"See how I did that?" Corbin said with a smug smile. "I wasn't pawing Ashlynn like I was trying to wrestle her. I was softly caressing her body. I didn't stuff my tongue into her mouth. It's all a dance, bro."

"Whatever," Trevor muttered.

Trevor would never admit to Corbin or his parents that he had always envied his brother. Corbin was outgoing, charismatic, athletic, and intelligent. Trevor was more reserved, had just started wrestling, and although he was smart, he just had to work harder at getting good grades.

He confided in me all the time about stuff like that. He felt inferior to his brother. He also told me he missed him. They had once been close, but a few years ago, Corbin discovered girls and didn't have as much time for him anymore. Corbin still hung out with him from time to time but not as much as Trevor wished he would.

"Look, Trev." Corbin sighed as if he realized he had thoroughly embarrassed his brother. "I'm sorry if I hurt your feelings. Just thought I'd give you a few pointers."

I could see the mortification in Trevor's gaze, especially when the girls giggled at him. I turned in his arms. "He doesn't need your pointers, Cor," I seethed as I put my hands on my hips. "Did you tell Ashlynn that she's just the flavor of the week? Come next week, you'll have another girl on your couch or maybe even in your bed. I've already lost count how many girls I've witnessed you 'practicing' on." I did air quotes before I turned to grab Trevor's hand. "Trevor and I can figure out what makes us happy without your pointers, thank you very much." I tugged on Trevor's hand. He gave me a thankful smile. "Let's go somewhere else."

Corbin was looking at me with narrowed eyes by the time I finished my little speech. Wyatt was laughing. Cara looked bored. Katie looked stunned. Emery looked mortified. And Ashlynn... Ashlynn was glaring at me.

I was about to dive into the water when Ashlynn snorted. "Sweetheart, maybe that's all I want, a good lay. Maybe I don't care if I'm just the flavor of the week," she mocked.

"Good for you." I clapped mockingly. "I'm sure your mom and dad are proud that you have zero self-respect."

"Lighten up, Ave," Emery huffed as if I had just embarrassed her.

"Don't talk about my parents," Ashlynn sneered. "Maybe your daddy shouldn't be running away from you guys all the time, and maybe your mommy should teach you to be as cool as your sister."

I felt like she had physically hit me as tears entered my eyes. The pain was still too new. Didn't Emery tell her about Mom? How did she explain her absence?

"Ashlynn!" Corbin barked out with a fierce look, all laughter gone from his features.

"My mother's dead, you whore," I said hollowly before I dove into the lake, not caring if Trevor followed me into the water or not.

He had.

Later on, Trevor and I spent most of the day avoiding everyone. No one tried to seek us out, which was fine with me. Trevor and I just had more time to make out without anyone bothering us while I licked my wounds.

Chapter 1

Present Day...

"Earth to Avery!" Sylvia crowed in my ear. "Why do you look like someone just ran over your dog, ate the last ice cream sandwich, told you the Monster factory blew up, or you just realized you were ragging after Danny Scully wanted to hook up with you? You just placed first! First!" she squealed.

I didn't have a dog. I preferred those strawberry shortcake popsicles over ice cream sandwiches. I lived off coffee, while she lived off Monsters. And I never had a crush on Danny, she had. She'd had crushed on Danny for years and knew he had a thing for me since freshman year.

"I am stoked," I said as I looked out of the fifteen-passenger van window, thankful when the driver started the engine. The sooner I got home to my bed, the sooner I could find a new band-aid. The old one just ripped off.

Sylvia had placed second in poomsaes, and still it hadn't fazed her. She frowned dramatically, then gave me a broad, creepy smile. She continued to make these freaky faces for several minutes. I knew she was just trying to cheer me up.

I attempted a smile, but I was struggling with it. Sylvia was usually really good at pulling me from my pity parties, especially when she was in this type of mood. She was the proverbial optimist.

Even when her life wasn't going the greatest, she always

found the positive: If she got a flat tire, at least she still had a car. She was late for class? Maybe fate wanted her to be late. She had a pop quiz she wasn't prepared for. Who cares? At least she passed another one.

Her optimism could be contagious sometimes.

"Beast!" my coach exulted as he hopped into the passenger seat. He turned in his chair and beamed at me, holding out his fist for a fist bump. "I think that sealed it. The Olympics are in the bag for you."

To most females in their early twenties, the nickname Beast would be an insult. To me, it was a well-earned nickname. Especially since Coach was one of the harshest critics to please. He was demanding, overbearing, insufferable, and I loved him for it. I didn't think I would have gotten as far in martial arts if it wasn't for him.

Without his coaching, I wouldn't be where I was today athletically. He had faith in me since he saw me compete six years ago. He nearly got me to the Olympics four years ago, and with his pushing and critiques, I was in better shape and faster than I was back then.

"Thanks, Coach." I tried to smile once more, but I had never been a great actor. I tapped my fist with his.

Dad and Mom used to say I wore my heart on my sleeves, while Emery was destined for Hollywood. She could convince you the sky was green, all with a straight face, or turn on the waterworks on cue. I had never learned the art of deception. As a child, it had amused me. As a teen, it had exasperated me. As an adult, it sickened me.

Coach Rich frowned. "What's wrong?"

"Nothing," I muttered. I looked out the window, urging my team to hurry.

Most of them had friends and family to kiss and hug goodbye. Even though the majority of the team had driven themselves or had friends attending, Coach insisted that we ride together on qualifying days.

In the reflection of my window, I saw Coach exchange a look with Sylvia. Her answer was a look of befuddlement and a shrug.

Sylvia and I met when I moved to Maryland eight years ago. She became one of my best friends almost immediately. There weren't any reputable gymnastic gyms locally, and our nanny Bernadette hadn't been willing to drive me to the closest gym over an hour away, so she had introduced me to her nephew. who was an amazing artist and I was enthralled enough to give it a try. Overnight, somehow, I'd gone from being a gymnast to a martial artist..

I had met Sylvia a week after I joined her Tae Kwon Do school. We clicked almost immediately. I was ecstatic to find out she went to my school, too, and more than happy to let her take me under her wing.

It was the first time Emery thought we needed to make new friends, not share our circle like we had done since kindergarten. She wanted to have her own identity. I understood, but still. I had felt isolated for nearly a week until Sylvia changed that.

Emery had become popular almost immediately. That was her. She loved being the center of attention. I liked having a small group of loyal friends. Always had, always would. I wasn't comfortable with getting recognition for the sake of getting attention. I thrived on the sparring floor, but I barely noticed the audience. I was there for the sport.

The last guy on our team, Simon, boarded the van with a broad smile and slid in next to Sylvia. "Killin' it like always, Avery." He smiled at me before leaning over Sylvia with both of his fists out.

"You too, Simon." I feigned another smile and tapped my fist against his.

Simon had been added to our team about three years ago. He went to the same college Sylvia and I did and was someone else I would credit my success to. He ate, slept, breathed training. He pushed me to become a better fighter.

When he sparred with me, he never held back. Unlike many men that I have fought against, he wasn't afraid to push me. I appreciated that. He beat me eight times out of ten, but I was okay with that. There was a reason they separated females from males in these tournaments.

"Drinks, tonight," he whispered loudly.

"Yes!" Sylvia squealed. "We need to check that new club out on tenth."

"Don't drink too much," Coach warned us.

I swear that man had supersonic hearing.

I shrugged. "Maybe. I still got to study for finals on Monday."

I was only using it as an excuse. I was never a big drinker. I would drink on occasion, but in my vulnerable state, I was afraid I would use it as a crutch again.

I knew what had happened last time I felt this... heartbreak. I went wild. I drank. I hooked up with random guys. Granted, it was only three guys, but it was three too many, in my opinion, since I never even established a friendship with those randos before sleeping with them.

Sylvia groaned. "No, just no! You've been too hard on yourself lately. You've done nothing but work, do clinicals, go to school, and train. We *need* tonight, Ave!" she whined.

It was true, I had been really focused lately, but I had a reason. The finish line was in sight. Today clenched plan A. Next week was plan B. If I passed all my finals, it was going to be official—I'd be an RN.

I had the luxury of not rushing my career thanks to my previous profession at modeling and my inheritance. Plan A was making it to the Olympics, since money wasn't a huge factor for me. The degree I was going to receive in nursing was my plan B. After I reached my first dream, I could pursue my other goals in life.

Right now, I needed to focus on Nationals which were right around the corner. After that, we would start competing internationally. God willing, in the next month or so I would be officially on team USA or working in a hospital several hundred miles away.

There were too many memories here in this state. Even a lot of good ones, but the bad had made all the good ones obsolete. I couldn't even go to the local coffee shop without remembering the last time Trevor had come to visit me and we'd snuggled up on the couch, making our summer plans.

Uncle Scott had eventually gotten orders to Andrews Air Force base. Trevor had moved near me by our sophomore year in high school, and finally we were reunited with our family and friends once more. They got a house near us, and Trevor attended our school. After a few months, Trevor and I had picked up where we'd left off the summer before. We became official.

When our college acceptance letters began coming in, we had to make some decisions. Did we make our relationship work, despite our different college choices, or did we break up? We decided to try and make our relationship work long-distance. We had been together for three years by that point.

We both received scholarships for two different schools. They were two hours apart, so it wasn't too bad to make the commute on the weekends.

We had made it work for almost three years, then in a blink of an eye, it had all went up in smoke. Or should I say, it went up in flames because I'd been burned.

"Are you going to answer that?" Sylvia asked me.

"Huh?" I looked over at her in confusion.

"Your phone," Sylvia stated, looking at me with more concern.

In order to get to my phone, I had to bypass that stupid, dreadful cardstock that had been cleverly concealed in a beautifully embossed envelope addressed to me. Earlier, on the way out the door of the three-bedroom apartment I shared with Sylvia and our roommate Lucy, I had spotted my mail in my basket and foolishly grabbed it, stuffing it in my bag in a hurry to get going.

I had been so busy lately and was never able to read my mail. So before the tournament, I headed straight to the van without stopping to talk to anyone as my teammates had. I had no one waiting for me and had come to terms with that fact long ago.

While I had waited in the van, I scrolled through social media, knowing Sylvia and my teammates had recorded my last match. It had been a tough one, and the other woman had made me work for the win. My hands had brushed my mail, so I thought I would get that out of the way first. I wish I hadn't.

If ignorance was bliss, I desired to remain ignorant. I would have been perfectly happy staying that way.

"Oh..." I startled, realizing my phone was in my duffel bag tucked under the seat. I tried to conceal the shaking in my hands, tried to swallow the tears that threatened to fall.

I didn't want to think about that stupid piece of mail or what it had included.

☐

I took out my phone and released a breath as I checked the first message.

Papa Bear: Just saw the video and pictures Sylv posted. You are a rock star! So proud of you!!! :-*

A real smile crossed my face. Dad was ecstatic when I

told him I wanted to join Tae Kwon Do. He always embraced my "tomboy" side. It had been no secret that I had been a daddy's girl since I could first walk. When he was home, I was always following him around.

Emery had been a mama's girl. They had been so similar. They liked everything "girly." It wasn't until the beginning of the school year that I decided to reinvent myself. I found out I actually *did* like looking like a girl. I started wearing makeup more, even owned several skirts and dresses.

Our brother BJ, however, kind of just went with the flow. His relationship with Dad was great now, but there had been many years he wouldn't even talk to him. The loss of my mother and Dad's constant absence had been detrimental to their relationship.

Me: Thanks, Dad :-* Are you still coming to my graduation in three weeks?

I looked off for a moment. Dad was coming home next week. I was graduating first, then BJ, then Emery. He had to do a lot of traveling when he was home this time, but I knew Stephanie, our new stepmom, wouldn't mind.

Dad had been mostly stateside for the last four years and had met Stephanie, a young widow, two years ago. She had two young boys herself. I wasn't ecstatic about their relationship at first, but I had grown to love the boys. The jury was still out for Stephanie.

It wasn't like she was a horrible woman. In fact, she was terrific for my father. She doted on him and breathed new life into him. It was just a bitter, hard pill to swallow, accepting a new woman when you believed your parents were soul mates. It was hard to acknowledge that my dad could love another.

At the end of the day, though, I had to accept it and accept it soon. Stephanie was pregnant with my little sister. It was kind of surreal, in so many ways, to know that I would be a big sister to a baby.

If I—I started to think but quickly shut those thoughts down. It hurt too much to think of that, even now. What had followed had been debilitating.

I focused once more on my conversation with Dad. A month ago, he was called overseas for a secret mission. I had no clue where he was or what he was doing, but I couldn't wait to see him.

Papa Bear: I wouldn't miss it for the world! Have you talked to Emery lately?

I sighed. He had been trying to mend our relationship for a while now. He knew we had grown apart long ago and even understood why I hadn't talked to her in nearly a year now, but he still held out hope that I would forgive her. I couldn't.

In retrospect, I knew the loss of Mom had changed Emery irrevocably. I knew the strain of not having our own separate identity for most of our lives and knew it had been hard on her. High school had been the beginning of the end of our close relationship. Her decision to go to another college had dug our grave. Her betrayal had nailed the nails in her coffin. She was dead to me.

I knew it was a bit dramatic, a bit Godfather-ish even, but I didn't care. Some things couldn't be forgiven. There were choices people made that sealed their fates in your life.

It hurt me more than anyone would ever understand.

Emery and I may have been night and day, but that whole twin telepathy thing had been real for us for many years. When I had my tonsils removed as a child, she had felt the pain I had gone through. And once, in our senior year of high school, she had gone skiing with a bunch of friends. I had woken up in a cold sweat, my leg in spasms. I told Dad I thought something was wrong. Less than an hour later, her friends called. She was in an accident and had broken her leg.

But where I embraced our connection, she had shunned it.

It wasn't the first or last time that had happened between us. I always felt this weird bond with her. Even though I was never willing to become who she wanted me to be growing up, I had at least embraced our differences. She hadn't. She always acted like I had been rejecting it one moment, then angry when someone confused her for me. She had always wanted to have her cake and eat it, too.

I finally responded to my father.

Me: No

I kept my answer short. He wouldn't push. He was awesome like that. I knew he would never give up, but he knew when to quit.

I continued to go through my messages, "feeling the love" as family and friends reached out to congratulate me on my win. My friends and family might not physically be there for my tournaments, but they were there emotionally.

I opened my next message, and my heart clenched once more. Reluctantly, I read it.

Aunt Pam: Congratulations, baby. I knew you could do it. Can you come to dinner next Sunday? Trevor won't be home...

Aunt Pam had taken on the role of my mother after Mom passed. She and Mom had been so much alike, and it comforted me to have her around. Uncle Scott and Aunt Pam had purposely purchased a house in the same neighborhood as us for that reason.

She had been so happy when Trevor and I started dating. She told me she always knew we were meant for each other and had confided in me that she and my mom had been planning our weddings since Tommy Messina had pulled my hair in the fourth grade, after which Trevor had punched him in the face, defending me.

She had helped Trevor pick out my promise ring during my freshman year of college. She shopped with him for my actual engagement ring. She always told me that Emery and I were the daughters she always wanted, but I was the daughter-in-law she hoped to have.

She had a great relationship with Emery, but I gravitated towards their family more. Especially on Sundays. I had attended church with them every week and had dinner with them afterward. Sundays were family days in the Cavalier household, whether Uncle Scott was there or not.

No plans were ever to be made on Sundays by the Cavalier boys. Even after Corbin joined the military, when he was home, he was always there.

I craved some normal family bonding. The invitation was always open for us to attend. When BJ was home on the weekends, he would tag along with me and Trevor. Emery had turned her back on that tradition by the tenth grade. She was too busy with her friends to care about family dinners.

I hadn't been to a family dinner since Trevor and I had broken up. I wasn't able to talk to Aunt Pam for months after the demise of our relationship. I had deactivated all my social media accounts until competition season began this past winter. I couldn't answer phone calls or text for weeks after we broke up—I just couldn't be reminded of all that I had lost.

With time, I eventually talked to her, but it wasn't the same. It would never be the same again.

Me: Maybe I can stop by for a little while. Mikey and I have a birthday party to go to.

Mikey was my youngest stepbrother. He was eight years old, and ever since he found out I was into martial arts, he became...attached to me. Dad got Mikey and Miller into martial arts, but Miller preferred the indoors and gaming. He went to classes, but he didn't love it like Mikey did.

Mikey quickly became my little buddy. Whenever I was at Dad's, I always made it a point to spend some time with my step-brother. He had suffered from my break up, too. I tried to make the three-hour drive home as often as possible. Mainly since my Dad was away, and Steph was so close to given birth. It was a great excuse to briefly escape from college life and help Steph out so she could have some much-needed time to herself.

I often took the boys out on Saturdays. We would hit up the arcades, movies, or pretty much anything else that gave Steph a few hours to herself. This weekend, the plans were to go to a place that specialized in climbing trees and ziplining. I was excited to see my brother BJ, too. He was just as stoked to accompany us.

I told Mikey I would take him to his friend's birthday party on Sunday before I headed back to college. I came to the realization that the busier I was, the easier it was for me to forget. Spending time with my siblings was the greatest way for me to keep occupied.

Aunt Pam: Please do. I miss you.

Me: I miss you too.

I bit my lip, trying to hold the tears at bay once more. One would think ten months was enough time to mend a broken heart, but it wasn't. Life had a way of laughing at me when I thought I was going to be okay again.

People never realized how much someone was imprinted onto their lives until they were gone. The simplest things—smells, sounds, shows, and songs—could dredge up old memories. I had given Trevor almost six years of my life as his girlfriend, and we had been best friends since our daycare days. That was a lot to forget, a lot to try to get over.

"No way, no way, no way!" Sylvia now squealed. "Please tell me this means what I think it means!"

I was brought out of my memories as Sylvia shoved her

phone in my face and continued to bounce up and down like a child strung out on too much sugar.

I took her phone, confused at what I saw at first, until I realized she was on Facebook.

Why, oh, why? Life, can you stop kicking me?

I didn't need what was in that card this morning. I didn't want to talk to Aunt Pam. And I definitely didn't need to see Corbin Cavalier's post. There was a reason I deleted him from my social media accounts.

Suddenly Sylvia frowned. "I'm sorry, Avery. I know you don't like to know what the Cavalier family is doing, but we're... still friends."

I really couldn't get mad at her. Sylvia had grown up in a broken home. Her life was worse than mine. My dad might have been gone all the time, and my mother had died, but Sylvia's father was in jail, and her mother was on drugs, an addict in the worse way. Sylvia had practically lived with me since we were fifteen, right after my dad had found out about her home life.

She got to meet Pop-pop, Nana, the Edens, and the Cavaliers the summer after I met her. Surprisingly enough, Wyatt and Corbin were able to take leave that summer too. They had joined the service together as their fathers had, and, ironically, they were still together to this day.

It didn't surprise me that Sylvia had fallen under the Mischief (Corbin) and Misfit (Wyatt) spell almost immediately. Sylvia was still just as boy crazy as Emery, if not more. She had lusted after Corbin and Wyatt immediately.

It was that summer that I realized the M & M–Mischief and Misfit– had changed. Where did the annoying boys and carefree teens go? In their place were men. Corbin had filled out. He had a large frame at six-foot-three and two hundred and twenty-five pounds of hard muscle. His long ash-blond hair had been shorn close to his head, due to the military. I'd also realized for the first time how unique his eyes were. They weren't soulful brown like his brother's. Instead, his eyes were a pale jade green one day, and a light steel-gray the next.

Misfit, Wyatt, had always been tall and lean. He was about six-foot-two, and before that summer, he had weighed around one-thirty, max. His first year in the military had helped him gain about forty pounds of muscle. He was still lean, but he had muscles where bones were once prevalent. The military also made him cut his glorious russet-brown, wavy hair. Unlike Corbin, though, he kept some length on the top of his head. I'd always noticed Wyatt's bright emerald green eyes since we were kids and still had never seen eyes as green as his.

"I didn't expect you to unfriend them," I admitted truthfully. "Just because I did, didn't mean that you had to," I murmured. I looked more closely at her phone. "What's this?"

It was just a picture of six rucksacks, six pairs of boots, and six M-4s leaning against the wall.

"Well," she had hesitantly. "It's Corbin's way of letting his friends and family know he's coming home."

Sylvia had grown out of her crush of M&M and had become friends with them. By her second summer at the campground, things had changed more so. M&M no longer treated us like pests. They hung out more with the men, but they still had time to hang out with us "kids."

Sylvia had exchanged numbers with them and soon were occasionally talking. Every time they deployed, we had sent M&M care packages. They had been part of some top-secret team for years now. For their last mission, they had left shortly after our Fourth of July get together—the one I had attended. This last one, though, I hadn't participated.

"That's great," I faked enthusiasm.

It *was* great, but I had been avoiding Corbin since my breakup. He had reached out several times, but in my irrational belief, I blamed him for Trevor's behavior. Trevor always looked up to him, and Corbin had always been a manwhore. Granted, Corbin never dated– that I knew of– and was still up front with the girls he hooked up with, but I had this belief that Trevor envied the variety of girls Corbin had been with.

It wasn't until after I had broken up with Trevor that I found out that the couple of times we had taken a "break," he'd been with other women. Whenever we took breaks, I assumed it was to get our feelings and heads sorted out. I loved Trevor. Never had I entertained the thought of being with another guy.

I had found out from Emery, since they went to the same school, that he had taken our breaks literally and found other girls to warm his bed. Her not telling me showed me how very different we were. I would have told her in a heartbeat. She honestly thought it had been no big deal.

We had taken a break, not broken up, twice. Both times she was aware of his behavior, and both times she never thought to tell me. If I had known last year that he'd done that to me, I would have called it quits then. So many things had happened between our break and the final break up. I would have still been hurt, but I didn't think I would be as devastated as I was now.

"He's been asking about you," Sylvia confessed quietly. "Wyatt too. They miss you."

I looked down at my hands. "It's hard," I confessed. "There are too many memories. I can't see Corbin without seeing Trevor. I can't talk to Wyatt without him talking to me about Cor."

Sylvia snorted. "I don't see how. You know Trevor was always the replica, while Corbin was the real deal. Trevor was...cute, but Corbin is hot."

I looked over at her, slightly surprised she was going down this road again. The last time we had hung out with Corbin and Wyatt was three years ago, and Sylvia had sworn they were vying for my attention. She was convinced they both liked me. At the time, I had laughed at her. I was happy with Trevor, and Corbin and Wyatt always treated me like a younger sister.

She had been Team Trevor back then. Now she had changed teams since Trevor had dragged me through hell.

"You know," she said slyly, "when we go visit Steph and the boys, we should swing by Aunt Pam's. I'm sure Corbin will be home by then. You know they're moving into their new place."

I sighed and looked around. I was happy to see my other seven teammates were animatedly talking amongst themselves or sleeping. It had been an early morning, and most of us had left ourselves on the tournament floor today.

"Aunt Pam asked me to come to Sunday dinner," I admitted quietly. "Trevor won't be there. I told her I might stop by."

Sylvia leaned in and hugged me. "Is that why you're so… down? You know it's been almost a year. I think it's time you stopped punishing yourself. And Aunt Pam and Uncle Scott, too."

The Cavaliers and Edens had taken to Sylvia immediately and now accepted her as family. With the ease that she fit in, one would think she was my sister. Hell, she was more of a sister than my *own* sister had become.

I reached down and withdrew the card once more. I pulled out the cardstock, and I felt my heart rip open. On the glossy cardstock was a professional picture of Trevor. His ash-blond hair perfectly swept to the side; his lean but firm body was leaning into the woman he had replaced me with. He was smiling down at her. The girl was looking up at him with a broad smile in return.

They wore complimenting outfits. He was dressed in a pair of khakis and a white button-up shirt. The sleeves were rolled up, revealing his forearms. She was dressed in a short white dress with thin spaghetti straps. The white was a sharp contrast against her tanned skin, and the length of the skirt was flattering on her long, shapely legs.

The way her head was tilted back and to the side was so familiar. Her medium length, dark brown hair was cut in layers and carefully curled to her shoulders. My hair was long and fell to right below my shoulder blades. I liked the simplicity of my hair, and unless I was going out, I never did anything with it.

Her makeup was done heavily, professionally polished, which made sense since she had several YouTube videos out on how to achieve a flawless look. Me, I was for simplicity. I wore makeup, but I preferred the natural look. Most of the time, all I needed was some mascara and lip gloss.

Her eyes were turned away from the camera, but I knew they were shaped like a cat's eyes, tilting at the corners and were a light amber color. Her hand was possessively touching his chest. A chest that once had been mine to touch.

"Are you shitting me?" Sylvia whispered in horror. "They actually had the gall to invite you to their... wedding?"

"It gets better," I said bitterly, my voice heavy with unshed tears as I showed her the little note that had come with the invite.

Sylvia gaped as she read the note. Her laugh was incredulous and angry. "You're kidding me, right? She wants you to be in the wedding?"

I nodded, wiping away the tears that had finally fallen. It was hard knowing your boyfriend of six years had cheated on you with another woman. It was perfectly reasonable to wonder why. It was easy to compare yourself to her. Typically, the other woman was so much more different than you in looks that you could understand the reasoning, even a tiny bit.

But imagine losing your man to a woman that looked exactly like you. In fact, identical. She might be more... high maintenance and have other hobbies, but in looks and mannerisms, we were indistinguishable.

The day I lost my boyfriend was the same day I'd lost my sister. They had chosen themselves over me. I could've eventually gotten over it, but things had only escalated from the original indiscretion. I understood they had been drinking; Trevor more so than all of them. After all, Trevor had been celebrating his successful finals.

The stories they'd told me were different, and Emery's had changed several times. Trevor said he was drunk that night and had put himself to bed. He woke up thinking it was me going down on him. He thought I had come to visit him.

Emery stated that *she* was drunk and had gone to find her flavor of the week who was in the fraternity with Trevor. They did have rooms beside each other. She said the room was too dark to realize her mistake.

I just couldn't buy the fact that, sometime during having sex, they hadn't realized their *mistake*. My sister said she was drunk, had continued to screw him, and then chose to stay in bed with him.

I had gone over there late that night, fragile and shattered in a million different fragments. Then I'd found them together. No one expected me that night. Imagine my surprise when I saw them both naked in his bed, the smell of sex still heavy in the air.

The house had erupted. Trevor begged for my forgiveness. Emery had pleaded for me to believe her, that she had thought it was her boyfriend.

I chose to walk away. I had so much going on at that time.

I had been at one of the lowest points of my life, and I couldn't face them. They both sealed their fate when I found out a few months later that they continued dating. If they had been so "genuinely sorry," they should have never continued what they'd started that night.

And now Trevor and Emery had the audacity to ask me to stand up with them at their wedding in a few months.

Chapter 2

It took me nearly to the next weekend before I felt somewhat...normal. The grueling week of finals was behind me and come next Friday, I would know whether or not I would receive my diploma. But even with the distractions, I knew I had aced everything.

"Are you ready?" Sylvia asked as she came into my room.

She had been acting strangely all morning, and I wondered what she was up to. When I had confronted her about it, she had denied my accusations. Usually, she was eager to visit my family but today was different. She seemed edgier and appeared too enthusiastic.

"Just about," I informed her. I eyed her suspiciously once more, before I placed a pair of jeans, a sweatshirt, a few tank tops, cut-off jean shorts, hiking boots, socks, and a few extra pairs of flip flops into my duffle bag. I hadn't emptied it entirely, but it was the only bag I had large enough to carry all my things.

"Why are you packing your sais?" Sylvia asked, laughing as she peered down into my bag.

Sais were weapons originating from Japan. Mine were approximately twenty inches long and had a handle like a knife. Each long shaft was blunt but effective in defensive maneuvers. From the handle were two side guards that curved out and up. A sais was initially designed to trap the weapons of an opponent.

In Tae Kwon Do, I practiced with swords, bo staff, and

sais. I was proficient in all three, but I was a master with the sais.

I shrugged. "I promised Mikey I would show him a few more tricks."

I didn't know if I had the time, but outside in my truck was a new set of sais I had just bought him. His birthday had been a couple of weeks ago, and I hadn't made my way down there since then.

"Let's go, let's go," Sylvia urged me. "BJ already texted. He's heading to his last classes!"

Last night, BJ had asked if we didn't mind swinging by his school and picking him up, since his jeep was acting up. It was on the way, so of course I didn't mind. We had always gotten along, and although we had spent a lot of time apart, we had become closer. He had become one of my best friends, and I was touched when he admitted the same sentiments after Trevor and Emery had betrayed me.

"Unlikely." I snorted. "But let me grab my toiletry bag and we can get going."

BJ had just gotten a new girlfriend, who he wanted to bring along, but her parents wouldn't let her travel the two hours with us, especially since they had never met us nor BJ.

I knew he wanted to stay on campus this weekend to be with her, but his loyalty to family was just as strong as mine. We took our promises seriously. He'd already promised Miller and Mikey that he was coming.

I smiled, imagining my brother. BJ was athletic, thanks to military school. He had been attending for the last eight years, but he was also brilliantly smart. He had a way with technology that I envied. He and Miller had a common interest in computers, and BJ had already started teaching our eleven-year-old stepbrother how to code.

While Sylvia and I took Mikey to his friend's birthday

party Sunday, BJ would be spending the day with Miller. The boys might not be our blood, but Dad loved them, and we had grown to love them too.

I grabbed my toiletry bag and remembered last Christmas when Sylvia had joked and said she knew we would be traveling a lot in our future and that was why she had purchased the bag. It didn't look large, but when you opened it up, it fit a lot more than you'd think. My shampoo, conditioner, body wash, loofah, shaving cream, razors, deodorant, some makeup, and even some tampons, fit in there with ease. It had a lot of compartmentalized pockets, making it easy to keep everything organized and together.

It would come in handy when traveling with the National Team, especially now that I had officially gotten the invite Wednesday night. Next month, I'd be heading to Colorado where my training would begin. I would officially be starting a new beginning. Well, *we* would be. Sylvia had been accepted for her poomsaes. She wasn't much of a fighter, but she was graceful in her forms

"I started your truck," Sylvia stated with a smile as she poked her head back into the room. "Also, I put your bag in there."

Sylvia had a little mini cooper, and there was no way we could all comfortably fit in there for the two-hour drive home.

My truck was my baby. I had bought it this past year with the inheritance my grandparents had left me. As if the year hadn't already been hard enough – because, you know, bad things come in threes – I had lost the only grandparents I had ever known. It had been a freak car accident that had immediately killed them. They hadn't even made it to the hospital.

I shook my head of my melancholy thoughts. "Let's go."

I really wanted to put my toiletry bag in my bag, but oh well. Ms. Impatience took the decision out of my hands.

We exited the room where Lucy was on the couch with her boyfriend.

Lucy was pretty cool, as far as roommates went. She always paid her portion of the rent on time and was alright for the most part. She just had an issue with taking things that weren't hers. She often took stuff from our closets without permission or ate the food on our shelves without replacing it.

Sylvia and I could have gotten a two-bedroom apartment, but there hadn't been any available when we were shopping a couple of years ago. We found Lucy on the message board on campus. She was looking for a room, and we had a room to give her, plus she alleviated our expenses.

Mom's life insurance had left me with a nice chunk of change, but I had always been cautious with my spending. Even after Dad gave me the college fund they had been putting away since my birth, I still couldn't splurge. I liked living modestly.

"Have you seen this?" Lucy asked in shock as we headed towards the door.

"What's that?" Sylvia asked.

I was still frowning over the fact that Lucy was wearing my sheer camisole top and short silk pajama shorts. I could see she wasn't wearing anything under them and it perturbed me. I had no problem sharing things, but the problem was she never asked, and in this, I wasn't cool with her wearing my intimate apparel.

"This can't be real news." Sylvia snorted.

"It is!" George, Lucy's boyfriend, insisted. "Those people are cannibals."

"With today's technology, it's probably all edited for a hoax. I just can't believe a reputable network is airing it," Sylvia said in exasperation.

Now my curiosity was piqued. I walked over to see what

looked like a video someone had shot with their cellphone, shaky hand and all. It appeared like they were in a hospital waiting room. I could see several people screaming and panicking as a man in a hospital gown was... Wait. Was he *eating* the face of a girl lying on the ground?

The girl was screaming and trying to fight back. I watched as two men, one a security guard, and the other a male nurse, tried to pull the psycho off the girl. The psycho turned and ripped a piece of the nurse's arm off. Blood projected everywhere as the nurse screamed in pain.

The screaming stopped from the girl before the psycho turned towards the person shooting the recording. I heard the recorder yell out curses and watched as the psycho advanced towards him. The closer he walked, the more I took in the details. He was of medium height, male, in his late thirties-early forties, pale. His flushed face was covered in blood, and his blue eyes were leaking... blood?

The recording was abruptly turned off, and the newscasters appeared on the camera. "When we tried to contact hospital officials, they were unwilling to comment on the incidents. All we know is that the government was called in, and the hospital hasn't been reopened since early this morning."

"I'm pretty sure this was just a one-off instance," the other news reporter stated, barely concealing his scoff. "Remember the bath salts incident years ago? Drugs can do funny things to a person's brain."

"See?" Sylvia stated with a smug smile. "Hoax or drugs. Right, Avery?"

"It's too much of a coincidence," Lucy maintained. "Six people in six different states with the same bizarre behavior?"

"Good thing it wasn't our state," Sylvia said flippantly. "We'll see you Sunday night, George and Lucy. Remember, no screwing in our beds," she teased.

Yes, the screwing in our beds had actually happened. I had been so infuriated when I had found out that they'd had sex on my bed one weekend. Without changing the sheets.

"Let's go, Ave," Sylvia pulled on my arm. "You agree with me, right? It's just a hysteria tactic."

I went to agree with her, but a shiver of unease prevented me from doing so. Usually, these feelings were accompanied by a phone call or text from Emery, but this time it was... different. I could be a very skeptical and analytical person, but something didn't feel right about this whole situation. No hospital was ever shut down over one instance. At the worse, they'd lock down for quarantine. No hospital administration could or would shut down a whole hospital without just cause.

"Avery?" Sylvia asked me with a raised brow.

"Right." I cleared my throat, though I didn't sound convincing. "No screwing in my bed," I added. "And Lucy, you can keep my pajamas now."

"Thanks!" she said brightly, oblivious to my ire.

◊

"Hello, boys," Sylvia flirted as she rolled down her window, giving the group of men smiles and waves as we passed. The men were running in formation, dressed in their physical fitness gear of black t-shirts and dove-gray shorts. They even wore matching black shoes and socks.

I loved the discipline and uniformity they represented. Even when a few of them turned their heads to smile and nod at Sylvia. I didn't blame them. She was a head-turner.

Sylvia was a beautiful Latina girl. Her mother had been Puerto Rican and her father, Mexican. Her skin had that dark olive color that rarely blemished. She had beautiful, long, curly, black hair, and had dark brown eyes to go with her gorgeous dark looks.

On top of having a pretty face, she had a cute, petite body. She was several inches shorter than my five-foot-eight, coming in at a whole whopping five-foot, two inches. I was considered athletically slim, whereas she was curvy. The only reason we could wear the same shorts and skirts was because she had what she called 'birthing hips' and my butt was... high and tight.

Besides Tae Kwon Do, I ran and lifted weights, too. Sylvia didn't like either and was content with aiming for gold in her poomsaes. Coach's requirements for me were a lot more demanding than her regimen. In order to get gold in sparring, I needed to be at the top of my game. Four years ago, I learned that the hard way. My endurance hadn't been where it should have been, and I missed my chance at Team USA by one match. *One!*

"*Boys* is right. They're probably babies," I jokingly teased her as we pulled into the parking lot of my brother's school.

The military academy my brother attended was one of the best schools in the country. It spanned over several hundred acres of land conducive for training "tomorrow's fighting force." They not only pushed education on their students but excellent physical fitness as well.

His school was adjacent to the college. More than likely, my brother would be attending there next year. I knew he was still on the fence whether he wanted to join the military as an officer or as an enlisted man.

"One time!" Sylvia whined loudly. "That was just one time. How was I supposed to know the guys that tried to pick me up were in high school and not college?"

I laughed. "You should have noted that they had the white stripe on their sleeve."

"You never told me!" she protested once more.

I laughed some more as I turned off my engine.

Truthfully, I had forgotten to tell her the difference between their PT uniforms when we visited BJ. The high school and college students wore identical clothing, except for a few barely-noticeable variations.

"How could you not tell?" I insisted for the hundredth time. "They had baby faces."

We had gotten out of class early, way earlier than BJ expected us. He was in his last course for the day. I figured by the time I signed him out for the weekend, he'd be done.

Most of the office staff recognized me by name and face since I'd been cleared to pick him up since I was able to drive. That and the fact that my father was a Lieutenant Colonel and well respected by over half the people here. For those who had never served with him, he was well known in this circle of professionals, and his reputation preceded him.

"They had muscles on top of muscles. You know very few guys looked like them at our school back then," she groaned. "If I would have known about all this fresh meat here in high school, I would have been coming with you all the time."

Before BJ had gotten his license, Trevor and I had been the ones to pick BJ up. It gave us some much-needed alone time. Sylvia had understood that we needed that time together, so she never asked to come with us.

"Why do you think we never told you?" I barely hid my wince over the "we" pronoun. I was no longer a "we." Now I was just a "me." I inwardly sighed. Just like that, my mind was back to dwelling over my heartache once again.

"Hello, hottie." Sylvia whistled as we neared the entrance, her attention on another male. She seriously had an overabundance of hormones when it came to men.

A tall man that was easily six and a half feet was heading towards the entrance as well. He appeared to be in his late twenties to early thirties, with bronzed skin that hinted at a non-Caucasian ethnic group. He was solidly built and reminded me of Channing Tatum in Magic Mike but much, much taller and darker. His black t-shirt was tight across his broad chest, and he walked with the grace of a dancer. His khaki cargo pants did nothing to hide his high, taut, biteable butt.

Whoa! Where had that come from? I really couldn't remember the last time I had lusted after a man.

"Hey, I know you!" Sylvia suddenly shouted. "Tacka!"

The man stopped, although I knew he had heard her the first time.

He turned, and holy hotness. He was beautiful. I never would have thought a man would be considered beautiful until that moment. He wasn't pretty in the pretty boy sense but more like a …a beautiful piece of art. I wasn't crazy about men with long hair, but his jet black, almost blue hair that fell almost to his shoulders was shiny and didn't detract from his sharp, honed features. His cheekbones were high, his nose sharp and narrow, but his lips…his lips were luscious, kissable.

Gah! Did Sylvia dose me with her extra hormones?

I could see his dark eyes, framed by outrageously long eyelashes, quickly assess Sylvia before he looked over at me. I couldn't help but squirm as I felt his eyes roam over my body. I felt horribly self-conscious. I looked like a bum compared to Sylvia.

Sylvia was wearing a pretty tube-top dress. The red fabric looked great against her skin. The cute red heels she paired with it drew attention to her shapely legs, and her hair cascaded down her back in large curls.

Me? I had opted to wear comfy clothes. I had on a pair of black biker shorts, with a form-fitting long sleeve white and black shirt. The only thing semi-cute about my outfit was the back, but he couldn't even see it. It was cut low, nearly down to the small of my back, revealing almost the entirety of my back and the black sports bra I wore.

I had a minimum amount of makeup on, and my hair was snatched up in a simple ponytail, with a thin headband completing the casually bummy look.

"I'm Corbin's friend!" Sylvia seemed oblivious to the fact that I felt like I was being dissected beneath a microscope.

I tensed at the mention of Corbin. I briefly closed my eyes and looked off into the distance. I could see the group of cadets nearing. I needed a distraction. A, I hoped Corbin was nowhere near, though I had no clue why he would even be here. B, I couldn't remember the last time I reacted to a man in this way. No, scratch that. I had *never* responded to a man in this way. Not even Trevor.

My gaze on him again, I saw a flash of recognition enter his eyes before they shuttered over.

"A friend?" he asked, his voice deep and gravely.

"Yes," she gushed. "OMG Ave, he's on Corbin's team. Welcome back!"

Now I knew why she had been edgy. She was hoping to run into them.

Corbin's teammate was silent, but that didn't stop her from continuing. "I sent you beef jerky, baby wipes, mac and cheese cups, and I made you the cake-in-the-jars. Well, technically Ave did–I can't bake for crap–but I sent it all."

I barely stopped myself from glaring at her. I should have known she didn't want twelve cakes-in-a-jar for her business statistics class. She knew how I had refused to send care packages this past year. I knew it was wrong of me, but again, I was irrationally angry at Corbin.

"Thanks," he said concisely.

"Is he around?" she asked hopefully.

"I'm going to sign BJ out," I said quickly before I hurried off, not caring to hear his response.

I felt their eyes on me, but I didn't care, I needed to get away from here. It was terrible enough having reminders everywhere. I didn't need to see the people who put those memories there.

☐

The principal, a Sargent Major on special assignment at the school, was eager to show me where my brother was. Apparently, BJ was in combat class. The usually stoic man was genuinely effusive in his compliments on my recent accomplishments; making the National Team was something he admired.

He knew it took a lot of skill, hard work, and dedication to get to the level I was at now. He told me how other visitors were in the school today, helping the junior and seniors decide their career paths. Most of the students had their minds made up, but people like my brother were still on the fence. BJ had a spot next door, but he could always enlist, if that was the route he chose to take.

"So, what's the likelihood of you sparring one of our combat veterans?" he asked quietly as we entered the gymnasiums.

I laughed until I realized he was serious. "Can I think about it and see what I'm working with before I make that decision?"

He smiled and nodded at me, indicating a few seats next to the doors. It was close enough to see the action but not so close that we were a distraction.

Inside, I could see approximately fifty students sitting on the mats on the outside of a ring, much like what I was used to seeing. Currently, there was a man dressed in a black shirt and khaki cargo pants grappling in the center of the ring with a student. It was clear the cadet wasn't going to win. Not because the man was that much bigger than the teen, but it was obvious the man was bred to be a fighter.

"There are about twenty joint operations specialists in our building as we speak," Sergeant Major continued to talk in hushed tones. "All of them are here as a favor, and a few of them just returned at the beginning of the week and wanted to help us with our students."

I really hoped Corbin wasn't among them. I had successfully avoided him for a year. By now, I could only imagine he had received the invitation for his brother's wedding, maybe even planned on encouraging me to attend and stand by my sister. I wouldn't. Not even if my father begged.

"I'm sure they are a font of knowledge," I murmured in return.

I believed it. Especially if everything Dad had told me was right.

About six years ago, a new task force of military was created. Before this task force was built, there were the Marines, Navy, Air Force, Army, Coast Guard, and all their guard and reserve units. Uncle Sam decided to take the best of the best from each service and create the Joint Operations Specialty Group.

These teams of six to ten people called themselves JOpS. Each team was comprised of a variation of all the branches. Dad had told me that these people were typically sent on missions that would always be considered top secret. The JOpS were a cohesive unit that was purported to be closer than teammates and more devoted than siblings, because they spent twenty-four hours, seven days a week, watching each other's six's- or backs.

He confided in me that these groups generally stayed together even after their deployment and missions were completed. They prided themselves on their camaraderie and closeness. Unfortunately, if one or two of their members caused any discord, the rest of the team could petition their superiors for a "swap out." Most of the time the petition was granted because they realized how important trust and solidarity were for these teams.

I honestly played with the idea of joining just to see if I could make one of these teams. Typically, the service members had to spend a minimum of four years in their career fields before their supervisors and superiors recommended them to be evaluated for the JOpS. It was a highly sought after and prestigious position to be in and just as competitive.

Wyatt and Corbin hadn't even been in for a full four years before someone recognized their potential and had placed them on a JOpS team. I knew that said a lot about them. They may always be M&M to me, but apparently they had another side of them I hadn't been aware of.

"They really are," Sergeant Major confirmed as we watched two new girls take the mats.

I watched as the JOpS woman and the high school student began their match. Within sixty seconds, the female on the JOpS team had me bristling in irritation. She was skilled, there was no doubt, but wasn't she supposed to be here in a training capacity? She was taunting the girl in the ring, and I could see the teenage girl's confidence getting shaken.

The last JOpS had patiently coached and helped his opponent during and after the match. I respected that so much more.

As a teenager, I was often bumped up into another age division to challenge me. I willingly chose that path. I even fought in divisions above my weight class at times, when specific tournaments allowed me to. Again, it was my decision. I was trained for that.

The teen in the ring hadn't asked to be humiliated and

publicly ridiculed. She also didn't deserve the too-hard hits aimed and inflicted on her.

I looked over at Sergeant Major and noticed the same frown reflected on his face.

"If she's game, I'll spar her," I whispered to the Sergeant Major.

He gave me a knowing smile and nodded, obviously not liking the way the JOpS was treating his students, either.

The JOpS in the ring was a dark-haired beauty with fair skin and was about an inch shorter than me. Where my muscles were toned and defined, I would never—and *could* never—bulk up like she had, even if I'd wanted to. Hit for hit, she could probably kick my ass, but I had something she didn't. I had strategy and speed going for me.

She looked as if she liked to get her opponent on the ground and use her strength. I would just have to make sure she never got me down.

Tae Kwon Do might not be a hand to hand sport, but I had been trained by some of the best Judo and Brazilian Jujitsu instructors in the world. For a while, I even had a coach for the USA team who tried to convince me to start training in Judo. I had enjoyed learning the other arts, but I loved the art of Tae Kwon Do most, so I had to let him down gently.

"JS Burns," Sergeant Major called out with a smile as we neared the ring. "I know I asked you to only spar with our cadets, but could I talk you into sparring a member of the national Tae Kwon Do team? I've always wondered how our training compared to the competition level."

Burns looked over at me and immediately grinned. I knew I didn't look like much. I was five foot eight and classified as a featherweight, weighing in at one hundred and thirty-two pounds. With my height, I appeared almost too skinny. Thank God I had a decent pair of breasts and a nice butt to balance out my petite frame.

"Is that a big deal?" Burns insulted me as she slowly perused my figure once more. "Of course, Sergeant Major."

"It is," Sergeant Major barely contained his frown. "I'll let you rest, and perhaps after the next match, we can have you females get in the ring."

My dad had run into a team of JOpS during his deployment and had come back cursing the insolence of their team lead. They had disobeyed a direct order from my dad, and in the end, half of his team paid the price with their deaths.

He supported the JOpS concept but didn't like how some of the bad seeds still found their way through the cracks. He always maintained they were necessary and helped cut through a lot of the standard military bureaucracy but acknowledged the program was still a work in progress.

"I don't need to rest," Burns stated with another cocky smile.

Sergeant Major looked over at me with a raised brow, and I gave him a shrug. "Harrison just came in from a long drive. We'll do another match, and you can be up next."

I smiled thankfully at him, forgetting that little detail. I didn't need to stretch, but it was probably a good idea. As I walked to the ring, I began to extend my arms. I saw my brother sitting near the front, and I couldn't resist giving him a loud resounding kiss on his cheek as I came up to him.

Some of the guys sitting near him snickered. PDA, or public displays of affection, was frowned upon on campus, but I knew Sergeant Major wouldn't care if I teased my brother with an innocent kiss. As predicted, he reddened.

"Hi, BJ." I smiled at him.

My nickname for him earned me more laughter and a few muttered innuendos. My brother hated his childhood nickname of BJ– for obvious reasons– and went by Bry now. On-campus he was generally called Harrison, as was the norm in military settings.

"Knock it off, Ave," he grumbled.

I smiled cheekily at him. I knew he was just acting embarrassed for the sake of his friends, who laughed at his expense. I dropped down next to him and began to stretch, grabbing my foot as I leaned forward to touch my cheek against my leg. I turned and looked at him.

I loved my little brother. We couldn't look more different, other than our height. Having tall parents, it was no surprise we were both tall as well. Two years ago, he had finally hit his growth spurt, so he was finally taller than me by three inches.

Like Dad, Mom had been adopted. We weren't confident what nationality she was, but the hospital she was dropped off at thought she was Polynesian. A Polynesian community surrounded the area she was dropped off in, so it probably was a reasonable hypothesis. Her dark hair, eyes, and tan skin tone had supported that theory. Dad was Caucasian, with sandy-blond hair and sapphire blue eyes. Our parents had been night and day in looks.

BJ had Dad's looks, but he tanned as Mom had. Emery and I were the spitting images of our mom in so many aspects, except my eyes weren't a genuine brown. Most people called the color a light amber, and in some lighting, they looked more golden.

"You're going to annihilate her," BJ murmured confidently to me as I switched sides.

"Aww, thanks," I teased him some more. "It helps to know you have that much faith in me," I said more seriously.

Our relationship was so easy and natural. I was thankful I had at least one sibling that just clicked with me. I had lamented several times that I wished he'd been my twin. Other than the occasional twin telepathy, Emery and I were nothing alike. BJ and I were too similar; it was scary at times.

"I do." BJ smiled at me briefly before turning back to the match in front of us. "I have a lot of faith in you," he continued murmuring. "I've been bragging to my friends since Wednesday. I've shown them your videos, and..." He blushed suddenly.

"And what?" I asked him as I nudged his shoulder with my own.

"And I had to change the password on my phone," he muttered with a scowl. "They kept trying to take my phone. Some of them were begging me for your number, and a few of them asked if they can come home with us this weekend. They think you'll hook up with them."

I stared at him in shock. "You're joking, right?"

I wasn't one of those girls that said I was ugly, just to fish for compliments. I knew by some guys' standards I was beautiful, but I never put in the effort most girls put into their looks. I lived in jeans and hoodies or jean shorts and tank tops. Oh yeah, and athletic gear. I kept my hair up on most days, because if it hung down my face too often, it annoyed me. I still couldn't cut it, though. Since I was such a tomboy, I felt long hair gave me a feminine look.

"I wish I were." He rolled his eyes.

"Well, they haven't met me," I said with a shrug. I'd hung out with enough guys to know my personality was off-putting at times. Simon, Will, and Abe, the guys Sylvia and I typically liked to hang out with, had no qualms listing my flaws, one being my independence. They had told me all men wanted to be needed and wanted.

I had only been in one real relationship, and that was with Trevor. I could never deny wanting him, but my dad and his had made sure I never needed a man. They had raised me to be independent.

It had hurt when I realized Trevor had the same grievance with me. One day, I had blown a tire and had pulled over to the side of the road to change it myself. He was upset that I hadn't contacted him to let him know. I hadn't seen the problem with it—it had been broad daylight in a safe area. And I knew how to change a tire. I couldn't understand why he'd been so upset.

Simon said most men liked predictable and stereotypical females. Most guys assumed I was like Emery but came to realize we were vastly different. I had never conformed to society's standards and beliefs in some areas. I couldn't pretend to be vulnerable to stroke any man's ego.

I wasn't crazy about going shopping. I thought roses and jewelry were a waste of money and preferred practical things instead. I preferred something I could use or eat; a favorite hoodie; a surprise cup of coconut-mocha latte; a picnic to a favorite place. I thought Trevor had understood all those things. Somewhere along the way, he had changed. Trevor wanted me to dress up and show me off. He wanted the four-star restaurants and the girl who texted him several times a day... someone needy.

BJ snorted. "And it's going to stay that way."

My brother was full of contradictions. One minute he wanted all men to stay away from me, and the next he was telling me I needed to start dating. He was overly protective while encouraging.

"Did you tell them the packaging may be... pretty but it doesn't reflect who I am?" I teased in a self-deprecating tone. "Sure, it's fun to think your girl could—or *can*—kick your ass, but reality doesn't match with expectations. Most guys can't take a hit to their ego like that."

BJ gave me a dramatic eye roll. "No, I didn't want to

encourage them. Had I told them the inside far exceeded the outside, they would have wanted you more. I didn't want them to realize that you are one in a million, and any *real* man would value that more than any superficial packaging."

I was surprised by his bold statement and almost teared up when I saw the conviction in his eyes. I realized then he knew where my deep-seated insecurity came from and was trying to convince me that Trevor had been an idiot. Sylvia had said the same thing, but it was easy for those who loved you unconditionally to see past your flaws.

"Harrison," one of the JOpS called me.

I looked up, startled to see the last match was over. I took a deep breath in and schooled my features. I needed to get my head in the game. Emotions had no place in the ring.

▢

Burns and I fist-bumped after the Sergeant, the instructor of the class, explained the rules. They were relatively simple and straight forward; one three-minute match, light contact only, no direct face hits, no groin kicks, no scratching, biting, or hair pulling. Points were awarded by clean hits, takedowns, how long you kept your opponent down, and forcing your rival out of the ring. The match was called after the three minutes, if your opponent tapped out, or if you were run out of the ring more than three times.

The whistle blew, and I immediately dropped back into a ready stance and leaned forward on the balls of my feet. If I remained flat-footed, it took more energy and time to react and leap into defense or offense. I lightly bounced up and down.

I didn't give her time to attack. I liked to take Wayne Gretzky's philosophy and apply it to sparring: *You will miss one hundred percent of the shots you don't take.* Granted, he was a hockey player, and I was a martial artist, but it still applied to my situation. I had three minutes to take as many shots as possible.

I immediately noticed how she kept one hand protecting her face, and the other crossed over her chest. She left her whole midsection open to my kicks. With quick succession, I did a double roundhouse kick. I led with my left foot, since my right foot had the power in it. I tapped her with enough force to let her feel my kicks but not enough power to be considered heavy contact.

She bent slightly over and grazed the padding, protecting her head from the top of my foot with another roundhouse kick.

I bounced back out of her range of motion. "If you leave your mid-section exposed, you allow your opponent the perfect opportunity to strike there," I called out loudly enough for most of the room to hear. "Your natural reflex is to lean forward to protect your stomach, leaving your head exposed."

I didn't want to humiliate her, by any means, but I wanted to give her the constructive criticism that she should've been providing the girl at least five years her junior.

She glowered at me and leaned forward, telegraphing her next movement. She wanted to get me on the ground. Her arms were stiff and extended somewhat out. My following action would probably be considered cocky, and brash even, but I had ten years of gymnastics and eight years of demonstration teams to make me believe my next move could work. I knew I had surprised her when I rushed towards her as she came at me. She tensed right before she went to grab me by my waist and placed her foot behind my own.

I leaped over her bent form, using her back as a springboard. My hands braced on the strong part of her back, bouncing off into a front handspring. I vaguely heard the surprised gasp around me, as I didn't give her the time to react. I crouched down and spun my right leg, hooking her ankle, and swept her feet out from underneath her. She fell, twisting her body, landing with a loud thud. I leaped up to a fighting stance once more, bouncing, always moving.

I watched as she tried to catch her breath on the mats. It sounded like she was trying to find her wind.

"If you want to know what your opponent is going to do next, watch their hips," I explained loudly. "I knew she wasn't going to attack me with her fist or feet because she was charging me. Sometimes you have to use your rivals' strengths against them. I know she's a strong girl and could easily take me down, but I used my strengths to my advantage."

I heard whistles and clapping around me, but I kept my face impassive.

There was no doubt in my mind that Burns was pissed when she rolled over and glowered at me. I allowed her to get up and saw that she had her hands up, covering her head and most of her midsection now. She wasn't rushing me, so I knew I was back on the offense.

I skipped in and quickly landed an ax kick to her shoulder, making sure my heel connected to her pressure point between her shoulder and neck. She swiped out to grab my foot, but I quickly pulled back, using my lead leg to land a push kick to her solar plexus.

She stumbled back, barely catching herself from falling over her own feet and landing on the ground once more. I took advantage of her floundering and darted in to place my foot behind her knees as I swept an arm to clothesline her across the chest. I barely skipped back in time to avoid her falling body. She landed on the mat with another thud.

"It's important to know your opponent's strengths and your weaknesses," I shouted. "I know a battle on the mats would not be favorable for me. There's a possibility I can find a submissive hold that may hinder her momentarily, but I'm not willing to put that theory to the test."

With more speed than I thought she had, she lunged towards me. This time she was able to grab one of my feet as she swept the other leg out from under me. Her foot came out to connect with my inner thigh, and I barely contained the yelp of pain I felt. I heard the crowd react in displeasure.

My training kicked in at the last second as the mat came rushing towards my face. I braced my hands out and pushed my body weight forward, tucking my head to my chest, I continued into the front roll, effectively dislodging her hand from my ankle.

I quickly turned once more, my left leg stinging. I was going to have a bruise there tomorrow, I had no doubt. My lungs were beginning to burn and I was becoming winded. My cockiness and her unexpected attack were catching up to me.

"Beast, beast, beast," I heard Sylvia's distinct voice begin to chant.

It caught on in seconds, as my brother's voice joined hers, followed by others. I smiled. My opponent sneered. She rushed, and I looked for my opening. A double roundhouse kick, followed by a spinning hook kick, grazed the side of her head.

A shrill whistle blew, indicating the end of the match, but she continued to charge. She grabbed me by the waist and pushed me down with her full body weight. Without a doubt, she outweighed me by at least thirty pounds, but I was sure it was all substantial muscle weight.

I felt the wind get knocked out of me and landed hard against the mat. Her face was full of fury as she snarled down at me. I had humiliated her. She cocked her fist back, aiming it to my face, and I barely had time to move my head from her intended target. Her knuckle grazed my cheekbone, and I felt the sharp pain radiate through my head. I gritted my teeth to keep from crying out.

The whistles continued to blow. She cocked her hand

back again. I knew I had to jump into action and fast. Several things happened simultaneously; I was able to scissors her knees between my thighs and twist with all my might, at the same time, two men looped their arms under her armpits and pulled her up and off me. She cried out as I pulled one way, and the men pulled her the other way.

I was pretty sure I jacked up her knee.

Chapter 3

"You were like Jackie Chan, Jet Li, and Bruce Lee wrapped up in one," Sylvia gushed as she swung her legs back and forth. "Maybe you're their love child!"

I snorted and shook my head.

After the fight was broken up, Sergeant Major rushed me to the nurse's office as the JOpS took care of their angry, insolent, wounded teammate. I was given two ice packs, one for the nasty welt on the inside of my thigh and one for the bruise forming on my cheekbone.

I hadn't even realized the bitch had a ring on. It had caught my skin, and what I had thought was sweat coursing down my face, had actually been my blood.

Now that the adrenaline was leaving my body, I was in pain.

I told Sergeant Major that stitches weren't necessary and just asked for the ice packs to go. We were now sitting in the back of my pick-up truck while we waited for BJ to grab his bags. Well, technically, I was lying down.

It was a beautiful spring day, and I wanted the fresh air. It was a little too warm in the cab of my truck, and I liked the feeling of the sun on my skin.

"Mission accomplished," I joked sarcastically. "I always wanted to be their love child."

"Seriously," Sylvia prattled on. "Where the hell did you learn some of that shit? Nowhere in the sparring guide book is front handsprings off your opponent's back permissible."

"Muscle memory, cockiness, demonstration teams," I said wearily. "You forget I did gymnastics for years, and the demonstration team is all about showing off."

I knew Sylvia meant well, but my head was beginning to ache. I wanted to ask her to quit talking for a little while, but I knew this was how she coped with stress. She had been worried about me. Where I became silent when stressed, she talked incessantly. It was who we were. I was okay with that. She was the yin to my yang.

"Harrison," I heard a man call.

"Holy hotness times three," Sylvia yelped.

I bit back my groan as I sat up. I had to school my features as I noticed Tacka and two other attractive males coming towards us. I recognized the average height and built body of the blond guy who I first saw sparring with the cadet. He had smiling blue eyes and looked like he would be easy to talk to. His other companion was taller and slim. He was dark where his friend was light, but his face was just as open.

They were cute, hot even, so why didn't they garner the same reaction Tacka had given me? I stuffed that in my *To be Examined Later* file as I realized what I was wearing—or should I say, what I *wasn't* wearing.

I really wish I hadn't been too lazy to grab another shirt. As it was, I was sitting in just my sports bra and yoga shorts. The ice pack had gotten cold on my face, and I had wrapped it in my shirt.

By the smirks on the men's faces, they had heard Sylvia's comment. Tacka's face, like earlier, was impassive.

I looked over at Sylvia, hoping to hide some of my embarrassment. "You know they heard you, right?" I murmured.

"Oh, I know," she nearly shouted with a broad smile.

"But Tacka shot me down, finals are over, and I haven't hooked up with anyone in like..." She looked up as if she were searching deep into her memory banks. "...three months. I need to blow off this extra steam, and you know I have a weakness for men in uniform!"

Sometimes I wished I could embrace my sexuality as she did or, at the very least, separate the action from my heart. I missed sex. Like, really, really missed it. The problem was, I hated casual hookups. I'd been there, done that, and despised it.

To Sylvia, the act was as normal as breathing. I could swear sometimes she was a man, with the way she treated most of the guys in her life as a once and done. She had a list of guys she might visit for seconds or thirds, but she always kept them at arm's length, saying she was in pursuit of the "authentic college experience."

I snorted as the guys didn't even try to hide their broad smiles. "Filter, Syl, filter."

"None, Ave, none," she retorted back immediately with zero shame. *Zero!*

"Hi," Blondie said, extending his hand to me first before taking Sylvia's hand with a receptive smile. By Sylvia's giggle, I knew he hadn't just shaken her hand. "I'm Cal, and this is my teammate Joe." He indicated the tall, slim, dark-haired guy before he tilted his head over towards Tacka. "And I guess you already met Axel."

Tacka, or should I say Axel, cleared his throat.

Cal rolled his eyes. "Anyways, how are you doing... Harrison?"

"I'm Sylvia, and this is Avery," Sylvia immediately informed him. "We don't go by the last names like ya'll do. And she's doing better now that you guys are here!"

Cal smiled at her once more before looking over at me,

and I realized he was still expecting an answer from me.

"I've been through worse," I said honestly, dropping the ice pack from my cheek. "It'll heal in no time."

Joe frowned before he reached for my face. Axel cleared his throat once more, and Joe quickly withdrew his hand after giving Axel an indecipherable look.

"We apologize for Burns," Joe said, looking back at me again. "It's hard to acclimate to our real-life when we return. Our last tour was hard on her, and she reacted inappropriately. Rest assured, as her team lead, I'll be handling the situation."

I looked at them in confusion. Axel hadn't even said a word to either man, yet they both seemed to be listening to him. If Joe was the team lead, why did he seem to hold Axel in a higher position? Even if Axel was a team leader, was he in a more elevated place of power than Joe?

I shrugged. I could empathize with Burns. My dad was strong and very private, but I knew he suffered from PTSD. He never spoke about it, but I saw the signs. I had heard him cry out in the middle of the night before Steph entered the picture.

I still didn't respect Burns, though. I believed she had character flaws that couldn't be attributed to possible transition issues. She seemed to enjoy the humiliation of cadets too much. PTSD and transitioning back to normal life screwed with your psyche and could make you act out of character but not in the way she had with the cadet.

"It's all good," I finally said when I noticed they were all staring at me. "Honestly," I said, holding up my hands. I bit back a sigh of frustration when I noticed their gazes linger on my breasts. FML. I didn't think that action through. I felt my cheeks warm before I mumbled. "I've been an athlete since I was three. I'm used to pain now. She barely touched me. I'm okay."

"Sergeant Major said you were part of the National

Team. What team is that?" Cal asked.

I looked over at Sylvia with a faint grin. I'd sic my mouth dog- not to be confused with guard dog- on them. She loved talking, and I wasn't in the mood.

"It means," Sylvia smiled at me, understanding me with zero words spoken. "That we are this close to the USA Olympic team in Tae Kwon Do!" she enthused as she held up her thumb and pointer finger about one inch apart.

"You're a fighter too?" Joe asked her with renewed interest.

Sylvia laughed, not in the least put-out. "Nope," she enthused, popping the P. "I compete in the poomsaes or forms."

She hopped up, brought out her phone, and began showing them a video she had of herself doing poomsaes. It was a series of beautiful, precise, powerful techniques using defense and attacking movements. It had a specific pattern to it, and you had to execute each move flawlessly. To me, it looked like a dance as she performed it. She made it look so stunning and natural.

I was good at doing my poomsaes, but Sylvia was terrific.

Joe and Cal hovered close beside her as she showed them the video, and I could see her reveling in their closeness. The guys seemed just as impressed, and Cal and Joe even clapped for her when the video was over. Sylvia beamed and dropped into an exaggerated curtsy. I smiled and shook my head at her as the guys laughed at her antics.

"Which way are you headed tonight?" Cal suddenly asked Sylvia as he pulled out his phone.

"Woodmore, right now. Not sure where we're headed tonight." Sylvia smiled coyly as she played with her phone.

"No way," Joe said in surprise before he turned to Axel.

"Isn't that where Cavalier's parents live?"

Axel gave him a raised brow.

I chose to close my eyes and lay back down. One— I breathed in— I deserved better. Two— I breathed out— I was stronger than this. Three, nothing could hurt me if I didn't let it. Four, everything happened for a reason. Five, patience was a virtue. Six, three months. Seven, my new life began in three months, and whether I made the Olympics or not, it was a new experience not associated with the Cavalier family in any way.

I continued to do my breathing exercises and affirmations as I vaguely heard them talking around me.

"We know Corbin!" Sylvia enthused. "He lives right down the street from where we're heading."

"Small world," Cal said. "Let me put my number in your phone. Text me, let's get together tonight."

"Avery, are you coming?" Joe asked.

"Avery!" Sylvia yelled at me.

I had to wait for my brain to process everything that had been said. "I have a little boy at home. I promised him pizza, movies, and PJs," I replied, opening my eyes as I looked up to the sky.

"He's not your son." Sylvia sighed. "He's your stepbrother."

"I have to wash my hair," I said next without skipping a beat.

"It won't take you long, plus it's time to get you laid, too. It's been too long for you. It's time to exorcise the demons," Sylvia cajoled loudly.

"I need to see a priest, then. Wait... I'm not Catholic." I frowned. "Do pastor's exorcize demons?"

"They're not real demons. It's time to get *under* someone to get *over* him," she nearly whined. "We need to go out."

We had played this game for too long. She was getting better. I allowed her to drag me around in months four and five of AT– or After Trevor. I hadn't liked who I'd become and the danger it put me in, so I began coming up with excuses for why I couldn't accompany her when she was on the prowl. I prided myself on being able to think quickly on my feet and finally stumping her. Unfortunately, she was catching on.

I had to act and say outrageous things to stun her into silence.

"Can't." I sighed, closing my eyes. "I like it on top, so if he's over me, it'll only make me claustrophobic."

"You can ride me," Joe immediately volunteered before I heard a loud *oompf* as if he had been hit.

Dammit. That backfired! Time to roll with the punches.

"Ran out of quarters to ride," I deadpanned. "Have you ever been to a Meijer's? Did you know that you can ride a horse for a penny? A penny!" I exclaimed excitedly. "Who doesn't have a penny? One time, I rode one sixteen times before the manager asked me to leave. And I had eleven more pennies in my pocket!"

"Umm, are you sure you're okay?" Cal asked with a frown in his voice. "Did you hit your head?"

"Don't let her fool you!" Sylvia cried in frustration. "She acts crazy to deter men from coming onto her. Avery didn't have eleven more pennies. She only had two left. She got kicked out because she was blasting Big and Rich's song, *Save a Horse, Ride a Cowboy* on her phone! There were kids around, some of them were waiting for their turn. It really wasn't appropriate, and the parents were getting upset!"

I had to bite my lip from laughing. Now Sylvia sounded crazy. The incident in question occurred in month five of AT, and I had been really, really intoxicated. The guys we had hooked up with that night wanted to take a road trip. Next thing I knew, we were on the road, stopping at places we had never been, and drinking heavily. Our DD... I shut down my thoughts. No, just no. Happy thoughts.

Joe and Cal began to laugh. "Most guys don't like crazy," Cal admitted with a laugh. "But you forget you're talking to JOpS. We bask in crazy! We're the kings of insanity!"

I sighed. Damn. It hadn't worked. And who liked crazy?

"Thanks for the invite, but I'm seeing someone." I feigned a look of contriteness.

"Who? You're not seeing someone! Come out with us," Sylvia insisted.

"Oh look, there he comes now," I looked over at BJ as he approached us with one of his friends.

"You're not seeing anyone," Sylvia said in exasperation.

"Am too," I deadpanned. "It's new."

"Are not. I would have known it." Sylvia stuck her hands on her waist.

"Am too," I continued.

"Bravo, let's roll," Axel spoke in clipped tones. His unnerving gaze was no longer on me, but it didn't make me feel as good as I thought it would.

"I'm gonna have to bail out tonight, guys," I looked over at Cal and Joe with feigned remorse, trying to avoid Axel's piercing gaze.

"You better be good to her," I insisted. "If you hurt her or push her into something she's not ready for, I'll hunt you down. I know things!" I did my best mean mug.

The guys looked like they didn't know how to behave with my erratic behavior.

"Seriously, guys, ignore her," Sylvia pleaded. "She's a fighter. I lost count how many times she has been hit in the head. Text me, Cal, and we'll get together." Then she gently began to push me towards the truck

"It's the eye of the tiger," I began to belt out, just to mess with Sylvia further. "It's the thrill of the fig-"

Sylvia clapped her hand over my mouth. "She's had concussions!"

One! I'd had just one. I wanted to refute her statement, but my mouth was still being covered.

"I'll text you in like an hour," Cal stated with a laugh. "Soon as I find out the plans, I'll let you know. You don't mind hanging with a group of us, do you?"

"The more the merrier." Sylvia grinned as she leaned over me, releasing her hand.

"The more the merrier. Get it? Wink. Wink," I yelled before she dove on me to cover my mouth once more.

"Ready, ladies?" BJ asked in confusion as the guys passed him. "Ave, do you mind if we drop Reid off down the road? He needs to pick his vehicle up."

I immediately hopped up. "Let's go! I'm thinking of pizza." I didn't bother climbing down from the tailgate. Instead, I launched myself off the side, further away from them. I winced in regret as my wounded thigh struck the truck.

"You okay?" I heard BJ and his friend ask as Sylvia snorted.

I cringed, feeling embarrassed for my lack of finesse. I handed BJ my keys as he threw his arm over my shoulder. "Just wounded my pride." I laughed, belittling myself.

"Hi, I'm Reid," Reid held out his hand, and I had to admit he was a good looking guy. "It's great to meet you finally."

I smiled up at him as I took his hand. "Likewise. I've heard a lot of good things about you."

Reid was like a big brother to BJ. He had taken my brother under his wing years ago and was trying to convince him to attend the college next door. We were supposed to meet on several occasions, but things always seemed to come up.

Suddenly, I had a feeling I was being watched. I looked up, and my smile dropped. Why was Axel scowling at me from across the parking lot?

⬚

"Why aren't you going out with them?" BJ cautiously asked after we dropped Reid off. "The boys go to bed at nine, and they're headed to Joe's at nine. You don't have to be on time."

As expected, Sylvia had immediately filled BJ in on her plans and had attempted to enlist his help on getting me out of the house as well. Almost immediately, her phone began vibrating with text. She continued to read each one aloud.

I shrugged, not wanting to admit there was no way I wanted to run into Corbin. Plus, I wasn't in the mood to be around all that testosterone. "I've had a long week. The idea of going to bed early and sleeping in sounds amazing," I said instead.

"You're a poor wingman." Sylvia pouted.

We were almost home and she had already had plans in place for tonight. I honestly didn't mind, though. Sylvia needed to go out. I liked to decompress in silence. She liked to unwind with excitement.

"I think you'll be okay." I stuck my tongue out at her, knowing she really didn't need me there.

In the past, I would have been there just to make sure she was safe, but as flighty as she could be at times, she had a good head on her shoulders. She would never put herself in a situation she couldn't get out of. Unlike me. Besides, even though she thought she was sneaky, I knew Wyatt had texted her already, and he would look out for her.

Wyatt had tried to contact me AT as well, but I had lumped him in with Corbin's pile. I didn't need anything to get back to the enemy, and Wyatt lived, worked, and was best friends with the enemy. Forget the fact he was my cousin; I knew where his loyalties would always lie.

The JOpS were all centralized in DC. They never had to PCS or TDY. They deployed so often the government had given them that one allowance. For the few that had families, they would never have to move them around. They could set down their roots near or in DC and never have to worry about the other things that came with military life.

Sylvia had informed me that, months ago, Wyatt and Corbin's team had purchased a home. Well, technically, they had bought a warehouse that had recently been zoned to residential, and they had planned to make it livable. I still thought it was odd that they all chose to live together. Didn't they ever get sick of each other?

I would never get tired of Sylvia, but, seriously, I needed my "me time" from time to time. I cared for my Tae Kwon Do team, but after a week of being with them, I got frustrated with them real quick.

"Did you get the invite?" BJ asked hesitantly.

I nodded. I didn't have to ask BJ what invite he was referring to.

Sylvia snorted. "Emery had the audacity to ask Avery to be a bridesmaid," Sylvia snarled.

BJ looked at me with astonishment. "You're kidding, right? They asked me to be in the wedding too but..."

"But they didn't screw you over," I said bitterly.

BJ frequently steered clear of conversations of Emery and Trevor. He was almost as angry at them as I was. He had chosen my side from the beginning, despite the fact I told him that I didn't expect him to. They didn't betray him. They betrayed me, and I wanted to be the "bigger" person. I didn't expect Dad, BJ, or Steph to choose sides. Emery was still family, and she hadn't hurt them.

"I told them no," BJ said, clenching his jaw. "I told them not to expect me at the wedding. You should have seen them at Christmas," he bit out. "At least Trevor had the decency to look uncomfortable, but Emery was up to her old ways."

I cringed, only imagining what she could have said or done. I didn't want to know, honestly. In fact, I never wanted to talk about them. They already took up way too much space in my thoughts.

"What did she do?"Apparently, Sylvia had no such qualms.

BJ looked at me dubiously. I sighed and nodded. Sylvia wouldn't quit until her curiosity was assuaged. Even if she pried the information from BJ later, I would still hear about it. She had a different approach to healing than I did. She thought if I listened to enough horrid and unpleasant things about Emery and Trevor, I would finally heal and get over my pain.

"She claimed that you always knew *she* liked Trevor and chose to pursue him first," BJ stated reluctantly. Sylvia scoffed. BJ continued, "She said that, every time you guys had a break, it was because of your stubborn pride and unwillingness to compromise. She alleged you drove him away. She claims that you left him at his lowest, and she was there to help him as any good friend would, and they didn't pursue their relationship immediately after that one drunken night."

Trevor might have been at a low point in his life, but I had been, too. More so. I didn't care to delve into that right now, though. If I told BJ, he would only hate them more.

Sylvia and I exchanged a look, and I shook my head. She glared back at me.

I sighed, rubbing my forehead. "Okay, maybe in the sixth grade Emery said she liked Trevor, but to be honest, she liked Corbin *and* a handful of other guys, too. Trevor wasn't interested in girls back then, and we always hung out more than they ever did. I never intentionally went into a relationship with Trev. We were nearly fourteen before we even had our first kiss. When Emery caught me kissing him, she never said anything. She was after Corbin at the time."

I shrugged. "Maybe I was the reason we took our two breaks," I admitted. "But that was only because Trevor was... acting funny. He would get cold. I wouldn't hear from him for days, and he always claimed he was busy, but he had time to go party with his friends or pledge to this or that fraternity. I never expected much. I didn't want one hundred percent devotion, but how much time does it take to send a simple text?

"I texted him daily, just to let him know I loved him or was thinking of him. I never demanded he not live his college experience. In fact, I encouraged it. When I asked him if he wanted a break, he gladly took it. Then, a few weeks later, he would come back and make some grand gesture and ask me to come back. And like a fool, I fell for his pretty words. Now," I said bitterly, "I think he readily agreed to those breaks because it gave him the freedom to hook up without the guilt."

Shaking my head, the pain smothered me, the emotions too raw. "And it's rich of her to claim he was in pain. That still doesn't excuse them for climbing into bed together. Even if they were drunk."

BJ reached over and squeezed my shoulder. "Everyone knows the truth, and they know Emery always loved playing the victim. Trevor is the blind and stupid one, Avery, knowing the way she is and staying with her anyway."

I bit my lip. Everyone thought they knew the truth, but they really didn't. Trevor, Emery, Sylvia, and I were the only ones who knew the whole truth.

I took a shaky breath. Dammit, I was tired of hurting! And so sick of giving them the power to still get to me. Every time.

〇

"Have you heard about this crazy stuff?" BJ asked as he turned up the radio.

The truck had been silent for the last twenty minutes as I composed myself. BJ had refrained from divulging any more information, and Sylvia seemed to be sucked into her phone as she texted her new friends.

At the mention of hospitals, I began to listen, my sixth sense getting piqued.

"...several hospitals are reporting patients are coming in with extreme temperatures of one hundred and four or more, after which, they exhibit signs of seizures. Doctors have said anywhere between five and thirty minutes later, the patients become violent, frequently biting the person closest to them. Sources tell me to avoid patients after they have a seizure. The moment they make contact with another person is when they seem to be transmitting the infection through their saliva," a female voice reported.

"Has your attempts to reach the CDC been successful?" a male voice inquired.

"They have refused all our calls," the woman said in irritation. "With twenty states now reporting these strange occurrences, you'd think something would be done or said."

"Of course not," BJ scoffed. "If there really were a problem, then they wouldn't want to cause mass hysteria."

"It's just a hoax," Sylvia added from the back seat. "If it were a problem, the American government wouldn't keep us in the dark. Fever-seizures aren't that uncommon."

"What kind of hysteria would occur?" I asked BJ.

He smiled at me. "You're only asking because I love post-apocalyptic books. A lot of people will probably try to leave well-populated areas. A significant influx of people would cause the roadways to become gridlocked. For those people that chose to hunker down, they'd realize they don't have enough food to last them for a sustainable amount of time, not beyond two weeks for the average person. When they run to the grocery stores, they'll already be wiped out. Most grocery stores don't have more than three days worth of food for their community on their shelves. Desperate people do desperate things, so then crime will ramp up. In an actual crisis, there aren't enough law enforcement to respond to everything."

"Please stop," Sylvia groaned. "You sound like Nana and Pop-pop."

"Why's that?" I asked in confusion.

"Pop-pop believed that something major would happen within the next five to ten years," BJ said slowly. "He became a prepper or survivalist, of sorts. He started stockpiling guns, ammo, weapons, food with long shelf life, and fortifying the campground to be more self-sufficient."

"Pop-pop was senile, and Nana was only humoring him." Sylvia snorted.

I looked between the two of them. I didn't know what to make of the situation, but something in me was telling me that Sylvia was taking this too lightly, and BJ might be onto something.

"What did Dad have to say about Pop-pop?" I asked with a frown.

It pained me knowing I hadn't made time to see my grandparents before they died. It was only a six-hour drive from my school. I had plenty of long weekends and could've made it work had I wanted to, but I'd been so self-absorbed. I thought I had all the time in the world back then.

Nana begged me to visit them the last Fourth, even promised to keep Trevor and Emery away from me, but I had been wallowing in my pity party. I wished I had seen them just one last time. I wished I could have told them how much I loved them.

"Uncle Scott, Uncle Mitch, and Dad were giving Pop-pop more suggestions," he suddenly shifted. "You know they inherited the campgrounds, right?"

I nodded, my eyes narrowing on him. He knew something. "Well, there *is* great fishing and hunting out there." I shrugged, not seeing the big deal.

"The last time I was home, I was in Dad's study..." BJ cleared his throat. "He bought over one hundred thousand dollars worth of solar panels."

I frowned. "For the house? Isn't that a bit excessive?"

"Not for the house." BJ shook his head. "When Uncle Mitch got out of the military, he bought a trucking company. He even purchased some warehouses. One of them is approximately fifteen miles away from the campground. That's where Dad shipped the panels to."

I was torn between being incredulous and shocked. My dad was more frugal then I was. Why would he have purchased that many solar panels, and why ship it there? Most importantly, how did BJ know all this?

"You hacked your uncles' and dad's computers?" Sylvia accused, laughing.

BJ ducked his head but smirked. "I fully expected Dad, Uncle Mitch, and Uncle Scott to scoff at Pop-pop, but they didn't!" he exclaimed. "They started acting funny," he explained. "You know as well as I do that they are privy to so much more than we could ever dream of. Things they could never tell us without compromising their careers, possibly their lives. What if the government knew something that they didn't want us to know?"

Sylvia started laughing. "And what if there are still aliens at Area 51?"

BJ mock glared at her. "If something happens, you're going to have to say BJ is the most handsome, smartest man I know, and no man will ever be as great as him."

Sylvia continued laughing. "Yeah, okay. If something happens, I'll even rub your gnarly feet for a week."

I smirked. Sylvia hated feet. Like, *really* hated feet. If you even came close to her with them, she freaked. One man had tried to seduce Sylvia by rubbing his foot against the inside of her calf, up to her thighs, and she flipped. She ran right out of the restaurant.

"Shh, listen," BJ stated as he turned up the radio and another report was being made.

Chapter 4

"Aww, man," Mikey groaned as we walked up to the doors to Treetop Adventures.

It took me a moment to realize why he was groaning. Right there on the door, it said the place was closed due to inadequate staffing. I imitated Mikey's groan. I was looking forward to our day trip, too.

"Now what?" BJ frowned as my phone rang.

I pulled out my phone and noticed it was an unknown number. I generally never answered them. I was happy with my medical insurance. My car's extended warranty wasn't about to expire. So, in short, unknown numbers generally equated to phone scams.

I was about to swipe red, but then at the last second decided I should answer it.

"Hello?" I cynically answered.

"Avery," Dad said immediately. "Where are you?"

"Well..." I frowned. "BJ, Sylvia, and I decided to take the boys to Treetop Adventures, but they're closed."

"Can you put me on speaker?" Dad asked.

I looked at BJ and Sylvia in confusion but did as Dad asked.

"Hey, guys, I need you to meet Stephanie at Costco's," Dad said without preamble.

"Um, sure," I said in confusion. "Now?"

"Does this have anything to do with what's been going on?" BJ asked shrewdly.

"You've always been too smart for your own good, son," Dad said cryptically. "And don't think I wasn't aware of your digging."

BJ and I exchanged wide-eyed looks. Was this real life? Was Dad saying things might head south? Sylvia still looked skeptical as she gnawed on her thumbnail. It was a habit I'd been trying to break her of for some time.

"Want us to go shopping for Pop-pop?" BJ asked.

"I think you should," Dad answered, relief in his voice.

"Then what?" I inquired.

"Are you still going fishing?" Dad asked in response.

There was only one place we ever went fishing, and that was at Sanctuary Lake, the campgrounds my grandparents owned. Dad always swore it was the only place he had luck catching anything. Poppop said that was because he stocked the lake, and the other water sources on the property weren't fished that often.

"That was the plan," I said in a small voice.

"Good, I gotta go, but I love you, Ave, BJ, Sylv, Mikey, and Miller." Dad's voice caught for a moment. "Take care of each other, and I'll try to be home as soon as I can."

"Love you," we all chorused before the phone was cut off. Miller remained tight-lipped. He was still struggling with having a stepdad three years later.

Sylvia looked at us. "Was he saying what I think he was saying?" She seemed afraid suddenly. "You guys didn't put him up to this, did you?" she asked hopefully.

BJ and I gave her a pointed look, and I saw her shudder out a response.

"Pop-pop's dead," Mikey said with a frown to BJ.

"What's going on?" Miller asked at the same time.

"Didn't you hear?" I tried to sound upbeat. "We're going fishing!"

"I don't like fishing," Miller grumbled.

BJ, Sylvia, and I all exchanged looks. We couldn't tell the boys the truth. They didn't need to know some weird virus was making people violent. We couldn't tell them that Dad thought things were bad enough that he wanted us to stock up and hunker down for a while until the danger passed.

"Yay!" Mikey danced around.

Miller and Mikey could pass as twins, but they couldn't be any more different. Miller was small for his age, where Mikey was big. They were precisely the same height, but Mikey was sturdier and tanner, since he was more active and was outside every chance he got. Both of them had hazel eyes and dark hair. Miller kept his neat and tidy, but it was a feat if Mikey even remembered to comb his.

"Well," BJ said in an upbeat tone. "After we go fishing, maybe we can work on that new game we're creating."

"Really?" Miller asked excitedly.

"Really." BJ's smile didn't reach his eyes as I saw the same worry I was feeling reflecting back at me.

⬚

Sylvia's phone went off the moment we got back into the truck. She immediately answered.

"Hey!" she said enthusiastically.

I had a feeling it was either Joe or Cal on the line. She hadn't told me anything about her night last night, but I knew she had accomplished her mission. She had been all smiles and coy looks since she came home this morning, dressed in the same clothing she'd left in.

If the boys hadn't been in the truck with us now, I'm

sure she would have already given me and BJ all the sordid details.

"We're going shopping—Avery's. Yeah, yeah, she's right here." Sylvia frowned.

I looked at her with a raised brow in the rearview mirror. I was the only other *she* in the vehicle.

I looked over at BJ, sitting in the passenger seat as he murmured into his phone. "Pull in there." BJ looked over at me, pointing at the gas station.

My tank was over half full, but I wasn't going to argue with him, especially not right now. I was sure he had examined everything. His love of post-apocalyptic books, combined with our families' recent behavior, would have made him go into research mode.

"It's for you, Ave." Sylvia shoved the phone at me before she hopped out of the truck. "Come on, boys. It sounds like we need to get a lot of snacks!"

Mikey and Miller didn't need to be told twice as they launched themselves out of the truck.

"Hello?" I said in confusion.

"Don't hang up," a deep, familiar voice responded.

"Hi, Wyatt." I sighed. "What's up?"

"Hey, Ave," he said, almost reverently before his tone became brusque. "Change of plans. There's a Costco twenty minutes away from your current location. It's en route to our destination. Head there. BJ will have the list you need. After you get what you can, I need you to go fishing."

"What about Stephanie?" I asked tentatively. "Plus, the boys, BJ, and Sylvia don't have their bags."

I hadn't taken my bag out of the side Ram boxes last night. I had been too lazy to grab it after dinner and didn't need it this morning. I still had some clothes in my old room, and

I had made do with them, just grabbing my hiking boots this morning.

"Don't worry about that," Wyatt insisted. "Get what you need at the store, and we'll bring their stuff as well. We're en route to get Stephanie as I speak. Don't come back here."

Unease gripped me. *Why not?*

"Seven cases of infected came into the hospital this morning," he said in a quiet tone. "It's not safe here."

"Okay," I barely breathed. "What about Aunt Pam?"

I may have avoided them for the last year, but I still loved them. I wasn't going to ask about Emery and Trevor, but if the family was reaching out to me, I'm sure they had already contacted them.

"We're taking care of that." Wyatt sighed heavily, his voice softer. "You just take care of the boys and yourself, okay?"

"Okay," I agreed, dread settling in the pit of my stomach.

I had to admit I had a morbid fascination with "end of the world" movies and TV shows. I had even wondered how I would've behaved in a similar situation, but that was all in fun. It was all fantasy, and should never have become a reality.

This was real life. There was no way to describe the crippling fear that had taken over me as I held the phone to my ear.

"How've you been, Ave?" his tone changed once more as I climbed out of the truck. "We saw your tournament match. You're a beast, girl."

I nearly missed my running board in my nervous haste. I may have gone a little overboard with how high I'd lifted my truck.

"Thanks," I said dryly. "Somehow, though, I feel like my dreams are slipping out of reach. What's the likelihood all this will blow over by the time I need to go to Colorado?"

He breathed heavily into the phone. "We can only pray it'll be handled sooner than later. When are you supposed to leave?"

"Three months," I replied glumly.

He was silent for several moments. "I wouldn't count on it."

I closed my eyes. "That's what I thought. Do you know why or what's going on?"

"We weren't given the full details, but—" suddenly Wyatt's voice cut off, and I heard a weird beeping sound.

"Wyatt?" I asked in fear. I looked down at the phone and noticed I had zero service and wi-fi.

"Did you're phone drop the call?" BJ came running out of the store with several gas cans in hand.

"Yeah," I answered him as I pulled out my own phone and looked at it. No service or wi-fi either. "What's going on?"

"They cut off communications," BJ replied grimly. "One of the steps to prevent hysteria is to cut off communications. They want to prevent rapid attempts of disseminating information; sharing information."

I didn't have to ask who *They* were. I looked at BJ in horror, feeling dread spread to my limbs, rooting me to the spot.

"Avery," BJ bit out, trying to reach me through my fog of anxiety. "Fill up the truck, then go inside, withdraw as much cash as you can, load up on snacks."

I looked at him, blinking in confusion. I heard his words, but they seemed to be on a lag. I felt like I was in an old Japanese- English subtitled film. His mouth was moving, but his lips and words weren't in sync.

"Avery!" BJ snapped at me, but his eyes were still kind.

"Now."

I snapped out of it, nodded numbly, and pulled my card out. I inserted it into the machine and started to pump gas into my vehicle. As it filled up, I went inside the store and saw the boys acting like they were on some grand adventure as they loaded up their hand baskets up with junk food they weren't usually allowed to have.

Stephanie was a physical therapist and was a health nut. I thought my diet restrictions were strict during training, but Stephanie took it to the next level. Her idea of snacks and treats was plain popcorn, granola, honey, and fresh fruit. She didn't even allow the boys to have sugary cereals. They had a choice between cereals like Cheerios, Chex, and other whole grains with no artificial sweeteners.

Of course, Dad, BJ, and Sylvia indulged the boys when they could, but Stephanie wasn't too thrilled about it. She wasn't a total tyrant, though. If the boys were at a birthday party or if the school gave them treats, she didn't deny them. She just didn't keep stuff like that in the house.

"Steph is going to flip," I warned Sylvia.

Sylvia shrugged and attempted to smile at me. "I'll tell her it's mine."

I pulled out the max amount my bank would allow me to from of one of my accounts before repeating with my other two accounts—yes, I had three accounts. I had one that my dad gave me for a college fund. One of the accounts had the money I earned from modeling. The last one held my inheritance.

I liked to keep them separate so that I knew how much money I was spending. I tried to tell Dad he should have held onto my college fund money since I had gotten a scholarship, but he insisted I have it for additional expenses.

Thankfully, Dad had always been a smart investor, and before Mom had died, she had been one of the most sought after supermodels. Not to forget the fact that Emery and I had modeled until we were twelve years old. Identical twin models that had our "exotic" looks had been sought after. In fact, they still were.

I had lost count how many times I had been approached to get back into that world, but there was a reason why Dad forced us to quit. He didn't think the money was worth it to our young impressionable minds back then, and now that I was older, I agreed with him.

At the tender age of twelve, Emery started starving herself. She heard some of the older girls equating skinny with pretty. She had dropped over twenty pounds before they realized she was on diuretics. She was living off of black coffee, celery, and cabbage back then. Our parents got her a therapist and pulled us out of the scene.

After blowing through her college fund in less than two years, she had gone back to modeling. Imagine my chagrin when she didn't bother telling me she was modeling again, instead finding out when I saw her on a cover of *Maxim*. Dad had been livid, but they compromised– even though she was an adult– and she promised to finish college before she pursued the career full-time.

She knew without Dad's help there was no way she could support herself modeling just yet. Even with a lucrative contract, there were no promises she could book the jobs she needed to survive off of it. There were no guarantees she would become a supermodel like Mom.

Emery learned that the hard way when she tried to ignore Dad one summer. She booked a few jobs but wasn't able to afford the apartment she shared with four other girls. She had to run back home with her tail between her legs.

I tried to support her at first. When I found out about her choice of career, I had been happy for her. I was glad she was chasing her dreams. I told her as much, but somehow she used it as a dig at me. She informed me she could get me a job as well if I dropped a few pounds and started dressing like a "girl."

"Holy cash," Sylvia breathed out next to me.

I smiled ruefully. She knew about my past. She knew about my college fund and inheritance, but I never told her how much each account held. The twelve grand I just withdrew didn't even put a dent into my accounts.

She was a scholarship girl, too, with no family to rely on. Her father was still in prison, and her mom OD'd our freshman year of college. Sylvia worked part-time and knew she could always depend on me to front her. She hated asking, but I never had an issue sharing my wealth. I just never told her how much I had.

I handed her a wad of money. "Put it in your wallet. From the sounds of it, we might have to split up when we get to Costco so we can get in and out quicker."

"What's going on, Avery?" she asked in a frightened voice.

"I don't know. Wyatt said it has something to do with the infected, and it's not safe to return home. The phones aren't working," I said truthfully as I began to gather my favorite snacks.

If this was the end of the world, I needed my hot fries, almond Hershey bars, and Starburst.

◻

"Miller, you're with me. Mikey, you're with Sylvia, but right now I need you boys to stay in the truck for just a few minutes," BJ said authoritatively.

I was surprised at how much my brother was taking charge. I knew he had it in him, but he'd always seemed too laid back to want the role.

The whole time we had driven from the gas station to

Costco, he had been writing down a list on three separate pieces of paper. He hadn't said much, and I could see the grim set of his mouth. I didn't know who he'd been talking to earlier, but they must have told him more than Wyatt had told me.

"What's going on?" I asked him immediately once we got to the tailgate of my truck.

"It's not good," he answered quietly after several minutes of silence. "Corbin told me more than he probably should have, but Dad and Uncle Scott were sent to a remote village in Africa. An entire town was found dead or just about. They looked like they had been eaten by people. What's worse is the village is missing some inhabitants.

"They were able to determine that some were carrying the infection by traveling to other villages, and a group of others that weren't in attendance when the massacre happened were also carriers of a virus. They were able to apprehend two of the people but knew others had slipped beyond their grasp, on planes, boats, trains, traveling to other countries. Three of them came to the US last week. They don't know what the virus is yet, but they know it can spread rapidly, as evidenced by recent news reports." He held out two mean-looking switchblades.

"So these people..." Sylvia's lower lip trembled and tears brimmed her eyes. "They're infected and want to spread their disease through *biting* people?"

BJ nodded. "Here, take these knives. Right now, it seems like well-populated areas are in the red zones, and we're not in one right now, but I don't want to risk it. Corbin says these... things cannot be reasoned with and have no qualms on killing you, or worse, infecting you. He says to aim for the head. This is the best I can do for now."

"So, they're like zombies?" I asked numbly. Inside, I was freaking out. Inside, I was terrified. But I knew I had to put it in my *To be Examined Later* file for now. I had to focus on getting what we needed, keeping it together for the boys, and getting us to safety.

"Who's zombies?" Mikey piped up as he came around the corner of the truck.

"No one," BJ said quickly with an affable smile. "I was talking about the game I wanted to create with your brother."

"Mom says no violent games." Miller frowned.

"I'll see what we can do," BJ stated as he handed us a list. "I say we make this a race. The first team that comes out here first, gets twenty dollars from the losers."

I could see he was trying to keep the boys from understanding what was going on, so I had to be the big sister here and help him. "Let's go!" I tried to feign excitement as I took off running.

I heard them following closely behind, the boys yelling that I cheated. I slowed down to a jog, looking down at my list. It appeared like I had a list of dry goods. Rice, beans, spices, honey, flour, yeast, powdered milk, etc.

I looked back and saw the dread and fear on Sylvia's face, but I knew she was holding it together for now. It was why BJ had told Mikey to go with her. She needed the distraction or she would fall apart.

I grabbed a flat cart as I entered the vestibule and headed towards the entrance. I looked around the store and worried my lip as I looked around— so many people. A Saturday afternoon trip to a huge box store didn't seem like a good idea, suddenly. I took a deep, calming breath and headed in the direction of the dry goods area.

I systematically began to load the cart with everything on my list. I added other items that I thought would keep and enhance the things we already had. It didn't take me long to fill the one cart, so I decided to grab another. I preferred to have too much than not enough.

I took my first cart up to the registers, noticing immediately the strange looks I was getting.

Ah. Right. It wasn't every day someone saw another person with ten bags of rice, eight sacks of flour and sugar, and all the other things I had piled high on my cart.

A male's nasally voice stopped me. "Excuse me..."

A middle-aged man stood before me. He had thinning hair and a slight paunch. I noticed his vest stating *Manager-Pete* on it. "What are you doing?" he asked me suspiciously.

"Shopping," I deadpanned.

"How do you plan to pay for all this?" he overlooked my cart.

I tried to act cool and collected as I pulled out my wallet. "Well, I have three cards with sufficient funds on it, and if not, I have cash, too," I stated as I showed Pete the stack of bills.

He gulped and nodded. "Why are you buying all these items?"

"Not that it's any of your business, but we have a family reunion to get to," BJ stated as he slid up behind me. His cart was just as full as mine. "Nana and Pop-pop are getting up there in age and asked us to pick up a few things." He pulled out his own Costco card and debit card from his wallet and handed it to the guy.

"I'm running back for more," I told BJ.

He nodded. "Okay, me too."

"I'll start ringing you up right now. One tab okay?" Pete said, suddenly eager.

"One's fine." I handed him my debit card as well.

He muttered something to me, but I didn't catch it as I went back to the vestibule and grabbed another cart.

"Twenty more minutes, then let's bounce." BJ looked

down at his phone. "It's too quiet in here," he whispered.

And for the first time, I noticed he was right. I had passed a lot of shoppers but hadn't discerned their silence. The tension was thick in the air, waiting for the first spark to burn the place down. I left him with a quick squeeze of his hand and a smile before I headed back to the canned goods.

I might have overdone it. We didn't need Ramen, Chef Boyardee, or some of the other items I snagged up, but I grabbed them nevertheless. I even stopped to pick up as many cases of Monsters I could for BJ and Sylvia, and cold coffees for myself.

I hoped we were overreacting. I prayed a week from now that I'd be laughing at us freaking out over nothing.

I finished piling up my cart and headed towards the front of the store. I saw books, activity books, and games near the checkout and impulsively bought some. I was ecstatic to find The Boxcar Children books that Mikey was getting into, and books about gaming for Miller. Hopefully, they'd keep them occupied for the next five or so hours up to the campground.

Sylvia and Mikey were waiting on us as I pushed my cart behind the other two. It looked like Pete had already taken care of me and BJ and was working on Sylvia's. She had more clothes and shoes than I thought were necessary, but who was I to say anything? Pete was scanning jeans, shirts, shorts, socks, shoes, and even underwear in various sizes as Sylvia placed them in totes.

It shouldn't have surprised me that Sylvia had been creative enough to think about that. They would be easier to stack in the back of my truck and keep everything consolidated and separated.

"I'm hungry," Miller stated as BJ came up behind me with another cart of stuff.

"We just had breakfast a few hours ago," I teased.

In my head, this was all one big game. Nothing terrible was happening, and we were going to be just fine. This was just a test Dad was giving us to see if we could react quickly. That this was no different then the elaborate scavenger hunts they'd give us as kids.

Uncle Scott, Uncle Mitch, and Dad enjoyed training little warriors when we were younger. They used to split us up in teams and send us out into the woods to find items that they had hidden. They'd hand us a map, a list, and a compass, challenging us to locate everything. The team that returned first got twenty dollars each from the brothers.

Most of us had thought it was fun. Katie and Emery, not so much. They really hated getting dirty, even as girls.

I had enjoyed it then, but this was no game.

"But I'm hungry again," he said in exasperation.

I handed him two twentys. "Why don't you get us two pizzas from over there and some drinks," I told him as I eyed the snack bar not even fifteen-feet away.

"Okay!" He beamed up at me before skipping off.

"Can I go too?" Mikey cried out.

"Go for it." I smiled at him.

He ran off happily. At least for now, they were unaffected by the tension buzzing in the air.

⧠

While Sylvia took the boys out to the truck, Pete was almost done ringing up the last of our items. BJ had suggested that Sylvia pull up to the loading zone. That's when we encountered the first proof that things were rapidly declining.

"Hey, Pete?" a woman a few registers down said with a frown. "Our credit card machine keeps declining the cards."

"I have enough money in my account," a red-faced,

angry man loudly exclaimed.

"Me too," another woman insisted.

Pete frowned and started to walk away.

"Can you please finish ringing us up first?" BJ quickly insisted. "We have cash, and we're already late for our family reunion."

BJ gave me a pointed look. First, communication had been taking from us, and now it appeared they were taking away our ability to use electronic forms of payment. I understood now why he had told me to take out cash.

They were trying to prevent hysteria but were only feeding into it.

"This will only take a moment." Pete shrugged.

"Seriously, sir," I stated firmly. "We have cash, and you won't have to even use your credit card machine for us. If you don't finish ringing us up, we're leaving, and you just missed out on a large sale."

Pete vacillated for a moment. "Stand by, guys," he told his cashiers. "I'll check out the issue in one moment. Let me finish with my customers."

"We need to get home too!" one man loudly proclaimed from the back of one of the lines.

"Sir, if you can just be a little patient," Pete hollered back. "I'm almost done here."

"Why can't *they* be patient?" a woman cried out. "You're taking care of kids that probably don't even have the money to pay for their stuff, while you have at least twenty of us waiting."

"Ma'am, with all due respect," BJ clipped out. "We've been waiting longer than you, and he's almost done."

Pete finished ringing us up, and I blanched at the total. Just like that, all my cash was nearly gone. BJ went to reach for his wallet, but I put a hand on his hand. "Save it," I murmured as I handed him my cash.

Pete looked at us suspiciously once more as he counted the cash.

"Let's go," I muttered to BJ as he grabbed the carts, dragging them behind him.

Sylvia came running into the store. "I locked them in," she explained, holding up the keys. "We should go, it's getting loud out there," she said quietly as she grabbed her carts.

I pulled one of mine behind me. It wasn't the fastest way to move, but I didn't trust anyone to leave it behind.

"Pete!" I heard someone cry out.

I turned around and watched as one of the customers collapsed into a seizure.

"Go!" BJ urged, and we took off as fast as we could.

I mentally calculated. We had five to twenty minutes before that person became violent, and I didn't want to be here when that happened.

"Someone call an ambulance. He stopped breathing!" I heard someone yell behind us. Seconds later, chaos erupted.

⬦

We were loading up the last of our carts when I noticed a younger family exiting the building. The man had blond hair, the woman had long dark hair, and the two boys resembled their Latina mother.

"I don't know what to tell you, Rosa," the man was saying irritably. "I have no cash. You know we don't ever carry cash."

"Luke, how are we supposed to get groceries?" Rosa whined.

"We'll just go to the next store," Luke said with a shrug.

"Excuse me, sir," Sylvia called out. "We have some food

we can spare just in case."

BJ and I exchanged looks.

Yes, we were altruistic. We'd volunteered several times in the past. We were generous by nature, but did we really want to give out food in front of a store full of people?

We already filled Sylvia in on our hypothesis as the siren sounded in the distance. We could hear the fire trucks, ambulances, and squad cars. The closest city was less than five miles away, and we could still hear them.

The match had been lit; it was only a matter of time before everyone realized our dire situation.

BJ sighed but quickly started to give them some of our food. I watched as he loaded one of our empty carts and loaded it with a case of ramen, Chef Boyardee, tuna, a bag of rice, water, and a few other items. Admittedly it wasn't that much, but I was starting to get antsy.

"Thank you so much," Luke exclaimed.

"Why are you giving it to us, and why do you have all this food?" Rosa asked us with narrowed eyes.

Sylvia's mouth dropped open at Rosa's waspish tone. "You're welcome," Sylvia snapped.

"Family reunion. Pop-pop won't notice it gone," BJ said curtly. "Let's go, girls."

I could feel the same tension I was feeling roll off of him.

"Can't you give us more?" Rosa insisted.

"Rosa!" Luke said in embarrassment.

"What? They have plenty!" she sneered. "I think they know something we don't. It seemed awfully convenient they had so much cash. They look like college kids, and they have *that* much cash in their wallets?"

Suddenly I saw a calculating look enter Luke's eyes. He was eyeing the truck and then us.

We needed to leave, like, now.

I grabbed Sylvia's arm and started to push her towards her door as I noticed more people coming out of the store, looking unhappy and empty-handed.

"Give us some more food!" Rosa went to make a grab the tailgate of my truck.

I gently pushed her back, noticing the crowd that had gathered. "Please, you're making a scene," I hissed. "Just take what we gave you and leave." I nodded towards the other people.

"Back off," I heard Mikey's small voice as he pointed his new sais at Rosa.

He'd gotten out of the truck?

"Don't point that at my mom," the little boy near Mikey's age yelled with a balled-up fist.

"Please," I insisted, trying to reason with her once again. "We gave you more than we had to."

Some of the people exiting had stopped and was watching on with interest now.

"You have enough for all of us." A tall, burly man started towards me.

BJ and I exchanged glances before he picked up Mikey and headed towards the passenger door at a run. I heard a shrill scream coming from the store.

I ran towards my door and dove into the front seat just as someone was pulling a few totes out of the bed of my truck. I put the truck in drive and pulled out, not bothering to buckle up as I watched the people converge over the three totes in the lot, fighting among themselves for the contents. In growing horror, I noticed people exiting the store covered in blood. Within moments, they attacked the unsuspecting looters.

I shuddered, feeling the contents of my stomach

threaten to come up. I heard Miller and Mikey cry out and knew they had seen what I had seen.

Chapter 5

"Okay, here's the deal, boys," I finally said as we merged onto the interstate. "Something's wrong. There are some very sick people out there, and they want to hurt us. We are going somewhere safe, but I want you to listen. Sylvia asked you to stay in the truck. Someone could have been hurt."

"I'm sorry." Mikey's lower lip trembled.

"Mikey, I'm proud that you were trying to protect us, but there were too many of them and not enough of us. Sometimes we need to know what battles to fight and what fights we should run from," I informed him gently.

Some might say I had mishandled the situation, but they weren't little. They were old enough and mature enough to understand that things weren't okay. I wasn't going to go into great detail, but I didn't want to keep them in the dark, either.

The moment we left the parking lot, the boys and Sylvia began to cry in earnest. I didn't have the luxury to break down, but my hands wouldn't stop shaking. I could see from BJ's grim expression that he longed to unravel too, but like me, he was shoving it to the back burner. He had pulled out a road map and was currently highlighting it.

"I'm sorry, Avery," Mikey apologized once more.

I reached forward and opened the box of pizza. I carefully grabbed the napkins from my glove box and handed it back to them. "I'm not angry, bud," I reassured him in the rearview mirror. "I just don't want anything bad to happen to you. Before you try defending us, let's wait until you're properly trained, okay?"

"Okay," he sullenly nodded.

"Shit," BJ muttered.

I looked ahead and cursed silently. The roads were locked up.

"The next exit is five miles ahead," he said. "Take it. I wasn't thinking. We should have taken the back roads, even if it took longer to get to the campground."

I took a calming breath in as I joined the queue of cars trying to get to goodness knew where. "No worries, B," I reassured him. "We'll get there."

I was hoping if I said it enough times and believed it, it would come true.

"Can I call my mom?" Miller asked in a quivering voice. He was usually such a stoic, unaffectionate, and serious boy. I never expected him to have cried the way he had. He had clung to Sylvia like he'd been afraid to let go. In fact, he was still leaning against her and holding one of her hands.

I sighed as I handed him my phone. "You can try, but the phone stopped working."

"What?" he cried out in panic. "We need to go back and get my mom and my baby sister."

My brows rose in surprise. I wasn't shocked that Miller was worried about his mom, but that he was concerned about his unborn sister. He had made it clear from the beginning that he was unhappy his mother had remarried and then had gotten pregnant. He had said on numerous occasions that he didn't want any more siblings.

"Don't worry, bud," BJ hastily reassured him. "Do you remember Corbin?"

"The Army guy?" he asked skeptically.

"Joint Force," BJ answered ironically. "But close enough.

He's getting her right now. He's one of the best people to look out for her. She's safe. We'll meet her at the campground."

I looked back to see Miller jerkily nod as he continued to tap at my phone.

"Is... is he by himself?" Sylvia asked hesitantly.

"No, Alpha Team and Bravo Team are together," BJ said. "They combined and split up to meet us at the campground."

"Joe and Cal will be there?" Sylvia asked excitedly.

I looked over at her in surprise. "That good, huh?" I asked her before turning my gaze back to the road again.

She rarely went back for seconds. Ever since she'd had her heart broken during our freshmen year of college, she was into no strings attached relationships. The fact that she was getting excited to see not one, but two guys, astounded me.

She gave me a dreamy smile in the rearview mirror. "Just wait until we're alone," she winked at me.

I groaned. "I'm afraid to find out."

"Me too," BJ muttered teasingly.

Honestly, I was beyond curious now. Who did Sylvia like more? Who had put that smile on her face this morning?

BJ suddenly reached out and squeezed my knee. I looked over at him and stopped the gasp from exiting my lips. "Miller, Mikey, on the floor. Don't get up and don't look out the windows unless we tell you to."

I was shocked and pleasantly astounded when they both unbuckled their seat belts and sat down without protest. I expected them to argue with me the first few times.

"Syl," I said quietly. "Can you reach into my bag and grab my sais, and can you grab those books for the boys to read?"

I'd had plenty of time to think as we were driving and knew if we ever had to enter an altercation with the infected, I wanted a weapon I was comfortable with. The knife BJ got me was great, but other than learning how to throw knives, I'd never mastered the art of using them in combat. My sais were an extension of my arms and gave me more peace of mind.

Out of my peripheral, I saw Sylvia moving to do my bidding. We'd purposely packed the front of the cab with items we might want or need for the trip. I hadn't planned on giving them the books until they grew restless, but I needed them not to focus on what was going on in front of us.

There were infected weaving in and out of the vehicles, pulling people from the cars. I counted at least twenty of them, but what was even more alarming was some of the bodies seemed to… reanimate and *join* the infected.

Sylvia handed me my sais, and I put them in my lap.

"Hey, Mikey," BJ nodded at me in understanding. "Can I have your sais?"

I had shown BJ how to handle most of the weapons I had taken up. He wasn't an expert with the sais, but he was more than proficient with them.

Mikey's sais appeared next to me and BJ grabbed them. "Thanks, little dude."

"Welcome," I heard his small voice reply.

"We need to get off of the highway," I muttered as I pulled my truck over to the shoulder.

"There's an access road for emergency vehicles up there!" BJ cried out excitedly.

I gritted my teeth as my tires bumped along the rumble strips. The sound and feel grated on my already taut nerves.

"I'm glad we didn't take my Mini," Sylvia quipped, her usual personality emerging.

"Good. I'm glad. Avery has little man syndrome," BJ jested.

"Hey," I bantered back. "One, no one could ever say I was

little by any means, I'm five-eight, for Pete's sake! Two, I just wanted a real truck, there's no harm in that. Ruth was over fifteen years old and on her last leg. I don't have to worry about Blanch breaking down on me."

BJ snorted. "Only you would name your vehicles."

"Why not?" I blinked jokingly. "I believe in establishing a great relationship with my rides. After all, they get me from point A to point B when I need them."

"Be honest," Sylvia insisted. "You purposely purchased a vehicle Trevor would have salivated over."

Funny how the end of the world put things in perspective. The thoughts of Trevor and Emery still hurt, but instead of the gaping wound I once felt, it was now just a mild sting.

I sighed. "Truth... yeah," I said with a shrug. "But that doesn't mean I didn't always want a big lifted truck too. It was either a lifted Jeep or a lifted pickup, and I figured a truck would be more practical in the long run for my needs."

BJ barked out in surprised laughter.

Sylvia giggled in glee. "Wow, you actually admitted it. Do you stalk Emery and Trevor's Facebook too?"

"No," I swore with a shudder. "I may be a masochist at times, but no. Just... no. Plus, you know I rarely scroll through any of my social media. The only reason I reopened my account was for my Tae Kwon Do stuff for Dad and family, and that's it. Even then, you are my unspoken publicist. Why?"

I was thankful they were distracting me as I weaved slowly around the traffic on the side of the road. In some spots, my truck easily navigated the grassy and stony areas. I could see some of the disgruntled motorists glare at me, but I couldn't focus on them. My focus was on the access road up ahead.

Sylvia and BJ started to laugh.

"They have his and her beamers now," Sylvia said. "Hers is white, and he has a black one."

My mouth dropped open. "Trevor hates cars," I said derisively. "Like, absolutely, positively despises them. He always claimed it too was hard getting in and out of them with his long legs."

I finally edged my way onto the access road and nearly breathed a sigh of relief. BJ was conferring to his maps once more.

Trevor may have changed from the teenager I whispered my dreams to, but I never thought he would change in this respect, too. To me, it was the equivalent to deciding your favorite season. Sure, you could enjoy other seasons, but your first love was always one over another. There were just some favorites that were intricately embedded in your DNA.

It all just proved, once again, that I hadn't really known him like I thought I'd had.

"Emery got her claws into him, and now she's changing him slowly but surely." BJ snorted.

I shook my head. "You know," I voiced aloud, "It doesn't hurt as much anymore, and maybe it took the end of civilization for me to make me realize I don't care. They deserve each other. Somewhere out there I'll find someone who will love me and takes me as I am."

"Amen, sister!" Sylvia cried out happily. I knew she had been waiting a long time for me to come to that realization.

"I know of at least two men who would," BJ said cryptically.

"Make that three," Sylvia said smugly.

"Who?" I asked in shock. No one came to mind off the top of my head. Who could they possibly know that was interested in me?

⬜

I should have known it was going too smoothly to last for long. I prided myself in being cautiously optimistic in most situations. It would have been too simple to escape that jumbled up mess we left behind without running into another issue.

It became abundantly clear about a mile off the interstate that we weren't the only ones who had decided to take the emergency access road. The problem was, this time we were blocked in from the cars ahead and the cars behind us. The ditch and forest on both sides of the thoroughfare blocked me in from going around the mess.

I heard Sylvia stifle a shriek and saw a group of infected heading our way from the thick stands of trees on both sides of us and from up ahead. She pulled out her knife and gripped it until I saw the white of her knuckles. The boys had been so silent, and I was thankful for their perceptiveness. I needed the silence to focus on my driving and to think.

I saw movement out of the corner of my eye as I realized that we were getting boxed in with the infected as they lumbered closer. I contemplated trying to force my way forward, but I didn't want to be that person, and I didn't want to damage my truck.

I turned my gaze back to the car in front of me and watched in dismay as a toddler's head popped up. His face was tear-streaked and red as he banged on the rear window. A young woman was being dragged from the driver's seat, kicking and screaming. The two infected that had gotten ahold of her were biting into her neck and arm.

I barely registered my back door opening and slamming shut before I saw Sylvia streaking across my windshield.

"No!" I cried out in horror. I didn't have time to think as I opened my door to chase after her. "Lock the doors and get in the driver's seat!" I yelled at BJ before I took off running.

I gripped my sais in my hand and was aware of the two

infected converging on me. I acted on pure instinct and from the theories of all the zombie movies I had watched.

I looked at the man closest to me. I tried not to think about who this person was before he'd become violent. He reminded me too much of one of my professors I had adored my sophomore year. I quickly shut those thoughts down as he lunged towards me, foam-like blood frothing from his mouth, and bloody tears pouring from his eyes.

He was too close! I put the blade of one of my sais along my forearm as a shield as I drove my other sai into the closest infected's eye. I cried out in horror as I felt the soft tissue give way too effortlessly under the blunt edge of the point. The popping sound made me flinch in disgust.

I tried to pull my sai back, but it refused to give way. I brought up my foot, giving the man a push kick to remove him from my weapon. He fell back with an audible crunch as his head made contact with the concrete.

I felt my stomach revolt, but I had no time to get sick right now. I had to get to my friend. I looked up to assess the situation once more. There were too many infected. I vaguely heard gunshots in the distance as I witnessed Sylvia slashing away at the infected.

"The brain, Sylvia!" I screamed at her as I whirled to take on my next attacker. "Aim for their eyes and temples." Her cheap blade was less than six inches long. I didn't think it would be adequate anywhere else.

I engaged in battle after battle for what seemed like endless hours. I heard the gunshots getting closer. I felt the sweat trickling down my face and back. I smelled the putrid, coppery smell the infected emanated. My breathing was coming in a ragged gasp, but I noticed that Sylvia had rescued the toddler and another smaller bundle.

I vaguely comprehended that BJ had taken a position at my back and was engaged in his own battles. We moved in circles like a well-oiled unit, eliminating infected after infected. The only sounds from us were our rasping breaths and the occasional grunt or snarl.

I felt like I was going to pass out any moment. Usually, I could literally run five miles and barely feel winded. I could spar six women in a row with scarcely a break in between matches and still be raring to go. I knew not much time could have lapsed, but it felt like I had been doing this for entirely too long. My mind was screaming for me to take flight, while my body was engaged in a fight.

"Harrison," I heard my name being barked out as I whirled around, looking for the next opponent, only to see BJ's blinding smile. Skeins of my long dark hair adhered to my sweaty face, and my chest heaved up and down as I gasped for oxygen to enter my lungs. I felt like a feral animal, cornered, as my primal instincts emerged. Surviving was the principal thought in my mind.

"Hallelujah," BJ cried out in triumph. "Thanks for helping us."

I still felt separated from the whole situation. Reality hadn't entered the haze clouding my cognizant thoughts.

"Avery, it's okay," BJ murmured, taking my shoulders in both his hands and gently shaking me. "We're safe."

I hazily registered the fact that Axel Tacka and three other JOpS stood before me. They were dressed and equipped, nearly identical, in their black t-shirts, khaki cargo pants, and black combat boots. They carried 9MMs – or pistols similar to them – attached to their left thighs and one in each shoulder holster. Knives were on each of their ankles, ammo was affixed to their belts, and they held M-4's at the low and ready. That was just the weapons I *could* see. I imagined they had more than that on them.

"Are you bleeding?" Axel asked gruffly as his eyes roamed up and down my body.

I looked down and noticed what state I was in. I was covered in blood splatter– or the equivalent of the infected's blood. It was a dark red, almost black, coagulated matter. It wasn't anything like what normally exited our bodies. My tank top was covered, and my jean shorts were no longer a faded light wash but a disturbing brown, black, and red color. Nearly every exposed piece of my skin had their blood on it.

"Get it off, get it off!" I freaked as I began to rip off my clothing.

In my panicked, wild thoughts, I imagined the saliva of the infected soaking into my skin. I needed to get it off as soon as possible, or it was going to turn me. Slowly but surely, my frantic thoughts were replaced by the reality surrounding me.

I vaguely heard an appreciative sound from a male's throat quickly followed by the gnashing of teeth.

"Clean this up, clear the lane," I heard Axel bark out.

"I'll be right back," BJ murmured. "I'm getting you a change of clothes and a couple of towels, Avery," BJ said more loudly as he tried to force me to look into his eyes, but I was too preoccupied with my surroundings.

I looked at the pile of dead bodies on the ground, and this time I was helpless to stop my lunch from coming back up. I held my hand over my mouth. I stumbled over the bodies and limbs, to the nearest patch of grass I could find. I fell to my knees just in time.

The acidity of my vomit stung the back of my throat, and tears rushed to my eyes. I lost the meager contents left in my stomach. My body shook as the rush of adrenaline left me.

Nothing but bile was coming up now, but I was unable to stop. My brain was catching up to my actions, and I felt the implications of all I had done. I was a murderer. Countless lives died at my hands without any misgivings from me as I committed the act over and over again.

I felt large gentle hands sweep the hair off my face.

"They're no longer human," a voice as rough as sandpaper proclaimed, reading my thoughts. "Tests have been done. Whoever they were before the infection, isn't there anymore. They have no feelings, no emotions, only the primal urge to eat and spread the infection. They have no qualms eating their friends, husbands, wives, children. They must be stopped. You did really good today. More than good, little warrior."

I blinked up into Axel's eyes as he handed me a wet wipe. I wiped it across my face. The baby powder scent helped soothe me some and helped mask the smell of my vomit and... death.

I didn't question how he knew all that. I had lived with my dad long enough to know some things were better off not examined. Once you started following the rabbit, you were bound to fall down the hole.

"Were you cut, bitten?" a man's voice asked from behind us.

I looked up and noticed a handful of people around the JOpS and BJ. I met Sylvia's gaze, and there were tears in her eyes.

"I'm so sorry," she cried. "I should have never left the vehicle. I–"

I cut her off and stood up. "The child was innocent. We couldn't leave him for infected food. You were behaving as any normal human being would."

The words not spoken hung in the air. Even with Axel's reassurances, I didn't feel human anymore. I'd lost my humanity the moment I slipped into that dark place that could kill over a dozen infected systematically. There were no thoughts in my actions, just a savage urge to survive.

I felt cold liquid being poured over my arms and noticed Axel was pouring a jug of water over them. The smell of alcohol hung in the air. I would have customarily protested the temperature of the water, but today I welcomed it. *Call it my penance,* I thought.

"Were you cut or bitten?" he asked once more as he rubbed my arms down with a towel.

I numbly watched as my skin was wiped clean.

I shook my head. "I don't think so," I muttered, shaking my head.

"I'm washing you down, just to make sure. Let me know if you want me to stop," Axel spoke quietly, as if he were soothing a frightened animal or child. I had heard him talk more in the last twenty minutes or so than yesterday afternoon.

His voice was pleasant. It was dark and rich, like a cup of strong coffee or smooth chocolate. I felt the tension wracking my body slowly dissipate by his dulcet tones.

"We put a splash of rubbing alcohol in the water," he continued talking to me. "It's not ideal, but we don't have anything else on-hand that kills germs effectively. We've been told their salvia can infect us, but only if they break the skin or if their blood comes in contact with open wounds, but I much rather be safe than sorry."

"I got you more clothes, Ave," BJ said quietly as he held up another pair of jean cut-offs and a black tank top. He had already changed, and I saw no blood on him. My eyes quickly assessed that he was unharmed. I sighed in relief.

"Thanks," I murmured to both of them.

"I'm going to put them right here." BJ placed them on top of a duffle bag I hadn't even seen next to Axel. "I'm going to help clear this out," he informed Axel. "Unless you want me to help her?"

I could see the discomfort in BJ's eyes. I nearly laughed at him before I realized I was dressed in my Wonder Woman bra and matching boy shorts. Yeah, I had a thing for character underwear. I loved my silk and lace sometimes, but my go-to undergarments were my simple cotton, somewhat quirky underwear.

I imagined my brother was relieved not to have to talk me down from this freak out in just my underwear. Granted, I showed just as much skin when we went swimming, but it wasn't like he was touching me in those conditions.

"I got this," Axel clipped out, his jaw tensing. "Go help my guys."

Axel continued his ministrations, and I tried to ignore the way my body was aware of his touch. How long had it been since I desired a man when I was sober? I quickly shut down my thoughts, realizing how inappropriate they were. Now was neither the time nor place for me to feel this pull towards him.

When he was done, he patted me dry with a towel. I tried not to notice how his hands seemed to linger on my hips, or how his long tan fingers came in contact with my skin at times. He slipped my shirt over my head, and then, as if I were a toddler, he helped me into my new shorts. I gently pushed his hands away before he could zip them up and fasten them. It felt too... intimate.

"Thank you," I said softly, then cleared my throat. "How'd you find us?" I finally asked, realizing it was too much of a coincidence.

I pulled a hair tie off my wrist, I had an obsession with collecting them there, and grimaced at the gunk on them. There was no way I could use them again. I ripped them off and watched them scatter to the ground. I then twisted my hair up and weaved it into a bun. It wouldn't stay put if I had to move a lot, but it would do for now.

"Your phones," he replied in an enigmatic tone. "Eden was able to use your stepmom's phone to get your location."

He reached into his cargo pocket and pulled out a hair tie and attempted a grateful grin. I surmised he knew the struggles with long hair too.

"Stephanie's okay?" I asked in relief. I knew she would be, with Wyatt watching over her, but it was like I needed to hear it verbally to feel better.

Axel nodded. "Let's get going," he said abruptly.

I looked around and started walking toward the small group that were on the side of the road. BJ, Sylvia, and three JOpS remained, murmuring among themselves as they hovered between a large black SUV and my white Dodge Ram.

The bodies were nowhere to be found, and the cars that had been blocking the path were pushed off into the ditch. Either I had lost a lot of time, or the JOpS and those who helped eliminate the infected had worked quickly.

I stilled, noticing Sylvia was now standing with a baby cradled to her chest. I blinked in confusion.

"They don't have anyone," she said in a small voice, noticing me. "I looked, Avery. I even went through their mother's phone. She just turned eighteen, and her oldest is three." She indicated the truck. "Both dads don't seem to be in the picture, and the last few messages she got from her stepmom made me believe she didn't have any family support. They're all alone. They need us."

I could see Mikey and Miller sitting in the front seat of my truck now, with the toddler sitting in between them.

Why was she behaving as if I would protest? She knew I had a softness towards children and animals. She even knew how much I loved my Pediatrics and Labor and Delivery rotation in clinical. Admittedly, I hadn't been able to touch a baby or hold them, but I knew I would get over that mental block eventually.

"Do they have their car seats?" I asked after a brief second of contemplation.

She let out a relieved sigh. "Chad put them in their SUV." She indicated the black Tahoe that was parked behind the truck. "I'm going to ride with them."

I noticed a man hunched over in the back seat of the SUV installing the carseats. I assumed he was Chad.

"I'm going to ride with you," Axel stated beside me, looking at me briefly before he addressed BJ.

Had I been more mentally present, I would have asked him if he was *asking* me or *telling* me. His overbearing attitude would have made me very snarky a few hours ago. When Dad was upset, or when Coach barked at me, those was their roles. I'd just met this guy. Who was he to command me around?

"We need to get off this road," he continued. "There's a rest stop about thirty minutes away. We'll stop there, compare our routes, and regroup. Maybe have a late lunch. Ready?"

Everyone nodded, and we started heading to my truck.

"Mind if I drive?" Axel looked over at BJ.

BJ started to laugh and shook his head. "Ask her," he said, climbing into the back seat of my truck.

"Go for it," I responded before opening my passenger door.

Maybe I had hit my head and not realized it. First I was following orders without questioning them. Now I was allowing a near-perfect stranger to drive my truck.

I was usually quite particular about who drove my truck. In fact, no one had driven it other than me until yesterday. But I was also realistic. There was no way I was in any condition to drive and was reminded more so as I stared at the young faces looking back at me.

"Get in the back boys," I told Miller and Mikey, ruffling their hair.

Miller pretended to grumble, but Mikey smiled up at me.

The toddler Sylvia had rescued, remained in the middle, and he peered over at me suspiciously before giving me a large smile, too.

I held my hands out to the adorable curly-haired, redheaded, freckle-faced toddler. He smiled at me as his tiny arms reached out. "Hey, handsome," I crooned to him. "Ready to go?"

He was so trusting and open as he hugged me. Toddlers were okay. But babies? They made me break out in cold sweats, made my hands shake, and caused me to panic. It hadn't always been that way, and I prayed I would get over it soon.

"Mama go?" he asked hopefully.

I closed my eyes, willing the tears at bay. "No, buddy." I swallowed. I remembered Sylvia holding a baby dressed in yellow. Did he love his brother or sister as I had at that age? It was hard to tell whether Sylvia had been holding a boy or girl. "Wanna go with your...?" I looked over and noticed one of the JOpS standing by with his arms extended. I assumed he was there to collect the toddler and put him in the other vehicle.

"Sister. She's Jenny, and that tot you're holding is Phillip," the man explained with a sympathetic smile. "Come on, Phil. Jenny needs her big brother." He produced a blue stuffed dog that Phillip cried out happily for as he reached for it.

I handed him off to the JOpS and watched them walk away. He was cute, and there was something seriously sexy about a man and a baby, but I felt... nothing.

So what made me desire the silent, strong man that sat in my driver's seat?

Chapter 6

We were pleasantly surprised to find the rest stop nearly empty. We found a spot in the back left-hand corner near the restrooms. BJ immediately pulled out some trays of food from the back of the truck and laid out the hard-boiled eggs, cheese, pepperoni, crackers, sliced apples, grapes, and nuts.

We found a couple of picnic tables under the trees surrounding the rest stop. It didn't take us long to get settled in.

I didn't feel like eating. I couldn't eat. Images of the infected dying by my hands were playing on repeat in my head.

"I grabbed some of this on impulse," BJ explained. "We should probably eat it up before it goes bad."

I examined the guys as they sat across from me, three of them I hadn't formally been introduced to. The man who had taken little Phillip from me was about my height, muscular, with dark hair, and eyes that were a startling blue against his tanned skin.

The man next to him was currently rocking the tiny infant, Jenny, in his arms. She looked so small and pale against his large, dark hands. He was built like a linebacker and was almost as tall as Axel but twice as big width-wise. His head was shaved bald, and he had warm dark eyes. There were lines around his mouth and eyes that suggested he smiled a lot.

Beside him was male who looked to be Filipino. He

was shorter than me but built like a bulldog. His dark hair was cut in the typical military fashion, and his brown eyes seemed alert and intelligent as he regularly surveyed our surroundings.

Sylvia came over with paper plates, which made me wonder just what else had we gotten today. I hadn't paid much attention to what we had loaded up when we were done shopping. I knew I had dry goods, and Sylvia had bought the clothing, but what had BJ grabbed exactly?

"Food is food. Thanks, man, we're starving." The man holding Jenny smiled as he shifted Jenny to one shoulder while grabbing some food.

"No thanks needed, Chad," BJ said with a smile. "If you guys hadn't come along, well..." He shrugged, leaving the words hanging in the air.

The Filipino guy snorted good-naturedly. "You're kidding, right? You guys had it more than handled. You're pretty sick with those sais, but your girl here was a beast."

Sylvia laughed as she handed Phillip a piece of apple. The toddler was safely ensconced in her lap, seemingly content to be held and eating. The way he was eating made me wonder when the last time he'd eaten a decent meal. "That's her nickname on the mats," she said. "And by the way, B and Ave are *siblings*, not a couple."

I felt Axel shift beside me and saw an indecipherable look cross his features.

"You're the martial artist that kicked Natalie's ass, aren't you?" Mr. Blue-eyes inquired in wonder as he assessed me.

"She doesn't look like much, but she really is a beast." BJ smiled at me as he bumped my shoulder with his own. He took no offense with the Filipino's observation. He preferred

Judo or wrestling to Tae Kwon Do or weapons, although he was pretty sick with the bo staff.

"*You* laid the smackdown on Nats?" Chad gave me an assessing look as well.

I shrugged self-consciously. "Not really," I said.

A bottle of water was placed in front of me and a plate of food. I looked over at Axel and saw his commanding, luminous caramel gaze on me. He looked like he meant business, and, somehow, I think he'd cause a stink if I didn't attempt to eat.

I sighed and picked up the bottle of water. I hadn't even realized how dry my mouth was. I also was reminded that I probably needed to brush my teeth.

"My sister's modest," BJ stated. "She just made the National Team and was headed to the Olympics."

Was. There wasn't going to be any Olympics anytime in the near future. I figured it would be my luck to be at the top of my game, only to have the dream yanked away.

"Aren't you a model too?" the Filipino asked, with something akin to lust in his eyes. "And you're the girl in the pictures in Cavalier's footlocker, right?

I saw Sylvia and BJ tense, and I almost laughed. I could tell they were getting ready to protect me or steer the conversation to safer topics. Had I been *that* bad? Had I been that sensitive on the subject of my sister?

I gave him a crooked grin as I tore a piece of my cheese in half. "My sister is the model, I'm the athlete," I explained as I took a tentative bite of my food. I didn't know if my stomach could handle it, but I'd try. "And if there are pics of me in Corbin's footlocker, it may or may not be me, but I doubt it. Emery and I are identical, and she and Corbin were closer to each other. So, it's probably Em."

"It's you," Axel murmured.

I looked up at him in surprise. How would Axel know?

My surprise was soon replaced with curiosity. The Cavaliers and Harris-Harrisons had always been close, especially after my mom died. We'd known Corbin our whole lives. He went from playmate to tormentor, to a teen who treated us indifferently. By the time his family moved near us again, he had joined up. He would come home to visit, but he never hung around that often. When Emery had gotten her license, though, she had hung out with him a lot when he was home.

From what I had gathered from her and Trevor, Corbin had acted like an older brother to her by then. She tried to get him to hook her up with his friends, and he shot her down. They bantered on Facebook a lot and tagged each other in pictures. I didn't have that type of relationship with Cor. I had been too wrapped up in Trevor.

So what picture did Corbin have of me, and how could Axel be so sure it was me? *Hello? Identical twins!*

Axel finally cleared his throat before he reached into his cargo pocket. "We should probably come up with a game plan. It's going to be dark soon, and if we don't reach our destination in time, we need to find a place to stay overnight."

"Why can't we drive through the night?" BJ asked in confusion.

Axel looked at Miller and Mikey. They had been quiet and was watching all of us intently.

"Hey, Mikey and Miller, let's hit the head... I mean, the bathroom," Mr. Blue eyes stated, standing up. Mikey and Miller groaned, obviously disappointed not to hear our conversation. "Wanna come with us too, Philly?" He turned to the toddler.

"Yes!" Phillip nodded. "Potty pwease," he requested in his cute little lisp.

Mr. Blue-eyes smiled and held out his hand to Phillip.

Jenny began to fuss once they left. Chad immediately stood with the baby cradled to his broad chest and walked towards the SUV.

"We know some things," BJ said the moment Chad walked away. "But we want to know it all. You guys know more than what you're letting on, and for our survival, we should know too. I understand OPSEC and all that, but let's be real, who are we going to tell?"

"Felix," Axel prodded after a few moments of heavy silence.

"No one knows where this virus originated from." The Filipino, Felix, leaned forward. "They think it may have been man-made. We heard rumors of a biological weapon being created for a little over a year, but every time we went to investigate these claims... poof." He made a noise with his mouth before he continued. "Alpha Team finally got a confirmation of the bioweapon, but by the time they located the village, it was too late. Everyone in the town was deceased, and they were only able to collect some data on the possible virus.

"They secured the village before the scientists were called in. With Alpha Team, we were actually able to find and locate some of the infected for the scientist to examine. They observed the test subjects to give us a better understanding of the virus once it establishes a host. They've been running the test and still trying to find a cure for the... infection. Before communications were dropped this morning, Harris told us the infected were more dangerous at night. They seemed to be faster, more intelligent. We really don't want to be in the open when the sun sets."

I gasped as I looked at BJ. He appeared as waxen as I felt.

"There's no need to be worried," Chad said as he returned with Jenny. The huge man was now feeding the baby a bottle. "We've encountered the infected over there, and we'll protect you until we reach our safe zone."

I barely registered how comfortable the large man was in taking care of the baby. He was caring for her with an ease that suggested he had done it before.

I felt tears burn my eyes once more as I covered my face. My dad wasn't any safer than we were. "Who's protecting my dad?" I stated hoarsely.

"Your dad?" Felix asked in confusion.

"Lieutenant Colonel Harris is our father," I said in agitation as things fell into place. "Is he even on his way home?"

"Colonel Harris is your father? But... isn't your last name Harrison?" Chad inquired with a frown. I could see the wheels working in his head.

From what I had gathered, he was on Bravo Team. If Alpha Team swept the village for the scientist, then they must have secured it for my dad. Did Wyatt and Corbin never tell Bravo Team their relationship with my dad, and where was Corbin's dad? He was deployed, too. Generally, they worked alongside each other.

They were two of the most brilliant scientists the military had.

Fear was gripping me once more. I felt light-headed and anxious. My dad could be in danger, and I didn't even know if Uncle Scott was with him. They always worked better as a team.

"My mother was Isabella Harrison- Harris," BJ stated numbly. "After the girls were born, she put them in modeling. They were nearly as hot a commodity as my mom. They modeled together until they were about twelve. Em developed an eating disorder, and there was a stalker after them. Dad thought it was best if they were removed from the spotlight. Mom got cancer and died. The stalker never went away. Dad then got orders to Andrews, and he decided to get their names legally changed to our mother's maiden name so they couldn't be found."

I saw the shock on all their faces. I never even told Sylvia about Marlon Gains. He was a memory I tried to bury. I had issues sleeping for years because of him. Em may have gone to treatment for her eating disorder, but I went to therapy because of what he had done to me. His obsession for Em paled in comparison to his fixation on me.

"I'm cold," I stated abruptly, feeling uncomfortable under their gazes. "I'm going to get my hoodie and brush my teeth."

I stood and walked stiffly towards the truck. I *was* getting cold, so it gave me the perfect excuse to get up.

There was a reason why I'd become so driven with Tae Kwon Do. I had motives I never admitted aloud to anyone but my therapist. I never wanted to feel powerless and helpless ever again. Martial Arts became my security blanket. The more confident I got in my training, and the more matches I won as a young teen, the better I slept at night.

I shuddered. Where was my therapist? I would love to talk to her right now. She was always such a great listener and put things into perspective. Most of the time, I just needed her to listen to me. I had made the mistake once of expecting support from Em when everything had been so overwhelming, and I regretted it still to this day.

I climbed into my truck and pulled out my bag. Right on top was my dojang hoodie. It was my favorite. It was black with my silhouette on the back, with my name on the front. I was doing a flying side kick in white. I liked it because no one technically knew it was my form on the back, but I knew. Coach had gotten all of us unique personalized gifts this past year. I silently prayed that, wherever he was, he was safe.

I leaned over and reached into the boys' bags next and grabbed their sweatshirts, too. I imagined they would be getting cold soon. It was still technically mid-spring, and even though it was comfortably warm during the day, the temps were known to drop at night.

Reaching into my toiletry bag, I pulled out my travel toothbrush and toothpaste. I got a bottle of water and rinsed my brush. It wasn't very practical to brush my teeth in a parking lot when a bathroom was fifty yards away. However, I was too lazy to take a walk and still wanted to be alone with my thoughts. When the disgusting taste left my mouth, I rinsed my brush, stuck it back in my bag, and then took a swig of water to rinse my mouth.

I was bent over, spitting the water out, when I felt a presence at my back. I was about to strike out but then froze when I felt cold steel pressed against my head.

"Not a word," a male voice hissed in my ear. I heard the gun's slide cocking back. "And don't you dare scream. Just give me your keys, and we'll leave here without hurting you."

Fear and reasoning battled inside my head. I could quickly disarm one assailant, but he had said "we."

"What's going on here?" I heard Axel ask from behind me.

"Just mind your own business," a shrill female voice sneered. "Move one more inch, and my husband is going to blow her brains out."

"Mom," I heard a young boy's voice cry.

"Shut up, Ben," another boy hissed.

Slowly recognition sunk in, and my fear was replaced by anger. "Really? Rosa and Luke?" I sneered. "We gave you enough food to last you at least two weeks. Is this how you repay people that show you good deeds?"

"Food you had *stolen* from us. You could have given us more," Rosa cried out hysterically. "You have so much of it. Now it's ours."

Of all the people to run into, we had to run into them? I thought. Where had they even come from? Had they been following us?

"Mom," the first boy continued to sob. "Please, they were nice to us. We should have left after they gave us the food."

I heard a resounding smack.

"Woah, woah," Axel said in a calming voice. "No reason to hit your son."

"How about you refrain from telling me how to raise my son," Rosa scorned. "Ben, Hector, get into the truck. Luke, grab her keys."

"Where are they?" Luke tapped the gun into my head, making me wince.

I went to grab my keys but felt the butt of the gun smack me in my head. I saw stars and cried out in pain.

"I said don't move!" Luke yelled.

Then I heard several bolts being pulled back.

"Touch her again and I'll fucking kill you," Axel said with deadly quietness.

Suddenly, I was being dragged around, now facing Axel, Mr. Blue-eyes, and Felix. They all had their M-4's raised and trained on Luke.

"All I need is the keys, man. She just needs to tell me where they're at," Luke's voice shook despite the confidence of his words. The muzzle of his gun dug into my temple. I knew with my body shielding him, he had a false sense of confidence. "Tell my boy where your keys are, and he'll grab them."

"They're in my pocket," I hissed out in pain as the muzzle dug further into my skin.

"Hector!" Luke called out. "Grab the keys from her pocket."

The older boy reached into my pocket and seized them. He held them up triumphantly. "Got them!"

"Now, here's what's going to happen," Luke stuttered out. "My wife is going to drive us out of here, and we're taking the girl to the rest stop exit Shoot at us, and you might hit the girl."

He pulled me to the tailgate of my truck as panic seized me. More agony shot up to my scalp as he dragged me backwards by my hair with one hand and held the gun to my head with the other. I cried out in shock and hurt.

"I said not to touch her!" Axel roared, raising the scope to his eyes. Felix and Mr. Blue-eyes began to talk to him urgently. I could see his strong jaw clench and unclench.

"If anything happens to my girl, know this," Axel finally rasped out. "I have the resources and ability to hunt you down. I will take your sons from you and make sure they're raised honorably while I feed you to the infected piece by piece."

A cold chill ran down my spine. I was glad he was on my side. I also hadn't missed his term of "my girl." I didn't want to examine the thrill at the thought of really being his girl.

I shoved my foolish thoughts aside and focused back on the situation I was in.

I knew he was just trying to scare Luke, to antagonize him. He had to pretend I meant something to him. Who would want to provoke a man that large and intimidating? No sane man, that's for sure.

"You do as I tell you, and I won't touch her again," Luke sniveled. "Climb up," he commanded me.

He released my hair and lowered the tail gate. I knew I had no choice but to obey him. I turned around and put my foot on the bumper of my truck before climbing in. I heard Mikey yell for me, but I kept my head down. I didn't want him to see my fear.

Luke climbed up next to me and leaned behind me. I didn't have the opportunity to jump out before his gun was digging into my back.

"Screw you, Tonto," Rosa cursed out from the driver's side window. She poked her head out and pointed another gun at the men. "Maybe if your girl wasn't such a selfish bitch, we wouldn't be taking everything for her."

Her racial slur made me snarl. Her ignorance knew no bounds.

My mind churned for a solution to the problem. I didn't want to give them all of our supplies, but I really, really didn't want to lose my baby, my truck. I must have overdosed on adrenaline today because I couldn't come up with the solution as my head pounded.

I heard my truck start, and soon we were pulling out of the parking spot. "Why does she treat you and your son like you're beneath her?" I scoffed at Luke as we drove at a slow pace towards the exit.

I refused to look at the people I left behind; their emotions would affect me and I needed to keep my feelings locked down. If this was my fate, then so be it, but I wasn't going down without a fight.

"She loves me and only wants what's best for us," he bit out, but I heard the insecurities in his voice.

"Whatever makes you feel better, I guess," I mocked him. "Rosa treats you like a dog. She speaks to anyone that contradicts her or makes her unhappy with disrespect. And we mustn't forget she slapped your son for speaking his mind. I guess everyone has to fall into line, or she punishes them."

"Shut up!" he screamed at me, and I knew I had hit a nerve. "Don't make me hit you again."

"Well, you could," I goaded. "But my man is JOpS. Do you know what that is? Heard of the rangers? How about the Seals? PJs? He's all that and then some. He's trained to be the ultimate human weapon." I tried to sell the lie but noticed how easy the words "my man" fell from my lips. I couldn't remember the last time those words came out of my mouth without cringing or feeling despair.

"Touch me," I continued, "and he'll hunt you down like he promised and make you regret you ever did."

"Rosa!" he bellowed.

She slammed on the breaks, and I tumbled back, stricking my spine against a tote. I bit back a curse.

"Get out!" he growled.

"Wait," Rosa said as she jumped out of the truck,

holding her gun towards me. "I want the sweatshirt. Give it to me."

I began to protest, but knew it was fruitless. I slowly removed it as I glared at Rosa. She didn't need my sweatshirt. She was just high on her power trip.

"Throw it here," she said with a scornful smile. "Maybe you'll share better next time."

She bent over and retrieved my sweater. She slid it on and gave me another smug smile. "So warm."

"If you believe in Karma, you're screwed," I said scornfully. "I just hope your sons don't pay for your greed."

Without warning, I heard the slide of her gun. I dove in the opposite direction, hearing it go off, and hoping she had a horrible aim.

Chapter 7

BJ, Sylvia, and Axel jumped out of the SUV and found me crying by the rest stop exit.

There was a small copse of trees and bushes on both sides, before it led out to the highway. I had crawled to one of the bushes and stayed there, clutching my knees to my chest. I knew it would only be a matter of minutes before help arrived.

"Did they hit you?" BJ cried out.

"No." I shook my head, wiping my cheeks.

"Then why are you crying?" Sylvia bent down in front of me. "If it's the supplies, it's okay. We have enough to keep us going for a while."

"It's not that." I sniffled as I pulled up the hem of my shirt to my nose.

"Your life is more important than your damn truck, Ave." BJ sighed in frustration. "If it makes you feel better, I'll steal you a better one."

I nearly snorted with laughter, imagining my once trouble-making brother boosting a vehicle. The academy had straightened him out and provided him the stability he needed that my parents wouldn't or couldn't give him.

"Blanch was a beautiful truck, but it's not that." I revealed my stomach once more as I wiped my running nose. I knew I looked like a hot mess, but I really didn't give a damn.

"Did they hurt you?" Sylvia hugged me harder.

"No. Not much, anyway," I cried out. "Rosa took my favorite hoodie."

I knew I was being totally irrational, but in my exhausted, distraught head, it was worth crying over.

BJ and Sylvia cursed.

"Seriously?" Sylvia sighed dramatically. "You're shitting me, right? Your black hoodie? The one with your name on it? The one with your silhouette on it?"

I nodded my head and mumbled my yeses into her chest. Suddenly she was shaking me.

"You have to be shitting me! You can't be the crazy one in our relationship. I am. You're not allowed to break down, Ave, because then I will, and then no one will pick up the pieces!" she began to cry. "And don't you ever scare me like that again. I thought I was never going to see you again. Then I hear a gunshot, and I find you crying... And you weren't crying over your fifty thousand dollar truck but your twenty-dollar sweatshirt. That's the shit I pull, not you."

"Umm, are we ready?" Felix asked as he leaned out of his window. From the laughter in his eyes, I assumed he had heard enough to realize I was borderline insane.

"Give them a minute," Axel commanded softly.

Felix rolled his window back up with a grin and a wink my way.

"We should get going," I cleared my throat, embarrassed now.

"No!" Sylvia insisted with her Latina stubbornness. She meant business. "Let it out now! You bottle that shit up all the time, and you hadn't seen your therapist this whole past year when you probably needed her the most! You lost your child, found out your boyfriend of six years slept with your twin sister, then lost your grandparents all within two months, and you barely cried then. Yet you're sobbing over a damn hoodie, and can't you cry like a normal girl, all ugly like? Can't you screw up on anything?"

"I did cry," I insisted. I almost laughed at her scolding me. I knew my face was red and my nose was running. I was a disgusting mess.

"Not in front of us, not to us," BJ said as he knelt next to me. "What baby, Avery?" he asked softly.

I stiffened, and Sylvia gasped, holding her hands up to her mouth.

"I'm sorry," she whispered in a horrified tone. "I've screwed up so much today! I offered that horrid bitch food, I put you in the middle of a hoard of infected, and now I'm spilling your secrets."

I stood up, wiping my face one last time, and took a deep breath. Meltdown over with. Time to close the door again. Time to compartmentalize my feelings. It was easier to cope that way. We had more important shit to worry about.

I debated not saying anything, but I could hear the hurt in BJ's voice. He and Sylvia were my best friends. Sylvia knew because she had to be there for me when I couldn't reach Trevor. She had driven me to the hospital, where I'd been advised to have a D&C. I couldn't drive myself, and she was by my side the whole time.

She had then driven me to Trevor's once I was released from the hospital. I just wanted him to comfort me. I wasn't mad that he hadn't been answering the phone. Imagine my surprise when I found my sister and my boyfriend in bed together.

"I was sixteen weeks pregnant with Trevor's baby," I began. "We wanted to wait until we were passed the first trimester to tell everyone. Then we figured if we waited a few more weeks, we could find out what the baby was. We were waiting for the Forth of the July bash to let everyone know. We ordered cute little picture frames with her ultrasound pictures in it to give to Aunt Pam and Uncle Scott and Dad. We even ordered one of those reveal cakes with pink in it."

I crossed my arms over my chest, feeling a deep chill hit me all at once. "I lost her. They had to take me to surgery. I couldn't reach Trevor, and when I went to his frat house after I was released, I found Em and him together. And you know the rest." I moved towards the truck, finished with the conversation. I was too emotionally raw.

"It was a girl?" BJ asked, his voice thick with emotions.

I nodded. "We were going to call her Bella, after Mom, and Mae, Aunt Pam's middle name." My voice cracked as I remember the fear I first felt, followed by the joy.

I knew Bella was going to put the Olympics and possibly nursing school on the back burner, but I was okay with that. Trevor had caught onto the excitement, too, buying her first shoes, a teddy bear, and it was his idea to do the ultrasound pics in the frames I had gotten for our parents.

"I'm so sorry, Ave." BJ pulled me close. "I wished you would have told me. I would have gone and kicked his ass and sent one of my girlfriends to kick her ass. How could they do that to you? You never deserved any of that, and they definitely don't deserve you."

"I guess you guys don't have to inform them you're not going to be in their wedding," Sylvia quipped.

I laughed in surprise, my sometimes inappropriate sense of humor finding amusement in her attempt to lighten the mood. BJ relaxed against me and started chuckling too.

"I can tell them I sent them a text, if we ever see them again," BJ bantered.

"I think my mailman lost my response before he turned," I added darkly.

"Ohhh..." BJ groaned loudly.

"Nooo!" Sylvia cried out.

"Too soon?" I asked with a raised brow.

"Yes!" BJ insisted while Sylvia looked deep in thought for a second.

"Well..." she drawled out. "He *was* a douche sometimes. He wouldn't give me my packages when I was standing right there! He made me wait until he relocked our box. So, if he turned, I'd say it was karma."

I sniggered, then sobered. He really was a horrible postal deliverer, but he didn't deserve to be infected. No one did.

"Let's go," I insisted, taking another fortifying breath.

BJ and Sylvia embraced me on both sides before we walked towards the SUV.

I was momentarily mortified when I realized Axel was still standing near the vehicle. He led me to the back and opened the back hatch. Four rucksacks were in the cargo compartment. He climbed in first and then held out his hand. I looked at it for a moment.

I didn't know if I should take it or not. I might have had one of the most stressful and emotionally exhausting days in a long time, but I could no longer deny the pull I felt towards him any longer. I craved human touch, and he was offering it to me. Even if it was for a little while, I'd take it.

I took his hand and let him to pull me up and settle

me between his legs. My back was cradled into his chest as he placed the steel bands of his arms around me, resting his hands over my midsection.

I closed my eyes, enjoying the feel of him. His body was hard but soft in all the right places. It was slightly disconcerting how natural and comfortable I felt in his arms after only hours of knowing him. I leaned my head back and sank further into him.

"Sleep," he murmured near my temple. His fingers began to caress my arm.

I wanted to protest and tell him I wasn't tired, but after a few minutes of his ministrations, I fell asleep.

Chapter 8

We had approximately one hundred and fifty miles left to Camp Sanctuary Lakes, but Axel told Felix to pull over when we neared a hotel that looked like it was off the beaten path. The sun was about to set, and we needed to find shelter. The idea of eleven of us sleeping in the seven-passenger Tahoe was unfathomable, plus the children were getting restless.

Felix, Axel, Sylvia, and Phillip were going into the motel first. They decided to take the toddler along to, hopefully, tug the heartstrings of the owners into giving us rooms. They took cash to offer the owners. More than a standard room would have cost, but we feared money wouldn't hold any value soon.

"I hope they have plenty of hot water," Josh groaned, rubbing a weary hand over his face.

After my brief nap, I'd found out Mr. Blue-eyes' name was Josh. I also found out more things I hadn't suspected. Felix was the talkative one of the group and divulged the fact that most of Alpha and Bravo had no family to return to, thus the reason why they eagerly accepted Corbin's and Wyatt's offer to accompany them to Sanctuary.

They informed us eight more JOpS were accompanying Corbin and Wyatt to our destination. They were traveling separately in hopes of retrieving the family members they did have. Unfortunately, I knew I'd be seeing Trevor and Emery, and soon. There was no way Aunt Pam and Stephanie would have agreed to come without them.

"A shower is much needed," I agreed. "Hopefully, they give them enough towels and toiletries."

"I'm sure Axel will ask. He thinks of everything," Josh said confidently.

"I'm going to hit up the vending machines," BJ said decisively as he reached into his wallet. "If they won't give us rooms, at least we can stock up on some snacks and drinks."

The hotel was two stories tall with the doors on the outside, and both floors had laundry and vending areas. It didn't look like the most up-to-date accommodation, but the place was clean.

"Can I go?" Miller asked excitedly.

"We'll all go," Chad smiled. "Josh, you think you can watch the baby? She's sound asleep."

Josh looked panicked for a moment before he nodded.

Chad chuckled. "Let's go." He lightly ruffled Mikey's hair.

"Do we have anything to put the stuff in?" I asked, checking to make sure I had my sais tucked in next to my hips. Luckily, I hadn't had them when She-bitch and Whipped-boy took the rest of our stuff.

"I think the twins have grocery bags tucked into the back cargo netting." Chad grinned.

Sure enough, I found cloth canvas bags in there. I wondered if the SUV owner was environmentally conscious, because he had more than ten bags tucked into the cargo net.

Wait. Twins? I blinked in confusion.

"The Rains boys are on Alpha Team," Chad explained, noticing my confused expression. "King nearly had an apoplectic seizure when East volunteered his vehicle. They're an interesting duo, and I'm sure they'll be excited to meet you."

His comment made me more curious as he opened the back doors for me. "Huh?" I asked as we made our way to the bottom floor vending machines.

"Your reputation proceeds you, Little Beast." Chad grinned.

The door to the laundry area was unlocked, and I noticed the six industrial-sized machines for washing and drying clothing. On the opposite wall were four snack machines and two drink machines.

"Here, boys." BJ handed them a twenty each, and I gave them some bags. "Have at it. Just don't get your hearts set on eating it all. We'll be back with your mom tomorrow, and I'm sure she's not going to let you eat like this anymore."

Mikey still cheered, but Miller groaned. "Can you hide it for me?" Miller asked BJ hopefully.

"Of course." BJ grinned wickedly before he handed me some cash. Chad held up his own money when BJ went to give him a wad of twenties but smiled his thanks.

Miller and Mikey cheered once more as they ran over to the machines. I walked over to the drink machines in dire need of some caffeine, Chad at my heels.

"What do you mean 'my reputation?'" I asked as I fed the machine a twenty.

"I'm close with Alpha crew," Chad explained. "Bravo Team is incredible, but I just get along better with Alpha, and Burns makes it challenging to be on a squad with her. Whenever we get sent on missions together, I just click with the guys better, plus, no offense, but Joe is a shit leader compared to Tacka. He–"

He shook his head, as if stopping himself from revealing too much. "Anyway, Wyatt and Corbin have been going on and on about you for years. We were coming home the day of your last tournament, and they must have replayed your video fifty times."

I reddened under his teasing scrutiny. I was surprised to hear that, that was for sure. "Well, we grew up like family," I informed him. "Our dads were adopted together, and we grew up like cousins. Plus, I lived with Corbin and his family for years and was practically engaged to Trevor, Corbin's brother."

Chad chuckled and shook his head. "So, you're one of thoooose girls."

I continued to feed the machine and push different buttons. I was pleasantly surprised to find Monsters in the vending machine. I rarely drank energy drinks unless I needed them, and I hadn't had caffeine all day. Therefore, I was in desperate need of one right now.

"What is *that* supposed to mean?" I inquired, befuddled.

"My sister was blinded by Trevor for years, man." BJ snorted, no longer pretending that he didn't hear our conversation. "She's loyal to a fault. She was blind to the fact that Wyatt and Corbin have had a crush on her since she was seventeen or so."

I snorted in astonishment. "Whatever, BJ. They were never interested in me. Emery chased Cor for years, and then Wy. They never showed any interest in her."

BJ and Chad exchanged looks before they started laughing.

"What is so funny?" I was starting to get annoyed, especially now that I was remembering the days Wyatt and Corbin used to tease us to get a rise out of us.

"The skinny twin?" Chad laughed. "The one with the eating disorder?"

"The one who always tried to use her looks to get by in life," BJ added.

"The one who intentionally stole her sister's man," Chad continued.

I gasped as my eyes narrowed, but BJ continued.

"She was always a piece of work, man. Modeling at such a young age filled her head with a lot of self-centered, overinflated ideas. Avery never was as invested in the scene, and Dad kept her well-grounded." BJ shrugged. "Emery was always intimidated by sharing the spotlight. I can't pretend to know what being the other half of an identical twin is like, but Avery forever took it in stride and created her own identity.

"Whereas Em," BJ went on, "felt like the only way she could be in the spotlight was to tear Ave down and push her out of it. I think she was and *still is* obsessed with being everyone's center of attention, that she doesn't even realize Avery never wanted any of it."

I was trying to process everything they were saying. Did Corbin and Wyatt harbor a secret crush on me for years? That was ludicrous! I understood Emery and I were different in personalities, but we were identical. Wouldn't that have been enough for the guys to at least attempt something with her?

As far as I knew, they never even tried to kiss her. If they had, I was confident she would have told me. She had fixated on them more when I started dating Trevor. Since our parents hadn't seemed to mind, she must've taken it as a blessing to land one of them.

I processed BJ's words next. I knew BJ had always felt Emery was a piece of work, but I never realized how well he'd has us pegged. His analysis was impressive.

"We have two rooms," Felix came bounding into the room, stopping my chaotic thoughts.

"But…?" Chad prodded.

"In lieu of payment and with several add-ons, the owners asked us to help them keep the motel protected tonight," Felix added with a shrug.

"Well, we already planned to rotate our sleep schedules anyway, so that's no biggie," Chad said.

"Let's go up to the room. Tacka is making the schedules as we speak, and we should get settled in before darkness falls." Felix held up a key with a room number on it, opposed to the key cards most places used.

"Come on, boys," BJ stated. "We'll get more snacks later."

⬚

The owners had given us adjoining rooms. Each room had two double beds and a pullout couch. They also gave us two playpens for the babies.

I was pleasantly surprised by the size, cleanliness, and amenities of the rooms. They weren't quite luxury suites, but they were a lot nicer than I expected for a hotel off the beaten path.

When I entered the room, I discovered the owners' teenagers, a boy and girl, unloading all kinds of things for us: a waffle maker, waffle mix, a skillet, a carton eggs, bacon, peanut butter, jelly, bread, butter, syrup, a toaster, bananas, individually packaged cereals, bottled waters, juice, and milk.

The room was already equipped with a mini-fridge, coffee maker, tea bags and coffee, so the additional items were beyond generous of them. Apparently, the owners were retired Army veterans and reluctant to leave their livelihood. They had family coming to stay with them, I'd been told, but in the mean time, they were somewhat vulnerable.

Axel hadn't hesitated in helping them, even before they had been generous. He let them know that we were leaving at first light, though, because we had people waiting on us, but the owner was thankful for any help given to them from experienced fighters.

Axel was sitting at a desk writing in a notebook when I entered the second bedroom. He was deep in thought, so I went through the adjoining door and figured I would get dinner cooking for us. My appetite had returned, and I was ready to eat.

I took the housekeeping cart they had piled all our stuff on and looked over at the boys. "Miller, I need you to put all this juice, water, and milk away in the refrigerator. Mikey, can you put all this stuff in the closet?" I pointed to all the non-perishable items.

"Okay," Miller agreed immediately. "Can I have a pop?"

"Go for it." I laughed, knowing Steph would hate how they'd been eating today.

"What'cha thinking?" BJ asked as he came up to the cart as well.

"Can you clear the desk over there?" I asked him. "I'm going to start dinner and need a clean surface area."

"Tell me what I can do," Felix said excitedly as he rubbed his hands. "I can't cook, but I can prep."

I laughed. "Perfect." I pulled out a large mixing bowl. "You mix the waffle mix and I'll cook it." I plugged in the skillet first, now on the newly cleared desk. As it warmed up, I set all the ingredients I was using on the dresser beside the television, which was currently on a cartoon for Phillip. Then I organized the other condiments and such beside the skillet, waffle maker, and toaster.

I washed my hands, thankful the sink was outside of the bathroom. Josh and Sylvia had wasted no time jumping in the showers the moment we all came up.

I stared at myself in the mirror above the sink and nearly groaned aloud. Dark circles were under my eyes, and my face looked pale. My hair was in desperate need of washing and brushing, but I had to prioritize everything. Soon, darkness would fall, and I wanted to make sure everyone was fed before we found out the watch schedule.

"Do you think we can wash our clothes tonight?" Sylvia asked, coming out of the bathroom in just a towel.

"We can probably manage that," Felix replied, eyeing her appreciatively.

"I'm sure we can give you some of our clothes to wear now until your clothes are washed. Would you mind throwing our stuff in as well?" Chad barely looked up from the cooing baby on the bed beside him.

"Deal," Sylvia said excitedly.

"Why can't she stay in her towel?" Felix mock groaned.

"Eww, gross," Mikey made a retching sound.

Felix chuckled. "That's what you say now, little man, just you wait. Avery, you're next, strip down to a towel."

Axel cleared his throat, shooting the other man a look.

"Just kidding," Felix muttered, looking contrite. "Sorry, Ave, but you can't blame a man for trying."

I laughed uncomfortably. "It's okay, I knew you were kidding. Sort of. You are a man," I teased, hoping to alleviate the tension in the room.

Was Axel trying to stake a claim on me? In the animal

kingdom, he would be the alpha. Every single man I had seen him in contact with seemed to bow to his requirements. Had he fought for his title, I wondered? Or did he demand it and they acquiesced, sensing his natural dominance?

I set a comforting hand on Axel's bicep and felt him physically relax.

He held out a t-shirt and boxer shorts to me. "You can shower next," he said quietly. "And if we want to start the laundry, we should probably do that now."

Josh came into the room next. He held out a pair of black PT shorts and a t-shirt to BJ. "Here, man. You can take a shower next in the other room."

"Thanks." BJ smiled and immediately left the room.

I looked up between Felix and Axel. They seemed fine with each other once more. I didn't want them to argue or fight over something so trivial as a joke.

"Sylvia, can you watch the bacon while I take a quick shower?" I inquired as I laid the first batch of bacon onto the skillet.

"Um, how quick?" Sylvia hedged.

Sylvia was great at cleaning, but she was hopeless when it came to cooking. Unless she could put it in the microwave, she had no clue what to do.

Chad chuckled. "I can man the bacon. Bacon's easy."

"You're such a domesticated man, Chad. You cook and take care of babies so well," Sylvia flirted. "How hasn't any lucky girl snatched you up yet?"

He grimaced. "Been there done that, and she took the kids with her," he said matter-of-factly. "She didn't think she was so lucky when I spent only half the year with her and the kids and the other half on missions."

Sylvia gasped. "I'm sorry. Do you get to see your kids?"

Sadness crept across his features. "They weren't mine. I was just the one who raised them for eleven years when their dad didn't want them. She never allowed me to adopt them, and the courts wouldn't allow me visitation because of my precarious position in the military."

I watched my friend embrace the tall, African American man and wished I could be as affectionate as she was. I knew what it was like to love someone so much that you tried to fight for them and still lose.

☐

I had cooked so much food that there were leftovers. My stomach was pleasantly full, and the children were already sleeping when the sun descended.

Axel pulled out his notepad and looked at us all. "Chad and Felix," he stated. "I have you on the first watch. At 0100 hours, I want you to wake me and Josh. I don't want you to engage the infected unless you have to. If at any time you feel overwhelmed, come and get us. No one needs to try and be a hero."

"When do you want me to take a watch?" BJ inquired readily. "I'm a good shot. If you let me use one of your weapons, I can help."

"Me too," I stated as I began to wrap the waffles carefully.

I didn't relish the idea of taking out more infected, but I felt like it was my duty to pull my weight around here. Pop-pop, Dad, Uncle Mitch, and Uncle Scott made sure I was more than comfortable around firearms. They taught us gun safety and took us to the range several times. I became very proficient with a rifle and a 9mm over time. I just never thought I'd ever

123

have to utilize the skills.

"I'm a horrible shot." Sylvia cleared her throat. "Guns scare me, but do you have something better than this?" She held up her little hunting knife.

Axel looked deep in thought for a moment before he nodded at Josh. Josh got up and left the room. It was like the man was telepathic, the way Axel just nodded at the men and they obeyed.

"You can take first watch." He looked at BJ, then to me. "You can take the second watch with Josh and me." Axel seemed reluctant but moved on, looking at the rest of the guys. "Right now, I think we should all sleep unless it's your watch. Josh and I will sleep with the children and girls. When you come in from your shift, come to this room."

Josh came back and dropped a large duffel bag onto the bed. "Pick your poison."

There was a plethora of guns and ammo in the bag. Josh opened a side pocket and withdrew a long sheath before he slid out a wicked-looking machete. "This is extremely sharp," he informed Sylvia. "Keep it in the sheath unless you plan to use it."

Sylvia nodded and smiled. "Thanks! I just wished I had my bo staff." She sighed. "I could make a point at the end and annihilate some infected ass."

The guys laughed at her eagerness. I cringed, flashes of this afternoon invading my thoughts.

"I'm sure we can come up with something," Chad reassured her.

She did a little happy dance, making even Axel's mouth tilt into a slight smile. I realized then that I couldn't wait for the day to see a real smile on his austere features. He looked beautiful in rest; I could only imagine what he looked like with a true smile.

Sylvia seemed to be taking the thought of annihilating their lives a lot easier than I was. She had taken out three of them with zero qualms. She believed the guys when they said they were no better than a rabid beast. I had seen that, sure, but I couldn't buy it yet.

"We need more formula." Chad frowned as Jenny began to fuss in the crib. "I meant to say something earlier, but it slipped my mind."

"There's a town at the foot of the mountains that we need to pass to get to Sanctuary," BJ said hesitantly. "We can try to stop there for some more."

"Does she need formula?" Felix asked with a frown of confusion.

"According to her mom's phone, she's five months old," Sylvia seemed just as mystified. "How long do babies need formula?"

"She'll need to stay on it until she's a year," I said, remembering my rotation with the pediatrician. "We can start her on purees at six months to supplement her feedings, though."

"How do you know that?" Josh inquired. His unease around babies was almost comical. If he weren't so playful with the boys and Philly- as he called him- I would've wondered if he hated all children.

"Nursing school. We had to do rotations in pediatrics," I said with a sigh. Who knew what it was worth now, though, when or *if* things returned to normal.

"You can kick people's asses, then fix them up." Felix whistled. "Keep talking dirty to me, baby, and you might finally make me take a knee."

Chad reached over, Jenny in one arm, and smacked the back of Felix's head with the other. "You have a death wish, son," he muttered his reprimand.

Silence fell, and Sylvia began to giggle as she gave pointed looks between Axel and me. She started to hum the wedding march. I ducked my head and continued to clean up our dinner mess. I smiled gratefully as BJ and Josh started to help me clean up.

"How well do you know the towns on the way there?" Axel asked, clearing his throat. "If we can find one that isn't heavily populated, we can stop there, too. And get a list of everything the children may need."

"Can you help me write the list?" Sylvia asked Chad.

"Of course," he replied, smiling.

"There are a few towns on the way," BJ stated after some thought. "We're already taking the route that avoids most of the heavily populated cities and towns, but some of those places still have the small mom and pop shops that are off the beaten path."

"Okay," Axel stated with a nod. "Let's get some shut-eye and get to our post."

☐

I was too wired to go to sleep, and Sylvia seemed to be in the same predicament. Josh sounded like he was already passed out. Within moments of his head hitting the pillow, his gentle snoring filled the room. I couldn't tell if Axel was asleep, but he hadn't moved on the other bed for some time now.

Occasionally, I heard shots go off and flinched each time. So far, none of them sounded like they were coming from directly outside, but still.

We were sharing a bed closest to the kids, who were stretched out on the couch and in the playpens. If it weren't for the guys and the kids, it would've felt like any other Friday night when we chose to stay in. It was a common occurrence for us to binge-watch our favorite shows, eat junk food, and gossip until we couldn't stay awake any longer.

In so many ways, Sylvia was the sister that I never had. Emery had stopped liking sleepovers with me by the time we were ten or so.

"I wonder if... everyone's okay," Sylvia whispered. "Stephanie is so pregnant and I...I just wonder."

"I'm sure they're fine," I whispered back, understanding the rabbit trails that our thoughts left in our heads. "You know Corbin and Wyatt will protect them with their lives."

I still worried about them, too, but I knew I couldn't be consumed with those thoughts. We had four children in our group that needed protecting, and if I didn't focus on them, I would be too distracted to give them my best attention.

"I hope Cal and Joe are okay, too," she whispered after several moments of silence.

"I'm sure they are," I teased. "Are you going to tell me who strikes your fancy more?" I knew she had been dying all day to tell me about her night last night.

She started to giggle. "Who *says* that? 'Strikes my fancy!' Promise me you won't judge me," she suddenly said.

I made the motion of the cross over my heart, despite the fact she could barely see me through the orange glow of the street light outside. "When have I ever judged you?" I smiled.

"Well..." she said hesitantly. "I fancy them both." She snickered before I realized she was serious. Her tone was hushed once more. "We just hung out at the new Alpha warehouse the other night. We were drinking–not a lot –playing pool, talking, and laughing. I swear I never laughed so much. They were just so easy to hang around with, and it was so easy to just be me, you know?"

"And then?" I gently prodded her. I knew what she meant. I knew how Sylvia slipped on her alternate persona when we were out. She wasn't different, per se, but she was more guarded and seemed to weigh her every word and action.

"And then one thing led to another, and we took it to a bedroom, where they both gave me the best orgasms I ever had!" she rushed out with a little squeal. "Seriously, I've been sexing *so* wrong until now."

I laughed at her inane word before I contemplated what she'd said for a moment. Oddly, I didn't even have to pretend I wasn't disturbed. She wouldn't have rushed into it without thinking about it. They must have made her feel really comfortable.

"Well, college *is* the best time to experiment," I finally said. I honestly felt no judgment. Cal and Joe made Sylvia happy, and it was all consensual.

"I don't think it was just… experimentation."

"Well, I hope they can make you happy," I said honestly.

"Can I tell you something else?" she whispered tentatively.

I wondered if I wanted to peek behind that door, because I had a feeling it wasn't something I wanted to know.

"Sure," I finally replied reluctantly.

"They share all the time," she said quietly. "Like the whole *team*. Maybe not all together or in pairs, but the teams like to have a female or two to…be with them."

I knew she was hinting at something else. Then it

struck me. If the Alpha Team and Bravo Team liked hanging out so much, they probably both engaged in these activities.

A flash of unexpected jealousy filled me. I never did jealously. I didn't even know envy was an emotion I could ever feel. After Trevor had found his popularity and the girls regularly threw themselves at him, I hadn't experienced it. Back then, I used to think if he wanted to stray, he would do so with or without me suffering that soul-eating emotion. I had to trust him to do right by me. In the end, he hadn't, but at least I didn't have to carry that ugly feeling around with me at the time.

I didn't know why the thought of some woman getting Axel's attention and, yes, even Corbin's and Wyatt's, bothered me so much all of a sudden. Up until tonight, I didn't even think Corbin and Wyatt saw me in that way. But if I were honest with myself, no matter how loyal I was to Trevor, I'd have to be blind not to notice how sexy Wyatt and Corbin had gotten with age. With maturity, they had even become more likable! I could more than see how women could be drawn in by M&M.

Wyatt really was a misfit. He could have been very popular in high school but always chose to hang out with the underdogs. He never liked to conform to social conventions and just walked to the beat of his own drum. He was also talented. He could sing and play the guitar better than most of the artists that played on the radio.

Then there was Corbin. He was mischievous. He was the one who liked to pull pranks and make people laugh. Unlike Wyatt, he stumbled into popularity and stayed. He was charismatic and charming. Aunt Pam always said he could sell ice to an Eskimo. He had a way of reading people and making them feel like they were the center of his universe if he chose to do so. He didn't even really have to try. He just was.

Now that my blinders had been removed, I could easily see how an attraction for them could grow, but I didn't want to be put in a position to come between them. Would I want them to share me, given the opportunity? And could I?

Plus, there was Axel to think about now. Today, after I'd had my collapse, he had quietly helped me compose myself and had comforted me without words.

Words rarely comforted me—I preferred actions. He had been all action, and I really enjoyed it.

He was the first man since Trevor that I ever imagined exploring a relationship with. His calm, comforting, solid and natural leadership abilities called to me. He seemed to know exactly who he was and was unapologetic about it, and I was surprisingly okay with that.

Would these men ever want me the way they had desired other women? Would they be satisfied with an arrangement they must have had in the past? They were stateside now, and the likelihood of them leaving anytime soon was slim to none. Would they want to settle down individually now instead?

"Was that too much?" Sylvia asked hesitantly. "I don't see the harm in it," she defended quietly. "It's all consensual. Plus, those guys deploy for months and months at a time. It's not like they can be in any type of conventional relationship, and they still have needs. It's a win-win situation for the woman, too. With the attention of four or five of the guys at a time, the girl would always feel... wanted. What girl wouldn't want to feel cherished and cared for by more than one man?

"There's a structure to the arrangement," she continued whispering. "The team have their rules, believe it or not. All that they ask is that the girl, or girls, are only with them while they're in this arrangement. They're a tight and close team, but they don't share well with others. If the woman wants out of the relationship, they just have to allow the team to know. It's a way for them to protect themselves, too. The group always uses protection and whatnot, but some of the guys feel comfortable relying on the woman's birth control if there's enough trust between them. If she stepped out of their arrangement and didn't use the proper precautions, it could impact the team negatively.

"One of the women that used to be in Tango Team got bored with her guys. She chose to step out on their arrangement and acquired an STD. When she came back, she didn't tell them about it, and two of the seven guys– who chose not to use condoms– caught it too."

I felt a surprising burst of desire streak through me. I could imagine the attention of Axel, Wyatt, and Corbin all at once, and I felt a warmth between my thighs. It had been way too long since I'd had an intimate connection.

Even the couple of months I had hooked up to fill the void inside me, it never worked. I still felt empty afterward. There was never any cuddling later– not that I wanted it from them, but still– and most of the time, I didn't even get an orgasm out of it.

Suddenly, I was filled with too many thoughts I probably had no business thinking.

"I can see how an arrangement like that worked for them," I finally admitted quietly. I almost applauded myself for sounding so casual, my voice not betraying my turbulent thoughts. "Do you think Joe and Cal would like an arrangement like that with you?"

"They hinted at it," she admitted, but I could hear the worry in her voice. "I wouldn't mind it, but you know me. I don't like giving my heart that easily, and I wouldn't want two men to break it at the same time if they decided they no longer wanted me anymore."

I had to get Sylvia out of her head. I knew she wanted this relationship, and even though I hadn't seen the guys with her yet, something told me that she needed them. She had been hurt long ago, and it was time she was loved and cherished again.

"Well," I said cautiously. It was a time for a little taste of her own medicine. "You know what I always say... you'll miss one hundred percent of the shots you never take."

She was silent for a second before I felt a pillow smack me across the face. "That's Wayne Gretzky's words, and you say that before every sparring match to yourself."

I laughed, knowing I had succeeded in easing her worries... some. "Wayne's a wise man, and he's right," I insisted. "Now go to sleep. I have to be up soon. Dream of your men. Dream of a man between your thighs and another one in your mouth."

She gasped. I knew I had shocked her with my "dirty" words. Typically, I was very private and guarded about my sex life. She was such an open book, and not only was my book closed, but it had a big lock on it. And what good had that done me?

Maybe with the world ending, I could recreate myself. Possibly, Avery Hope Harris could be reborn. Avery Hope Harrison allowed others to create her. Perhaps she could rise from the ashes that Trevor and Marlon, my first monster, had left her in.

Chapter 9

"Avery, sweetie," I heard his voice croon to me. "You want to be famous, don't you? Take your top off."

I looked down at my thin arms. They were shaking.

I was sitting on a stool in the middle of the room, a stark white screen at my back. It was the background of the shots I'd just taken. The wooden floor was worn beneath my bare feet.

I was wearing a white button-down shirt and a navy-blue pleated skirt for the back-to-school advertisement I'd just modeled for.

"No," I insisted quietly. "I don't want to be famous."

"Avery," he commanded, his voice harsher. "Take your top off, or I'll bring Emery in here."

I looked at Marlon. It had been said that Lucifer was the most beautiful and talented angel in heaven. Before he'd fallen from grace, he had been one of the most favored angels of God.

Most people imagined the devil as ugly, with red skin, horns, and a forked tail. But I believed he looked like Marlon Gains. A handsome, dashing man with hair so blond it almost looked white. His eyes were a bright blue that would rival the sky on a sunny day. Very fit, he took care of his body. Yet when he smiled, you could see the devil lurking within.

"No, please don't," I sobbed.

"One...Two," Marlon began to count.

With unwilling fingers, I unbuttoned my top and pulled it off.

"Now your bra," he insisted.

He had been so friendly to me at first. He'd given me advice, listened to me. When he got my cellphone number, he would text me sweet messages. He always brought me my favorite candy. He was always telling me how beautiful and smart I was and made me feel special. Then one day, he changed.

"Please," I begged him. "I don't like it when you take pictures of me like this."

I was so confused the first time he'd asked me to take off my top and pose in my bra. He showed me the pictures of the beautiful models dressed in less than the modest white cotton bra I wore. I'd thought it was okay.

Eventually, I knew it wasn't okay. It started with my shirt. Then it was my skirt. It progressed to my bra, and now Marlon wanted me to remove my undies. He hadn't touched me yet, but I knew it was a matter of time.

"Then I'll get Emery in here. She wants it more," he harshly said as I hesitated. "She'll do anything to become famous."

I had to protect Emery. I couldn't let him take pictures of her like this.

Once, I had felt beautiful, now I felt ugly, humiliated.

I sobbed as I took off my bra.

"Good girl." He smiled in satisfaction. "Put your hands on top of your head. Let me see those beautiful, perky breasts."

I sobbed and placed my hands on top of my head. The cold, air-conditioned room made my skin erupt in goosebumps, and I felt my nipples go erect. Shame washed over me.

"Now you're panties." His voice was filled with a strange

huskiness.

He was one of the most sought after photographers. Magazines called him to ask him who he would shoot for their advertisements. I had been so honored when he wanted to shoot me by myself. All my shoots, until recently, was done with Emery. We were sought after by so many.

The camera clicked numerous times. I caught the gasp at the door and met Emery's wide eyes. She looked horrified.

"Run!" I screamed.

Her scared and horrified expression spurred my actions. I realized I didn't need to stand here and listen to Marlon.

"Close that damn door," Marlon screamed at her.

She ran. She didn't look back. Marlon was distracted. Then I ran.

I ran and ran, with him screaming at me to return. He forgot to lock the door this time. He couldn't stop me from leaving. I needed to tell Dad. I couldn't allow that man to humiliate us and take advantage of Emery.

I knew if I didn't say something soon, he'd make Emery do it like he made those other girls.

My breath was coming in gasps, but I couldn't stop. I ran down the stairs, past the startled people, out into the parking lot. The hot black asphalt burned against my tender, bare feet, but I had to keep going.

Suddenly, someone slammed into me from behind. I fell with a scream.

"No!" I wailed. "No more! Please! No more!"

"Avery," I heard an urgent male's voice in my ear.

I thrashed around, trying to get him off of me. I needed to tell someone! Wild sobs wracked through my body as I felt pain in my legs and arms. The asphalt bit into my nearly bare skin, followed by the night's cold breeze.

Wait. Why was it cold, and why was it night time? The sun had been shining just moments ago. It had been so hot!

"Avery," the male urgently whispered. "Little warrior, wake up."

And just like that, the vestiges of my dream wore off. I was suddenly aware of the male body lying on top of me. So much bigger than mine, so powerful, but gentle. I could smell his spicy and masculine scent coming off of him. The same smell I had been breathing in since I put on his t-shirt earlier.

"Axel?" I asked in hesitation, with mortification and realization sinking in. My throat was raw. It hurt. I must have been screaming again.

I gazed around as best I could and saw that I was on the ground in the middle of the woods. I could feel the pain in my feet and the sharp sting along my legs and arms. I had run in my sleep. I hadn't run in almost six months, and before that, it had been years.

Suddenly, I heard a loud, shrill scream, followed by deep bellowing yells. The sounds were... eery, creepy, non-human, yet too human-like.

"We got to go, little warrior." Axel popped up suddenly, and without another word, he scooped me up and threw me over his shoulder.

He took off running like I weighed nothing.

The screams tore through the night air once more. I felt Axel tense beneath me, but he continued to run.

"Who is that?" I asked him shakily, knowing the answer but hoping I was wrong.

"The infected," he responded, not even sounding out of

breath.

"I'm too heavy. Let me run. I don't want to weigh you down."

"Hush, you weigh nothing." He was firm with his words, gentle even, but I knew better than to insist he put me down again. He ran for what felt like hours, but I knew it couldn't be that long. I didn't know what building loomed ahead of us, but I knew it wasn't the hotel.

How far had I run? How long ago?

We arrived at the building as another scream sounded closer. With quick movements, I was set down. Axel leaned my back against a wall. I could feel the cold night air rapidly cooling my overheated body. The remnants of my dream had left me shaken, and my heart threatened to beat out of my chest.

With a click, I heard a door open behind me, right as I saw the first infected break the treeline.

"Axel!" I hoarsely cried as I pulled him into the open door with me.

He quickly slammed the door closed as the first infected smashed against the door. The door rattled on its hinges, and I stifled the scream that rose to my throat.

"Avery, I need you to find things to put in front of the doors and windows," Axel said softly but firmly. "They become more like predators at night—their sense of seeing and hearing increases. I don't trust the door, but the windows look shatterproof. We found that, sometimes, if we went out of sight, we become out of mind. If they can't see us, hopefully after some time, they'll wander away."

I nodded numbly, wincing as my feet reminded me of my nightly run. When I'd first started running in my sleep, I used to wear shoes to bed. I hated waking up, not knowing how far I had run or where I was, with my feet all torn up. I had no sense of preservation when I was in that frame of mind.

I surveyed my surroundings and realized we were in a pharmacy of sorts. I noticed the coolers of sodas near one of the walls. It wasn't too big and looked like it was on wheels, so I laid down on the ground to unlock the wheels.

"Good thinking," Axel softly praised as he helped me shimmy the soda cooler out of its spot.

He took the unit from me and pushed it towards the front door like its weight was inconsequential. I hobbled towards the register, hoping they had those little flashlights I could use to see better. The illumination from the street and the coolers gave me some light but not enough to see clearly. Searching around, I successfully found a little flashlight that put off a surprising amount of light.

As I walked down one of the aisles, I saw some large poster board and duct tape. I poked a hole through the middle of the packaged tape and slipped it over my arm before grabbing an armful of posterboard.

On my way back to the front, I noticed a stand of car air fresheners. He said they had a keen sense of smell. What if we confused them? Masked our scent? I didn't know if they could smell through the glass, but I was willing to give it a try.

I limped back to the windows, trying not to jump as a hoard of infected began banging on the doors and windows. Their screams felt like ice water being poured into my veins. I tried not to look directly at them in fear of freaking myself out more. I had to pretend they weren't there so I could remain calm.

I grabbed handfuls of air fresheners before I began laying the poster board on the ground. I tore off strips of duct tape and placed them on the posters. One by one, I started putting them on the windows, with the air fresheners attached to them. I flinched each time I felt the vibrations against the glass, but I continued systematically covering the windows.

Axel returned to my side and began helping me until all the windows were covered and were at arms' height above Axel. With no words, he then picked me up and carried me towards the back of the store. Light filtered from a hallway. I hadn't even noticed he had propped open a door.

I wanted to protest about him picking me up, but, truthfully, I was full of embarrassment and in pain. No matter how many times the police, perfect strangers, or my dad found me, I always felt fear and mortification. No one knew what it was like to be prisoner to your own mind until they'd experienced it themselves.

When someone saw a person with a broken leg or a large bruise, it was typical for them to garner sympathy. When a person suffered from depression, bipolar disorder, stress disorders, or any other mental health issues, no one could see it. It never gained the same automatic sympathy.

I'd lost count of how many times people looked at me like I was attempting to gain attention. Endless people behaved as if I could magically think happy thoughts and be miraculously "cured."

It was like breaking your arm and asking someone to take you to the hospital, and they, in turn, looked at you and said no, questioning why you broke your arm in the first place, that you should've been more careful.

In the real world, something like that would never happen.

With my mental health issues, I'd heard people tell my

dad that I should've been locked in the room at night. People had suggested sticking me with drugs, not knowing if that would help me or give me long term side effects. Ultimately, the number one culprit to my running was stress-induced. They suggested I eliminate my anxiety. As if I'd willingly sought it out.

If anyone could tell me how to avoid stress, I'd love to do just that. It wasn't like I was on the street corner like a hotdog vendor yelling, *'Stress, stress, come give me your stress!'*

Tae Kwon Do and meditating helped me a lot, but my disorder was so unpredictable. I ran at twelve years-old. I ran off and on for two months after I lost my daughter and Trevor. I dove into my training with a vengeance. I tried to wear myself out.

This time, I imagined that the combination of the infected, not feeling safe, and thoughts of Marlon tonight had triggered it.

Axel sat me on a countertop in a large one-person bathroom. Somehow, he'd managed to get everything to help me clean up while I hadn't noticed. This was becoming a habit of his.

"I'm sorry," I finally croaked sheepishly. "How far did I run? Are we near the hotel?"

He carefully began cleaning my wounds. I hissed as I noticed the multiple lacerations on my legs, arms, and feet. He put a bucket beneath my legs and proceeded to pour peroxide on all my wounds.

"I'll try to be gentle." He frowned as he noticed my hiss of pain. "We're only a few blocks from the hotel, and I say you ran about three miles tonight. I-" he began, then shook his head. His eyes hooded so that I couldn't look into them. "You nearly outran me, and I'm fast."

He said it with zero bragging, more like fact.

"I never knew how to take things by half measures," I said self-deprecatingly. "I couldn't just do gymnastics, I had to be the best gymnast in my school. I couldn't just do well in school, I had to become valedictorian. I only made salutatorian, but I was okay with that. I couldn't just do Tae Kwon Do, I wanted a gold medal from the Olympics. I can't just sleepwalk, I have to sleep *run*."

"How often does it happen?" he asked as he moved onto the multiple lacerations on my arms.

Something in him made me want to confess the secrets only my therapist, my dad, and the judge knew. Mom had died by the time I admitted to Dad what happened. Dad put me in therapy right away, and the judge put Marlon in jail.

BJ thought I had been stalked. Emery thought I had lured the handsome, talented photographer, costing her career. I was a minor, so barely anyone else knew the truth.

I hadn't talked to my therapist in over a year. I didn't want to rely on her anymore, but I'd been foolish to believe I hadn't needed her.

Somehow, I knew if I talked to Axel, he wouldn't tell a soul. In fact, I had a feeling he carried around his own secrets that were locked in tight.

"As soon as we were born," I began to explain as I closed my eyes and leaned back against the mirror, "the world wanted to see the identical twins of the great Isabella Harris. A gossip rag even offered my parents half a million dollars for our first infant photos. Mom convinced Dad it would be an intelligent way for them to start our college funds. So my mom did a photoshoot with us, donated half the money to orphanages and fostering organizations, and the other half went into our accounts.

"By the time we were a year old, another magazine wanted us to do a birthday party shoot. Again, half the money went to children charities, and the other half went into our accounts. We continued to model over the years, but Dad said no more than two photoshoots a year because he wanted us to have a normal life. But at around twelve, Emery started insisting she was old enough to decide how many jobs she could take. Dad bumped it up to *four* shoots, *if* they didn't interfere with school.

"I didn't want to do it anymore, though. I loved gymnastics, school, riding bikes with my friends, and hanging out with them. I hated the attention we got, even on military installations. But they didn't just want Emery, so she begged me to model. Exotic-looking twins sold more copies of magazines. I reluctantly agreed, and somehow, someway I caught the eye of Marlon Gains.

"Suddenly," I said grimly, "he wanted to take pictures of me... just me. He said Emery could be hard to work with, and I followed directions well. He gave me treats, made me feel special. I wasn't just the Harris Twin or the other twin. I was *Avery*, only Avery. Very few people ever made me feel like I could be an individual.

"I loved being a twin, but I'll be honest... it sucked not having my own identity at times. I hated when people automatically assumed I should be like Emery, or questioned my sexuality because I wasn't girly like her. So, I was flattered when he told me I had that *it factor*."

I closed my eyes. "Eventually, he was asking me to remove my clothing for him. He threatened to do it to Emery if I didn't listen. One day, I'd had enough and ran and ran. When his assistant caught up to me, he threatened my family and me."

I heard him mutter a curse, but I continued.

"Not too long after that, Mom and Dad found out about Emery's eating disorder and pulled us out of modeling until she got better. I began to sleep run then. I would wake up miles and miles away from home sometimes. A friendly farmer found me in his pasture the first time. He called the cops. The cops called my mom, since my dad was deployed. It happened two more times, before I started getting afraid to sleep, which only made it worse. Mom started getting ill, and I thought it was because of me. I always tried to make my parents' lives easier because BJ was a troubled kid who missed his dad, and Emery always needed more attention."

Opening my eyes again, I looked down. "I asked my sister at first to sleep with me. I tried to tell her that what Marlon had done to me had affected my sleep. She insisted I had seduced him, that I was now regretting my actions. She blamed me for our loss of careers.

"Trevor, Corbin's brother, my ex, was my best friend. I finally asked him if he could sneak out of his house at night and sleep with me. Most nights, he did. I ran a few times, but he was able to stop me before I even left the yard and placed me back in bed.

"After a while, I thought I was getting better, but then Mom got diagnosed with an aggressive brain tumor. I was devastated by her prognosis. Dad came home, so Trevor couldn't sleep with me. That stressed me out, and I started running again. Eventually, I told Dad. Dad pressed charges. The judge found Marlon guilty, since I wasn't the only girl he'd made pose naked and worse. We moved. Dad changed our names, yet stress and not enough sleep can still trigger them.

"When we moved in with the Cavaliers, for a while it seemed to make them go away for good. I had a few episodes here and there, but I found that Tae Kwon Do and meditating helped. I went nearly four years without another incident. Then I had my miscarriage, lost my sister, best friend-slash-boyfriend, and it started again.

"I realized if I drank a lot, I didn't run, but too many hangovers taught me it wasn't an ideal solution. Then Sylvia slept with me most nights, and for the nights she couldn't, I installed locks above my bedroom door and over my windows. I locked myself in at night. The problem with that, though, is that I feel no pain when I'm in that state. I vaguely realize it's happening, but it's like my mind doesn't know my body's hurting itself."

I held up my knuckles, where I'd punched through the glass of my bedroom long ago. The thin white scars covered my entire right hand. I leaned forward and pushed up my shirt, indicating the scars on my back I had gotten from climbing out the window onto my fire escape.

"I woke up in the hospital with these. I even had to go through a slew of drug tests before they retained my records, proving I wasn't on drugs... just stressed."

"Do you always scream before you run?" he asked as he gently spread an ointment on my scratches.

I looked into his dark eyes and saw no judgment in them. He didn't look like he thought I was crazy. I saw no pity. If anything, his eyes held understanding and even determination. It set me at ease. I nearly sighed in relief.

He proceeded to wrap my feet in gauze and then slid a pair of socks onto my feet. Next, he wrapped bandages on the areas with multiple lacerations. I looked like a mummy from my elbows, down to my shins.

"No," I admitted. "I know when I do, because my throat hurts, like it does right now. I've been told I can get really loud.

Other times I just run. Sometimes, I didn't even know I was running. The only way I knew was because Trevor took off my shoes. I used to sleep with shoes on because I didn't want to screw up my feet."

"Is it always... him you dream of when you run?" he inquired.

I shook my head. "No." At his skeptical look, I continued. "Tonight I dreamed of him, but sometimes it's manifestations of other fears. Standing in front of over one thousand members of the student body, naked, as I had to give a speech. Hearing my mom call for me and running to find her so I can save her. The dreams aren't always the same subject matter."

He lifted me and began carrying me back to a room that looked like a break room. Like the bathroom, it seemed fairly nice and clean, considering that it wasn't the largest of stores.

He sat me on a couch and grabbed a bottle of water, some ibuprofen, and handed them to me. I smiled my thanks at him before I took long pull of water. He sat on the edge of the couch next to my hip.

"If you'll allow me to, I'd like to make sure one of my men, or me, is with you at night." He picked up my hand, and I was surprised by his tender gesture. "You woke up screaming, and before I even knew what was happening, you were running out the door. Felix tried to stop you, but you elbowed him in the eye. A pack of infected was near the hotel, and you ran right past them. You drew them after you. Luckily, you decided to scale a fence, and it slowed them down some."

With a look of contemplation, he gently traced my barely discernable scars on my knuckles. The touch of his long bronzed fingers was both soothing and nerve-wracking.

"I was able to reach you on time, Avery, but I'm not sure

about next time. The world we used to live in was dangerous, but things have changed. We don't just have to worry about the normal predators, ones like you thankfully survived, but the infected now, too."

Now I felt further embarrassment. I'd hurt Felix? I could only imagine the chaos I had caused tonight. I never wanted to be a burden.

"I'll ask BJ and Sylvia to watch over me until..." My voice trailed off. My episodes didn't have an expiration date. There wasn't any guarantee of getting better, ever.

"What about my men and me?" he asked softly as he traced his thumb on the inside of my palm. "We all carry demons as well and wouldn't mind helping you with yours," he continued as if he understood my self-conscious reservations.

I gulped. My mind was going back to the conversation I'd had with Sylvia. Was he asking me on the premise of watching over me, or was he asking me to enter an unusual arrangement with him, Corbin, Wyatt, and the rest of the Alpha Team?

"I heard you tonight," Axel finally admitted raspily.

"Uh... okay?" I asked in confusion. *Which time?* I thought. I'd said a lot tonight.

"With Sylvia," he added, releasing my hand.

My eyes widened for a moment, and he looked at me with intense scrutiny.

"It's true," he said. "We've shared women in the past. The boys more so than me, but I need to find release at times, too." He sighed and clasped his hands together, looking down at them, then back at me. "The last woman we shared didn't work out. Sylvia's right. We value trust and honesty above all else." He stopped as if he was gauging my reaction.

What *was* my reaction? I should feel... offended, possibly

disgusted. Instead, I was curious.

"Is it all the time?" I inquired. "Only when you're deployed? Do you return home and then become, I don't know, monogamous?"

He smiled ruefully. It wasn't a huge smile, but it was the closest I'd ever seen him smiling fully. He really was a handsome man. I sat up and impulsively pushed a lock of his hair off his face. He typically kept it in a low ponytail, but it was free right now.

My action seemed to surprise him. He seemed to tense at first, then visibly relaxed. "About five years ago, the female on our team pitched the idea to us. She fit in well with us. As you know, we are with each other all the time. We kind of slipped into this open relationship that worked well for all of us. It was a convenient arrangement. Being a thousand miles away from home without the usual conveniences of meeting people can affect you emotionally and psychologically. We found comfort in it, and surprisingly enough, we became a better team. A stronger team.

"When we got home," he continued, "she went out to blow off some steam and met another man. She let us know she thought it was going somewhere, so she broke it off with us. We tried various arrangements since. It's been a trial and error of sorts. We had two women that fit in... well, with our group, but then one started getting jealous because they felt the other one was getting too much attention and vice versa.

"Eventually, we found what worked best for us, once we realized we needed to set up ground rules. We ask our girl to have no favorites or at least not so that we can tell. No engaging in sexual activities with anyone but us. We know we're clean. We know we would never put each other in harm's way."

I knew I was clean and their choice to get tested reassured me. I was also on birth control—I wanted to control when I got pregnant the next time.

"Have they always left you, the women?" I found myself asking.

He grimaced and shook his head. "No, there were some that started dissension in the group, so we asked them to leave. My team members are more than coworkers. We're family. Very few people can understand the demands of being with us. We can be called up at a moment's notice. You can't depend on us to make all the birthdays and the holidays, we can't make promises, and we're always running towards danger, instead of away from it. In order to make sure my men and I return home safely, we have to be a family, and anyone that wants to tear us apart can't be with them or me. We all understand that. We've lived by that creed for the last six years, since our inception."

I finally gathered enough courage to ask what was in the back of my mind. "Are you telling me this because... you want me to enter in an arrangement like this with your...team?"

Again, another crooked smile that made me melt. He really needed to smile more.

He nodded. "I know Corbin and Wyatt have cared about you for years. I knew they put your happiness and Trevor's above their own. The moment they found out that he had cheated on you with your sister, they nearly put our whole team in jeopardy a few times. They haven't been themselves since last June."

My eyes widened. That was when I'd lost everything, nearly everyone.

"Until recently, I never even knew they liked me," I admitted quietly.

He laughed. He actually *laughed*, and it—and him!—was so beautiful.

"I've come to the realization, Avery, that you have no clue who you are or the effect you have on others."

I laughed, too. "What does that even mean? I know exactly who I am. I think it's you who is blind."

He shook his head again. "I'm not. Corbin and Wyatt aren't, and I'm pretty sure King and East are more than intrigued with you."

"How?" I asked, mystified. "I mean, Chad told me that they'd seen some videos of me competing, but that's not real life."

He shrugged. "Maybe not how you see it, but it's ours. We tend to know what we want and just go after it. After all," he smirked at me, "you miss one hundred percent of the shots you don't take."

A surprised laugh burst from me, and I covered my mouth. I shook my head, not knowing if I should be perturbed that he had eavesdropped long enough to have heard my words from earlier.

Soon, humor was replaced with thoughts of doubt. "The world *has* changed, like you said. You guys don't have to run off at a moment's notice anymore," I said softly. "Maybe with time, you'll want to settle down and be normal. And isn't it presumptuous to think the guys would *want* to enter into an arrangement like that with me?"

"Once the boys find out you're sleep running, they're going to insist on you sleeping near us," he said firmly. "I'm going to ask you to sleep near at least one of us at all times. If anything were to happen to you, I know Corbin and Wyatt would go berserk. I saw how they were when they thought you were emotionally hurt, and it wasn't pretty." He grimaced. "My team wouldn't be able to go through that, and we've been through a lot worse."

He turned further towards me and braced his elbows on his knees. I knew he was weighing his next words.

"I want no lies between us and the team. I'm not going to glamorize what we have, because it still takes work to *make* it work, but when it is working, it can be more than satisfying. I want you to understand, Avery, the situation you're in now. Soon as Wyatt and Corbin see you again, I know they'll no longer hold back."

He smirked then, and it almost looked...cocky. "They'll be pursuing you with everything they've got. If you want me to protect you from them, from me, let me know now. Otherwise, Joe and his team can watch over you, and they know better than to mess with you. Hell, I'm pretty sure Chad has already decided he's half in love with Sylvia, and he's already your unappointed big brother."

I stared at him in stunned silence. A million questions ran through my mind, but only one came to mind right now. "Why would I need protection from you or them?"

He leaned forward so that his mouth was inches away from mine. His eyes were so dark, the black nearly taking over. "Because," he nuzzled my cheek, "once you give us the green light, Avery, nothing will stop us from wanting to get between your shapely thighs, gripping that tight ass, and then driving our hard cocks into you."

My mouth had gone dry at his words, my skin tingling with everywhere he touched. He didn't strike me as a man who talked dirty. It just went to show me, yet again, that he was a complex man with many layers.

"Most of us have different vices... fetishes even," he went

on. "Wyatt and Corbin like to take girls together most of the time. They like to see who can make the girl come the most in one night." He nuzzled my neck some more. "The twins like their individualism but don't mind sharing, every now and then. King is an exhibitionist. He loves the thrill of taking a girl in somewhat public places. He gets a rush from having to concentrate on staying quiet, yet doing everything that makes a girl want to scream."

He nuzzled the back of my ear and ran a hand along my bare arm. "East is our romantic. He has no... odd proclivities and seems to know when our girl just needs a cuddle and a sweet fuck."

I felt the wetness between my thighs, finding it hard to breathe. Axel's words fed fuel to my imagination. I never had two men at once, but I could see how Corbin and Wyatt would make it an experience I would always remember. I hadn't even met the twins yet, and I was intrigued.

Could I enter a relationship with a group of men so quickly? A year ago, I was pregnant and engaged to one man. Today, the world was collapsing around us, and I was entertaining the idea of letting *five* men take care of me.

"What about you?" my voice came out husky, whether it was from a raw throat or arousal, I couldn't tell.

His mouth hovered above my own. "I'll show you once you decide whether or not you will be with my whole team and me. There's no rush, though. If you say yes now, I'll give you a small taste. If you accept us all, I will show you, apocalypse or not. I'll make sure you'll have my undivided attention all night long."

"How will you show me now?" I whimpered.

How had our conversation shifted so quickly? How had it gone from revealing my disorder, to having five men take care of me, in every sense of the word, in less than sixty seconds?

He growled in the back of his throat as he shifted against me, his erection pressing against my leg. "I don't kiss, and I don't go down on a woman. It's far too intimate an act for me. In fact, I can't remember the last time I did or even wanted to," he husked in my ear. "But if you say yes and if you will let me... I need to taste you. I want to bury my tongue between those strong thighs and drink from your petals. I want you to ride my face until I taste your sweet honey."

His lips moved against my mouth with a kiss that belied his words. If he didn't kiss, then he must never need any practice, because it was the best-closed mouth kiss I'd ever received.

I didn't think I could get any wetter. I didn't even know if I could think straight. He hadn't even touched me yet, and I felt dangerously close to having an orgasm right there.

He nipped at my bottom lip, and I gasped. His tongue dipped into my mouth, and I sucked him in. I wanted to touch him. I needed to feel him.

He groaned against me as I sat up and straddled his lap. With one hand, I weaved my fingers through his long, soft black hair, and with the other, I explored his body.

I had wanted to touch him earlier, but I didn't want to embarrass myself if the feelings weren't going to be reciprocated. Now that I knew he desired me as much as I did him, I freely touched him. I felt his erection and moved my heat towards it, rocking against him. I gasped, both at the feel of his long thick member against my clit and because of his sheer size.

"Fuck," he muttered before he pulled back from my lips. He bent his head and grasped my braless breasts, seizing one and lifting it to bite my nipple.

I wasn't expecting it, so I cried out, but the pain was soon followed by pleasure. I moaned and rocked my hips in earnest against him. "Again," I begged him.

He cursed once more before he suddenly pushed me from his lap, stood up, and began pacing. I could see his erection pressing against his cargo pants. His breathing was ragged as he looked at me. I leaned back, confused by his actions as he bit the pad of his thumb, his nostrils flaring.

I said nothing, feeling like he was having an inner battle with himself.

"Say yes so I can reward you," he finally commanded. His pacing stopped.

"Yes," I said with zero hesitation. I lifted his borrowed shirt in one fluid movement and opened my thighs, allowing Axel the chance to take the boxers off of me.

I couldn't remember feeling so alive, nor being so close to an orgasm so quickly. I knew I overthought things when it came to sex. With Trevor, *I* had been the problem over half the time. There were some nights I couldn't get out of my head long enough to orgasm, no matter how hard he had tried.

Right now, with Axel, I was in this moment with him.

He growled out once more before he was down on his knees in front of me, stripping the boxers off in one movement. Groaning, he looked down at my naked thighs. He dipped his long digits between my lips, slipping a finger over my slit.

"You're dripping down your thighs. You're so wet for me," he murmured, his eyes full of desire. He growled once more before he buried his head towards my core.

There was no teasing. Axel went straight to business. His words replayed in my head. He might not have gone down on a lot of women, but he was beyond a master at it. He seemed to know exactly what my body wanted as he alternated between licking my slit, circling my clit with his tongue, lightly nipping, and flicking his tongue against it.

"Axel," I cried out as I buried my hands in his hair. "You're gonna make me come," I mewled, thrusting my hips against his mouth. He placed my ass in his warm palms and began to help me work my core closer to his mouth.

I cried out his name once more. I thought it already felt amazing, but the way he was manhandling me was a major turn on.

He groaned in satisfaction before he lifted his gaze to mine. "Then come for me," he rumbled against my mound, sliding two fingers into my wet opening and latching onto my clit.

He pumped his fingers into me, stretching me, making me gasp. His thumb circled my swollen, sensitive clit. After a few short movements, I saw black behind my eyelids before the bright lights exploded. The tension that had been building between my thighs burst in my stomach, and I could've sworn my whole body went paralyzed for a few seconds as I cried out his name.

"Good girl," he murmured against me before he cleaned up my juices with his tongue. "I have never tasted anything better," he growled.

When his tongue accidentally grazed my clit, I made a noise and tried to get him away from my oversensitive area.

He chuckled, and I smiled at the sound. He sat up before he gave me a long, lingering kiss. I could taste myself on his lips. Again, I was reminded that, for someone who didn't kiss or go down on a girl, he was definitely beyond excellent at both.

"The sun should be up soon. I think I saw some formula here, and we should probably get a few more things," he nuzzled his nose against mine.

I smiled at the tenderness he was showing me. I wanted to reciprocate the favor. I pulled away from him before I grabbed him through his pants and leaned forward to whisper in his ear as he had done in mine. "Let me suck your cock and make you feel better. Let me taste your come like you tasted mine. Let me make you feel as good as you made me feel."

He hissed between his teeth, and I felt him stiffen in my hand, felt him sway against me for a second.

Instead, he abruptly stood up, clearing his throat. "Little Warrior, as tempting as that sounds, we've tarried long enough. I'm sure your brothers and friend are more than worried about us. We need to gather supplies and get out of here."

I frowned, immediately realizing how selfish I was being. I grabbed Axel's t-shirt and slid it over my head. I had put not only myself, but Axel as well, in danger tonight. I had made my family worry, putting us all at risk by putting myself first. Had Axel not stopped me, I would have gladly gone down on him and begged him to take me. My own release had been put above others and common sense.

"Whatever you're thinking stop." He knelt in front of me, then kissed my lips gently. "I want nothing more than to feel your mouth around me, to slide into you." He adjusted his erection, which was still very hard, as if to prove his words. "If we were at Sanctuary right now, I'd have to brake all my rules and take you with or without you accepting my team, but sadly duty calls." He kissed my nose and smiled.

I nodded and kissed his mouth briefly, still feeling bereft.

Chapter 10

"What are you doing?" Axel asked sometime later as I wrote 'eight tubs of formula' down on a notebook I had found.

"I'm figuring how much we owe them. BJ has some cash left, we can swing by and pay them before we leave," I said with a shrug before I placed them in a book bag I had found.

So far, my list looked like this:

Notebook   2.39
Pens   1.59
Bookbags (6)   119.94
Tampons (10 boxes) 100.76
Pads (14 boxes) 168.68

I had started rounding up at this point because I still had to do the math, plus I hadn't attributed taxes yet.

Condoms (11 boxes) 170
Formula (8 tubs)   240

Axel leaned over my shoulder, perused the list, and started to laughed heartily. I was too stunned to react at first. He had the prettiest, straightest white teeth I had ever seen and... crinkles! He had eye crinkles! Could the man get any more beautiful?

He surprised me by wrapping his arms behind me. "Little Warrior, you are so... refreshing. You do realize money is useless now, right?"

I frowned. "I know, but this was someone's livelihood. I don't feel right just taking their stuff with no... payment."

He kissed the spot between my neck and shoulder before he reached in his back pocket and withdrew a wad of hundred dollar bills out of his overstuffed wallet. "I'll put this in the office if it makes you feel better, but I read their communication binder," he said, pointing toward the phamarcy's back room. "I have a feeling Mrs. and Mr. Edwards aren't coming back. Cathy called out because her husband was sick, and Kurt refused to stay since Bill, Ned, and Cory were no-shows and weren't answering the phone. That was two days ago. No one's been here for two days."

I nodded, somewhat mollified. "Okay."

I turned back around before filling the bags with baby food, diapers, and wipes. I systematically filled the bags with all the things I thought we might need, from first aid kits to toiletries for us all.

Axel came back with a bin that looked like a laundry cart. "We can start filling these up. I found a work van at the back door, and before you ask, I wrote out a check. I'm good for it." He smirked at me with a wink.

Who was this man? I was amazed at the transformation he'd gone through. He was teasing me, touching me. For a man who didn't kiss or go down on his partners, he was very demonstrative.

"Well, I'm sorry if I don't have a penchant for stealing," I replied pertly as I stuck my tongue out at him. "How was I supposed to know the owners were gone?"

"Don't stick that out unless you want to use it," he warned me with a faint smile.

"Oh, I wanted to use it." I licked my top lip. "I wanted to lick that big cock of yours like a lollipop and then suck on you like a popsicle until you filled me with your sweet treat, but you denied me," I said saucily.

His eyes darkened, and he couldn't hide the erection

157

pressing against his pants as he visibly swallowed. "Be careful the games you play, Little Warrior," he said quietly before he started to walk away with his bin. "Oh, and make sure you pick up more condoms," he said over his shoulder, "...the largest size they have, too. Because when it's time, I'll be using them and you won't be able to walk the next day."

It was my turn to groan in frustration, wet yet again. I wanted nothing more than to feel Axel stretching me.

⬚

The sun had risen only an hour before we finally packed up and pushed the cart to the van. It was a newer model van and still smelled new, with lots of room in the empty back and even had built-in shelves.

"What do you think happened to the people who owned this?" I asked softly as I buckled up.

He leaned forward and synced his phone to the bluetooth. He scrolled through his phone until Imagine Dragons' *Believer* came out of the speakers surrounding us. I nodded and smiled. I typically liked to listen to a variety of music, but I had been on an Imagine Dragons kick recently. Before my matches, over a week ago, I had *Thunder*, *Whatever it Takes*, and a few others on loop, pumping me up for my fights.

"I think," he finally said, cautiously, "that I don't like to think about what happened to them. We can spend all day tormenting ourselves with those kinds of thoughts. I much rather live in the present and protect those I can."

He put the van in drive and drove down the alley. We hit a few potholes, but the suspension in the vehicle made it barely noticeable.

I nodded. "You're probably right," I said quietly.

It took us less than five minutes to reach the hotel. We entered the parking lot to see four other vehicles now parked near us, and a small group of people were dragging bodies of the infected to a ditch near the road.

"What will happen to them, the infected?" I asked, scrunching my nose in distaste. Even from this distance, I could smell their putrid scent of rot and copper.

"They need to be burned," he answered concisely.

The closer we got to the hotel, the more I felt Axel physically slide back into his former role. Gone was the teasing, affectionate man I knew, replaced by the stern, stoic leader.

"Are they... contagious, even in death?" I inquired as we opened the doors.

He frowned, seemingly debating his response. "I won't pretend to understand the virus or all of its effects, but we had to put down several of the strays that roamed the village. Without the people throwing them scraps, they became desperate for food..." His voice trailed off, and I filled in the rest.

I was torn between cursing my curious mind and empowered to know the truth. Right now, knowledge was power, and I refused to feel more helpless than I already felt.

"Avery!" I heard my name called out in relief, before Mikey and Miller launched their bodies into my arms.

I felt Mikey's wet tears against my shirt, and Miller had a death grip around my waist. I pulled them in tight and felt the trembling in their little bodies.

"Hey, guys, I'm okay," I murmured to them. "I'm sorry I scared you. I had a bad dream, and I didn't know what I was doing."

"I'm scared to see what you *would* do if you knew what you were doing," Felix said dryly as he sauntered over.

I gasped, placing my hands over my mouth. Any embarrassment I may have felt over my actions was quickly replaced by horror. Felix's right eye was nearly swollen shut, and the entire area around it was painted in angry shades of blue, purple, and black.

"I am so sorry, Felix," I whispered in mortification.

Felix scrutinized me for several seconds before he smiled. "It's all good, but be warned, woman. In the future, I'm going to tackle your ass and not worry about gently waking you."

"That won't be necessary," Axel said dryly. "I already have a plan in place, and my team will ensure her safety."

I felt my cheeks blush red as Felix gave me another small, knowing smile. "Well, you know that the Bravo Team always has your back."

"I'm going to kill you! Bring you back to life and kill you again!" Sylvia yelled from my right.

I couldn't help but smile as the little firecracker stomped towards me, BJ only steps behind her. "You can try," I teased her. "But until you outgrow my pocket, I don't think you'll do much damage."

BJ embraced me as Sylvia stopped to growl at me. I always joked that we were such an odd couple. She was so short, and I was so tall. She would tease me in return and say I should just get one of those purses for dogs so I could carry her around. I replied that I wouldn't need a bag when she could fit in my pocket.

"I should stab you," she growled.

"I love you, too," I replied with a smile. "I'm sorry I scared you. You know it's not intentional." I frowned.

She hugged me, trapping the boys against me. I felt her warm tears on my chest, and I patted her back comfortingly.

"Welcome back." A tall, lumberjack of a man walked towards us with a broad smile. "I'm happy to see you found her safe. Boys, my girls just made some cookies. Why don't you run and get your tins." He looked at Miller and Mikey.

"Thanks!" Miller yelled, taking off at a run, not even stopping to ask if he could have any.

I frowned again. We had been too lenient on their sweet intake the last couple of days. Stephanie was going to have a conniption when she found out they hadn't had any vegetables and barely any fruit in our care.

"I'm Duke." The burly man held out a hand.

"Avery," I murmured, returning the shake as I looked the man over. I'd never seen hair so red. The beard that fell to his chest was just as vibrant. He had a broad open face. I liked him immediately. Some people just had this...vibe about them that put you at ease, and he had it.

He gave me an assessing look. "There's a pound down the road about a mile to the left. We're headed that way now. You need a dog," he stated decisively. "Let one of them pick you, and you'll have a friend to help keep you from running."

I immediately realized this was the owner of the hotel. The guys had returned to the room last night, telling us about the nice but interesting character that owned the hotel. If this man was the owner, then that meant he was the Army vet. Did he, too, suffer mentally? Why was he telling me I should get a dog?

He reached down and ran a comforting hand over his... dog?

I didn't know how I had missed the ugly dog behind the lumberjack—it was hard to miss. He was missing an eye and almost a whole ear. My immediate reaction to him was revulsion, but soon I saw the beauty in his sleek gray coat, his thick muscular body, and the calming golden eye that regarded me as if he could see into my soul.

I always wanted a dog, but my parents didn't think we were responsible enough to care for them as kids. The Cavaliers had a yellow lab, up until a few years ago, but it wasn't the same. Then my apartment complex wouldn't allow any dog over ten pounds, and I wanted a dog, not a... toy.

"For real?" Sylvia gushed as if she'd forgotten her ire at me, wiping her eyes with her hands. "Do they have small dogs, like a Chihuahua, a Yorkie, maybe even a Pomeranian?"

"Right now, we have a brother-sister pair that can't be separated," said a kind-faced woman who walked over to us. "I think they are a mix of Boston terrier and Pomeranian; sweet dogs, but most people didn't want both of them. I volunteer at the shelter. The owners abandoned them. I don't want them starving to death in their kennels and," she hedged, "I don't want to release them if they can turn." She frowned. "Duke and Liza are going to take some of them, but they can't take all of them, and my husband will kill me if I bring any more dogs home. I already have five. I want to place the dogs before nightfall, as they seem to be a natural deterrent against the foamers. I heard them all night last night, those foamers, circling my home, but they wouldn't come up on my porch. I kept my Rotties out there all night, patrolling the porch."

"We'll take them!" Sylvia said enthusiastically. "I even have their names picked out." She gave me a wicked smile.

I groaned, certain I didn't even want to know. I looked over at Axel and noticed he now held a large box of supplies.

"It doesn't hurt to test the theory out," Axel said cautiously. "But it is your land, your place. It's not up to me to make that decision."

Huh. I wasn't expecting that response. Sure, the land was in Dad's and his brothers'names, but in my head, it was always Nana's and Pop-pop's.

Axel had taken the lead in most decisions up until this point. I just assumed he would make a decision whether or not we were going to try and fit a few dogs into our two vehicles. They were packed enough as it was.

"I think we should get a few," BJ said cautiously. "But where are we going to fit them?"

"We have the van now." Axel patted the vehicle. He handed the large box of supplies to the red-haired man. "We ended up in the pharmacy down the road. It looks like the owners are gone, and the employees stopped showing up to their shifts. I left a significant amount of cash on the desk," he cut his eyes towards me, "and grabbed a few things. I put together a box of things that may be a hot commodity soon—antibiotics, a few bottles of pain killers, alcohol, and I noticed the Mrs was smoking some Marlboro lights. I got a few cartons of those as well."

I barely noticed Duke laughing until he uncovered his mouth. "Thanks! She'll appreciate that. You left cash on the desk, though...?"

"She made me." Axel smirked at me. "She didn't want to steal from good, hard-working people."

Duke continued laughing, and I noticed a few others had joined us by now and was participating in the mirth as well. I felt my face redden.

"Stop it." A petite African American woman came pushing her way through the people. "Stop embarrassing that girl," she said in a deep southern accent. "It's honorable!" she insisted, taking my hand and squeezing it. "My name is Liza, and that brute is my husband."

"Avery." I attempted to smile through my chagrin.

They had to be the oddest couple I had ever seen. Liza was as dark as Duke was light, and tiny where he was huge.

"New world, new rules," Liza said softly. "It's not honorable to steal from the living or in occupied areas, but if a store is left open with no sign of ownership, it's...free game."

"You're right," Duke said, wiping his eyes. "I'm sorry for being an ass, Avery, but after what I've seen in all my forty-nine years, I never knew people like you still existed. How'd you get the van?" his mouth twitched as he looked over at Axel. Somehow I didn't think he was done teasing me.

"I wrote a check." Axel grinned before he took me into his arms. I was surprised he'd embrace me in front of the others. "The last time I checked my bank account, I had more than enough to cover the cost."

Liza snorted. "Let me know when you can access your accounts, because I can't even make a simple phone call, let alone withdraw money."

I grimaced. Where did all that money go, and if the world were to return to normal, would I be able to access mine? Was our currency system now obsolete?

"We should probably get going. Thank you for the hospitality, but we're in a race against the sun," Axel stated as he looked over at Josh, who was just now joining us. "We'll make a quick stop at the pound and see if any dogs want to come along with us."

"The truck's packed, and what dogs?" Josh said with a confused expression.

"You guys talk amongst yourselves. Finish getting packed up for your trip," Liza commented. "I'm going to steal the girls away. My sister-in-law owned a boutique and brought a lot of her inventory. We're going to get these girls some clothes!"

I looked down at my t-shirt and boxers. That was probably a good idea.

"Oooh clothes!" Sylvia cried out gleefully.

"Sounds good, hon." Duke smiled. "Hurry back, though. They really should get going to their safe place. Just wished I could talk you guys into staying." Duke sighed dramatically.

"If we didn't have family waiting on us, we would gladly accept," I heard Josh say as Liza and Sylvia dragged me away.

I felt a sharp sting on my butt as I walked away, and I whipped my head back around. Axel grinned and winked at me. Did he just spank me? And did I like it? I glared at him before sticking my tongue out at him. His eyes darkened with promises I couldn't wait to indulge in.

☐

We left the pound with seven dogs, supplies from the near-by vet clinic, and several bags of dog food. Four of the dogs were now riding with the kids, Sylvia, Chad, and Felix, and three of them were with the rest of us, in the van.

In the time that I had taken a shower and gotten dressed, the guys had a bench-seat installed on the sidewall of the van. Apparently, Duke had an old, broken-down van, so he gave us the seat to use in ours. Currently, BJ and Josh were sitting on it. BJ's labrador was lying at his feet, while Josh's pit-lab puppy was curled up in his arms.

It was more than endearing to see the guys act like kids as they chose a dog to come home with us. Only Axel and Chad had elected not to select a dog and had followed me around as I picked out mine.

"I think we should call him Goliath," I stated as I ran a hand over the massive head of the black beast that had taken residence between our bucket seats.

"Goliath was arrogant and got taken down by a mere boy," Axel scoffed.

Axel tried to act dismayed when the black, seven month old pitbull and Neopolitan Mastiff mix had chosen me. He immediately called him a horse and informed me he would not be cleaning up after him. But as the miles passed, I observed him reach down and pet him several times.

I had taken Duke's advice, letting the dog choose me. Formerly named Prince, the black beast had picked me. I knew immediately he was mine and I was his. Despite being an older puppy, he had no issues following us out to the vehicles and had immediately jumped into our van without any urging.

"Then *you* come up with something better," I challenged him.

It was strange, bantering back and forth with Axel. It was almost like we were a real couple. Around the others, he still behaved a certain way, but when we were alone, he slipped back into the man that had seduced me on a couch in the back of a pharmacy.

"Deogee," he replied with a straight face.

It took me a moment to let the name roll around in my head. "Ugh, no!" I slapped at his arm playfully. "Seriously? Who names a dog, D-O-G? Could you get a little more creative?"

He smirked at me. "What? I like it. He's a dog, and I think Deogee fits him."

I rolled my eyes at him and drew my legs up to my chest, hugging them to me with my arms. I noticed his appreciative gaze on my legs and couldn't help but feel...pleased. Even with my "war wounds" from last night, he was checking me out!

Liza had insisted that even though it was the zombie apocalypse, I could still look cute, and I secretly liked feeling more womanly. She had given us a large canvas bag full of cute clothing. Nothing practical, but I was sure I could find some time to wear them.

Currently, I was wearing a pair of light jean cutoffs with frayed ends, and a black off-the-shoulder crop top that showed a decent amount of my tanned midriff. She'd also given me a fitted, lightweight leather jacket. On my feet was a pair of black gladiator sandals.

At the women's insistence, I had even left my hair down. It had been some time since I'd felt so feminine. It was all well worth it, though, whenever I noticed Axel's gaze on me and all the looks that followed.

I only had one brief, awkward moment when Jules, Liza's sister-in-law, commented on my beauty and told me I should have been a supermodel, telling me how much I looked liked the legendary Isabella Harris. Danika, Liza's daughter, then chimed in, saying I reminded her of that girl that was on the cover of last month's Cosmogirl.

I then had to admit my relationship with Emery and my famous mother. They almost seemed starstruck, and it made me... uncomfortable. It was one thing to garner attention for my athleticism than for my looks; I much preferred to be known for something I had worked hard for than something I had been born with.

"How about Onyx?" I said with pursed lips.

"You want to name our black dog after a black stone?" he queried with a raised brow.

A thrill ran through me at his reference to the dog-formerly known as Prince– as *our* dog.

"It's fitting," I grumbled.

"So is Deogee," he smirked. "Bane?"

I actually liked that name. "I'm not sure I want to name him after a character that was a comic book villain, but the name fits." I smiled. "What do you think, bud, wanna be called Bane?" I asked the dog.

He looked up with his big pitty smile. He had the shape of a pit bull's blockhead, but he was bigger and had the excess layer of skin that most Neos had.

"I think you like it, too, huh?" I grinned as Bane nudged my hand.

"How do you know about Bane? The movies?" Axel ran his hand over Bane's smooth fur.

I scoffed. "I may or may not have gone through a comic book phase."

He laughed. "First, a Salutatorian and now comic books." He shook his head. "Next you're going to tell me you were a mathlete."

"Science club." I sniffed.

He let out a surprising roar of laughter. "You're pulling my leg!"

"B!" I yelled to the back.

"Yes, A?" he called back.

"What did I do in high school?" I turned slightly so I could see BJ better.

"Umm, what do you mean?" he asked as he leaned forward with a confused expression.

"What clubs, sports, that sort of thing was I in?"

"Oh." He smiled with understanding. "Let's see. Tae Kwon Do, Basketball, Yearbook Club, and Science Club."

I turned back to Axel and gave him a smug smile.

He laughed once more and shook his head, then lowered his voice, leaning towards me. "I don't think I've ever eaten out a geek before. Now I know why I lost the taste for pussy. It hadn't come from the right place. I need another taste soon, see if it's as good as I remembered."

I felt warmth infuse my cheeks. But then my eyes narrowed as I realized he was purposefully riling me up.

I peered in the back, to make sure we weren't being heard, then looked back at him. "JS Tacka, you shouldn't start a war you can't, or won't, win."

He smirked. "There's a reason I was the youngest appointed Team Lead ever at twenty-four," he said smugly. "I doubt you can beat me."

I did the math in my head. He said he had been with the JOpS since its inception. If he had been twenty-four then, he was now thirty. He was almost eight years older than me. I had to admit the age gap was kind of thrilling.

I gave him a sweet smile. "Oh, how the mighty will fall."

☐

"What are you doing?" he husked as I knelt beside our seats.

Bane had curled up at my feet to sleep about twenty minutes ago, opening up the area for me to utilize.

"What does it look like I'm doing?" I asked him as I grabbed his belt and began to undo it.

He bit the bottom of his lip. "The boys can see you," he husked out.

I had occasionally been checking in the back for some time now. I saw that Josh and BJ were getting more and more tired as the miles passed. About twenty minutes ago, we had pulled onto a stretch of country road. BJ had stretched out a sleeping bag and was currently lying on the floor between the shelves and laundry bins, his new dog curled up against his legs. Josh was stretched out on the bench seat with his puppy on his chest, the dog's head tucked under Josh's chin.

I may or may not have grabbed a Polaroid camera with a lot of refills from the store. And I may or may not have snapped a picture of the guys in rest. Also, I may or may not have already labeled their names on each photo and tucked them into the pocket of my new backpack.

My therapist long ago, had suggested I pick up a camera and start taking back my power. She thought if I was the one taking the pictures, I could learn to heal. Surprisingly enough, it had helped, and I actually became fond of photography.

"The boys are sleeping." I smirked, using his word for the guys. I thought it was funny, him calling them that when he himself couldn't be much older than Josh, and BJ was nineteen, not exactly a boy.

I unbuttoned his pants and slid his zipper down. He was

already hard.

"Lift your hips, big man," I commanded him.

He hissed out and lifted his hips slightly. I shimmied his pants down over his narrow hips, down to his thick thighs. I wasted no time in freeing his cock out from his red boxer briefs. He really was massive, like frighteningly so. I grasped the warm, smooth, hard flesh appreciating the feel of his length.

He stifled out a moan, and I knew I needed to have him in my mouth soon. I didn't want the guys to wake before I helped him find his release and was thankful for the bins hiding me from the back. If either one of them stood up, though, they would easily see me.

I watched as a drop of precum appeared on the tip of the head. I wasted no time licking it, and his thighs bucked against me. I hummed in approval at the taste of his saltiness against my tongue. I continued licking him, drawing power and confidence from his stifled grunts and groans. When I felt like I had lathered him enough with my saliva, I lowered my mouth down over him.

He hissed once more, muttering my name. I continued to lower my mouth until he hit the back of my throat. I tried to open my throat up wide to accept more of him. There was no way I could swallow the whole length of him, but I was going to try. I flicked my tongue out against him.

His muffled noises let me know what he liked, and I felt myself getting wet, knowing I pleased him. I began to bob my head up and down on him. My fingers couldn't completely wrap around him, but I still mimicked the motions of my mouth anyway. I increased my rhythm, nearly choking on him as I took him deeper.

His fingers found their way through my hair, and he began to tug gently. It incited me on ever further as I purred against him in pleasure. He muttered a curse and his legs began to shake. I felt him tense beneath the hand I had braced on his thighs.

"I'm going to come... swallow all of me, Avery. Don't you dare waste a drop," he commanded with a thick, raspy voice.

"Fill my mouth with your come, choke me with it," I mumbled around his cock.

He groaned out. With fevered movements, I continued to pump him into my mouth. His shaking increased against me. I took the hand I wasn't stroking him with and gently cupped his balls, playing with its heavy weight, applying enough pressure without it being painful. I felt his balls draw up hard and tight.

He jerked against me, made a deep sound in the back of his throat, and began to come. He spilled copious amounts of his seed into my mouth, and I swallowed down every last bit of his salty but sweet substance.

His breathing was coming in heavily. He cursed long and low as the shaking in his legs subsided. His cocked jerked one more time, and I waited a few seconds. When I knew he was utterly spent, I took one long last lick, finishing at the tip.

He let out a surprised laugh and a protest at the same time. I knew his tip was super sensitive and smiled at myself. It was payback for what he had done to me earlier. When I looked up at him through my dark eyelashes, I could see the knowing smirk on his face.

I popped up, smiling, like I hadn't just gone down on him. "So, do you want vanilla, mocha, or white chocolate frappuccino?" I asked him, referencing the bottled Starbucks coffees I had in a cooler for us.

"Mo-" he cleared his thick throat. "Mocha," he finally said.

"Coming right up, JS Tacka." I gave him a saucy wink as I slipped into the back to grab the drinks.

Chapter 11

"Hey, Ax?" Josh called up in a groggy voice.

"Yeah?" Axel called back.

"I think we need to pull over." He moved up, so now he was situated between the two seats. Bane hadn't moved from the spot curled up at my feet. I didn't know how the seventy-pound dog found comfort in such a tight space. "Felix keeps flashing his lights at us."

I looked out of the side view mirror, and sure enough, Felix was turning his lights on and off. It was somewhat difficult to notice in the bright light of day. Axel sighed but pulled over.

We should have already been in Sanctuary over three hours ago. We had hit a town that wouldn't allow us to pass through. We could have easily overpowered the little podunk civilians running the roadblock, but we didn't want to cause any trouble. That detour had caused us an extra half an hour.

As we approached another town, Axel's sixth sense had kicked in. He thought it looked like a trap had been laid up ahead. With his past, I wasn't going to doubt his instincts or experience.

He had decided to go around that one too. That added another forty-five minutes, at least, but we were thankful to have taken it, because we ended up getting shot at and chased after. They finally gave up as we exited the road running parallel to their town and the original highway we had been on.

It had confirmed Axel's suspicions that the town was laying traps for any travelers that moved through their town. The car that had been chasing us down had an odd symbol spray-painted on its hood. We saw similar painted vehicles on the opposite highway traveling the other way, and they too tried to make us crash. I didn't know what their ultimate purpose was, but it couldn't be good.

If not for Axel's and Felix's expert driving, I wasn't sure we'd have escaped unscathed. Once we had reached a safe distance between them and us after several miles, we had finally pulled over. The kids were hysterical, and we had to calm them before we could get back in the vehicles.

We ran into one other stretch of road that we chose to avoid because all the dogs started acting strangely, and we knew then to trust them. That deviation wasn't as long, but it was time we still didn't want to waste.

We had just left the city limits of the closest civilization to Sanctuary. It marked the last thirty to forty-minute drive to our destination. BJ had just woken up, and I could see the excitement in his eyes and feel the anticipation that radiated off him.

A feeling of excitement and sadness had been warring in me. I was excited because Sanctuary indicated safety and had so many happy memories attached to it. But I felt a deep sadness because, for the first time in nearly twenty-two years, Nana and Pop-pop wouldn't be greeting us after our long journey. I knew their memories would linger everywhere, along with regret. I longed for Nana's warmth and nurturing way and Pop-pop's indulgent and wise ways.

Sanctuary was where I'd spent many summers learning a lot of life lessons, where I ran barefoot for a whole three or four weeks. It was where showers were optional and not required, and where the smell of sunscreen and sunshine clung to us like perfume everywhere we went.

At Sanctuary, competition thrived. Relays were held to see who could swim the fastest and furthest. We went fishing to see who caught the most fish and the biggest. Tournaments were conducted to see who the best shot of the summer was. It was no wonder I was so competitive.

Sanctuary Lakes Campground was the epitome of everything great about summer. Some people preferred the winters there. They had high hills to go sledding or tubing on, and the hunting was excellent. Me? I thought winters paled in comparison to the summers.

"What's up?" Axel asked out the window as Felix pulled up beside us.

Felix looked agitated, edgy even. "Easton's Tahoe was back at that shopping mall, along with Burn's Jeep."

"Did you see Amy?" Josh interrupted from the back. I turned to see his eyes wide with fear.

"No, man," Felix answered. "They were too far away, and there was a group of infected pouring into the building. I think they're trapped, man."

I looked at Axel.

He closed his eyes and cursed silently. "A shopping mall? Why such a large, heavily populated area?"

Chad leaned over from the passenger side. "I smell Jade and Natalie all over this. I guarantee they went inside and the guys went to bail them out."

"Let's go," Axel clipped out, his jaw tensing as he started driving again.

Moments earlier, he had been riding high from the blow job I had given him hours before. Sure, he had been irritated when we had to deviate from our original route, but he had still been in high spirits. Now his leader persona was back in place, and Axel Tacka, the man, was no longer visible.

"Shit." Josh slapped the van floor. "Who the hell invited

Jade and Natalie? The paperwork was submitted for their reassignments weeks ago! Trouble follows them wherever they go. They're not team players, and they've put our teams in danger time and time again. They should have been kicked out of as JOpS long ago. I swear to all that is Holy, if Amy has so much as a scratch on her because of them, I'm wringing their fucking necks."

His eyes were wild, and I could feel his panic rolling off of him in waves. I was surprised by the mild mannered man's outburst. I wondered if Amy was the girl they shared on his team, minus Cal and Joe.

"Joe's always treated the girls differently," Axel murmured enigmatically. "He has a soft spot for them."

"You don't treat Amy any differently," Josh sneered. I knew his scorn wasn't directed at Axel but Joe. "Maybe Joe needs retraining, too."

"Deep breaths, man." Axel gripped the other man's shoulder with the hand that wasn't driving. "We'll get them out. You forget Amy's mine, and my boys are in there."

My brows rose, but I remained quiet. I knew Alpha Team was currently a team of six. They had just lost their other members a few months ago to reassignment. I guessed it surprised me that a woman rounded out their team.

Axel's comment seemed to deflate the other man's anger. "Yeah, you're right. We'll fix this."

"Are our weapons loaded?" Axel asked Josh.

I had personally watched Axel reload and check the weapons before we all rolled out, but I could see he was trying to give Josh a purpose, redirecting Josh's fear and panic. It only solidified my belief that Axel was an observant leader.

"I'll check," Josh mumbled.

We pulled up to the shopping mall, and from our vantage point, I could see precisely what Felix had seen. The mall was large and sprawling. It was foolish even to attempt going in there with a small team, JOpS or not. There was too much room inside for the infected to hide, and the place was too big to defend or procure any items we might have needed. Whoever had made the senseless decision to go in there had been acting irrationally.

There were three vehicles parked near one of the entrances, and already the infected were pouring through the open doors. I counted at least fifty of them filing into the opening.

"BJ," Axel called.

"Yeah?" BJ asked as he moved forward in the van.

"The boys told me you hit twenty-two out of twenty-four shots last night," Axel stated matter of factly. "What did you shoot in the academy?"

"Expert," BJ said without hesitation.

"I'm dropping you off at that water tower. It's about two hundred yards to that entrance. I want you to climb up and pick off all of the infected going in or out of the building. Do you think you can do that?" Axel asked.

"Yes, sir!" BJ almost seemed to preen from Axel's confidence in him.

"Eyes open, though, make sure you don't hit any of our men or women. Copy that?" Axel inquired.

"I can do that," BJ reassured him.

"Good," Axel clapped his shoulder. "I have faith in you," he added.

BJ smiled at his compliment.

"Here, man," Josh handed him a sniper rifle, along with several additional magazines.

Axel found a parking spot far enough away from the infected. The other vehicle pulled to a stop beside us. Chad hopped out of his vehicle and advanced towards us.

"What's the plan?" Chad asked as he slid open the van door, Felix following closely behind him.

"I'm putting Boy Wonder up on that tower," Axel stated, and BJ beamed at the nickname. "He's going to pick off all those infected near the entrance. I think you should park the Tahoe near the tower as well. We'll leave Slyvia with the kids, but BJ can still keep an eye out for them. Tell Sylvia if she thinks they're in danger, though, just to leave. Go to Sanctuary. We'll get BJ back, and you can ride with us if need be. I'm going to circle the building and see if there are any other entry points. Once we figure out the best point of access, we'll go in there and locate our teams."

"Copy." Chad and Felix nodded.

Chad reached behind him and handed me my sais, handles toward me. I cried out in surprise. In my rush to leave this morning, I'd completely forgotten to check for them. I grinned when I saw that the points were no longer blunt but sharpened into sharp points.

"I thought this would be more practical for offense." Chad gave me a hesitant smile.

"It's brilliant," I gushed. "Thank you!" I wanted to hug him, but the other guys were blocking him.

Axel looked over at me with an enigmatic look. "You don't have to go if you don't want to," he stated gruffly.

I vacillated for a moment. "I want to." I nodded decisively. By my assumptions, there were roughly five to ten people trapped in the mall, versus at least fifty of the infected. They needed as much help as they could get.

Axel nodded slightly, his face blank of any expression. "BJ, hop out and have Sylvia take you over to the tower. Remember, vigilance."

BJ nodded firmly before hopping out. He paused and

leaned over to kiss me on the cheek. "Too the moon," he murmured.

I smiled at his reminder of the words Mom used to tell us.

"And back," I whispered in return.

⬦

"This is the best spot," Axel murmured as we neared the door.

We had examined all the doors and realized this was the only door the infected weren't milling around. The long narrow hall appeared to be where the offices were located. With any luck, we could assess the situation without the infected noticing our entrance.

Chad, Josh, and Felix had already dispatched the few infected stragglers that had been back here, so we didn't have to worry about watching our backs.

I bent down to make sure my boots were laced up correctly and tucked in a new blade. Then I zipped up my jacket to my chin. If I was going to continue volunteering on these missions, I needed to get a jumpsuit or something. The thought of having infected blood on me again was already making me queasy.

A part of me wanted to back out right now, but on the other side of that door, Corbin and Wyatt were outnumbered. They were my family. I should have never allowed Trevor's association with them damage the relationship I had with them.

Axel wedged the door open. "Ready?" Axel looked at us, his eyes alert, focused.

"Speak the words, Rev." Felix nodded.

"Let us bow our heads," Chad rumbled. "Dear Heavenly Father," he prayed. "Put Your hands upon us so we may fight with Your strength. If it is Your will, give us the sharpness of mind, and the hands and feet we'll need. Please put your protection over our brothers and sisters inside and over us. Amen," he finished.

"Amen," everyone replied at once.

I was surprised by their actions. I knew spirituality and faith could be such a touchy subject for some. They seemed to embrace it, and honestly, it comforted me.

"The harder the battle," Axel held out his fist.

"The sweeter the victory," Chad, Josh, and Felix responded as they bumped their fist to his.

"Say the words, Avery," Felix insisted. "Bump the fist."

It took me a second to realize they wanted me to say the same words they had.

I blinked and nodded. "Okay," I said hesitantly. "The sweeter the victory," I murmured, bumping their fist with my own.

"Let's go." Axel put his hand on the handle and slowly opened it. "On me," he murmured, looking at us all intently. He suddenly paused before he leaned over and kissed me. His lips were firm but gentle. "Eyes open," he murmured against my ear. "Be safe."

I nodded, shocked by his actions. For a man who didn't kiss, again, he was demonstrative in front of his men. "You too," I whispered back.

When I pulled away, I saw Chad and Felix smiling broadly at me. Josh still seemed preoccupied with thoughts of his... girlfriend. Felix gave me a wink, and Chad reached out and ruffled my head like I was a child.

I mock growled at him as I ducked out from under his large hand. I pulled my hair back into a ponytail. I would need it off my face.

Axel slipped inside, and I immediately heard the shots,

grunts, and yells echoing in the halls. The lights above us were too bright, reflecting harshly off the tiles. Our footsteps seemed to bounce off the walls and seemed too loud to my ears.

Axel made his way through the hall faster than a walk, but not quite a jog. I fell into step behind him and Felix, but stayed in front of Chad and Josh. When Axel reached the end of the hall, he held up a fist before he leaned forward. I saw him take a deep breath as he looked over at Josh.

"I have eyes on Amy," he said.

A relieved smile crossed Josh's expression, and I saw some of the tension leave his body.

"Go left and take Chad with you," Axel directed.

Josh went off with a grin, Chad following close on his heels.

"We'll go right," Axel said before he took off at a jog. I pulled out my sais, keeping them down by my sides, conscious of the now sharp points at the ends.

The inside of the mall was three stories tall, with a floor above us and one below. The high ceilings had skylights, illuminating the center of the mall as the sun poured in. I looked down, observing a man and woman on top of a carousel shooting at the infected milling about below them. I watched as Chad and Josh exterminated any infected between them and the carousel.

The mall once was one of the busiest malls in the county, due to its location. Most of the area surrounding it was underdeveloped, and a lot of the people that sought refuge in the country or rural areas came here to do their shopping. On any given time or day, the mall and the grocery store- right across the road- were reasonably busy.

I imagined when the first infected entered the mall, it had been a free for all, resulting in the infection spreading rapidly, like sparks in a dry forest. I tried not to think about the people that had come here to meet up with their friends, watch a movie, get a quick bite to eat, buy their dress for prom...

I shook my head of my dark thoughts.

Breathe in. Focus. Breathe out. Be here.

We didn't even make it ten-feet before the first group of infected came out of the store to our left. I cleared my head and tried not to let the fear of the infected control me. I would not feel empathy towards them. I had to believe that any humanity in them was absent. Now focused, I turned the switch off in my head and slipped into the zone.

I began to work my way through the infected systematically. I tried not to look too long into their bleeding eyes and foamy, blood-frothing mouths. I shut out the noise of their primal growls, hisses, and screams. I ignored the smell that made me nauseous. I moved as if I were in dance, positioning myself so that I could take out two of the infected at a time. I kept my jabs shallow, aiming for their eyes, temples, and soft spots below their chin. The points made it easier for my sais to sink into my targets without getting stuck.

With Felix by my side, we continued clearing the store. I lost sight of Axel, but I couldn't worry about him right now. If I sought him out, I knew I would be unfocused. There was no room for distraction.

"Clear," Felix called to me as he checked the dressing rooms of the sports store. He disappeared for a second, and the next thing I knew, a gate was being lowered, closing off the store.

"Smart," I commended him.

He gave me a cocky grin and wink. "No use clearing out the same area twice."

I nodded and turned around. We ran another twenty-feet before I spotted Joe and Cal with their backs to each other as they tried to fight off a pack of twenty or so infected. I ran to the furthest side of the huddle, while Felix began taking out the ones closest to us.

I aimed for their ears and the soft spot between the neck and skull, jamming my blade up and into the brain. Bodies began to fall. My eyes met Cal's for a moment, and his eyes widened in confusion and surprise.

My chest was heaving by the time we dispatched the group.

"Avery?" Cal asked in confusion before his gaze turned to Felix. He grinned. "You could have warned me about Bitchy Sobby Barbie." He finally turned back to me.

They looked horrible. Cal and Joe were covered in blood and seemed on the verge of collapsing. Their breath came out in great gasps. I wondered how long they had been here.

I was confused for a moment before realization dawned. I grimaced. "So, you met Emery?"

"I wish we hadn't." Joe made a wry face before he brought Felix and me in close. He kissed both our cheeks. "Thanks for saving our asses."

I tried not to cringe at the sweat and other unmentionable liquids he might have smeared on me in his affection, but I recognized the relief in his eyes. It was akin to kissing dry land after being set out to sea for months. He must have thought the end was near, and here we appeared. I couldn't fault the man for his affectionate nature.

"It's not the first time, and I'm sure it won't be the last," Felix said cockily.

A scream, decidedly human, rent the air. I chose not to think about the fact that my sister was nearby and took off running in the direction of the desperate shriek. I heard the slaps of shoes following closely behind me.

We rounded the corner, and I saw Burns, aka 'not my biggest fan,' striking down the infected with a wicked-looking curved blade. There was a beautiful Asian girl taking shots with a handgun. Her long dark hair was pulled back in a ponytail, and her face was carefully made up with heavy dark makeup, accentuating her beautiful dark almond-shaped eyes.

My breath caught when I noticed the man. He was ruggedly handsome. Even from this distance, I could see that he was slightly taller than me. His physique reminded me of a runner's body; not bulky but not thin either. I could see his muscles ripple and strain against his black t-shirt, but it wasn't glaringly obvious, more subtle. He was using weapons similar to a kama, and I had to admire the grace with which he moved.

He had a riot of pale blond, loose curls with natural-looking caramel highlights. I noticed how attractive he was, with his roman-esque nose and full pouty lips. Suddenly I found myself wondering what color his eyes were.

As I watched, I saw the beautiful Asian girl slip and fall as she ran away from the hoard that tried to close in on them. I ran forward and began to immediately stab, duck, feint, and move through the bodies separating me from the girl on the ground. She was screaming as she tried to fight them off with her now empty, useless gun.

I assumed she was out of bullets, since she was just striking out with the butt of the gun. I finally made my way to her as one of the infected lunged for her neck. I tried to disregard the fact that the infected was once a young girl of twelve or so as she jerked beneath my blade, crying out with an animal yell. When she slumped forward, no longer alive, I dragged her off and reached down for the knife I had in my boot and handed it to the Asian girl.

"Here," I breathed out.

I expected thanks or a smile. Instead, she sneered at me. "Done crying, Princess? We told you to stay in the truck."

I was momentarily stunned until I realized she wasn't talking about me. "Wrong sister. You're welcome," I said sarcastically as I turned to assess the situation once more.

Joe, Cal, and Felix worked together like a well-oiled machine. I could tell that they were accustomed to working together.

I watched as Natalie Burns struck one of the infected in the neck and kicked out at his knees. He collapsed, but he continued to squirm around as she moved onto another infected without finishing the man off. The squirming man began to crawl towards the curly-headed blond.

"Rains!" I heard Felix cry in warning.

"Blondie!" I yelled, seconds before the infected grabbed him by his ankle. Blondie lost his balance, tried to regain it again, but caught his heel on another downed infected. He came down with a resounding thud on the ground, the side of his head making contact with the hard tiled floor.

He looked momentarily stunned as he laid there, blinking, and turned his head slightly towards me. The most unique shade of seafoam green eyes, framed in long, light-brown lashes, gazed at me in confusion. *Holy crap, his eyes were mesmerizing!* Then they shuddered closed.

I snapped out of it, realizing the danger hadn't passed. A burst of adrenaline struck me as I jumped over a few downed bodies. The infected had pulled himself up and was dragging himself up Blondie's body, his mouth gaping open to take a bite. Bloody foam dripped onto Blondie's t-shirt. I dove towards him.

I missed my target, though, and struck the infected across the cheek. His skin peeled back, releasing coagulated dark red and black ooze. That seemed to piss him off more, as he lurched at me with surprising speed, roaring at me. His knee pinned my left forearm as he went to dive on top of me. My sai clattered on the ground, just out of reach. I tried to scramble up but was only able to make it to my knees. I had to strike out with my other sai, but it could only reach the infected's foaming mouth as he gnashed his teeth at me. I cocked my foot back, and with all the strength I had, I did a roundhouse to his temple, making sure the steel toe of my boot struck him.

I didn't wait to see if the move had hurt him. He staggered back, bloodied eyes rolling back into his head, and finally released my pinned arm. I dove and struck out with my other sai, driving it through his ear.

I sat up trying to desperately suck air into my lungs, as deep jarring shudders wracked my body. *Holy crap! I nearly became infected food!*

The sound of grunting penetrated my dazed, shocking thoughts. I realized two burly infected men had Felix pinned up against the wall by his arms while he struggled to kick out at them. It was enough to shake me from my frightened stupor.

I quickly assessed the situation. At this angle, I couldn't strike both infected at the same time. So I ran, trusting my instincts, and leaped over some downed infected and into the air a few feet away from my intended target. Turning my body at the last second, I extended my leg out and did a sidekick to the closest infected's temple. He staggered to his right like I had hoped he would, and stumbled into his buddy. I landed, and with narrowed vision, I struck out with both my sais, landing my left sai into the first infected's temple and my right sai into the neck, up the skull, and into the brain.

I spun, checking for the threats behind me, my lungs seeking the air it so desperately wanted. There was a pile of bodies strewn about. All the infected had been neutralized. There had to be over fifty of them. I felt the bile rise into my throat but shook it off.

Blondie was sitting up and clutching his head as another man with glossy, black, loosely curled hair, wrapped his arms around the blond's head and kissed the top of it. The man murmured something to the blond, who nodded. They looked like a sexy couple. If it weren't for another man already intruding my thoughts, I would've been attracted to either one of them—if they had been interested in girls, that was.

I didn't know how Axel had weaseled into my thoughts and affections so quickly. However, he was there. I had only known him for less than forty-eight hours, and already I felt we were... linked.

The sound of angry whispers brought me out of my musings. I turned to see Natalie and the Asian woman looking my way. Natalie was glaring at me. The Asian was looking at me with a barely concealed sneer.

"You're welcome still." I smiled sweetly at her once more. "As a thank you gift, I'll take chocolate, preferably with almonds," I said flippantly.

Seriously, what was her problem? I'm sure my sister had left a bad taste in her mouth. However, the woman knew I wasn't Emery. Whatever beef she had with my sister should not extend to me, especially after I saved her from being *Infected* food.

"Holy shit, thank you, Ave," I heard Felix mutter as he ambled up behind me, embracing me from behind. I could feel his body rising up and down against my back, shaking slightly. "I didn't want to be one of them."

Cal and Joe stared at me with open mouths. "She's like Buffy the vampire slayer," Cal breathed in awe. "She flew over all those bodies without hesitation and did some Hollywood shit."

"I just wished I had that on camera. No one would believe that shit was real unless they saw it," Joe incredulously said as he wiped his face.

I laughed weakly, feeling the energy begin to seep out of me. "Are we even now for the bruise?" I teased Felix. I knelt by an infected, trying not to examine them as I found a section of their clothing that wasn't soiled in blood. I used it to wipe the blades of my sais. I exhaled through my nose. Their smell was pervasive in my nostrils.

"More than even," he muttered in relief. "I owe you a life debt."

"Avery?" I heard my name at the same time a female voice cried out for Axel.

I turned my head and had to blink twice before I realized he wasn't a mirage. He was tall, built like a football player, wide shoulders, broad chest, narrow waist, long legs, and muscular all over. His ash-blond hair had been shorn close to his head, and a few days' growth of facial hair covered his strong jawline. Eyes that changed from light green to gray assessed me as if he were seeing a ghost.

I vaguely noticed the Asian woman running past me and launching herself at Axel. I blinked in shock but wasn't able to compute the hollow feeling in my chest as I was nearly barreled over by Corbin.

"Corbin," I cried out as my sais clattered to the ground.

The moment his arms wrapped around me, I felt... home. My body seemed to melt into him instinctively.

His presence no longer represented pain; instead, it signified security. He was the boy who'd once cleaned up my boo-boos when I fell off my bike. He was the teen who helped me fix one of my mom's favorite lamps before she found out I had broken it playing ball in the house. He was the "nearly adult" who sat next to me at my mother's funeral, holding my hand in his.

How had I not seen how much he had been there for me growing up? Sure, Trevor had been my best friend, companion, even my shield, but Corbin... Corbin had been my protector.

I threw my arms around his neck as he lifted me. He squeezed me tightly to his hard chest. I wrapped my legs around his waist, not caring that we were both covered in blood, sweat, and other disgusting things. I felt him take a few steps before my body connected with the wall. I noticed his arms were trembling, and I felt a wetness on the side of my neck.

After several moments he pulled back. His eyes were red as if he had been crying. "How?" he asked in wonderment.

I was confused by his strong emotions and shocked when his mouth crushed down on mine. He wasn't gentle. When he nipped my lip, I tasted the metallic taste of my blood on my tongue. I gasped, and his tongue drove into my mouth with ownership. My brain told me to push him away. But my body recognized how right he felt.

I gripped his shoulders, tempted to shove him away, when I noticed the delicious warmth of his skin under my fingertips. His powerful muscles rippled under my hands. My body won, as I surrendered to his skillful lips. I softened my mouth against his, returning his kiss. After some time, he groaned and pulled back. I noticed his ragged breathing first before I realized I could barely breathe myself.

"How are you here?" he finally rasped once more.

"I came with Axel and the men. Sylvia, BJ, Mikey, and Miller," I explained to him, mystified. I was rambling. I never rambled unless I was nervous. "And... oh yeah, we found these kids and got some dogs, too."

I heard Wyatt's gasp right before I saw him stagger back into Axel and Chad. "Avery? But... you're dead..." Both Axel and Chad were struggling to keep him upright.

Wyatt's usually gelled, russet-colored hair was standing on end like he had been running his fingers through it a million times, and his emerald green eyes were red, like he had been crying, too. There was an unhealthy pallor to his typically fair skin, and the spattering of brown freckles across the bridge of his nose and cheeks stood out starkly.

"What are you talking about, Wy?" Axel gently prodded the stunned man.

I vaguely realized that Axel no longer had the Asian girl plastered against him. I made a mental note to ask him about her later. Our... thing... was still in the infancy stages. I assumed he was unattached. After Trevor, I wasn't going to be so blind anymore. If he wanted to be with her, then I was out, regardless of his pretty words and willingness to share me.

"How?" Wyatt muttered, capturing my attention once more. "We saw your body. You were dead!" Wyatt cried out.

Chapter 12

"We saw your truck, so we all pulled over," Corbin began to explain as we went out to the vehicles to grab the rest of our party. "We passed a guns and ammo store, and Mom swore she saw your truck in the parking lot. I looped back around, and Steph confirmed it. When we saw you—no, someone wearing your sweatshirt-" he stopped and shook his head. "There was a woman with dark hair, a blond-headed man, and a little dark-haired boy," his voice rasped.

He rubbed his face, suddenly looking tired. "We couldn't recognize them. The infected did a number on them. So, yeah... She had on your shirt, then? The man must have had on BJ's desert tan boots and fleece jacket. The little boy... he had on Miller's favorite Green Lantern t-shirt. We went searching for Sylvia and Mikey. We looked for hours. By then, we thought we should let the rest of the team know what was going on. They were told not to come here because I knew it would be overrun."

My stomach roiled. "Rosa and Luke, they stole my truck. They had another little boy, Ben. You didn't find him?"

"Aunt Pam thought she saw a dark-haired boy, but she was so distraught. Steph, too," Wyatt muttered before he was hauling me into his arms.

I didn't tense against him but allowed him to take comfort in my arms. He held me close while he buried his head in my neck. "You're alive," he muttered against me, his lips brushing along my jawline.

How did this become the new norm? I accepted their familiarity and embraces as I never had before. I was also completely okay with the little kisses– or in Corbin's case, not so little kisses. This hadn't *been* us in the past, so how were we slipping into these roles with such ease?

"I'm alive, yes!" I laughed as I embraced him in return.

My families were huggers. We weren't always, but Aunt Pam and Aunt Carol grew up in average, loving homes. They had to reform my dad, Mom, Uncle Mitch, and Uncle Scott and had made them huggers, too. Then they all taught us to be huggers.

It was nothing to embrace our cousins when we saw them or when we were leaving. As kids, it was comfortable; as teens, it became more perfunctory. I didn't think I'd ever considered how it would feel to be in Wyatt's or Corbin's arms, but now, without my single-minded thoughts of Trevor, I had to admit it was beyond lovely. I couldn't deny the awareness that prickled across my skin.

I didn't care that we were in the middle of a parking lot, or that it was in front of Axel, Corbin, Felix, and Chad. I let Wyatt take comfort in my arms, and I permitted myself to feel pleasure in his touch. He peppered kisses along my jawline, and I ran my fingers through his hair.

"Wyatt! Corbin!" Sylvia cried out.

I looked up to see Sylvia climb out of the Tahoe and embrace Corbin, laughing, and crying at the same time.

"Am I cleared to come down?" BJ yelled down from his position up on the tower.

Axel merely nodded and waved him down. I could see the smile spread across BJ's face, even from this distance, as he clamored down. I knew he was just as excited to see Wyatt and Corbin, too.

Sylvia ran over to us next and hugged Wyatt. He

embraced her with one arm, seemingly unwilling to let me go just yet.

The back doors to the Tahoe opened, and Mikey and Miller came tumbling out, holding the leashes of the Rottweiler, Jack Russell, and Sylvia's ugly but cute dogs.

"Can we walk the dogs?" Miller asked. "They really need to go."

"Stay near us," I called back.

"Okay," they simultaneously responded before they walked over to our van.

"And keep their leashes on them!" I added. We had no clue if the dogs would run off, and I'd hate to lose them right after we had just rescued them.

"Dogs?" Corbin laughed. "Where the heck did the dogs come from?"

"A shelter." I smirked. "A woman we ran into was a volunteer at one. She thinks they unsettle the infected. We couldn't let them starve to death in the shelter, and it was worth checking out the theory."

"I should go get the babies," Sylvia chirped. "They were getting restless."

"I'll grab the princess," Chad eagerly volunteered as he followed her.

I smiled at his retreating back. He loved that baby, and we could already tell Jenny adored him, too.

"*Babies?*" Wyatt added with a raised brow.

I frowned, feeling sad. "We found Phillip and Jenny on the way out here. Their mother was... taken by the infected. Sylvia rescued them before they could become infected food. The mom was only eighteen, with no real family to speak of."

I saw the grim expressions settle on their faces. No one wanted to think about the helpless that had no one to rescue them.

A loud, low bark erupted in warning before I saw Bane charge towards me. Once he reached me, he circled me, whining loudly. He made me feel lighter, a balm to my troubled soul.

"It's okay, boy," I crooned. "Were you a good dog?"

"That's not a dog, that's a horse," Wyatt teased.

I smiled. "I know, and he's just a puppy!"

"How are we supposed to feed him?" Corbin smirked.

"We got food." I feigned a sniff.

"Bane did well," Axel stated with a satisfying twist of his lips. "He didn't chew up anything or have any accidents; however, your side of the door now has claw marks embedded in it. Looks like he didn't like you leaving him."

I kneeled and stroked Bane's coat. "Want me to train you, Baney boy, wanna come with Mama when she's out kicking infected booty?" I hummed. I was pleased to see he didn't seem to need a leash. Perhaps he'd be one of those dogs that wouldn't run.

"She's baby-talking a dog," Corbin mocked, talking out of the side of his mouth to Wyatt. He held out his hand and I stood up, taking it.

"And that's a surprise?" Wyatt quipped back. "She used to apologize to the nightcrawlers before she put them on the hook, and then thank the fish when she caught them."

"She did not," Axel remarked with mock horror.

"Not surprised." Felix smirked. I could tell he was still shaken from his near-death experience.

"She used to apologize and thank the deer we used to hunt, too." BJ joined into my roasting as he extended his hand to Corbin.

Corbin took it and did one of those weird male rituals

of shaking it, pulling him in, and slapping his back as he embraced him. "I heard you've improved you're shooting." Corbin smiled at him.

"Didn't you see all those bodies we had to climb over to get out here? That's why I call him Boy Wonder," Axel added with his look of pride. "The kid's a sniper."

I saw the flush of pleasure come over BJ's face. I knew he was trying to act "manly" as he received his compliments.

"He got expert in the academy," I bragged on him.

BJ turned red some more. Wyatt laughed and pulled BJ into a manly hug next. "He always was a good shot, I imagine the academy just made him better." Wyatt clapped him on the back loudly.

"We should get out of here, you guys smell," Sylvia said, wrinkling her nose but smiling as she jostled Phillip on her hip.

Chad was slightly behind her, patting Jenny's little back. I noticed he had wiped down and was wearing a new shirt.

I looked down at myself, noticing I was in desperate need of a shower, too. I removed my jacket and placed it on the hood of the van. I made a mental note to wipe it down later.

I heard an appreciative sound and noticed Corbin, Wyatt, and Axel watching me. So far, I was glad to see Axel had no qualms with seeing me in Corbin's or Wyatt's arms. Maybe he really didn't mind seeing me with his men...

I shifted, slightly self-conscious. It was nice knowing they desired me but still such a new concept for me to process. In theory, it sounded great; in practice, it seemed a lot more complicated.

"I think we should stay here tonight," Axel finally said, pulling his gaze away from me, as he looked down at his watch. "We have about seven hours of daylight left. We still need to clear and burn the bodies, and we can't guarantee that we're not going to run into any issues heading to the campground.

We can get anything in here while it's secured. I'm not sure if it would be wise to return once the locals realize it's clear. I'm going to come up with a game plan and need everyone to meet me in the food court in fifteen."

He turned to Felix. "Find a spot we can keep Mrs. Cavalier, Mrs. Harris, Sylvia, Avery, and the kids. The women and children don't need to see the carnage in there."

"Copy that," Felix said without hesitation as he took off running back towards the mall.

"I'll help with the cleanup," I said with a frown.

Axel sighed as he put his hand on his hips. "You're a civilian."

I raised my brow at him, walking back towards the circle of sorts they had formed. I was conscious of Wyatt's and Corbin's gazes still on me. "I'm a civilian that helped make that mess, and I'm sure you expected BJ to help as well." I imitated his stance, putting my hands on my hips, too.

Axel scowled at me. "BJ went to the academy. He already had one foot in the door and the training."

I scoffed at him. I knew he was just trying to give me a break, but I also knew if he weren't involved with me, he would still expect me to pull my weight.

"I'm helping, you can't stop me," I said mutinously, crossing my arms over my chest.

I think I heard Corbin stifle a laugh, but it was quickly covered up with a cough. He stepped up behind me and wrapped his arms around my waist and lowered his chin on my shoulder.

It felt so natural just to lean back into him. It was hard to concentrate on my ire towards Axel with Corbin's body so near.

I could see Axel's jaw work as he had one of his inward battles.

"Mommy!" Mikey screamed out unexpectedly as he took off at a run.

Miller was steps behind him with six dogs hot on their heels. I turned to see Steph and Aunt Pam breaking away from a group of a few civilians and JOpS. They were both sobbing. Steph opened her arms and her boys fell into them. I felt my eyes water at their reunion and smiled before Aunt Pam's petite frame barrelled into me.

"Oh, Avery, I thought you were dead!" she sobbed, pinning me against Corbin's chest. She pulled my face down to hers so she could kiss both of my cheeks. "I saw your long dark hair, your truck, your favorite hoodie with your name on it! BJ!" she called out.

"Yes, ma'am," he dutifully replied, coming over without her voicing her request.

Soon, all four of us were in a hug, and tears were shed. Corbin was rubbing his mom's back and mine, murmuring reassurances.

"My babies, I missed my babies," she kept repeating, sobbing. "I thought I would never see them again."

"I'm here now," I reassured her. "I'm sorry I've haven't called or texted that much. I'm sorry I was taking my...hurt out on you. No more. I promise."

She pulled back and looked at me. Tears were coursing down her face still. "It was okay to heal, baby. I understood. I just didn't want to push you, but I wanted you to understand I will always feel like a mother to you, more than an aunt."

I swallowed back my tears. "And I'll always look at you more than an aunt." I tried to stem the tears from falling from my eyes. "I know I'm lucky, not only to have had my mom, but you, too. You were just as much a mom to us as she was. We never... I never doubted your love for me."

She began to cry again in earnest once more.

I heard a throat clear and saw Trevor's solemn gaze on me. "Avery." He held his arms out.

He hadn't changed much in the year I had last seen him. He was still maybe two inches or so taller than me. He'd stopped wrestling long ago, so had lost some of his muscle mass, but still looked in great shape. His ash-blond hair was still shorter on the sides but kept longer on top, parted and gelled to one side. His soulful brown eyes were the same, always so expressive. He never could lie without his face giving him away.

I wasn't going to count his lies of omission. I never outright considered him cheating on me, so I had never asked. Had I asked back then, though, I'm sure it would have been written all over his face. I wish I would've asked him before we got pregnant. It would've changed a lot of things and probably wouldn't have ended in one of my most significant heartbreaks.

I continued my perusal of him. Even his clothing style was still the same. In our senior year of high school, he started to dress preppy and was fastidious in his looks. Despite the fact we were in the middle of an apocalypse, his khaki shorts were wrinkle and dirt free. His white polo shirt and white shoes were still pristine, as if he'd just purchased them.

I stared at him and felt...empty. There was no sharp, suffocating pain left in my heart. In its place was just sadness; not because he'd broken my heart in the worst way possible, but because I missed the best friend I'd once had. I realized now I no longer missed him like I would have for a lover but as a dear friend. And for the first time, I felt like I could learn to forgive him. My unwillingness to do so had put me in shackles. I hadn't been free from my self-imposed prison since the day I walked out of his frat house.

We'd never have the relationship we once had, and I knew there wasn't going to be an immediate absolution. I predicted it was going to take time. I wasn't ever going to forget, but it was time I made the right steps to free my soul and let go of the pain, anger, and hurt I felt.

As I warred with myself, I hadn't noticed that Corbin had taken a protective stance between his brother and me. I looked up at him and smiled.

"It's okay." I patted his chest, then whispered, "He might be the man that hurt me, but he's still the boy that used to be my best friend."

"Are you sure?" he said with a frown, searching my features, cradling my cheek. "If you need–"

I cut him off and smiled once more. "I'm sure."

Trevor's eyes looked confused and somewhat inquisitive as he looked between me and Corbin. A sheen of tears filled his eyes which were full of regret, uncertainty, and... longing. With his arms open, I could see his silent plea, asking me to step inside them. I sighed but moved towards him, one step at a time.

"Trev," Emery sharply admonished as she sidled up to his side and then in front of him. Trevor sighed, dropping his arms, and didn't make an effort to embrace me again.

"Hey, Twinsy," Emery said, smiling wide at me, the welcoming emotion not reaching her eyes.

"Hey, Em," I said a bit stiffly.

I didn't know why it was harder to imagine forgiving her. Maybe it was because, unlike Trevor, she was blood. We had shared a womb for nearly nine months. Or possibly it was because I knew she had pursued Trevor all along, with the sole purpose of taking him away from me.

Something within me had a feeling Emery hadn't been drunk that night like she had said she was, and no matter how many explanations I heard, I still didn't believe she *accidentally* stumbled into his room. She had been over to the house enough to know exactly what room he had stayed in.

"Is that it?" She raised a perfectly arched brow at me.

I knew that look all too well. She was itching for a fight. She needed to twist it around as if I had been at fault and she the innocent.

It was surreal, at times, to see myself when I stared back at her. The dark hair, tanned skinned, amber eyes that tilted like a cat's, the slightly upturned button nose, the bow-shaped lips, and heart-shaped face. Our differences were only apparent when we stood next to each other. Our hairstyles and bodies were imperceptibly different. Her hair was in layers, unnoticeable in the chic ponytail she wore. She was also ten to fifteen pounds lighter than me and didn't have the muscle tone I had.

I shrugged and smirked at her, knowing it would get under her skin. "Yeah." I turned and looked at Axel. "When are we having this meeting? Aren't we losing light?"

▢

After Axel had held his meeting and laid out all his expectations, I began to go through the infected's pockets and belongings. He wanted as many keys retrieved from the infected and their vehicles moved to the furthest point of the parking lot. The cars would act as a barrier of sorts, with mere inches separating each vehicle. He only wanted one lane open for our departure in the morning.

He'd also expressed his wishes for each adult capable of driving to take a vehicle–if they didn't already have one –to Sanctuary Lakes Campground. Each transport would be packed with anything we found in the mall that we wanted, as well as the items we'd need.

Axel wasn't too crazy that Sylvia and I had insisted on helping with clean up, but he still put us to work. He figured getting car keys from people wasn't too hard of a task.

"I wanna thank you for saving my life," the blond-haired man with the riot of loose curls called out, now running up beside me. "I'm Kingston, but you can call me King." He held his hand out to me.

I shouldn't have been shocked to realize the blond I found so attractive was the infamous King. I had already heard so much about him that it was slightly awkward to be meeting him when I already knew his sexual proclivity and been driving around in his Tahoe.

Should I pretend I didn't know who he was, I thought, *or lay all my cards out on the table now?*

Not for the first time, I wondered if Axel's assumptions about the guys' interest in me were correct. I had yet to see him wrong, but had he read the situation correctly? How could two guys I'd never met... want me? Everything they knew about me was through Facebook videos and Wyatt and Corbin.

I smiled in return. "It was no problem. I'm Avery, but I have a feeling you already knew that. It's good to meet the man who wants to be an environmentalist but is unwilling to sacrifice too much and has a thing for public sex."

Why had I said that? I wanted to slam my hands over my mouth, but it had just slipped out as I contemplated how to interact with him.

I suddenly needed to hide from my outspokenness, so without waiting for his response, I went back to my task at hand. I bent over and reached into the infected's pocket, looking for his keys. I smiled in triumph as I felt the keyfob in there. I grabbed it and his wallet and took out his cash and ID, placing the cash and IDs inside the new backpack I'd found in the sporting goods store. The wallet I threw in a rolling bin behind me. Then I marked the infected with a permanent marker to let the burn team know he was ready to be carried out.

King threw his head back and laughed, causing me to look at him. His eyes danced with mischief. "The first one is something I don't flaunt around, and I'm curious how you knew that. The second one is no secret, but I wonder... who told you that? Were you asking about me?"

It was my turn to laugh out loud as I arched my brow at him, moving on to the next body. "You have canvas grocery bags in a vehicle that guzzles gas, and a girl has to have some secrets, so I'm not telling you who or how I found out that you're an exhibitionist."

He smirked at me before watching as I picked up a woman's purse. It was leather, pink, with gold "C" designs on it. It was very feminine. When I opened it, I realized it was more like a diaper bag. There was a hand pump, nipple pads, nipple creams, diapers, and various other baby needs, as well as three wristbands dated thirteen days ago. I frowned when I realized one of the wrist bands matched the name of the man's wallet I had just rifled through.

"I thought you were supposed to be getting keys," he stated as he held out his hands for the keys attached to one of my belt loops with a carabiner. King was one of the people moving the vehicles. He playfully placed his head on my shoulder, peering over it, thankfully pulling me from thoughts that could spiral me into a deep depression. "What are you doing with the cash and wallets?"

I sighed. Sylvia and I had decided to deviate from the directive given to us. Through my musings, I wanted to retain some of my compassion. We agreed that there was no humanity left in the infected, but maybe someone, somewhere would be looking for these people, wanting answers about their whereabouts. We figured they should at least know if they needed to stop searching, and they'd never be able to identify anyone from ashes after the bodies were burned.

We were going to try and collect any identifiers of

each infected. Afterward, we would cover the advertisement marquees at the entrance of the mall and affix their identifications to them. Sylvia was artistic and creative, and she was already thinking about the words she was going to paint above the boards, words that we hoped would bring some closure to their loved ones, if they were still out there.

We were going to put their personal effects near the boards, too, just in case their loved ones wanted them.

"They don't need their money anymore," I explained first. *Might as well let him laugh at me now,* I thought. "When I go shopping, later on, I'm going to pay for my stuff with the cash I find."

He started to laugh, and I shrugged.

"Wait," he said after several seconds. "You're serious."

I nodded, rolling my eyes. "As a heart attack."

He began to laugh once more. Every time he went to open his mouth to speak again, a fresh round of laughter emerged from his mouth.

"I wanna know the joke," a smooth baritone voice said from behind us.

I turned around and noticed Axel, then my gaze went to the owner of the voice standing beside him. I didn't school my face fast enough to hide my surprise.

I've heard of fraternal twins, but I never thought I would ever meet a set like the two in question.

Kingston Rains was almost identical to his brother in every way except for his coloring. Looking at King, I would never think he was of mixed race, what with his light-blond hair and light skin tone—not fair, per se, but he was lighter than me, and I was Caucasian and Polynesian.

Easton, on the other hand, was distinctly mixed. If I had to guess, he was a mixture of African American and Caucasian, but I wasn't sure. Guessing ethnicities could be so tricky. His warm-brown skin was maybe a shade or two darker than my bronzed shade. And unlike his brother, his soft, loose curls were black. However, on closer inspection, I could see the blondish highlights streaked in his hair, and they, too, looked natural.

I suddenly had a flashback and realized he was the one who had been kneeling over his wounded brother. At the time, I had almost mistaken them for lovers. His body language had been so protective and gentle. Now I realized that he just had an intense bond with his brother, and seeing his brother in that condition must have frightened him.

"I'm white chocolate, he's the milk chocolate," Kingston husked in my ear.

I blushed. "Sorry for staring," I finally stammered. "I know what it's like to have people stare, and I hate it."

"You're beautiful. Of course you're going to get stares," Kingston quipped with a wink.

I rolled my eyes at his attempt at flirting. He was cute, and he knew it. I had a feeling he was used to charming people to get his way. It was working, but I wasn't going to let him know it.

"Wow." I blinked at him with great exaggeration. "I bet that works with the girls all the time. If you're charming and act oblivious, they underestimate you and lower all expectations, never suspecting your calculating nature at all, unless you choose to reveal it to them. You knew I was talking about the whole twin thing. How people stare at you, dissect you, and try to figure out ways to tell you apart. In your case, though, you guys look identical, just different color palettes."

Both men chuckled, and I saw even Axel's lips lift into a grin.

"I shouldn't be surprised," Kingston said with a rueful smile. "Wyatt did warn me her astuteness rivaled Easton's."

Easton held out his hand and smiled gently. "I'm Easton. It's a pleasure to meet you, Avery, finally. We've heard so much about you over the last few years. I feel as if we already know you."

I noticed that Easton had the same unique seafoam eyes his brother had, but his eyes held a more reserved look...a certain intelligence. Not to say Kingston didn't have a look of cleverness, but Easton had the eyes of an old soul.

"I hope it was all good things," I gave the clichéd response.

Easton's mouth twitched with another smile. "So, what was the joke?"

Kingston looked at me once more and started laughing. I rolled my eyes and knelt next to the bodies, repeating what I'd been doing since I began stripping them about half an hour ago.

Kingston laughed. "She's removing their cash, identifications, and putting their wallets and purses in that bin. She wants to pay for everything she takes, but Avery has yet to tell me why she's holding onto their identifications and belongings."

I looked up to see Axel and Easton regarding me with curious eyes. I sighed.

"Someone out there might come looking for their loved ones," I explained tentatively. "We need to burn the bodies, to stop the spread of infection, but what happens if people are out there looking for them? They'll never be able to identify them through ashes. We're giving some of their families closure. They can stop wondering *what if*. Sylvia and I are going to put their ID's or anything uniquely theirs up by the bulletin boards, along with their belongings."

"I think that's a brilliant idea," Easton said decisively. "I'll go tell the rest of the cleanup crew the same information."

"Thanks, Easton." I smiled at him.

"See you later, Avery." Easton walked off with a nod and smiled.

Josh called out for Kingston's help then, and King told him to hold on, giving me a wink and a mischievous smile. "So, if I were to pick something out for you, would you accept it, or would it go against your moral dilemma?"

I shook my head at him. "Make fun all you want." I rolled my eyes. "You have to stand for something, or you'll fall for anything."

He gave me a slow once-over. "I stand for a lot of things, goddess, and I think I'm gonna have so much fun showing you that." He licked his bottom lip and headed Josh's way.

I wasn't sure how to take his words, but I had a feeling he was letting me know he was interested—more than responsive, in fact. I shook my head, clearing my thoughts before I turned to look at Axel.

He was now standing at the railing, looking down to watch the clean up below. I could see the tension radiating off him and paused what I was doing to walk over to him. I removed the rubber gloves I'd found and reached out to him. When I laid my hand on his shoulders, he tensed at first. I began to massage his shoulders and felt him relax against my hands.

I noticed Jade's-the Asian girl- gaze on us from below, and she was sneering at me. *No surprise there.* She eyed my hands on him, and I thought I saw her snarl.

Without me asking, Corbin and Wyatt had filled me in on their past relationship with her. They seemed quick to reassure me during our meeting, after she had tried to drape herself across Axel and he had commanded her away from him. I had to hide my smile when he'd shot me a look as if to reassure me.

"We're almost there," I whispered now in his ear. "We'll get there soon enough. You're doing a great job protecting us all. You were born to be a leader, Axel."

Somehow, I had a feeling that his tension was based on the fact that we weren't close to being safe yet. Sure, we had taken care of a hoard of infected in the mall, but what was tonight going to bring? We still had no clue what our position was going to be at Sanctuary Lakes, but at least we knew nature would protect us or, at least, shield us from most threats.

He personally felt responsible, not only for his "boys" but all of us. He might have known war, but this war was new to him. I had seen him in edgy-alert mode ever since he rescued us on that access road, but since we had arrived here, his rigidity had risen. I'd only heard snippets of his meeting with a handful of the JOpS, and I was sure that what I hadn't heard had bothered him, putting him the most on edge.

The moment the duties had been doled out, he'd called the JOpS meeting. He had taken Joe, Corbin, Kingston, Natalie, Jade, and another JOpS by the name of Garth into one of the offices reserved for mall management and had laid into them. Whatever was said, I knew Kingston had no qualms informing Axel what had happened earlier in his absence.

Apparently, Garth, Natalie, and Jade had decided to take it upon themselves to ignore Joe's direct orders of bypassing the mall. Joe hadn't thought it wise to stop there since they were so close to their destination. Natalie, Garth, and Jade, however, had turned off and entered the mall before they could be stopped.

Joe had no other choice but to go in to assist them. Even if it had been a suicide mission, the JOpS had an unspoken rule of never leaving one of their own to fight alone. They would all rather go down together than return from a mission with a possibility that "their man" could have been saved otherwise.

Joe could have technically wiped his hands of Jade and

Natalie. As it was, they had been at a meeting yesterday morning with their commanders about removing both girls from the team—which they had approved—right when we had received the call to evacuate to Sanctuary.

Rumor had it, Jade and Natalie overheard some of the conversation Joe had with Chad on the phone. The girls followed Joe. They hadn't made their presence known until last night. If Joe didn't have such a bleeding heart, he would have told them they weren't welcomed to follow them.

Garth was technically Team Charlie, but, again, he was a JOpS. He had been hanging out with the group when the call came through, so Cal had invited him along, not realizing to what extent things would escalate.

Axel had ripped the culprits a new one- like the gossip went- warning them that it was their first and *last* warning. If they stepped out of line one more time, he'd said, the promise of safety would be taken from them. He told them he couldn't afford to have people on his team that he didn't trust and that couldn't obey orders.

He drew a line in the sand. JOpS or not, his priority was his direct family, then the civilians. He felt their primary duty was always the civilians at home. Now that the battlefield was here, their duties shifted to the homefront.

After several moments, Axel finally turned in my arms, shaking me from my thoughts. He pulled me in tight. "I needed that, thanks," he murmured in my neck.

I didn't know if it was from my ministrations or my words, but he didn't look as stressed anymore, and I was glad I was able to help him, even if it was for a little while.

Chapter 13

I didn't think I'd ever felt so exhausted in my entire life. My head was starting to throb, my limbs felt heavy, and I was pretty sure I was laughing and giggling more out of pure exhaustion than humor. My body was trying to tell me I was tired, but I couldn't listen to it yet.

My usual mixture of adrenaline, serotonin, epinephrine, endorphins, and dopamine in my brain was thrown out of whack, so I was laughing at nearly everything. Luckily, Sylvia was on the same sleep deprivation high, because she was laughing just as much as I was.

As we worked alongside each other, we talked, joked around, and found laughter in almost everything. It must have been our coping mechanism in this new world we'd found ourselves in, on top of sheer exhaustion.

We managed to clear out all the infected by sundown, dumping them into empty dumpsters before setting them on fire. While the bodies burned, the food court area and the center of the mall were cleaned and sterilized to the best of our ability. The smell of bleach had been so strong that we had to air out the rooms by opening up all the nearby doors. We also lit many scented candles, placing them throughout the area.

Most of the food court tables had been pushed up against the entrance doors, save the two that we'd use in the morning. All the windows had been covered just in case, too. The now empty court held our air mattresses and bedding, nicely placed in the middle for an operative defensive position.

Teams of four would be taking shifts patrolling the mall for any potential outside threats. Two snipers were stationed up on top of the roof as our ultimate lookouts and first line of defense. After everyone went "shopping," the metal accordion gates had been located and erected.

So far, the many rows of meticulously parked vehicles in the now-tight circle on the perimeter seemed to be holding back most of the infected. It was an excellent strategy on Axel's part, and the guys made sure to commend him for it numerous times.

I learned a lot more about Axel in those moments. He was a strong, well-respected leader. Even Joe seemed to hold a high reverence towards him and deferred to him on most matters. The praises sent his way never seemed to go to his head, either.

The way he handled opposition was commendable as well. Natalie, Jade, and Garth were clearly not happy with him. They seemed to make everything so much more complicated than they had to. But Axel remained firm with them and challenged them to complete their tasks.

He was consistent, fair, and genuinely seemed to desire our safety, even the Terrible Trio- the name Sylvia and I had given Natalie, Jade, and Garth.

Sylvia and I had just finished putting up the last ID, when we stepped back and looked at our handiwork, feeling satisfied yet also filled with a great sense of loss. There were too many people on the board, all senselessly dead because someone out there had decided to play God and create a biological weapon of devastating consequences.

We hugged each other and silently cried as we looked upon the results of the infection's depravity.

Sylvia had written, 'Hold onto the Love, Not the Loss' above the bulletin boards. Surprisingly, once everyone had found out what we'd been doing, almost everyone wrote words of encouragement or sympathy on the walls surrounding the boards. A row of battery-operated candles had been turned on and placed on a long narrow table in front of the bulletin boards. I wished we could have done more, but I was glad we at least did something.

Bane whined as if he knew I was hurting, nudging the back of my legs. The dog hadn't left my side, or Axel's, since being released from the store that the kids, Steph, Aunt Pam, and Emery had been holed up in while we took care of most of the cleanup.

In this part of the mall, footsteps were easily heard. We didn't tense, though; between the guys, Cal, and Joe, we were never alone for long.

Sylvia and I quickly wiped our faces of tears when Corbin and Cal came around the corner. Everyone else, except for the six people on duty, had been sound asleep for the last hour or so.

"Come on, girls. Bath and bed," Corbin bade.

"You gonna join us?" Sylvia asked boldly, coming back to life. "Will you wash my back, Cal?"

Both men laughed and shook their heads, but it was Cal who spoke up first. "Come with me, and I'll wash more than just your back." He winked at her.

"Promise?" She smiled coyly.

There had been a lot of flirting going on between Sylvia, Joe, and Cal throughout the night, but they hadn't had much time to spend together. She had been lamenting to me all night long about the impossibility of being with two men. She wanted to be with them, but she didn't understand how an arrangement like that could last.

I still hadn't had a chance to talk to her about *my* new predicament. I felt like I was bursting at the seams to tell someone. It felt like every time I found an opportunity to finally broach the subject, one of the guys would come around to "check" on us. They would stay and chat, and for once, Sylvia seemed to be oblivious to the fact that the guys were more than flirting with me. There was an underlying sense of anticipation and sexual tension that she seemed to not notice at all, what with her mind so occupied by her own situation.

"Promise." He smiled. "I just got off of my shift and I'm free. I'll show you where I got us set up for the night." He suddenly looked uncertain about his presumptuous actions.

"Lead the way, prince charming," she said giddily.

"Yeah?" Cal smiled broadly.

"Yeah," she said before she skipped forward. "Night, Cor and Ave."

"Don't forget I slipped condoms in your bag," I teased her, retreating back.

Sleep deprivation was loosening my tongue.

"I hope you gave me an entire box," she sang back, "because I plan to use all of them!"

I groaned. "Too much," I yelled back.

"That's what she said." She turned around and walked backward, grinning at me.

"She would never say that!" I joked back. "There's never enough."

I heard Corbin make a low grunting sound, and I saucily winked at him.

He grinned and shook his head at me.

"True story," Sylvia said solemnly. "Well, I'm hoping to get *too much* right now. Night night," she chirped once more.

"Mind if I accompany you to the restroom?" Corbin asked as they disappeared around the corner. He held out his hand, and I took it without thought. "I won't even offer to wash your back unless you want me too," he flirted.

I leaned my head against his arm. "Does any of this feel... weird to you?" I asked softly as I gently squeezed his hand.

Corbin and Wyatt had barely let me out of their sight, and whenever they found a chance, they were touching me. Our connection seemed to grow in so many ways, and the more time I spent with them, the more... *right* it felt. Everything felt so natural, like the way things were supposed to be.

"Nope," he said immediately, lowering his voice as we walked past the food court of sleeping people. "It feels like I'm finally getting the chance to show you how I've felt for years. I think in a way, I've always noticed you. I lived in denial for years. The summer you kissed my brother, I didn't like it, and I didn't know why.

"So I joined the military and got some distance away from you, but you crossed my mind often. When you started Tae Kwon Do, Mom kept raving about how you skipped a belt, won a tournament, or aced another test. She liked bragging about you. She always loved you like her own. And when she didn't mention you, I felt down and didn't know why.

"When I came home on my first leave, when the rents moved to Maryland, I came back and saw you were with Trev, and for the first time in my life, I was jealous of my kid brother. I told myself it wasn't jealousy, that it was just irritation over Trevor pursuing a relationship with you that had the possibility of ruining the relations between our families if things went south. I kept telling myself I was a pervert for having a crush on someone so young. I tried to convince myself that it wasn't an attraction towards you. I tried to forget you and became more of a... manwhore."

I snorted, and Corbin gave me a sidelong glance and a rueful shrug of his shoulders before smiling. For as long as I knew him, save for when we were at Sanctuary- after the summer Trevor and I kissed- he had come alone, but I knew he wasn't without female companionship.

"The last time you were trying out for the Olympics," he continued, "about four years ago, Mom told me that you had a crucial match in Virginia. Wyatt and I decided to go. We didn't tell Mom, just in case we were called up, but it turned out they couldn't make it anyway. Mom had to get Dad from the airport, and Trevor had his finals that week. But Wyatt and I made it and we got to see you in your element.

He stopped suddenly and turned towards me. He cradled my face in his large hands, threading his fingers through my hair. He tilted my head up to meet his penetrating gaze. The actions elicited a slight tremor through my sensitized body. He gently caressed my cheek with his thumbs.

"I think at that moment, I realized my feelings for you had...evolved. You were no longer a little girl anymore but a woman. Wyatt felt the same way but came to that conclusion sooner than me. But he didn't think I'd be okay with him wanting my brother's girlfriend, or the fact you'd just graduated high school."

My lips parted as he traced them with a calloused thumb. It was if the air were being sucked from the room again, but for better reasons. His thumbs were rough, whereas my lips were soft. I liked the contrast of textures. He seemed to notice it as well, as I watched him sink his teeth into his bottom lip for a moment.

"You occupied my thoughts continually for years, Avery," he confessed as I gave in to the urge to flick my tongue out and taste him. He closed his eyes and groaned before continuing. "I watched you from afar, telling myself it was just from the perspective of a big brother, a protector. Eventually, I felt like we were never supposed to be. You loved my brother, and he adored you. You guys had been best friends for years, and it just made sense if you both became more. I don't think I realized how wrong he might be for you until after your first break up. I knew he loved you, and I think he will *always* love you, but he's always been his worst enemy," he said cryptically."

A small satisfied smile curved his lips as I placed a kiss on his palm.

He opened his eyes. "I think this is our season, Avery. It took me some growing up to realize you are what I always wanted. So, yeah, all that to say this feels right to me. This feels like a missing link was finally found."

I digested his words and found myself agreeing with him. I even noticed his use of the pronoun *our* and not *my*, and that maybe this *was* our season.

I smiled at the reference to one of Mom's and Aunt Pam's favorite bible verses. When things didn't go our way as kids, they would say it wasn't our season. Eventually, they went so far as to get matching tattoos of the words along the outside of their ribs. They picked their favorite parts in the scripture, not using it all, of course, but it was from Ecclesiastes 3:1-8. I had it memorized, as it made me feel closer to my mom.

"'For everything, there is a season,'" I began to murmur the verse, "'and a time for every matter under the Heaven: a time to be born and a time to die; a time to plant and a time to pluck up what is planted; a time to kill and a time to heal; a time to break down and time to build up; a time to weep and a time to laugh; a time to mourn and time to dance; a time to cast away stones and a time to gather stones together...'"

Corbin joined in the last part of the verse with me, "'...a time to embrace and time to refrain from embracing...'"

We looked at each other and smiled.

"Is that the only part you knew?" I teased.

He shook his head and lifted his shirt. My breath caught. Along one of his ribs was the part my mother loved the most: *a time to weep and a time to laugh.* In tiny lettering, he'd put her name and the years she had been alive. I knew my mom had meant to him what his meant to me. I was just surprised he chose to honor her that way.

He turned so I could see his opposite rib and my breath caught again.

A time to kill and a time to heal.

I had a feeling those words had a deeper meaning for him. He was part of an elite group that worked covert missions. One didn't survive on a team like that without getting blood on their hands.

I felt tears warm my eyes. "I always wanted to get this one." I traced the same tattoo my mom had against his ribs with my fingertips. I heard him grunt and felt his skin ripple beneath my touch. I shook off my melancholy and smiled up at him. "Maybe if we find a tattoo artist in the apocalypse, I'll get this one, and on the opposite side, 'A time to mourn and a time to dance.'"

He grinned at me. "Funny you should say that... Kingston so happens to be an undercover artist, and I'm pretty sure he can find the equipment to hook you up."

My eyes widened. The blond, trouble-maker didn't strike me as an artist. "That would be awesome."

"I'll tell him that." He chuckled. "With his resourcefulness, it shouldn't take him to long to find everything he'd need.

I was excited at the thought of getting my first tattoo with him nearby, especially since he'd honored my mother in one of the most permanent of ways.

Stopping in front of the family restroom, he withdrew a key from his pocket. He opened the door and stepped back, placing a hand on the small of my back and gently guiding me into the room. The lights were turned off, but vanilla scented candles lit the whole room. In the middle of the space, one of those portable hot tubs was bubbling away. I gaped at the transformation.

"We know how hard it's been on you the last few days, so the guys and I thought we'd do something nice for you." He leaned over and picked up a shower hose that was attached to the sink head. "I installed the showerhead, while Axel, Kingston, and Wyatt filled up the tub. Easton got you shampoo, body wash, and all that. Towels and clean pajamas are over there." He pointed to the back of the door and a little shower caddy. "And I," he held up a two-piece bikini, "got you a swimsuit just in case you wanted company in the hot tub after you take a shower."

I was stunned by their sweet gesture. Axel, Corbin, Wyatt, Easton, and Kingston had honestly put the thought into spoiling me. No one had ever gone to such lengths to do something so thoughtful for me. To have them collaborate and do all this made me think they really were serious in pursuing a relationship with me.

King and Easton had pretty much already expressed interest in me as the early afternoon transitioned into the evening and then into the night. We were at the get-to-know-you stage, but they both had admirable and desirable traits I could see myself being drawn to.

They were a year younger than Axel, at twenty-nine. Easton was brilliant– like, on a genius level. He had graduated from medical school and was a resident before he joined up. The only reason he joined the military was because Kingston was joining.

He seemed a bit on the introverted side and gave me the impression he was always soaking in everything around him. He didn't speak much, but he wasn't severe and stoic like Axel. He leaned more towards "laid back."

Kingston, on the other hand, was unconstrained and slightly unbridled. I had no doubt he was brilliant, just in a different way, and he was definitely prone to mischief.

Kingston, Wyatt, and Corbin proved to be a dangerous trio of mischief already. Earlier tonight, after everyone had eaten and washed up, the trio had decided it would be funny to put together a gift basket for Amy and had left it on her air mattress, the one she'd blown up for her and Josh.

In the gift basket were several items they'd pilfered from Spencer's. Glow-in-the-dark condoms, flavored condoms, a sexy nurse outfit, lubes, edible underwear, fuzzy handcuffs, vibrators, and other sex toys. She had turned bright red, especially after Steph and Aunt Pam started suggesting other sexual aids, offering to get her some more.

That kind of backfired on Corbin, though, because Felix made sure to ask if Aunt Pam had used any of those aids when Corbin had been conceived. The two men had nearly ended up getting into a fight over that, with Corbin grossed out at the thought of his mom and dad getting it on.

"You don't have to say yes," Corbin said now. "I know how tired you are, I just wanted to sit and talk with you for a while." He seemed so hesitant, and I had *never* seen Corbin unsure of himself. If anything, he usually had an overabundance of confidence.

I smiled at him. "Sorry, I was just thinking that this is possibly the sweetest thing anyone has ever done for me. You guys really know how to spoil a girl. Let me wash up. And I'd love your company."

He smiled beatifically. "Are swim trunks optional?" He waggled his eyebrows suggestively.

I crossed my arms over my chest and raised a brow at him.

He laughed. "Hey, I can be sweet. I never said I was a saint." He gave me a bold wink. "Just knock on the door when you're ready for me to join you."

〔

When Corbin returned, not only was his big beautiful body on display in his low-slung swim trunks, but he'd also brought a bottle of Moscato and a bluetooth speaker to hook his phone up to. He turned on a playlist with Shawn Mendes, Ed Sheeran, and other "easy" listening music as we relaxed together.

Being with him, I felt like I had stumbled into the best of both worlds. We could reminisce about the past, and we had already seen each other through the awkward years. There was also the comfortable familiarity with each other, making the conversation flow with ease.

Then I got to witness the passionate, flirtatious side of him.

I was laughing at a recounting of one of his basic training stories when I noticed he hadn't joined me in laughter. I looked over at him, and there was an indecipherable expression on his face. One minute he was sitting next to me, and the next, his fingers were threading through my hair. He tilted my head back, and his piercing gray-green eyes were lit with an inner fire.

"Tell me to stop now, Ave," he muttered as his breath caressed my lips.

My eyes widened momentarily at the raw desire in his eyes. I'd already had a taste of him, and I couldn't deny that I was already hooked.

I shortened the distance between our lips and kissed him. He let out a soft groan as I nipped him before tangling my tongue with his. His massive body pushed me against the side of the hot tub, and I gasped as I felt his arousal pressing against my core.

His large hands began to caress my responsive skin. He stroked my waist and stomach before palming my breasts. His thumb rubbed against the erect peaks of my nipples, and I moaned as heat unfurled deep within.

He grabbed my hips and pulled me closer before he began nibbling on my neck. I gasped and threw my head back so he could have better access. He seemed to innately know what spots were most sensitive and responsive as he licked, sucked, and scraped his teeth against my erogenous areas.

"You taste so delicious," he groaned.

"So do you," I responded before moving restlessly against him.

My hands explored the hard planes of his body. My fingernails scraped against his back and scalp. The sounds he made in the back of his throat encouraged me to continue exploring him and enlightened me further. He wasn't shy, letting me know what turned him on. With each kiss, stroke, and caress, we fed our cravings which spurned us further on. It was like a drug, but luckily there was no danger of overdosing, because I didn't think I'd ever get enough of Corbin.

I was so close to capitulating to my desires and was so turned on. Plus, I was curious to see if being with Corbin would be as good as kissing him. I was fully aware that he knew the art of seduction rather well.

If someone hadn't knocked on the door of our oasis, we would've been seconds away from sealing the deal.

"Someone's in here," I called out, unable to conceal the frustration from my voice.

Corbin growled then laughed before nuzzling my neck. "We should probably get some rest."

We both hopped out. He handed me a towel before grabbing his own. I watched in fascination as he dried off his hair before moving onto his body. *How could the simple act of drying off be so sexy?*

He smirked at me before he handed me my pajamas next. "I'll turn around. This time." He winked.

I laughed and rolled my eyes before drying myself off. I slipped out of my bikini and into the PJs Easton had picked out for me; blush-pink silk pajama bottoms and a matching camisole top trimmed in black lace. I had to admit I liked Easton's taste. The outfit was both cute and sexy.

"You can turn around," I informed him before I picked up a brush off the vanity.

He wasn't done getting dressed. I looked in the mirror, totally giving in and peeking. He had a nice, high, taut ass, with those cute little dimples at the tops of the cheeks. I was giggling to myself when he turned.

His hot gaze fell on me, and the desire in his eyes made the wetness between my legs return, the aching heat settling in my stomach once more.

"Stop it!" I laughed, my voice husky from desire.

"I can't help it," he growled, hurriedly redressing in his uniform of a black t-shirt and khaki cargo pants. "You're just so damn sexy." Suddenly he was on me, swooping me up and pushing my back against the wall. I wrapped my legs around his waist.

I was a tall girl, and positions like this could be awkward. I always felt too tall and heavy for any guy to attempt this position, but twice in one day, he'd had me like this. I liked it. A lot. He did it so effortlessly, and it felt...primal.

His mouth captured mine, and I nipped at his bottom lip as I ran my fingernails against his scalp. He growled once more, and I slipped my tongue into his mouth. He was still aroused, and I could feel his hardened length brushing my nether lips. He wasn't as large as Axel, but it was still a large, impressive size.

I rubbed against him, gasping as the knock sounded

once more. I heard Bane let out a single bark.

"Stand by!" Corbin growled out to the knocker. "There are other bathrooms, you know!"

The only answer was another knock.

He sighed. "Later?" he asked me hopefully before brushing my lips once more and stooping to affix his weapons to his body.

I smiled, feeling on cloud nine and slightly giddy. I picked up my own sais. Axel had made me something to carry them with ease. It was reminiscent of shoulder holsters but longer and reinforced in consideration of my blades. It was just another thoughtful gesture done for me today.

"Most definitely." I bit my bottom lip. The cards were now on the table—no doubting it now.

He grinned, sliding on his black combat boots, and grabbed our bags before he took my hand. He opened the door, and I stopped short, feeling some of my euphoria fading. Emery was standing against the wall in a white negligee. The shadows of her nipples and bare mound were on full display. She had her arms across her stomach and was tapping her foot in irritation.

I refrained from rolling my eyes. My silk PJs might not have been the most practical nightwear in the Infected Apocalypse, and to some, might be considered sexy-ish, but I wasn't blatantly flaunting my sex.

"What were you guys doing in there?" she asked waspishly.

Corbin snorted. "I don't think that's any of your business, Emery."

I had noticed at dinner that Corbin was definitively standoffish with Trevor, but he was outright cold to Emery. Emery had continued to try to draw him into the conversation, and he either ignored her or answered tersely. It bothered me to see how much it hurt Aunt Pam to see her sons at odds with each other, and her "daughters," for that matter. But I knew she wouldn't push any of us to behave a certain way.

There was just so much that had occurred over the past year to make it all just go away. I was going to try, but it was going to take a great deal of effort.

Corbin squeezed my hand and began to lead me towards the heart of the mall.

"Why didn't we have showers and a hot tub?" she called out peevishly.

Corbin froze and retreated a few steps. Between clenched teeth, he hissed at her. "Everyone is sleeping, stop screaming like a harpy. No one stopped you from doing it yourself. We're not here to pamper you, princess, and the faster you realize that, the easier it'll be for all of us."

Her eyes filled with tears, and I nearly snorted. They were her theatric tears.

"I don't know why you are so mean to me," she said "You are one of my best friends. Trevor and I made a mistake, but we're together now."

"You want the truth Emery?" He gave me an apologetic smile before addressing her. "I used to regard you as one of my friends, Em. I knew you wanted me, but I still cared about you. I overlooked a lot of your flaws, but the way you betrayed your own family was unforgivable. I guess I should be thankful. You did us a favor. However, it doesn't forgive your sins. You purposely took advantage of Trev in his inebriated state. You betrayed your own damn sister. You have always been selfish and manipulative, but that topped it all."

"I didn't take advantage of him," she insisted. "I've never been as selfish or manipulative as Avery." Big crocodile tears fell down her cheeks. "She came to you hoping you would save her. She probably didn't tell you she forced Trevor into my arms. She has you fooled. It was an honest mistake!"

"It's no longer a mistake if you repeat the action. And don't get it twisted. Your sister was never the selfish one. You forget I knew some of your sorority sisters," he warned her.

"They lied!" she looked panicked for a moment.

"About what, Emery?" I asked with a narrowed gaze. That was telling. He hadn't even said *what* he'd heard or learned from her sorority sisters. Something told me Corbin knew a lot more details about that night than I did, and I had long since suspected there was more to the story.

"Nothing!" she insisted. "Plus, it doesn't look like it matters anymore! You guys are obviously together. It looks like one brother is good enough as the other, right?" she inquired snidely to me.

I felt Corbin stiffen beside me.

I sighed heavily. "Corbin and I... just happened," I said, squeezing his hand reassuringly. "It was never intentional on my part, but I'm not sorry about it. For the first time in nearly a year, I am genuinely happy again. The fact that you're trying to turn it into something ugly shows me your real character. You really, really hurt me. We shared the same womb. We're sisters! And not once did you reach out and tell me you were sorry. Trevor called and texted me constantly, and you didn't even text me once."

I saw her eyes narrow. I guess she didn't know that, but what did she expect? She would come in, sleep with him, and he would forget all about me? All about Bella? I had just lost his baby. A baby I knew he'd wanted. I had seen the crushed look and devastation in his eyes when I had left his room that morning for the final time.

"I hope you're happy with what you did to us," I added passionately. "Your actions didn't just affect us, you drove a wedge between our families. And sadly, you'll never own up to it."

"It was *you* who made people pick sides," she hissed at me.

I shook my head, smiling sadly at her. "I'm done. This conversation isn't going anywhere." I turned on my heel and began moving towards the hall.

"I'm sorry Trevor chose me! I'm sorry you can't be happy for us!" she screamed at my retreating back. "I'm sorry you're so desperate to become a Cavalier you're whoring yourself out to Corbin! Get over yourself, Avery!"

I snorted but refused to turn back around. I knew she wasn't done trying to make a point. Corbin stopped me before we reached the top of the escalators and pulled me in close. He kissed me softly, conveying to me another message.

"I won't pretend I'm sorry they screwed up," he muttered honestly against my cheek. "I wish they hadn't hurt you, but I'm glad I get to try to be the man you finally deserve. I'm happy that my military brothers, best friends, seem happier when you're around, too."

I reached up and gripped his face, his stubble surprisingly soft against my hands. "I won't pretend painful memories won't resurrect from time to time, or that I'm completely over it, but I know I'm over Trevor. I'm excited to explore my feelings with you, and with them. All of you have made me happy, each in different ways, since you came back into my life."

He smiled and kissed me gently once more. "We need to be up in, like, five hours. Let's get to bed. Can I share your bed with you?" he inquired.

Earlier, when we'd went in search of beds, Wyatt and Corbin immediately secured a mattress for me and put all the bedding on it after they got two mattresses for Steph, Aunt Pam, and the kids to share.

I smiled and nodded. "I'd like that."

He smiled in return, kissing me again. "I like this kissing thing with you," he teased.

I laughed and shook my head at him. "Ditto."

I was almost to the escalators when I realized Bane was no longer behind me. I stopped and looked back. He was sitting in front of one of the stores. It took me a moment to recognize it was the one that Felix and I had first secured. Bane's head cocked from one side to another before he let out a long low whine.

"Come on, Bane," I called softly.

He looked at me, ran a few steps towards me, and then back to the gate.

"Bane, come," Corbin said in a more commanding voice.

The dog hopped back on his hind legs and let out a loud whining bark before he landed back on all fours. He turned once more and began to paw furiously at the gate.

I sighed and made my way over to him. "There's nothing in there, bud," I crooned. "Do you need to go potty? Let's go get your leash, and we can go potty."

We had found a grassy area between two parts of the building that we quickly blocked off for the dogs to use at any time. Four of the seven dogs were potty trained. Josh was already frustrated by his dog's lack of training. Luckily, Amy seemed to have more knowledge about puppies, because she had no qualms about taking the dog out often and giving him a treat when warranted.

Bane seemed semi-trained, but he'd already had an accident. In retrospect, it really wasn't his fault, since I had missed his pacing before he had gone. Axel and I then agreed to alternate taking him out. Well, Axel *informed* me we were splitting our duty. Who was I to argue? Especially since he was helping me out.

"Was that room cleared?" Axel asked, appearing as if my thoughts had conjured him. He looked tired, and I knew he had only slept briefly. Like the night before, he had scheduled himself for the most challenging shift—the shift between the two.

Today, with the amount of JOpS and BJ to help, they had split it into two shifts, with a group of guys straddling both shifts. Axel was one of the straddlers.

"Felix and I cleared it, and then Felix did the last sweep," I said as I reached down to unhook the lock we had in place. It wasn't latched, but it was on there.

The store sold sports memorabilia and jerseys. No one seemed keen on getting any of that stuff, so the store had never been reopened.

"Stand by, Avery," Axel warned. "On the count of three, lift the gates, okay?"

I nodded as I heard both men pull the charges on their weapons.

"One...two...three," Axel murmured.

As soon as the gate was lifted, Bane went bounding inside the store. He approached a wall of clothes and jumped towards it, whining and huffing a low bark.

I pushed him aside and slid back the bottom rack of clothing and saw nothing. Then I heard it—a soft mewl. I pushed aside the top shelf of clothing and saw a baby carrier tucked in the back corner. I pulled it down, and nestled inside, was a newborn baby. She was dressed in a pink frilly outfit, and she had had a shock of thick black hair.

I cried out, noticing the sunken look around her eyes. She looked like she wanted to cry, but no tears fell, her mouth moving with no sound. She appeared to be raising her little fist, but it only twitched.

"I need an IV stat and saline solution!" I cried out as I set the carrier down gently, unclipping her from the contraption. I gently slipped my hands under her limp body, making sure I supported her head.

Since Bella, I hadn't wanted to touch a baby. That's why I hadn't even looked much in Jenny's direction. It had been a painful reminder of who I had lost. There was a long time after my loss that I couldn't even watch a diaper commercial without tearing up. I would have to change the channel if pregnancy or babies were even mentioned. People never realized the possible triggers of everyday things until a crisis occurred.

All my misgivings were thrown out the window as I stared down at the precious baby. She couldn't weigh more than nine pounds, and her body was so fragile. I began to cry in earnest as I nuzzled her cheek. "Hang in there, pumpkin," I murmured desperately. "Don't give up on me yet. You've lasted this long, don't you dare give up on me."

"I'll get the supplies, you find Easton," Axel urged Corbin.

I vaguely heard both men run off as Bane leaned in, whining, trying to nudge the baby and lick my tears. "Sit, Bane," I commanded him as I moved over to the counter in the store. I cradled the baby in one arm as I pulled down a soft plush blanket with the University of Michigan logo emblazoned across it. With shaking hands, I spread the blanket out on the counter as best as I could with one hand.

"Please, pumpkin," I continually begged her. "Please hang in there."

Once the blanket was spread, I placed her on it. Her eyes were closed, her breathing labored, her body listless. I removed her clothing, my actions taking a lot longer than usual because I couldn't stop trembling.

I stripped her down to her diaper and slowly began to examine her. Her diaper had a faint yellow stain on it, but it was bone dry. She was severely dehydrated, and it was a miracle a baby that young had survived at least twenty four hours of not eating. She should have already been dead.

"Oh baby, please keep fighting," I murmured to her, using my arm to wipe my eyes and nose. "You didn't make it this long just to die on me now. Please, sweetie!"

A depression I hadn't felt in months engulfed me. Watching her tiny little body fight for life brought back too many painful memories. I may have never physically met my daughter, but my dark thoughts had taken me places after I'd lost her. I wondered what her last moments were like. The what ifs and the unknowns had been nearly insurmountable.

Losing Bella before I had even met her was one of the hardest things I had ever lived through. I had been so excited about her arrival. The day I lost her, I had the occasional back pains and mild stomach cramps, but the doctor told me that it was normal. I went to bed early that night and woke up to some of the most excruciating pain I had ever felt.

Covered in blood, and I had called out to Sylvia. An hour later, I found out I'd had a placental abruption, and there was no saving my little girl.

I began to pray in earnest that *this* little girl would make it.

Chapter 14

I was leaning into the baby, praying and begging for her to hang in there, when Easton came running into the room. He had a sand-colored duffle bag with him, with a red and white cross on it. Axel and Corbin were steps behind him, carrying two large boxes.

Easton took one look at the baby, and I saw sadness enter his eyes, the same hopelessness I was feeling, but he still withdrew items from his bag. He took out some gloves and a stethoscope.

"I have a lot of stuff I scavenged from the pharmacy," Axel said gravely. "The vet tech at the shelter gave me a lot of stuff, too, but I don't know what you need, Doc."

As Easton did his examination, I began pulling things from the box. I found the gravity bag and saline solution carefully packaged in their boxes and pulled them out, setting them aside. I continued grabbing all the other stuff we needed. I was more than pleased to see what we had to work with, so many useful things in there. I was looking through the needles when Easton came to peer over my shoulder.

"Let's try that one," he said, pointing to the smallest one. "She's severely dehydrated, Ave," he warned me softly.

"I know, but she didn't survive this long without being a fighter." I didn't even try to stave off my tears.

He nodded and began to set up the bag, solution, and drip tubing. He found an empty clothing rack to hook the packet to. I pulled out the gauze, medical tape, alcohol pads, hot pack, and tourniquet. I took a deep calming breath. The doctors and nurses that I had done my rotations with commended me on how well I placed a needle. They joked and said I must have been a phlebotomist in my previous life.

The only problem I was having now was I was overly emotional, and she was in such critical condition. I'd also never had a patient this tiny.

When I felt like I had a handle on my emotions, I finally walked back over to her. "Hey, baby girl," I murmured to her. "We're going to try to help you, but you have to keep fighting."

I lifted her little hand and put a heating pad on it. It felt like hours before I could find the vein.

"Are you sure you want to do this?" Easton asked softly.

I knew he was worried about my emotional state, but I felt like I had to do it. I nodded and cleared my mind. I tried not to think about my tiny patient or how her life hung in the balance.

I wiped the area with an alcohol pad and carefully removed the cap on the catheter with one hand, tightly pulling the skin around the IV site with my other. I made sure to keep the catheter parallel to the baby's skin and inserted the needle. A hint of blood in the catheter's applicator indicated that I hit the vein directly. I then continued to advance the catheter.

Easton handed me the tape to secure the needle in place.

"Good job," Easton praised me. "You've done this before."

I gave a shaky laugh and nodded. "Thank you, and yes, but the youngest patient I had was maybe eight or nine. Not... this age."

"I'm impressed," he commended me once more.

If I wasn't so worried, I might have preened under his praise. He handed me the rest of the stuff to complete her

IV. I opened the IV line and ensured the fluid was dripping into the chamber. I checked for leaking and swelling at the IV site, relaxing marginally when I realized it was a successful insertion. I then secured the IV line with additional tape.

Easton adjusted the drip rate and then smiled at me. I smiled in return. I knew we weren't out of the woods yet, but we did as much as we could for her right now.

"I found something," Kingston stated, running into the room.

He had a kitchen cart and a clear plastic bin with a bassinet pad lining the bottom of it. It looked similar to what they used in the NICU, and I was surprised by his ingenuity.

"I made sure to wipe it down with antibacterial wipes," Kingston reassured us.

"We'll move her to that," Easton said soothingly. "Depending on the severity, it may take several hours before I even consider her stable."

I nodded in understanding, but as he reached for her, I quickly bypassed him. "I'll get her," I told him.

Kingston rolled over the cart, and I carefully lifted her into the container.

"It's so tiny," Kingston breathed in wonder. "I didn't know they came that small."

I couldn't help but smile at his awe. "They come smaller than this sometimes," I informed him.

"How old do you think…" He looked around. Without her pink dress on, it was hard to tell whether she was a boy or girl, so I understood his dilemma.

"She is–" I stopped and closed my eyes, memories flooded me, my heart dropped. "–thirteen days old or so." I tried to stop the emotions from overwhelming me. "Her mom and dad must have been shopping nearby," I said quietly as I double checked to make sure all her tape was affixed in place, then grabbed a soft shirt from a rack and covered her, keeping her warming. "They probably knew they couldn't protect her out in the open, maybe hoped they could come back for her. They shoved her into a place they thought would be safe from the infected. They didn't make it far, though. Rhett Michaels and Donna Michaels."

I had noticed their relationship the first time I came across their names. I then remarked about it to Sylvia as we were hanging up their ID's. I even wondered aloud if they had gotten a sitter to watch their newborn baby because, thankfully, no babies were found. It was terrible enough—No. I couldn't think like that.

I swallowed and continued. "They were right outside these doors when they were infected and later... dispatched."

"The Coach pink bag with the gold Cs on it," Kingston finished grimly. "I'll go get it," he offered.

"Thanks." I tried to smile as Easton stepped up, verifying the drip once more. "She was a breastfed baby," I said into the silence. "She didn't have any formula in her bag. Just a handpump."

"We'll find a formula that agrees with her," Easton promised. I was thankful he was planning for her future like I was.

"Or... if you're not opposed to a wetnurse," Steph spoke from the doorway, "I can nurse her once she's ready. My milk is already coming in, and I tandem-nursed the boys. If not, I can pump the milk for her so you can feed her."

I turned to see my stepmother walk, or should I say, waddle, into the room. She stopped by the makeshift bassinet. With one finger, she gently traced the baby's soft cheek as tears filled her eyes.

Stephanie looked barely older than me, which was no surprise, because she was only ten years my senior. She was beautiful in a classical way, with light brown hair and pretty dark blue eyes.

Stephanie got pregnant with Miller during her senior year of high school. She got married shortly after graduating but lost her husband overseas when the boys were seven and five. My dad had been his commanding officer. She and Dad had struck up a friendship. He would help her on occasion and helped her navigate her husband's death.

A couple of years later, they ran into each other again. Stephanie had been working on base as a physical therapist, and they started hanging out. Next thing I knew, my dad was telling us he was getting remarried. It had been hard to accept.

"Nursing can induce labor," Easton said cautiously.

"I'm thirty-six weeks pregnant," Stephanie said resolutely. "If Madeline wants to come now, so be it. The antibodies in my milk may be more beneficial for this sweet thing right now. Especially if she was already nursing."

Easton gave me an inquiring look. I knew he was giving me the chance to make that decision. I knew the ongoing debate about breastfed vs formula-fed, but at the end of the day, I knew breastfed was best, no matter how I felt about it personally.

I bit my lip and swallowed, my feelings and memories too close to the surface. "If you're okay with giving it a try, I'm okay with that, Stephanie. I know some women aren't compatible with pumps."

Stephanie smiled and nodded. "I can care for her, too... if you want," she said hesitantly.

I shook my head immediately. "No. No, thank you. I really appreciate the offer, but I want to care for her."

"Avery," Axel said, surprising me. I had forgotten Axel and Corbin were here. "If you–" he began. He had watched me break down too many times already. He must have seen the pain I felt when I first lifted the baby from the carrier.

"No, Ax." I shook my head, cutting him off. Then I looked at Steph and Corbin.

They had never known about Bella, and that was another guilt I had carried around for months. I had longed to talk to Aunt Pam about my miscarriage. However, I also knew Stephanie had had a miscarriage before she had gotten pregnant with Madeline. Both women had experienced miscarriages, and in Aunt Pam's case, several of them. There were times I wished I had talked to them through my dark periods.

I knew part of me thought this was a second chance, of sorts. That God, fate, destiny, had brought me this sweet baby girl, but I knew she would never replace my baby girl or make things magically better. There had to be a reason Bane, the dog that had picked *me*, had found her, and that out of all the names I had come across today, her parents' names had stuck with me.

"I was—" I cleared my voice. "Trevor and I were expecting. At first, I didn't want to tell anyone because of the whole first-trimester taboo. Then we decided to announce it to everyone at the annual family trip to Sanctuary Lakes." I swallowed my tears down. I felt warm arms encircle me and knew it was Axel by his spicy scent with mint undertones. I leaned back into him, glad for his support. "At our sixteen-week check-up, I found out she was a girl. We decided to name her Bella Mae, after Mom and Aunt Pam. Six days later... I lost her." I was fighting my emotions as I looked down at Axel's arm around mine.

I heard a gasp at the door and looked up to see Aunt Pam; her eyes were filled with tears. "I was going to be a grandma?" she asked tremulously.

"Mom," Corbin gently said as he approached her.

She pushed his arms away and came towards me. "But

why, Avery?"

I knew what she was asking. I didn't know how to tell her why we hadn't told her. At the time, it had seemed like the best thing to do. We wanted to surprise the family as a whole. We didn't think there was a massive rush, because we had been out of the "danger" zone, and we wanted to let Nana, Pop-pop, Dad, Uncle Scott, and Aunt Pam know in person.

"You know I had three miscarriages," Aunt Pam whispered as she patted my cheeks. "I know how hard it is. How hard it still is! We could have talked about it. I could have been there for you."

"When did you lose the baby?" Corbin inquired almost icily.

I looked over and noticed his green-gray eyes were very, *very* icy gray. I knew his anger wasn't directed towards me, though. He must've done the math. He knew now that it was around the same time.

"It doesn't matter, Cor." I shook my head decisively. "It's all water under the bridge. I've decided to move on."

"Was it before or after he cheated on you?" he insisted.

"Corbin, please," I whispered as I heard Aunt Pam's gasps.

"Cavalier," Axel said in warning.

Corbin took a deep breath and shook his head before storming out. Kingston came into the room, carrying the diaper bag. He looked in confusion at Corbin's retreating back, then handed me the bag.

"Thanks," I croaked out.

I looked at the baby, the diaper bag, and then Corbin's retreating form. I was so torn. I wanted to run after him, but I didn't want to leave the baby either.

"Go watch him," Axel murmured to Kingston. "Make sure he doesn't go near his brother until he's cooled off."

Kingston looked confused but ran off without question.

With shaking fingers, I placed the bag on the counter and opened it.

"I won't like the answer, will I?" Aunt Pam finally whispered as she peered down at the baby with sadness. The nurse in her was checking the IV and the dripping tube.

"The answer won't change anything," I murmured in a pained voice.

"I don't even know what I can say to make things better. I-" Aunt Pam began.

"There's nothing to say, Aunt Pam. I love you, and I will *always* love you. You are not a reflection of Trevor's behavior in this." I took a deep fortifying breath in. "Trevor is a grown man and responsible for his own actions. I know he wasn't in the right frame of mind when he was initially with Emery.

"Things will get better," I promised. "Maybe not today, maybe not tomorrow, but I have resolved to no longer to carry the weight of unforgiveness around. I will never forget what they did to me. I'll work on forgiving Trevor, and maybe, one day, even Emery, but right now, she hasn't asked it of me. She still believes she didn't do anything wrong."

Aunt Pam sighed and patted my arm. "You're mom always said your heart was bigger than hers," she said almost bitterly before looping her arms through Steph's. "We should go to the restroom and then back to bed. You need your rest."

Stephanie patted me on the shoulder. We weren't close, by any means, but I had an affection for her, and I loved her boys. I knew she was trying to build a relationship with me. Maybe it was time I forgave her for trying to take my mom's place, even if she never wanted the position. She never even tried. She never deserved the feelings I held towards her. She made my dad happy, and that's all that should matter to me.

"Thanks, Steph, for everything." I smiled at her.

She nodded and smiled back at me.

I sighed again and reached into the bag, looking for anything to identify the sweet girl fighting for her life.

I finally came across the three hospital bracelets. I placed the larger ones on the counter before examining the smallest one. I blinked several times. My knees began to shake. My vision started to close in. The name Isa May Michaels swam before my eyes before I lost all consciousness.

〇

His slim, muscular arms were wrapped around my middle from behind as we laid in bed. I felt his hands trace my bare belly with a gentle touch. "What about Isa Mae Cavalier?" he asked as he kissed the back of my neck.

He knew how sensitive that spot was. I groaned and arched my back into him. I felt his erection press against my rear.

"Really?" I groaned out in laughter. "Again?"

He flipped me onto my back. His perfectly styled ash-blond hair was now mussed from the sex we'd had earlier. A lock of it was falling in his eyes. I liked him most like this. He looked more like the boy I once knew; less like the man that believed he needed to make a lot of money, drive the right car, and wear the right clothes to be successful and more like the teenager I had fallen in love with at sixteen.

Back then, our dreams had been so different. I was going to be a nurse– which hadn't changed– and he was going to be a teacher. We wanted to move to the city and make a difference there. He always loved working with kids, ever since we began volunteering at the Boys and Girls Club.

After meeting some of those underprivileged kids, we wanted to make a difference in the world. Our dads and my mom knew what it was like not to be loved, to be abandoned. Most of those kids lived in broken homes. They needed people like us to remind them that they mattered.

The summer before our senior year, we had been invited to one of Emery's friend's family home. Her dad was an architect. They were clearly well off. Trevor was immediately enamored with that lifestyle, and just like that, he'd decided he wasn't going to be a teacher anymore.

Then when we started to apply for colleges and the scholarships began to roll in, he chose to go to another school. I was okay with that, but I knew it was going to take work on our part.

"My baby is carrying my baby." He smiled wickedly at me. "How can I not want you all the time?"

With those words, he drove into me. I closed my eyes and groaned. I loved having sex. I loved the feeling of him inside me. I just found it hard to find my release sometimes, and when Trevor was in this mood, I knew he was seeking his own. He pushed into me, setting a slow but deep rhythm.

"I can't believe you're gonna be my baby momma. Do you want to get married before the baby or after?" he asked.

I laughed, wrapping my legs around his waist. "Mmm, maybe before. We can just hit up the Justice of the Peace, and maybe when the kids are older, we can have a real wedding, and they can be our ring bearers and flower girls."

He paused in his thrusting movements, his eyebrows knit, "You want more than just Bella Mae?"

I paused, frowning slightly. "Yeah. I want three, maybe four. You just want one?"

"Well," he said hesitantly, still moving his hips. "I figured we'd both have careers that kept us busy, but I guess we can hire a nanny."

He leaned forward, kissing me, shutting down our conversation. I tried not to think about the fact he seemed so blase about nannies raising our children. With having dads who were often deployed, we were both raised in almost single-parent households, yet our moms still handled it. If Mom hadn't died,

Dad would have never hired a nanny.

I didn't see why we couldn't both work and take care of our children without hiring live-in help. Parents did it across America all the time.

His movements quickened, and I forgot my thoughts as I clutched him. "I love you," he cried out before spilling into me. He collapsed on top of me, kissing my shoulder. "I really am a lucky man to have such a beautiful woman carrying my child. You're my best friend, Avery, the best thing that ever happened to me."

I smiled at him, my cross and upset feelings forgotten. "Bella Mae," I finally agreed.

He smiled. "Mom's gonna love it." He got up, padding to the bathroom, his lean runner's butt flexing with each step.

It felt like I was just dozing off when the bed dipped beside me. He had been in the bathroom for a long time. I smiled and looked up sleepily, my tiredness of the first trimester still kicking my butt.

I heard a baby crying in the distance.

"Trev, can you get the baby?" I inquired sleepily.

After several beats, I heard the baby crying again. "Trev?" I mumbled disgruntedly.

I then heard Trevor's discombobulated voice, like it was coming from afar. "Run, Avery, run."

"What, why?" I asked in confusion as I blinked the tiredness out of my eyes.

"Run, Avery, run," he repeated.

I looked up at him and gasped. I tried to scramble away from him, but my legs got tangled up in the sheets.

Trevor advanced towards me, tears of blood pouring down his face, bloody foam coming from his lips.

The baby began to scream in earnest now.

"Run, Avery, run!" Trevor now screamed at me before he

lunged.

"No, please, no!" *I screamed in terror as I finally freed myself from the sheets.*

I tumbled from the bed and began to run as I threw open his bedroom door. Wait. Where was I? I didn't recognize his frat house. The baby wailed once more.

I heard the door slam behind me and turned to look over my should. Trevor was screaming my name.

"Please, please!" *I begged him as I began running towards the stairs.*

I felt something or someone tugging on my pant legs. When did I get dressed?

I felt my barefoot catch on something, and next thing I knew, my feet were taken out from under me. Something gritty and rough dug into my hands as the baby continued to cry. Another sharp pain in my knees had me crying out in pain. Arms encircled me from behind. Strong arms.

"You're okay, relax, you're okay," *the voice murmured in my ears.*

"No, please, no," I cried out.

"Avery, it's me, Wyatt, you're safe," he murmured.

I heard an excited yip, followed by a low bark.

"Wyatt?" I murmured in confusion. *When did Wyatt get here?*

"What happened?" I heard Easton's voice next.

Wait why was he here?

I shook my head, the remnants of my dream disappearing. I groaned as I slowly opened my eyes. "How far did I get?" I sighed in embarrassment. My hands stung, and my knees throbbed. I looked down and noticed I had bits of asphalt in my hands.

Bane was whining and nudging me.

I frowned. How had I even managed to get outside? It was a question that never had an answer, every single time.

☐

I looked around and noticed I was in a room I didn't recognize. I was on Wyatt's lap, and Easton was sitting in a chair in front of me. A sizeable first aid kit was sitting next to him on a desk. The door banged open, and Axel and Corbin came into the room.

My humiliation increased as I felt their eyes on me. Easton rolled his chair closer and began to dab my hands gently. I hissed, feeling the sting of the medication.

"She shouldn't have gotten that far," Axel clipped out concisely.

"How far?" I asked before looking around the room and seeing little Isa in the corner. "Oh! How is she? How long was I...sleeping?"

I remembered now, blacking out after seeing Isa's name. It was such a coincidence for her to have a name similar to my daughter. It was one of the names we had thought about for her.

"She's coming around, Avery." Easton's face softened with a broad smile. "Our little girl really is a fighter. By the afternoon, I hope we can feed her some real sustenance."

I felt an overwhelming sense of relief fill me.

"You were only out for about three hours," Wyatt said slowly, making no move to remove me from his lap. He then cleared his throat. "Is anyone going to tell me what happened?"

"I...sleep run," I told him in a quiet voice. "It's triggered by stress."

"How long have you done this?" Easton said with a frown as he began to clean my other hand.

"Since I was about twelve," I said, shifting uncomfortably. I felt Wyatt place one hand on my hip, while the other one began gently rubbing my back.

I didn't want to tell them why the running began. It was too early in the day, and I was still emotionally raw from the earlier revelations.

"It comes and goes," I confessed instead. "I ran on and off for about a year, and then it stopped. There's no cure for it. No medicine has ever worked. Tae Kwon Do, running, and meditating works sometimes, but stress overrides all of it."

"But if you sleep next to someone, it helps, right?" Easton asked.

I nodded, still feeling embarrassed.

"Will you be okay if we...sleep next to you until you feel less...stressed?" Easton asked gently.

"I don't want to feel like a burden," I admitted quietly.

Corbin sighed loudly. "You won't be a burden. I'll gladly lay with you."

"Me too," Easton said with a touch of pink entering his cheeks.

"Me, three." Wyatt squeezed my hip.

"I'll come up with a schedule," Axel stated.

Axel and his schedules. If the situation weren't so severe, I would have teased him about it.

"For now," Axel added. "I think it's time we started getting everyone up so we can hit the road."

"I'll start breakfast," I mumbled.

"No, you'll rest here," Axel said with a no-nonsense tilt to his chin.

I sighed. I wasn't going to win that argument. No use engaging Axel in one.

Chapter 15

I peered down at Isa and softly stroked her cheek. "We were going to call my daughter Bella Mae after my mother, Isabella, and Trevor's mother, Pamela Mae," I explained to Easton as he emptied the first aid office in the mall. "We contemplated naming her Isa Mae for a moment. Finding out Isa's name... shocked me—what a coincidence for her to have the name of my baby. We chose that name because my mother was Isabella Harris."

From his expression, it was no surprise to him. "I knew who you were long before Corbin and Wyatt told me about you," he softly said. I noticed the tinge of pink in his cheeks was back. "My brother and I saw you and your sister on the Teen Choice Awards when you were twelve or so. King had a crush on Emery, and I..." He didn't finish, and I filled in the blanks. I smiled at his openness at the risk of his own embarrassment.

I could imagine a younger Kingston having a crush on Emery. In a lot of ways, they were the same. Both were extremely outgoing and gregarious. They liked being the center of attention and had an aura that drew people to them naturally. I wondered if he still had a thing for her.

I felt warmth enter my cheeks but then remembered the chaos of that day all too well. Marlon had known the producer of the show and had gotten us a hosting spot.

"That was when our careers were at an all-time high,"

I explained ruefully. "Disney and a few other talent agents wanted us to cross over to the acting side. Emery and Mom wanted it. Dad and I did not. Then something... happened, and we left that world for good." I wasn't ready to tell him about Marlon and his pedophile ways.

Easton gave me a gentle smile. He had this energy about him that felt so relaxing. I could imagine I could sit in his presence for hours without feeling any discomfort.

"I think you guys broke Kingston's heart," he said, "when he found how young you were. He used to have pictures of you two on the wall of his bottom bunk. I tried to remind him you guys were young, but he didn't care." He gave me a rueful shrug.

"So what your trying to tell me is that I should tease Kingston that he had a crush on Emery, who was seven years his junior?" I teased him.

He laughed. "I say save it for your arsenal. You may need it someday." He gave me a conspiratorial grin.

I laughed and nodded. "I'll keep that in mind. Hey, East?" I said tentatively.

"Yes, Ave?" he asked, pausing in his movements.

"I've heard kangaroo care for a young infant can sometimes make them healthier. Do you think if I carry her on my chest, skin to skin, it can help her? I know I'm not her mother, but maybe..." My voice trailed off.

He gave me another warm smile with a nod. "I don't think it would hurt to try. Kangaroo care isn't only done with mothers. It's done with fathers, too. I just want to make sure we're careful to watch her IV. Do you have a button-up shirt? It may be easier to transfer her to your chest." He suddenly cleared his throat. "I can, uh, get one of the women to help you, if you like, after instructing them on what to do."

My eyes widened. I hadn't thought of that. I finally

smiled and shook my head. He was such a gentleman. "Doc, if you don't mind seeing a pair of boobs, I don't mind showing them to you so we can make sure it's done correctly."

He took a step forward, surprising me with his closeness. He lowered his head so that our eyes met. *Damn, he had some beautiful eyes.* The caramel tone of his skin only made them even more startling.

"I don't think I'd be able to look at them in a professional capacity," he admitted huskily.

I gave him a crooked smile. "I'll go get a button-up shirt," I told him boldly. I didn't have one, but I knew where to find some. I'd make a quick trip to one of the stores right outside the office and grab a few.

I watched him bite his lower lip before I slowly turned away from him.

What was wrong with me? I'd had Axel between my thighs two nights ago. Then I had him in my mouth yesterday. Last night I had Corbin's tongue in my mouth, and now I was entertaining the thought of Easton gazing at my breasts.

Was I so loved starved that I was rushing this? Had I been in a famine for so long that, the first time I find five highly attractive men desiring me, I was willing to feast? Was I moving too fast? Should I have been taking my time in getting to know them?

I was so deep in thought I didn't notice Jade, Natalie, and Emery until I nearly ran into them. I backed up and hoped they'd move on. They hadn't seen me yet, and I was okay with that. I didn't need their negativity in my life right now.

"Their interest in her won't last long," I heard Natalie scoffing.

"I'm pretty sure it just a pity fuck," Emery added with a laugh. "Trevor always said she was unenthusiastic in bed. Why do you think he cheated on her so often?"

I felt a twinge in my chest. I really hoped Trevor didn't talk about our sex life to my sister. I wouldn't say I was unenthusiastic in the sack, but I knew my inability to have an orgasm had bothered him. He had thought I wasn't that into sex, and when he wanted to be daring, it made things even more difficult for me to come.

No one wanted to be thought of like a dead fish in the sack. I didn't believe Trevor would have discussed such intimate details about our sex life, but then, I never thought he would have cheated on me, either. I didn't know what the truth was, nor whether Emery was making up things to make herself look like the more... interesting twin.

"Is it true you slept with him while they were still together, Emery?" Jade laughed, no recrimination in her voice.

"No," Emery sounded shocked. "They were on a break. She'll lie and tell you differently, though. She's always felt insecure and jealous of me. She was such a tomboy, and no guys wanted her if they could have the better version. So, no. Trevor had texted me and wanted me to come over to party with him and his frat brothers. When I got there, he was flirting with me all night. He invited me back to his room and told me how he'd always wanted me but didn't think he had a chance, so he settled for her."

I knew some of her stories were all lies, but I wondered if Trevor had really called her over. They had hung out often, and his frat brothers had a thing for the sorority girls. Did he plan on seducing her that night? Was that why he wouldn't text me the whole day?

Both girls laughed. "The boys will get bored with her real quick then," Jade said smugly.

When had they become such good friends? Maybe it was when they all realized they had a common enemy. Not that I did anything to deserve it. I may have humiliated Natalie, but perhaps she shouldn't have been such a twat to that cadet.

"Corbin and Wyatt love to share, and if she can't satisfy one man, she won't be able to satisfy both of them," Natalie said snidely.

I frowned. Had Natalie been with the boys too?

"Like, together?" Emery asked. I looked around the corner to see her shudder with interest. She was basically salivating. "Are they...good?"

"The best." Natalie grinned.

I blanched. I knew they weren't interested. I knew the name of the game, but did I want to face two girls for goodness knows how long, knowing they'd been with all the guys I was interested in?

"I don't know. I've always been partial to Kingston and Axel, myself." Jade gave her a knowing smile. "If you like it rough, Axel knows exactly the right amount of pain to give you to bring you pleasure, and Kingston," she made a deep sound in the back of her throat, "is a freak. When he's in the mood, he doesn't care where or what you're doing. He'll pull down your pants and fuck you right there."

"Kingston can be yummy at times," Natalie agreed. "I just wish Axel would kiss me or go down on me. He's a bit selfish."

"Well, I like a little roughness, and kissing can be so overrated. When you say anywhere, does that mean anywhere at all?" Emery's voice was breathless. "And which one's Kingston? The blond or the brunette?"

"Why?" Jade asked with a laugh. "You'll leave your vanilla boyfriend and try and help us get our men back? I guess it may take all three of us to keep them interested. They are a bit insatiable at times."

Emery laughed back at her. "Have you ever had them all at once?"

Natalie and Jade laughed.

"Easton and Axel really aren't into the group thing, but Wyatt, Corbin, and Kingston are always up for a little group fun," Jade answered.

"You're asking an awful lot of questions for a girl who has a fiance, Emery," Natalie said a bit snidely.

Emery snorted. "Trev was always the consolation prize. My sister has always wanted what I wanted. I wanted Corbin first, then Trev. Since she knew she couldn't get Cor, she moved onto Trev. Now that he's mine, she's moved onto Corbin. But I'm sure if I talk to Trev, he'll be okay with sharing me," she said flippantly. "You need to tell me everything, though... what each one of them likes. Lace, leather, a lot of ass, a lot of tits? I want to know it all." She was nearly purring.

All her lies and her attitude revolted me, and suddenly I felt sick to my stomach. I closed my eyes and leaned my head against the wall. I wasn't going to compete for the men's attention. Maybe it was time I stopped things before it got too far.

"You know it's rude to eavesdrop," a masculine voice purred in my ear.

"It's call reconnaissance," I whispered back, nearly jumping out of my skin. "It's always good to know who your friends and foes are." I straightened, needing to get away from Kingston. I had a lot to think about. It had been foolish to have even entertained the idea of me with five guys.

With my head up, I moved towards the girls. I had no other choice. The store with the flannels I needed were in that store.

All three of them looked at me with varying looks of hate. What I ever did to my sister, goodness knew.

"Tick-tock," Jade taunted.

"Blub, blub, little fishy," Natalie added with a laugh.

Emery laughed. "Oh! I get it. A clock, like time, is running out, and she's like a fish in bed," she clarified.

What were they, twelve? I thought. I rolled my eyes, choosing to ignore them.

"Hey, girls," Kingston drawled suddenly.

I cringed, not realizing he was still behind me.

"Hey, Kingston!" They giggled simultaneously.

I continued ahead, but I still caught his words.

"Just want to let you girls know, just in case you get any wild ideas in those little heads of yours... my brothers and I would never, ever be interested in any of you, now or ever again," he said almost coldly. "The fact that you have to tear down a beautiful, intelligent, strong woman to make yourselves feel better is just one of the reasons why you're all ugly, small-minded, weak women."

"Oh come on, King," Jade said in a pouty voice. "We didn't even know she was there! You know we're just joking around. We didn't mean anything by it. Want us to take you to the dressing room? We'll show you exactly what you're missing."

"You knew, all right," he bit out. "That's why you were having a loud conversation in the spot you'd seen her last. And as far as any invitations go, never again."

Tears of hurt, humiliation, and confusion threatened to fall.

"Avery," he said quietly, following me into the store. "They're jealous of you and will do anything to tear you down. You don't really think it was just a coincidence they were in the part of the mall they knew you were in, right?"

"It's not a big deal," I muttered, looking around the shop.

It was almost summer, so not a lot of stores had flannels or long sleeve button-ups for sale anymore. I grabbed one of the deep shopping bags the store had available for its customers and moved towards the back.

"We shouldn't be judged by our past mistakes," Kingston stated resolutely.

"Okay." I shrugged, refusing to meet his eyes as I began sifting through the racks.

"Let's go, people," I heard Chad bellowing. Moving out in ten!"

I quickly shoved shirts into the bag, and impulsively grabbed some leather pants in my size as well. They were faux leather, but I was sure they'd clean up as well as my leather jacket had. When Axel had returned it to me, I was surprised that not a drop of blood had remained.

"Why do I have a feeling those girls ruined what we could have had?" King grumbled.

"We didn't have anything." I finally sighed. "Look, I like to consider myself as a realist. I should've known better. I don't like to get hurt, Kingston. I've been hurt enough to last a lifetime. I was only fooling myself in believing five, highly attractive men would stay interested in me for long." I turned then and looked him in the eye. "You guys discarded sex on heels and one of the strongest girls I've ever met. And now you have the more feminine, sexually confident version of me wanting you."

I shook my head. "I can't compete with that," I whispered before running off.

󠀠

I knew I had confused all the guys, save Kingston, when I refused to ride with any of them. I didn't want to tempt myself further. It was better if I ended things before it started —well, continued, in the case of Axel and Corbin.

"Wanna talk about it?" Sylvia gently prodded from the driver's seat of my truck.

I was beyond ecstatic to be reunited with my truck, Blanch. That family had left a mess in it in the short time they'd had it, but Wyatt and Corbin had cleaned it out really well.

"There's nothing to talk about," I muttered as I gently stroked Isa's cheek.

With the help of Steph and Aunt Pam, I had secured her to my chest with a baby wrap. It brought her in snug to my chest, and I still had the use of my hands. With her so close, I could feel each rise and fall of her chest. She hadn't woken yet, but color had returned to her cheeks, she was breathing more comfortably and didn't feel limp or lifeless.

"Then why do you look like someone kicked Bane?" Sylvia inquired.

At the mention of his name, Bane popped up from the back seat. He had been lying on the bench seat while Sylvia's dogs laid on top of him. She still wouldn't tell me their names, but I still had a feeling I wasn't going to be crazy about them.

"I would hope no one would kick my baby boy." I turned to look at him.

"Deflecting and diverting won't help deter me. Is it Axel, Corbin, or Wyatt?" she gave me a pointed look. "Who do I have to cut?"

I would've laughed had she not looked serious. She was weirdly protective over me, more so after Trevor.

I looked out the window as we passed the last convenient store at the foot of the mountains. I saw movement near the store and thought it looked like a little boy with dark hair. I could see the flash of a white t-shirt and a pair of dark jeans before it disappeared into the broken door of the store.

"Stop!" I yelled suddenly.

Sylvia slammed on the brakes. I braced my hands on

the dashboard, nearly crushing Isa to my chest. I cursed at my thoughtlessness as I heard the squeal of tires behind us. Good thing we'd only been going about thirty-five miles an hour.

I looked back, and I knew my heart was beating over a hundred miles an hour. We were the sixth vehicle in our procession of cars. Everyone, save Steph and I, was driving solo. Chad was driving Steph and the kids.

I breathed out in relief, thankful that my impulsive decision didn't cause the vehicles behind me to crash.

"What's going on?" I heard Axel bark out immediately over the radio.

Axel had found enough radios for each vehicle. He'd located them in the security office in the mall. They weren't as good as military-grade radios, he'd said, but they had the capability to stretch for miles and were better than any of the ones they could find in the stores.

"Pull in there," I insisted breathlessly.

Sylvia gave me a wide-eyed look but turned in. I picked up the radio and handed it to Sylvia.

"Tell them I thought I saw Ben," I told her before I pulled my sais out from the holsters I kept on the seat beside me.

I had only seen the boy twice, but it was long enough to know his mannerisms, size, and height.

"Avery, wait," Sylvia insisted, mystified, as she parked. "Who's Ben? Why don't you call Axel, and did you forget you have a baby hooked up to your chest?"

A rapping on my window made me start. I turned to see Wyatt standing on my running boards.

"What's up?" he asked as Sylvia rolled down the window.

I glared at her, and she gave me a pointed look back. "Tell me, or I'll continue doing stuff like that."

"The little boy, Ben," I explained to Wyatt without meeting his eyes. "I saw him run into the store. He just lost his family. He's all alone."

"Ave." Wyatt frowned.

"Please just get Ben," I muttered. "We can talk later."

He nodded and left.

"I need to know what's going on," Axel bit out once more through the radio.

"We're checking the Quick Stop Shop for a child," Wyat told him.

"Copy that, who has your six?" Axel returned.

"I do," Amy stated as she showed up next to Wyatt.

"I'll canvas the store for any usable items," Josh spoke up next.

I had recently learned that Josh and Amy were engaged and were supposed to get married this fall. They had been together for nearly three years and were such a cute couple.

"I'll have his six," Felix added.

"Copy that, everyone else get moving," Axel commanded.

I watched as the other vehicles began to move up the mountain.

"Talk," Sylvia insisted.

I sighed. Sylvia wouldn't give up until I told her. "There's not much to talk about," I muttered. "Reality came knocking, and I'm answering it."

"Way to be vague," she huffed at me. "Deets. Now."

"Do you know if Joe and Cal ever hooked up with Jade or Natalie?" I asked her suddenly.

"Yeah," she said with a shrug. "There's a reason why Joe was filing for them to be moved off of the Bravo Team."

I gaped at her. "How can you be so... okay with that? Women who get used, then discarded when they're not wanted?"

Sylvia snorted. "Don't let them fool you. Their arrangement and the paperwork had nothing to do with each other. Those girls are manipulative. They were initially on Bravo Team but found out about Alpha's... *proclivities*. They latched onto Alpha first. After being overseas for nearly a year, the guys got lonely. They girls slept with them a handful of times, then tried to cause discord in the group, even making up lies to kick Easton out of the group. So Axel made the decision to stop hooking up with them, since they were the cause of most of their issues.

"Needless to say, Jade and Natalie were pissed. Axel tried to be diplomatic and reminded them it wasn't a permanent arrangement. They still tried to cause discord among the group and attempted to seduce just the men they really wanted. Apparently, they never showed Easton any attention, and there were times Wyatt was excluded in their affection as well. It didn't work for the team.

"When the girls returned home, they got Easton arrested for attempted rape. They had assumed *he* was the one behind their dismissal. Luckily, Easton was in the clinic on the night in question and was recording his findings from an infected they had found."

My mouth was hanging open as she continued.

"They tried to pitch a similar arrangement with Bravo Team, pulling the same stunt when they decided that they no longer wanted Chad and Cal. They filed a complaint against the two. In the military, the women can cry wolf and be believed. Most of the time, the guys will be on probation of sorts and removed from duty until they are proven innocent, *if* they're proven innocent. Each of their complaints were filed anonymously, so Alpha Team didn't know who Easton's accuser was. If Josh hadn't overheard the girls conspiring against Chad, no one would have known. That's when Joe submitted the paperwork. No one trusts them anymore. They *can't* be trusted."

I gasped in shock, my animosity towards the women growing. I didn't have much time to process my feelings, though, before I saw Amy exiting the store. I sighed in relief as I saw Wyatt carrying a struggling Ben closely behind her.

"Ben," I yelled, rolling down my window.

He stopped struggling long enough for his eyes to dart around and find me. His eyes looked haunted, and his face crumbled the moment he saw me.

"Come on, Ben," I called softly. "You're safe now."

He nodded as his little body was wracked with sobs. Amy patted his back, and he was led into her vehicle.

"Poor boy." I frowned. "His parents were horrid, but he still loved them."

Sylvia made a noise of consent.

We watched as Felix and Josh exited the store with several cases of items. Wyatt ran back inside and returned moments later with a dolly of cases as well. They made a few more trips, and I wondered where they squeezed it all in.

Most of the vehicles had been packed to the brim of things we retrieved from the mall.

"So, what have the girls done now to poison the well?" Sylvia asked after several moments of silence as the guys got back in their vehicles.

Wyatt eased back onto the road, and we joined the procession once more.

"The guys like me," I mumbled. "This morning, the girls were talking about them, including Emery, and I got... jealous and insecure. I felt like, if they could be so easily disregarded, then so could I. I'm...I'm not ready to be hurt again."

"All five of them?" she took her eyes off the road for a moment to gape at me.

I nodded.

She started laughing. "You lucky bitch!" she hooted.

Totally not what I expected to come from her mouth. I glared at her in response.

She finally stopped laughing and looked over at me, giving me a stern look. "I don't think they'd ever hurt you. You forget, Corbin and Wyatt have crushed on you forever, and I've seen the way Axel looks at you when you're not looking. I think they're already halfway in love with you, Ave. I'm not sure how Easton and Kingston fall into it all, but from what I've heard, they're admirable men. They're guys who you want on your side."

Her expression softened. "If you go through life worried about the what-ifs and scared people are going to hurt you, then you're not living, Avery. There are no expiration dates on love. Sometimes it works, and sometimes it doesn't, but you will never know unless you try. Enjoy the moments you have and stop worrying about the future.

"This *apocalypse* has taught me to stop expecting people to let me down. I lived a life with an abusive, alcoholic father that is rotting in prison because he killed a man for his next high. My mother checked out and turned to drugs. They couldn't care less about me. I always thought it would be better to leave before I could be abandoned. But I was only half living that way. I don't know if Joe and Cal will stay with me forever, but I know they make me happy now, so I'm going to focus on that. I'm going to focus on all the things that can go right and stop thinking about the things that can go wrong."

She grinned and looked at me again. "A wise woman once told me you'd miss one hundred percent of the shots you don't take. So, are you going to sit on the bench because you're afraid to take a shot and play, or are you going to suit up and jump into the game?"

☐

I must have dozed off, because the next thing I heard was a squawk on the radio.

"Home sweet home, Harris-Harrisons, Edens, Cavaliers, and friends," I heard a familiar male voice say over the radio.

His voice carried a lot of relieved emotions.

I sat up and smiled, my sleepiness quickly dissipating. "Uncle Mitch," I breathed out. I looked down and noticed Isa was still deep in slumber. I patted her little bottom and readjusted my shirt.

"You forgot Cortez," Sylvia huffed into the radio with a smile.

"No one can forget you, Mama," Aunt Carol piped in.

"Hi, Aunt Carol!" Sylvia squealed back.

I smiled at my best friend. I loved how easily she had fit in with my family.

I looked up ahead to see we had caught up with the rest of the caravan and were now stopped on the narrow two-lane road leading down to Sanctuary Lakes Campground.

Sanctuary had always been a hidden gem. There was only one road that led in and out of the campground. You had to take a nearly fifteen-mile trek up a winding mountain road, and then, on your descent back down, you had to find the two-lane road that was easy to miss unless you were familiar with it.

Once you turned on that road, you had to take the gradual ride down. There was a stand of woods to the left and the rock face of the mountain to the right, at the entrance. After several miles of the most beautiful sights, the sign to the campgrounds could be seen. We were parked in front of that right now, but instead of the welcome sign, we now faced a tall, ten-foot or so, wrought iron gate.

I blinked in confusion. *Where had that come from?*

As I watched, I saw a man descending from what looked like a lookout tower situated in the trees to the left. From his gait, I immediately recognized it was Uncle Mitch. He was now surrounded by four other men, each with weapons strapped to their chests.

"Dorothy, I don't think we're in Kansas anymore," I said in surprise. "Was this like this in July?" I asked her.

Sylvia shook her head. "Nope," she answered, popping her P. "But from what BJ was stating, I'm sure they had been planning this for some time. With Uncle Mitch retiring last September, I'm sure he started making improvements as soon as he could."

"How long do you think they've known about this biological weapon?" I asked with a frown. The thought had crossed my mind several times, but I had filed that one away.

Sylvia snorted. "Alpha and Bravo have been in search of it for the last two years, with Charlie, Delta, and Echo teams joining the quest this past year."

I gaped at her. "How..."

She gave me a sheepish look. "The boys talk a lot. I wasn't supposed to say anything, but I had to tell you."

The gates opened, and soon we were making the downward trek to the campgrounds. The rock wall to the left gave way to rolling hills of forest. A copse of trees draped almost like an arch above us.

I saw two men ascend the lookout nest as the others jumped on quads and started riding alongside the caravan. I gaped as I got a better view of the lookout. Now that we were below it, I could see that it was at least thirty feet in the air and looked like a glorified treehouse. It seemed more extensive than my apartment from the outside.

"There it is!" Sylvia cried out excitedly as we crested the next hill.

I looked out, and both relief and sadness filled me. Sanctuary Lakes Campground was nestled in the valley of three mountains and got its name for the five lakes situated on the two-thousand acre plot. From our vantage point, you could see the man-made lake to the right, where we used to swim. The cabins that once housed the campers were about fifty yards behind it.

There were a total of fourteen cabins, all with fireplaces, and large enough to house sixteen bunk beds, or thirty-two campers, each. The bathrooms and showers separated the cabins, and right behind them was the kitchen and dining area.

Beyond the cabins were the barns and paddocks for the horses, and a short jaunt through the woods was another man-made lake they had created a few years back—an outdoor water park, of sorts. It had a zip line, inflatable water obstacles, and water trampolines.

We continued down the mountain, and the first parking lot opened up to the left, where the information center was. Nana and Pop-pop had built a restaurant and a sizable gift shop-convenient store there as well. The restaurant had become popular among the locals, not just vacationers, who visited just as frequently as the guests that had stayed here.

Right now, the parking lot seemed full of vehicles, yet I couldn't see anyone walking around like I typically would have.

In fact, it was slightly unnerving to see how empty everything looked. It was a week after Memorial Day. Usually, it would be buzzing with people; people enjoying the horses, bike paths, canoeing, kayaking, and the other activities offered here. But other than a small group of children near the playground, I didn't see anyone.

I continued to look around as we cleared the copse of trees and saw Nana and Poppop's two-thousand square foot cabin on the top of one of the hills. At the foot of it was the hall.

The hall had been an addition that my dad had suggested they open, roughly five years ago. It was created for weddings and big gatherings. Erected out of logs, the building was top-notch, with a commercial kitchen, a massive fireplace large enough to take up nearly half of one of its walls, and an expansive area to fit and house a wedding party of five hundred.

It had been a smart investment, because, even in the dead of winter, couples had rented it out, and in the summertime they had the use of the hall and several prime locations for an outdoor ceremony.

We ended our journey at the foot of the hill where the recreation center, laundry mat, and the arcade was. The large parking lot we parked in led in three different directions: the left was where people camped among the trees, whether by tent or recreation vehicles. The right led up and around to the campers' cabins, and straight ahead was where families or hunters could rent the log cabins that offered up to six bedrooms.

There was so much more to the camp, but with the expanse of land, hills, mountains, and trees, it was hard to see it all. It now hit home why Dad and the uncles had deemed this as a safe place, a sanctuary. The mountains and the single entry point made it easily defensible. That and you could completely live off the land, with the right equipment, knowledge, and supplies.

Sylvia barely had the car in park before she was leaping out and running towards Aunt Carol and a few women who'd exited the recreation center. I took my time, exiting the truck, mindful of baby Isa. I opened the back door, and Bane immediately jumped down to stand next to me.

Sylvia's two dogs needed help getting out, being smaller than Bane. I had no qualms letting them out as well. After Miller had accidentally dropped their leashes earlier, her dogs had stuck around, and Sylvia was pleased to find out that, like Bane, they weren't runners either.

I rubbed Isa's back as I grabbed her saline bag, careful to keep it elevated. I paused to look at her and gasped. Her beautiful dark blue eyes were staring back at me.

"Hi there, beautiful," I crooned happily as tears filled my eyes.

"How's our little girl?" Easton hesitantly asked, startling me.

He kept referring to her as *our* girl, and it was starting to grow on me. Corbin and Axel had shown a lot of concern for her, but I knew Easton was already emotionally invested. It had forged a bond between us. This tiny little girl's life had hung in the balance, and with our combined efforts, she was recovering. She really was a miracle baby, a fighter.

I unbuttoned a few more of my buttons to show him the little bundle peering up at me.

"Hi, there little fighter." His smile rivaled mine as he peeked down at her. "We should get her somewhere so I can check her vitals, see if she will take some milk, then we might be in the clear to remove her IV. Her color already looks better to me. I think your idea of Kangaroo Care was brilliant, Avery."

I smiled back at him and angled myself so that I could place my arms around his waist. I felt him tense for just a moment before he began to rub his hands up and down my back, lowering his head next to mine.

"What's this for?" he asked with a chuckle. "Not that I'm complaining."

"For helping me." I leaned into him the best I could with

Isa between us. "For helping Isa. For just being you."

I felt the vibrations of his chuckle once more, before Isa chose to let out a pitiful whimper.

We both jumped back, looked at each other, and began to laugh. My tears were happy tears as they coursed down my face. I'm pretty sure I saw tears enter his own eyes as he embraced me again. He took the saline bag with one hand and my hand with the other. I squeezed it, thankful Sylvia had spoken her words of wisdom to me.

I was done worrying about what might happen. It was time I just enjoyed the now moments.

Chapter 16

"You look like you were born to do that," Aunt Carol commented with a beatific smile.

We had been busy since we'd arrived, and right now was the first time I'd gotten to sit and just *be*. We were seated in the wedding hall, which Aunt Carol had determined was the best location for mealtimes until we could figure out all the details of caring for over fifty people.

Stephanie and Aunt Pam had migrated to the large overstuffed chairs and couches near the fireplace. The sitting area was comfortable and gave us a great vantage point of most of the outside. All the windows were open, letting in the fresh late-spring air.

I looked up and met the sad and sympathizing looks of Aunt Pam and Stephanie. They had taken the couch across from me. I swallowed the pain down and smiled.

"Thank you, Aunt Carol," I told her.

I shifted Isa in my arms. I curled my feet under me and gave her the bottle Steph had prepared for me. I was so thankful and surprised to find out that she had started to pump for Isa last night, and instead of the colostrum she'd expected, she was producing the fatty milk Isa probably needed. The female body never ceased to amaze me.

"I feel like it was destiny that this little one and I met," I explained to them quietly.

Aunt Carol was family, and I'm sure somehow, someway she would hear about my miscarriage, but I wanted to be the first to tell her.

"I lost a little girl nearly a year ago. We planned to name her Bella Mae, after we'd debated on calling her Isa Mae. Imagine my shock when I found out this little girl's name was Isa May with a Y," I explained quietly. "I know she'll never replace my little girl, but I think all people come and go in our lives for a reason. There's definitely a reason she came into my life. Maybe she's here to help me heal."

I saw the bright sheen of tears in the eyes of the three women as they looked at me.

"Please don't cry," I insisted.

"Oh, Avery," Aunt Carol breathed before she squeezed my hand. She then took the armchair between the two couches. "I know the loss of a child. I don't know if you remember Wyatt, Katie, and MJ's younger sister, Bethany. You must have been four or five at the time when she was born. She had congenital heart disease. They couldn't fix her."

I nodded my head. I vaguely remembered attending a funeral with a tiny casket. I remembered the sadness, remembered my mom, Nana, and my aunts hugging and crying a lot. The men had wandered off to drink and smoke their cigars on Nana's porch once all the strangers had left. Us kids were left with very little supervision. Katie and Wyatt had been sorrowful, but MJ had been a toddler back then.

Aunt Carol and Uncle Mitch had three "natural" children. Wyatt was the oldest, followed by Katie, and then MJ. It was easy to forget that they had a fourth child at one time. I had been so young.

"There's not a day that goes by that I don't think about her, but I know she's in a better place," Aunt Carol continued. "God has brought others into my life now as well, and I don't think we'd have ever thought about fostering children if it hadn't been for her. Now look at us. We've loved and cared for over fifteen children, and I've adopted two of them through that experience! I don't love my Bethany less by loving the others. Our hearts are amazing things, Avery. It shows us there are endless ways to love."

Her eyes got a far off look for a moment, and I saw sadness there, then worry. I knew she was thinking about her son MJ, and all the children she had loved along the way, wondering and probably fearing where they could be now. I often found myself thinking about the people I cared about and praying they were okay.

MJ was at college on the west coast. Luckily, Uncle Mitch was able to contact him and tell him to come home immediately. Last time they talked to him, he was at a friend's house. Even in the best conditions, it would take days for him to reach us. Now with the world in shambles, it was going to be downright treacherous.

"Mom, when's lunch?" James came running into the hall as if his mother had conjured him.

James was a small but robust ten-year-old. He was half African American and half Irish. He had light brown skin with a surprising amount of freckles across his nose and cheeks. His hair was a riot of reddish-brown curls, and his eyes were a warm hazel. I'd always had a softness for the sometimes overly rambunctious but affectionate child.

It was somewhat ironic that, despite no blood relation and a slight difference in skin pigment, he resembled Katie, Wyatt, and Aunt Carol in so many ways. They all had freckles and that radiant reddish-brown hair. His hazel eyes even resembled Katie's and MJ's.

Aunt Carol shook her head with a smile. "Soon as the men are out of the meeting, James."

Once we had arrived, we had emptied all the vehicles of community items, storing them where Uncle Mitch told us to. Then BJ, Corbin, Trevor, Wyatt, Axel, Joe, Uncle Mitch, and a few of his men went up to my grandparents' old house. They invited me along, but I had elected to stay and help Aunt Carol, Aunt Pam, Stephanie, and a couple of Aunt Carol's friends, Trudy and Winnie, make a cold lunch.

Aunt Carol had shown me the greenhouses that they had erected at the end of last summer, which were already producing enough vegetables to create the salad we made. Along with the salad, we had put out some lunch meats, cheeses, tuna fish salad, bread, and homemade potato chips.

Sanctuary had closed and locked its gates after Uncle Scott's call on Saturday. Thankfully, a large order for the restaurant had been previously placed and was delivered to the restaurant that Friday. That left their pantry, walk-in freezer and refrigerator nearly fully stocked.

We had every intention of using the restaurant food in the coming weeks, but we knew with some of those items, once they were gone, that was it. Eventually, we'd have to come up with a solution to last us for the long haul, then prepare for the worst and pray for the best.

I knew that the food situation was one of the reasons why they were having a meeting. Axel had jumped in with two feet, like always, suggesting the meeting. He wanted to come up with a list of all their needs. Together, they'd come up with worklists, security detail, supply runs, and housing assignments.

If left to their own devices, Corbin and Axel predicted some of the people here wouldn't contribute to the new community. Uncle Mitch, Uncle Scott, and Dad had already begun to anticipate and plan for such an event. Thus, all the changes around here and all the new stuff I was still learning about.

It was no surprise that Kingston, Easton, Chad, Felix, Cal, Josh, and Amy immediately jumped in and were currently inventorying everything in the food and supply buildings. The buildings behind the wedding hall were new too. They had the building erected, but Uncle Mitch and Eddie, one of his best friends, didn't have the time or organizational skills to get it prepared for long-time use.

Corbin and Axel hadn't been wrong: the moment they'd left for the meeting, Emery, Garth, Jade, Natalie, Katie, and her boyfriend Nico, plus a few of the people that had been here, had already wandered off.

"Okay." James sighed dramatically before he turned to leave. "I guess we'll starve to death."

We laughed at his dramatics as he went back outside.

Mikey, Miller, Ben, James, and a few other children had immediately taken off together the moment we'd parked. There was a small playground by the recreation center. If I were to look out of the many windows in the front of the building, I could easily see them. Fifteen-year-old Gloria, the Eden's other adopted child, had volunteered to watch them with a couple of her friends.

I was kind of glad for James' interruption from our earlier conversation, and soon we began to talk about some of the other changes that had been made since last July. However, it seemed like the men had kept the women in the dark for the most part.

Aunt Carol had previously assumed they were preparing to have the restaurant converted to a farm-to-table concept, so the new additions, like the greenhouses and the pole barns– which I had yet to visit– hadn't seemed strange to her.

"I think the menfolk are returning shortly," Sylvia interrupted with an exaggerated southern drawl, poking her head inside the hall's doorway.

We all got up and met her outside. She had Jenny and Phil in a double stroller. She, too, looked like a natural, with two babies in tow.

"Did you see them?" I asked hopefully. Honestly, I was hungry. I was starving, even. I hadn't eaten breakfast, so my stomach was angrily reminding me.

"They're headed down the hill right now." Sylvia grinned. "Can I ring the bell, please, please, please?"

"Go ahead." Aunt Carol laughed.

Sylvia squealed before she took off running to the end of the sidewalk. There were three dinner bells. One up at my grandparents' house, one up at the campers' cabins. And the last one was at the recreation center. Each one had a distinct sound, but the one by the cabins carried sound the farthest.

Jenny let out a wail of fear, while Phil cried, and Isa jumped when the bell began to carry. Aunt Pam immediately picked up Jenny to calm her down, while Aunt Carol gently pushed Steph to the side to pick up Phil.

"You're too pregnant, woman," Aunt Carol teasingly grumbled. "Let's keep Madeline in there a little longer."

Steph groaned jokingly. "I'm ready to stop feeling like a beached whale now. She was already weighing in over seven pounds at last week's checkup." Then a look of fear entered her eyes. "How am I supposed to have a baby with no hospital? No doctor."

"Well, you know I'm a Labor and Delivery nurse," Aunt Pam gently reminded her as she rocked Jenny up and down.

Aunt Pam was the main reason I'd gone into nursing. She was now a Nurse Practitioner and had no plans of retiring anytime soon. She loved her career, and I felt her passion.

"Easton is a medic too," I spoke up as I placed Isa on my shoulder to burp her. I was more than happy to see that she'd taken another two-ounce bottle. "I'm not sure what his specialty was, but we can ask." I closed my eyes, enjoying her sweet baby smell as I gently patted her back.

Aunt Carol made a sound of appreciation. "If I were

twenty years younger and single, I would be chasing after those twins. Make me the meat in their sandwich."

My jaw dropped in shock before a burst of surprised laughter left my lips.

Stephanie and Aunt Pam laughed uproariously. Aunt Pam, Aunt Carol, and Mom had never shied away from talking about their sex lives, but they had put boundaries on what they said around us when we were younger. For instance, saying, "if the sock is on the door, do not disturb" or "he really knows how to rock my world!" Gross, but innocent, comments like that. Though they never went as far as talking about being *the meat in the middle of a sandwich*!

"Girl," Aunt Pam finally breathed, "you'd still be fifteen years older than them."

Aunt Carol mocked sniffed. "Then I'll be the cougar wanting to teach those boys a thing or two."

I continued to laugh in shock while the other two laughed like this was nothing new. I refrained from telling her I was sure it would be the other way around—the guys seemed to have taken sexual freedom to another level. Even shy, reserved Easton.

"What did I miss?" Sylvia came running to us with the same boundless energy she'd had before all the crap had hit the fan. Her mood had dramatically gotten better since when we'd gotten here. Now that she was safe, she was back to her usual self.

"You don't want to know," I jokingly groaned.

Aunt Carol tsked at me. "I was just telling the girls how I wouldn't mind being the meat between the Rains boys' sandwich."

Sylvia let out a mischievous laugh as she gave me a pointed look. "Being the meat between a sandwich can be so amazing. Especially if you're with two men who know what they're doing."

"Do tell," Aunt Carol sliding closer, Phillip content at her shoulder.

"Please," Aunt Pam added, leaning towards her.

Sylvia went inside, waiting as we followed, and took a seat on the large stone coffee table in the middle of the sitting area. She sat Indian style and clasped her hands in excitement. All we were missing was a bowl of popcorn, from the looks on the women's faces. I just continued to gape at them in shock. Who were these women, and what had they done with the women I'd grown up with?

◻

I was pretty sure I still had a look of bemused laughter and shock on my face when Wyatt and Corbin entered the room. The girls were still avidly listening to Sylvia's new arrangement between her two men. Her back was to me, so she didn't even see them come in.

Isa was now safely tucked into the portable bassinet. Her little thumb had even made its way to her mouth. I stared in fascination at her every now and then. It was when I was checking on her for the fiftieth time that I saw the guys walk through the back screened-in porch.

Wyatt sat down first, on my left side, and then Corbin to my right. The couch still had plenty of space, but they both insisted on sitting nearly on top of me. Aunt Pam, Steph, and Aunt Carol were too enthralled with Sylvia's retelling of having Joe and Cal together to pay much attention to us

"Your moms are freaks," I whispered to them.

"How do you think I became one?" Wyatt whispered back before he nuzzled my neck.

I bit back a moan as his lips brushed an especially erogenous area.

"Spending most years with romance novels and

vibrators can do that to a troop's wife," Corbin murmured in my other ear before he lightly bit the space between my shoulder and neck.

I literally bit the inside of my cheek to cover that response. I had never been bitten, and I never thought I'd like it. I was wrong.

"Did you like that?" Corbin husked in my ear.

I jerkily shook my head in denial. I was a big fat liar, but I didn't know the game they were playing. Before they'd gone up to the main house, they seemed to be keeping their distance from me.

"If I were to dip my hands inside your shorts right now, would you be wet for us?" Wyatt whispered in my other ear.

"Stop," I begged them breathlessly while Wyatt began to trace my bare thigh with his fingers.

"Are you done being mad at us for something we didn't do?" Corbin demanded.

I sighed. "Yes. I'm sorry," I whispered.

"Joe is a total breast man," Sylvia was saying. "He has a way of biting and tugging on my nipples that nearly makes me orgasm every time, and Cal has a talented tongue, if you know what I mean."

"Mmm," Aunt Pam hummed. "I know what you mean!"

I heard Corbin choke on...air?

"Did you take one in the exit and entrance yet?" Aunt Carol asked with interest.

Wyatt grunted now. Both seemed to be taking a break from tormenting me.

"Yes." Sylvia giggled at her terminology. "I was a strict exit-only girl until they showed me how... great it is."

"I've always wondered if Mitch would let me... you know, invite another man into the room so I could experience that. Double penetration, maybe even triple, has always intrigued me. I already got him a girl for us on his birthday one year…" Aunt Carol sighed dramatically.

"Oh, mom!" Wyatt cried out suddenly, making Aunt Pam, Aunt Carol, and Sylvia yelp and jump up in surprise. Steph just covered her mouth in mirth. "There are just some things kids do *not* want to hear about their mothers."

I began to giggle, hiding my face in Corbin's chest. "I warned you," I crowed out as Corbin buried his head in my neck. His chest was rumbling with laughter against my cheek.

" I just thank all that is good in this world that I didn't hear my mom's confessions." Corbin rumbled with laughter.

Wyatt glared at us, and I continued to laugh as Corbin began to wipe tears from his eyes.

"Wyatt Eden!" Aunt Carol put Phil on one hip and a hand on the other. "You weren't immaculately conceived. Are you saying you wouldn't want to know I was having my world rocked when you were made? It's time you know your mom loves sex and lots of it."

"*Mom*," Wyatt groaned, seriously looking aghast now. "Please stop. I can't *unhear* those words."

"Honestly, you're all grown now, and why should we hide something so natural from you guys?" Aunt Pam sniffed in Aunt Carol's defense. "I can tell you how and when Corbin was conceived."

"Don't you dare, Ma," Corbin growled in warning, suddenly out of laughter.

"Corbin was conceived at a UB40 concert!" Aunt Pam shouted. "We didn't wait to go to the bathroom or the car. We went at it right in the middle of the concert. I turned around, sat on your daddy's lap, and rode him while they sang, '*I Can't Help Falling in Love with You.*'"

"Ma!" Corbin growled out. "Stop, please."

"They act like they're such sweet angels," she went on, totally ignoring him. "I'm pretty sure I caught that Ashlynn girl giving Corbin a blow job before they left for boot camp. And I remember catching Wyatt in bed with that slutty girl... what was her name again?" Corbin glared at her, but she continued, looking at Aunt Pam. "Oh! Should we tell them about the time we got high and then we—"

"No!" Uncle Mitch quickly interjected.

Where had he come from? He must have been there for some time, because his face looked red from laughter, too.

"Storytime is over for now," he quickly added. "Let's eat! Everyone is on their way in now."

"Let's," I agreed as I looked at the shocked and stricken faces of Wyatt and Corbin.

I knew their minds were conjuring up the many scenarios of the time their mothers were smoking weed together, and based on their expressions, it must not have been pretty.

I started to laugh again. "Feed me! I'm hungry," I told the guys.

"I'm hungry, too." Corbin leaned over at the same time Wyatt did.

I realized they were going to dish out some payback for my laughing at their expense.

"We'll feed you, if you feed us," Wyatt whispered in my ear.

"Would you like to suck on Wyatt's cock while I eat you out, or would you like to suck me dry while Wyatt gets to eat that pussy of ours?" Corbin suggested.

I turned my head into Wyatt's neck. "Please stop teasing me," I pleaded.

"It's no tease," Wyatt growled. "We already have a crib

being set up in our cabin. We'll lay Isa down, and then we'll deliver on all our promises. Would you like to come for Corbin and me, together?"

"Just say yes and we'll go now. We have two hours before anybody will come looking for us," Corbin added. "I think we could do a lot in two hours."

I shifted in my seat, glad that no one seemed to be paying us any attention, as Wyatt began to caress my thigh.

I stood up. "Let's go." I was done waiting.

If it all crashed and burned, then so be it, I thought. But life was too short to not enjoy the moments given. Our current situation was showing me that now more than ever.

They both growled in satisfaction before Wyatt scooped Isa up, gently cradling her in the crook of his arm. They followed me towards the door. Corbin put an arm around my shoulder, and Wyatt put his hand on the small of my back.

We were exiting the back door, hoping to avoid the rest of the people, when Trevor appeared. We all paused momentarily on the screened-in porch.

I felt Trevor's gaze on me before he turned to look at Wyatt and Corbin. "Why are you insisting that Avery stay in a cabin with you guys?" he growled out.

Corbin sighed and rubbed the bridge of his nose. "You aren't her keeper anymore, Trev."

"She's still my best friend and–" Trevor insisted.

"And nothing Trev," Wyatt cut him off. "Best friends don't do what you did to Avery. You knocked her up and then cheated on her with her sister? Where were you when she lost her baby? Sylvia told me *she* was with her, that *she* had to take her to the hospital."

Trevor's jaw dropped. He looked at me with sad, soulful brown eyes. "You told them that you–"

"Trevor!" I called out in warning before he could continue his tirade. Only Sylvia knew, and I would've never told Corbin and Wyatt about that day—I never wanted to turn the brothers on each other.

But Trevor didn't heed my warning as a bright sheen of tears entered his eyes. "You'll never know how much I hated myself for not charging my phone and checking it. If I had known you were losing Bella, I would have never started partying that night."

"Please stop, Trevor!" I pleaded. "I didn't tell them!" I insisted.

"Oh, hell no," Corbin cursed quietly, understanding finally entering his eyes as I looked at him. "You're telling me you screwed Emery the same night Avery was losing the baby?" The cold fury on his face was chilling.

Corbin yelling was formidable. Corbin cold and quiet like this? Dangerous.

Trevor blanched. "I never planned any of that," he whispered. "I loved Avery. I still do. I was stupid. I shouldn't have drank that much. I haven't touched alcohol since that night for that very reason. I lost everything that night." His eyes were pleading with me to believe him, and... I did. But it didn't explain why he was still with Emery. People didn't repeat mistakes.

"Avery and Bella were my future," Trev said. "I went to our bench on her due date," he whispered to me as tears fell down his face. "You never came."

We had a bench in our parents' town. It was where all our highs and lows had been shared. It was where he'd told me he'd made varsity wrestling. It was where I'd told him I'd made the Junior Olympics. It was where he had told me he'd gotten his scholarship, and where I'd told him about mine. He told me he would marry me on that bench, with a promise ring. I gave him my first sonogram there, with a simple note that said,

It's time to ask... with the watch he now wore, engraved on the back with the words *Will You be my Baby Daddy?*

I felt my tears coursing down my face and barely noticed Wyatt stroking my arm. "It wasn't our bench anymore. You don't repeat *mistakes*, Trevor. If you really cared about me or Bella's memories, you wouldn't have continued a relationship with Emery." I felt Corbin embrace me gently.

"Emery was there for me, Ave," Trevor said, his voice trembling with emotion. "She let me cry on her shoulder, made me go to classes, made sure I ate, made sure I took a shower. I was a total wreck after you left me, after we lost Bella. I always loved Emery, just was never in love with her. Then I realized if I couldn't have you, then she was the closest I would ever get. You weren't answering my phone calls or texts!" His voice shook more. "Is this your way of getting over me, because I'm still not over you? Is this what this is, payback? I start dating your sister, and you start dating my brother, or is it Wyatt now?"

I brushed my tears away, feeling his hurt and truth. "No, Trevor. You wrecked me. The three months I spent sleeping around and nearly getting molested– when I made the mistake of drinking too much– was my *getting over you* phase," I said in a whisper. I saw the devastation on his face and felt Wyatt and Corbin both stiffen beside me. "Me with Corbin or Wyatt or anyone else at this time, is the *I'm over you* phase. I'll always love you, and I hope you and Emery find real ove, but the day I realized it wasn't just her but at least four other girls, I fell out of love with you. Love like yours hurts, Trev. Love shouldn't hurt like that."

And that was why high emotions and me didn't mix. I blurted out things that should stay in the shadows.

With a shaky sigh, I wiped my eyes and turned away. "Can you take me to our cabin?" I muttered to the guys.

"We were on a break, Avery!" Trevor cried plaintively. "I

didn't look for those other girls. They came to *me*. I didn't think I had to remain faithful to you if we weren't technically together."

"Then why did you continue texting me?" I bit out. "Why did you ask me if I was seeing anybody? You got jealous when you found out I had a study date with Neil. Meanwhile, you're hooking up with girls left and right. You were pulling away from me, so I let you go. I know now that we got together too young. You were in college, surrounded by beautiful girls. You were curious and maybe even frightened by the thought of me being your first and last. Unlike you, I was perfectly content with that."

My voice softened. "I genuinely believe you were too drunk to realize you were sleeping with Emery that night. Even I think she made you believe it was me. However, the damage has been done. You chose to walk out on our relationship several times. Now I'm choosing to walk away from you, permanently. I'm hoping with time, we can become friends. Maybe. But I'll *never* give you my heart again."

"Please, Ave," he pleaded.

"Let's go," Wyatt said gruffly to me before turning on Trevor. "Just quit, Trev. You know you fucked up. Do you really believe you deserve her, let alone her forgiveness?"

"Yes. I do, actually," Trevor said mutinously. "You're worse than I am, Wyatt. You have a constant stream of women in and out of your bed. You're a bigger manwhore than I could ever be. Corbin and his friends are no better." He then looked at me again. "You don't realize they're going to hurt you worse than I ever could, Avery."

I made a buzzing noise. "Wrong," I stated with conviction. "In the short period I've known them, and in *all* the time I've known Corbin and Wyatt, they were many things, but being a liar wasn't one of them. If they ever felt the need to move on, they wouldn't continue to string me along. They wouldn't lie to me about their feelings. Can you say the same?"

"So, you really are staying with all five of them..." Trevor stated incredulously. "You know what they do with women, don't you?"

Corbin turned on him, furious. "First, she knows. Second, we won't ever damage her like you have. And third, she's running again. Wanna tell her what happened the last time she ran?"

I turned my shocked gaze on him. *What* had happened?

"You always took on the mantle of her knight in shining armor, Trev," Corbin continued. "You may have loved her, but you always took her love for granted, letting her put you on some damn pedestal that you didn't deserve to be on."

Trevor blanched. "You promised," he whispered earnestly.

"What did you promise, Corbin?" I asked in a cold tone. I *so* was done with the secrets, so done with the lies.

Trevor had hidden so many things from me, knowing they'd hurt me but had always justified his actions. We were broken up. He forgot. He was drunk.

I refused to start another relationship on the same footing.

"Tell her," Corbin insisted.

Trevor shook his head. "No. You promised!"

"What happened the last time?" I demanded, nearly hysterical.

"Fine, dammit. It wasn't me!" Trevor cried, his jaw set in anger at his brother. "Avery... It wasn't me who carried you back to the house or tucked you back in bed when you ran. One night, I lost you. You were sleeping beside me, and in the early morning, you weren't. I had to tell someone. Corbin went out looking for you. He found you. The second time it happened was when you were living with us. I may have fallen asleep with you, but Corbin always slept on the floor after we fell asleep. You never left the house again."

I turned startled eyes on Corbin. Had he done that for me? He'd never told me!

"Are you happy?" Trevor muttered bitterly. "Now I'm a complete monster in her eyes."

I sighed as I went to Corbin and leaned against him, trying to convey with my touch how much he meant to me. I felt hollow and drained of all emotion as I turned in Corbin's arms and faced Trevor.

"I don't think you're a monster, Trev. I know you'll always be the man who brakes when an animal crosses the road. Who will still run up ahead to open the door for older women, or give a helping hand to the frazzled mom in the grocery market. Your heart was always good. It was the influences around you that began to poison your brain.

"I meant what I said. I still love you. The good times I had with you outweigh the bad, and someday I hope that we can be friends again. Just don't push me or try to turn me against the guys. Right now, I'm... happy, and if you ever loved me, you would want me to be content. I'm tired of... despising you. We're going to see a lot of each other in the upcoming months, maybe even years, and I don't want our families to suffer anymore. I want us to be able to coexist in peace, and maybe, one day, we can talk and laugh like we used to."

Chapter 17

"Can we *not* talk about the time I was getting over Trev?" I muttered as I took a seat on the leather couch.

Uncle Mitch had given us one of the cabins used for bigger families and for hunters. There was a sizable kitchen, with a living room and dining room as soon as you walked into the house. The master bedroom was tucked over to the left with its own bathroom. To the right, another room, complete with a queen bed. Straight ahead were the other two bedrooms, a bathroom, and stairs that led up to the loft. The loft could be used as a recreation area or bedroom, and it too had its own bathroom.

"Have you talked to anyone about it?" Wyatt asked.

Wyatt had put Isa in a crib that had already been set up in the corner of the room next to the master.

I nodded mutinously, knowing that was a no to my request. Wyatt and Corbin weren't going to let it go. "I went through a phase where I wanted to see... if something was wrong with me. I got drunk a lot and hooked up with a few guys. One night, Sylvia and I were on a road trip. We were with these guys who were in a couple of our classes. They brought along a guy that volunteered to drive for us. When we got tired of driving, we stopped at a hotel that had one of those large suites. My hookup and I were in one bedroom, and Sylvia and her partner were in the other room.

"I had an aversion to cuddling. Especially with the guys I hooked up with, no matter how drunk I got. So, later I left the room to get some space. I forgot our DD was crashing on the couch bed, so I curled up on the love seat. I woke up to him offering me water. I don't remember anything after that. I was so sick the next morning, felt like I had the flu, even for days afterward. I thought my drinking had caught up with me. My misdiagnosis, combined with my plummeting grades, made me decide I was done seeking out meaningless sex and alcohol.

"A few weeks later, our DD was busted for slipping women date rape drugs." I heard them both growl, but I continued. "I started having these flashbacks. I don't remember much. Eventually, I sought out a crisis counselor on campus. By then, the guy had admitted to all his crimes. I wasn't on the list, but when I was able to confront him in prison, he admitted to slipping it into my water. He says he had drunk too much by that point, though, and wasn't able to get it up. I don't know if I believe him or not. I remember things. I just don't remember the whole act..."

I shrugged and stared down at my hands.

"Do you have..." Corbin began tentatively. "Are you afraid of men?"

I twisted my lips bitterly. "I haven't let a man touch me in months. Well, except you guys. I haven't had sex, consensual or otherwise, in over four months. If you're asking if I'm afraid of you..." I paused and dug deep. My actions of late would negate that theory. "No, no, I'm not. Actually, since Axel came into my life, I felt an... awakening."

I'd had my breakdown after I found out about the DD. That's why I'd gone to a counselor. He had been helpful in showing me how to process my feelings. The counselor helped me realize that the more I feared intimacy, the more power I was giving that scumbag.

Memories of what the girls had said about me in the mall replayed in my head, and I decided to give them the full disclosure.

"Trevor was my first. We were sixteen when we had sex for the first time. It was awkward. He didn't know how to hold out. He usually came before I could find my own release. We experimented, learned what each other liked, but to this day, I still have a...problem. I can't come all the time. I knew it frustrated Trevor. I don't think he had those issues with the other girls. But I like sex. It feels great to me. I tried to see if I was...broken, and I really think I am. Only one of those guys I hooked up with after Trevor could give me an orgasm, and I was drunk out of my mind, which, I think now, was the only reason. I finally got out of my head."

I looked up, and Corbin and Wyatt were both watching me with indecipherable looks. It was Wyatt who suddenly spoke.

"Sweetheart, I don't think it was you. With the right partner, you can come over and over and over again. Sometimes it just takes a little patience and skill, but it can be done. We can show you. When you're ready," he hastily added.

I gnawed on the inside of my cheek. He seemed confident that it wasn't me, and I wanted to see if he was right. I stood up and slowly began to unbutton the oversized flannel I was wearing, revealing the Superman bra underneath. Next, I moved my hands to the clasp of my jean shorts.

"There's no rush Ave," Corbin said huskily, but his eyes were lit with an inner fire. I could see his appreciative gaze roaming the swell of my breasts that were pushed up over my bra, then onto my narrow waist, my four-pack abs, and the flare of my hips where my jean shorts sat low.

I said nothing as I unbuttoned my shorts and unzipped them, allowing them to pool at my feet. My underwear matched my bra, the S perfectly hovering over my mons.

I heard Wyatt moan before he stepped up behind me. "Tell us how far you want us to go, Ave," he whispered huskily before his lips found the side of my neck. His tongue darted out, licking my flesh before he nibbled on it.

I groaned the moment he found that sensitive spot behind my ears.

Corbin stepped forward, sandwiching me between his and Wyatt's bodies. "This is all about you," Corbin huskily murmured before he began nibbling on my throat.

Their words and their lips turned me on. I could feel the tension settle in my lower belly. A delicious ache spread down to my very core.

"We can be perfectly content just feasting on you, hearing you scream as you come apart on our tongues," Wyatt said as his hands roamed down my back, down to the swell of my hips and finally to the front of my waistband. His fingers teased, just above my pubic bone.

I found my back arching towards his fingers. My skin felt like it was on fire. Corbin's lips were leaving a trail of heat wherever he touched. Wyatt's fingers made my skin jump in anticipation.

"I want to take these sweet tits out and suck on them, bite them, lick them. Would you like that, baby?" Corbin asked as he began to trace my already erect nipples in lazy circles.

No one had ever bitten my nipples before. I was intrigued.

I moaned. "Please."

Wyatt released my bra before his lips continued to trail kisses down the nape of my neck and down my spine. I felt the cool air brush against my nipples and heard Corbin growl out in satisfaction.

"They're perfect," Cor muttered before he laved one of my nipples with his tongue. He did the same to the other side, and I began to rock my hips restlessly against Wyatt's fingers.

I cried out when Corbin finally latched onto one of my peaks. He scraped his teeth against my sensitive nipple before tugging. The sharp pain wasn't…unpleasant. In fact, it felt like a string was tied to them and my core. I felt my ache grow to insurmountable proportions.

"Please," I cried out when Corbin switched to my other breast.

"What do you want, sweetheart?" Wyatt inquired as his fingers traced the outside of my panties.

I found myself separating my thighs, giving him better access to where I really wanted him to be.

"I can feel her heat through her panties, Cor," Wyatt moaned out. "Avery,' he said then, in a slightly commanding voice. "Do you want me to feel how wet you are?"

I nodded eagerly.

Corbin chuckled deeply. "So responsive," he murmured, tugging my nipple with his teeth. "Do you want just his fingers, or his mouth too?"

They paused, and I nodded.

"Use your words," Wyatt commanded once more. This dominant side of Wyatt turned me on. He was the laid back one. He never demanded anything from anyone.

"Both," I moaned out when I realized they weren't going to continue unless I told them what I wanted.

Corbin growled while Wyatt hummed his approval. "Take her to her room," Wyatt ordered Corbin before he strode past us.

Corbin lifted me and followed Wyatt. His long strides ate up the distance in no time. My eyes widened in appreciation when I saw Wyatt, now shirtless, standing by the bed. He emptied his pockets next and put some things on the nightstand. I had no time to appreciate the room before Corbin was placing me in the middle of the bed.

I turned my head to look at the muscles in Wyatt's chest

flex in movement as he unbuttoned his cargo pants. He made no move to remove them as he looked over and smirked at me. He knew I liked what I saw. He wasn't nearly as broad or big as Axel or Corbin, but he still had excellent muscle tone, six-pack abs, and defined arms.

"Do you like what you see?" he asked with a small smile.

"I haven't seen it all," I said boldly. I think I surprised us both.

"How much more do you want to see?" Corbin asked as the bed dipped beneath his body weight on the opposite side of the bed.

Before I could answer him, he captured my lips. His lips weren't gentle or as exploring as they had been last night. Today, he was demanding a response. He wanted to stake a claim and let me know how turned on he was.

As he continued kissing me, I felt hands caressing my feet, then my calves. "So much muscle," Wyatt hummed appreciatively. "So strong and beautiful." His hands trailed the inside of my knees, and I jumped at the unexpected pleasure it brought. His hands continued to trace feather-light caresses up the inside of my thighs. I opened my legs up with no shame.

I heard him tsk at me as his lips hovered over my thighs and felt the heat of his breath. Combined with his knowing touch, it was driving me insane. I drove my hips up and off the bed.

"Tell us what you want, baby," Corbin insisted once more. "Tell us how far you want us to go. This is all about you."

"I need you both naked," I gasped. "I want Wyatt's fingers in me, and his mouth on my clit. I need you biting and sucking on my nipples."

"That's what we wanted to hear, sweetheart," Wyatt hummed in approval moments before I felt the cool air on me and my underwear being removed.

I heard Corbin groan, and my head turned to see him shucking off his clothing, not caring where they landed. "Tell me how she tastes," Corbin licked his lips seconds before I felt Wyatt give me a broad stroke of his tongue.

I cried out, my eyes closing, my hips arching up towards his mouth. My body was on fire. I needed to quench this thirst within me. They were the only ones capable of doing that right now.

Wyatt moaned against me, the vibrations of his mouth made my clit throb in pleasure and pain. "So good," Wyatt finally stated after several strokes of his skillful tongue. "She's so wet for us, feel her, Corbin."

Wyatt shifted, so his mouth was latched sideways on my clit. He alternated between flicking his tongue on my nub and circling it. Before his words could sink in, I felt Corbin insert a finger in me.

He hissed out, and I looked up at him. His eyes were dark with passion and desire. "She is so damn tight too." He bit his lip before he slipped another finger inside me. I felt myself stretching against his fingers, sucking him into my body. He groaned out a mixture of pleasure and pain. He pumped them in and out as Wyatt continued his ministrations. "Her tight little cunt will milk us dry."

Wyatt's hum of pleasure and Corbin's dirty words elicited another carnal response in me.

I was shocked to feel the build of tension in my lower belly so soon. I moaned out my pleasure. "Please," I whimpered.

"Your wish is my command," Corbin growled as he curled his fingers up. His fingers found my G-spot. It was something I had only heard of but thought it was too elusive and challenging to find. As his fingers expertly circled that special place, I felt the pressure inside build to astronomical proportions.

I had only ever known the gentle build to a delicious release up until this moment. When the tight ball of pressure unwound, it wasn't a calm ball unraveling. It was more like an explosion. An explosion akin to fireworks, firing off behind my eyelids. I screamed out my orgasm, seeing the bright colors fill my vision.

I heard them both groan out in pleasure as Corbin gently withdrew his fingers from me. He immediately placed his lips on mine, sipping from my lips as if he were tasting a fine wine. Wyatt put his whole mouth on me once more, gently licking my juices from between my thighs. When his tongue touched my clit, I shuddered and whimpered.

My whole body was shaking from the after-effects of the delicious release. When some of the tremblings subsided, I pulled my lips from Corbin's and nuzzled his neck like a contented kitten, purring against his throat.

"I want to return the favor," I informed him before climbing down his body.

I admired his body as I settled between his thighs.

"This was about you, baby," Corbin feebly protested.

"I want to do this," I insisted before I looked over my shoulder at Wyatt. "I want you to take me from behind Wy," I looked at him through heavy lids.

My body was humming with exquisite languidness, but I was still hungry for more. Having both of them work to bring me pleasure filled me with a sense of thirst I feared would never be quenched.

"Are you sure, Ave?" Wyatt asked, suddenly the man I was accustomed to and not the demanding lover I had known just moments ago.

"Yes," I said without hesitation as I took Corbin's cock into my hands. He hissed as I felt his warm, smooth flesh jump between my fingers.

It almost felt like an out-of-body experience. I couldn't believe I had my hands wrapped around Corbin. He was Trevor's older brother! A part of me was fully aware that we were adults, but the other part of me still couldn't believe that this was Corbin, the boy and teenager I'd grown up with. For a brief second, I couldn't separate our past from the present. Sure, we'd played games and hung out, but it had been some time since I considered him a friend. As we got older, we'd grown apart, and he was just "my boyfriend's older brother."

He gasped my name, yanking me from my astonishing thoughts.

I licked him several times, hoping to lubricate him before stroking him up and down. He really was an impressive size. He continued to make sounds in the back of his throat with each stroke down his steel length. I looked at him through my eyelashes as I finally lowered my mouth down on him.

He bucked against me, groaning out my name, a sound between a prayer and an entreaty. I tried to fit his whole length into my mouth, opening my throat up wide as I felt the tip of him hit the back. I pushed down further, feeling the tears enter my eyes as I tried to take more of him down.

I felt Wyatt's reverent hands on my hips, his thighs against my own. I released Corbin's cock from my mouth and looked over my shoulder and noticed Wyatt was sliding a condom down his length. He pushed the tip of himself in me, and I nearly gasped. He was thick. I could feel him deliciously stretch me out as he pressed inside me further. I knew he wasn't entirely in before he hissed out a curse.

"You weren't lying, bro," he hissed out. "I don't think I felt anything tighter in my life," he cursed out softly.

His words only incited me. I felt... empowered and inflamed by his words. I pushed my hips back into him as I went back to work, sucking on Corbin, up and down. I felt his hand tangled in my hair as Wyatt groaned out in pleasure.

Wyatt was so thick, and he was stretching me full. I knew he was waiting for me to get used to his size, but I was almost wild with desire. I needed more. I leaned forward and then slammed back on him. I heard him curse before he began to drive into me with long, deep strokes. With every thrust of his hips forward, I pressed down on Corbin's cock.

I relished the feel of us as we worked in perfect symphony, finding a rhythm that pleased us all. I could think of nothing but the feeling of Corbin in my mouth and Wyatt's full, deep thrust as he learned my body. Wyatt gripped my hips with the perfect amount of gentleness and strength.

"Holy shit," Corbin bit out. "I'm going to come."

"Me too," Wyatt groaned out. He leaned forward, bracing my hips with one hand while his arm reached around me. My still sensitive clit throbbed and jumped as his fingers knew precisely which moves to take me to the edge once more.

"Do you want to spit or swallow, baby?" Corbin said in a strained voice.

"Let me taste all of you, give me every drop," I mewled around him as Wyatt's hips began to slam into me. His movements were frantic and wild, while his fingers rubbed out a rhythm my body seemed to recognize.

With a few more flicks of his fingers, I was pushed off the edge and spiraling down the abyss once more. I moaned as Corbin roared out his release. His cum nearly choked me as I found my own surrender. I quickly sucked him down as Wyatt continued to drive into me a few more times.

"Oh Avery," he cried out as I felt him buck against me. He grabbed both of my hips almost painfully as he drove into me a few more times.

When he collapsed on top of me, I finally collapsed myself. I laid my head on Corbin's firm thigh, trying to catch my breath. I could feel the subtle sheen of sweat clinging to our bodies. My limbs quivered with the aftershocks of the mind-blowing sex I'd just had with my childhood friends, turned now into...partners...lovers?

Corbin reached down and began to gently push my hair off of my face. My scalp tingled at his touch, having always been sensitive to my hair being played with. Goosebumps erupted across my skin as I moaned in pleasure.

I felt Wyatt finally shift slightly off of me. His fingers lazily drew against my sensitive post-coitus skin.

"Is this okay?" Wyatt suddenly asked as I felt him tense beside me.

I felt Corbin tense, too, and I was confused for a moment. I then recalled the words I'd told them, how I hated cuddling after sex. It was true. It always felt too intimate, too wrong, like a great big lie. But with them it was different. It felt *too* right.

"More than okay," I said with a yawn. "I've never done that before." My eyelids suddenly felt heavy.

"Made lo-" Corbin started to say in amusement before he hastily corrected himself. "Had sex with two men?"

I laughed as I shifted my arm to trace his other thigh with my nails. I heard him hiss and felt his skin twitch beneath my fingertips. "That too," I said dryly. "What I meant to say was I've never orgasmed so closely together."

"Never?" Wyatt asked incredulously.

"Nope." I yawned once more. "Sometimes I would have sex eight, nine times a week, and if I was lucky, I might orgasm once."

"You're kidding, right?" Corbin inquired with a frown in his voice. "That much sex and only one orgasm. Was he...were they five-minute men?"

I shook my head. "No," I said, suddenly feeling awkward

about talking about my past sex life with two men that I'd just had sex with—one of which was the brother of my ex. Was there a period of waiting that should be observed, I thought? Or should I never talk about it?

"Talk to us, Ave," Wyatt urged gently. "We all have a past, and as long as we're not bragging or criticizing each other, it's good for us to know what you like, and you should know what *we* like."

"Sometimes it felt like we spent hours in bed," I finally said after much deliberation. "Him lasting was rarely the issue. It was me not being able to respond. I'm broken. Don't be surprised if I can't come next time. And I'm okay with that, though. It felt really, really nice."

I heard Corbin scoff while Wyatt laughed, placing a kiss on my shoulder. "You're not broken, sweetheart," Wyatt soothed. "In fact, your body is very responsive. I liken sex to music. If you don't play the rights notes, the song will never sound right. But if you learn to read the sheet music and continue practicing, a symphony can be made."

I smiled; leave it to the musician to correlate music to making love. "Do you still sing and play, Wyatt?" I suddenly asked as I closed my eyes, lulled to slumber by Corbin's hands in my hair and Wyatt's fingers tracing my back. The warmth of their bodies surrounding me made me feel like I was in a cocoon.

"Yep. Do you want me to play for you sometime?" Wyatt sounded pleased by my question.

I think I mumbled a response, but I wasn't sure. Sleep had pulled me under.

◻

I didn't know how long I slept, all I knew was the next time I blinked, my eyes opened to a dusky room. I tried to seek out the source of what had woken me. Corbin and Wyatt were still in bed with me. I was cradled on Corbin's chest, and his arm was still embracing my head, his fingers weaved through my hair. Wyatt was pressed to my back, and his leg was draped over my thighs, with his arms wrapped around my waist.

I heard the slamming of a door and a loud feminine yell. Then a softer, quieter, male voice. I was still trying to figure it all out when our door was flung open. I cried out in surprise. Both men stirred beside me.

Emery's mouth popped open before a cruel laugh escaped her. I saw her eyes narrow, and jealousy and cruelness lurked in the depths. "I always knew you were a slut."

I was still stunned by her presence in my doorway, and I was thankful someone had draped us in sheets.

"Says the girl who stole her sister's fiance and who pledged her sorority by giving all the frat boys blow jobs." Corbin's voice was thick with sleep, but as I looked at him above me, his eyes remained closed. "Get out of here, Em. Avery doesn't need your brand of poisoning. You already did enough." He kissed the top of my head and gently squeezed me.

"Sorry, guys," I heard Easton say.

I startled, feeling my cheeks redden. It was one thing to be caught like this by my sister, but something entirely different being found like this by Easton.

"She burst in while I was bathing Isa and she wouldn't leave," he said, standing behind Emery. "I guess we need to lock our doors around here. Now, please leave, Emery." His voice was clipped, stern. So not like his usual demeanor.

"What did you do to Trevor?" Emery ignored them, her gaze on me still.

"Get out of here, Em," Wyatt sat up, making sure the sheet stayed draped on Corbin and me. "Why are you such a miserable bitch? You wanted Trevor. You got him. You win. It's too bad he doesn't love you like you thought he would, but it's nothing to do with us."

"He's not eating again, and it's your fault, Avery! He won't even let me...help him!" Emery shrieked out like a wild banshee, causing Isa to cry out in displeasure from the other room. Easton gave Em a dirty look and left to go to the baby.

"Not my problem," I deadpanned. "You wanted him. Have him. Why are you so worried about him, when just this morning you were scheming on how to get Axel, Corbin, Wyatt, Easton, and Kingston in bed?"

I heard the two men scoff in disbelief.

"Trevor was always mine!" she hissed, her face turning red. "You've always wanted what I wanted. That's why you chased after Corbin and Wyatt next. You're just so desperate for my scraps, aren't you?"

Corbin and Wyatt laughed as they looked at each other.

"You chased, but we never wanted you. In order for us to be your scraps, you would have had to have us first," Corbin said cruelly. "The sad thing is, Emery, you've never been satisfied with what you had. You've always hated being a twin. You hated sharing the spotlight, and then it grew into something poisonous. Once you realized Avery was perfectly capable of surviving without you and was able to forge her own path, that still wasn't enough. Your obsession with Avery is unhealthy. You leave toxicity everywhere you go, and the sad thing is, you have no interest in recognizing your own failures. You need to work on that or you'll never be happy."

"Now, please leave," Wyatt stated. "This is the last time we're going to ask you nicely. The next time I will be removing you forcefully."

Emery huffed and turned on her heel before whirling towards me once more. "This isn't over, and you best believe I'm going to tell Aunt Pam and Aunt Carol you're screwing both boys."

I felt my face pale, and she smiled smugly, knowing she got me. Almost.

I lifted my chin. "Go for it. They already can't believe half the words that come out of your mouth. You have lied so much and so often, I'm not even sure you know what the truth is anymore."

"We'll see," she scoffed before turning away once more, passing Easton who'd come back into the room.

"Well, she's a delightful woman isn't see?" he said dryly as he situated Isa on his shoulder. She was dressed in just a blanket.

I looked over at the clock. It was nearly dinner time. "Holy crap! Was Isa awake when you got here? I should have fed her an hour ago."

Easton shook his head and smiled at me. "I came back a couple of hours ago, and she was still sound asleep. I went and got some milk from Steph and came back. I woke her, and she ate like a champ." He placed Isa on the bed.

"Hey, pretty baby," I cooed as I sat up. "Were you a good girl for...Easton?" I asked. She was wide awake and very alert. It warmed me to see the color returning to her face.

"Uncle Easton," Easton said gruffly. He was shifting uncomfortably, and I looked down to realize the sheets had pooled at my lap. I squeaked, reddening once more.

Wyatt and Corbin laughed at my expense, and I glared at them.

Wyatt shrugged. "What? It's Easton. He's a doctor, it's not the first time he's seen a pair of tits."

"Not all tits are the same," I huffed.

Easton actually let out a cough of laughter. "So true, and I have to tell you, Ave, you have the best I've ever seen."

I gaped at his unnatural forwardness.

"I'm gonna get our little girl here some clothes and a diaper. Get dressed, Avery. You skipped breakfast *and* lunch. You can't skip dinner, too," Easton commanded before he whistled out of the room.

"He's rarely bossy." Corbin laughed at my dumbfounded look. "If he gets bossy, it only means he cares."

"You know he likes you, right, Ave?" Wyatt asked tentatively as I extracted myself from the bed, resituating Isa so she now laid further down the bed.

I looked over at him, unsure how to respond. I cleared my throat. "Yeah, I guess so."

"And how do you feel about him?" Corbin gently probed.

"Besides the fact that he's scary smart and sweet?" I hedged. I was usually timid after sex. I trained in gymnastics for years and had no compunction jumping, flipping, and everything else in miniscule fabric, but completely nude, I felt self-conscious.

I was surprised to see my duffel bag and several of my shopping bags piled in the corner near my dresser. Now that I could look at the room better, I noticed the king-sized bed I'd just left and the two nightstands on either side. A large vanity, complete with a dresser, was across from the bed between the bedroom door and a closed door which I padded over to. I found a small tiled bathroom with a stand-up shower, small vanity, and toilet.

I needed a quick shower. I had ran last night and just spent part of my afternoon having sex with two men. I blushed and looked at myself in the mirror above the sink. I didn't recognize myself. My hair was wild, and my amber eyes shone brightly. There was a flush to my skin I never recalled seeing.

"You look beautiful," Wyatt murmured from the doorway.

I jumped, yelped, and then ducked my head. "Thanks," I murmured shyly.

"Too bad the shower is too small for all three of us," Corbin stood behind Wyatt.

I tried to hurriedly avert my eyes as I noticed they were both in their naked glory, and both looked to be more than ready to go again.

I heard Corbin chuckle, and I refrained from sticking my tongue out at him.

"You didn't answer our question," Wyatt gently prodded me as he shifted from foot to foot. He suddenly looked...hesistant.

"What question?" I asked, seriously mystified.

"Easton?" Corbin reminded me.

"Oh. Yeah," I said before I closed my eyes and sighed. This was so not a normal conversation. Typically, the man you were with wouldn't like the thought of you with another man. Yet Axel, and now Corbin and Wyatt, seemed concerned about whether or not I could accept all of them like they were a package deal.

I had told Axel I would try, and after meeting the guys, I understood how tightly their lives were woven together. It bothered me that Jade and Natalie could have had a perfect thing going if they had only accepted them all.

"Yeah," I said finally with a nod, feeling the conviction deep within.

I could imagine, in the grand scheme of things, Easton would be the man I needed when I wanted to decompress in silence. There had been times I wanted company but *silent* company. Sylvia never knew how to let me process things without pushing. Sometimes I had needed that, and other times I needed the exact opposite.

"Really?" Wyatt asked hopefully.

I nodded before I turned on the shower. "Yeah. He's smart, and he doesn't seem to have to fill the silence with chatter. Sometimes I like the silence but with company," I clarified.

Corbin flashed me one of his brilliant smiles.

I smiled crookedly at him before I stepped inside the stall, turning around to rinse myself. I didn't have my toiletries, so the little travel size containers would have to do for now. I was hungry, and the faster I washed, the faster I could eat.

"We'll be right back," Wyatt said over the sound of the water. "We're gonna hop in the other showers."

"Okay," I called over my shoulder.

Why did this feel so...normal? Emery's words made me tense for a minute, but then I shook myself out of my anxious thoughts. I'd cross that road when or if I got to it.

Chapter 18

The walk from the cabins to the central area of the campground was a long one but refreshing on such a beautiful day, but I imagined we'd need to think of alternative means of transport when the weather got colder.

"On our next supply run, do you think we can find some quads or ATVs?" I asked as I carried Isa against my chest and held onto Wyatt's hand. I was somewhat surprised and pleased at his insistence on taking my hand as we all walked. "I know we have a few here, but not enough."

"It on the list," Wyatt confirmed. "Dad says they have a few, but he wants the people on security to have the use of them first."

"Understandable. When is the next run?" I asked next.

When they didn't answer fast enough—even Easton!—I looked at them and saw something pass between them. "I don't like lies," I immediately bristled.

Corbin sighed. "Tomorrow morning."

He wasn't telling me everything. "And you guys are heading out and leaving me behind," I concluded, understanding dawning. "I'm a grown woman. I can decide whether or not I go."

True, I had an aversion to killing the infected. It still made me sick doing it, but I knew I was good at it. I wasn't even cocky about it. It was just a fact. I would be needed more out there than here.

Plus, the idea of sitting here and worrying about them nearly overwhelmed me. I didn't want to lose them yet. I had a somewhat inane belief that, if I were there, I could control the situation better.

Wyatt sighed. "It's safe here. We just want you to stay safe."

"It's my decision to make," I seethed.

"You're not trained," Corbin said half-heartedly. From the look in his eyes, I had a feeling he hadn't been behind the idea.

Lightbulbs, complete with sound effects, went off in my head. "Axel," I seethed. "And you and you." I pointed at both Wyatt and Easton.

Easton immediately ducked his head, but Wyatt stared back at me defiantly. "There's nothing wrong with wanting to keep you safe. We don't want to worry about you *and* focus on the mission."

I snorted. "I can handle myself just fine. I don't need you worrying about me. In fact, if it weren't for me, I'm pretty sure Kingston and Felix wouldn't be here! I know you guys have shared women in the past, women you've worked with. Did you wrap *them* in cotton balls and stop them from doing their job?"

I heard Corbin hide a laugh, before Wyatt and Easton glared at him.

"That was their jobs, Ave, and they were trained," Wyatt shot back.

"Like Natalie?" I yelled. "It was her fault that Kingston nearly got bit because she didn't finish her kill. Like Jade? Because I'm pretty sure she was running away from the fight, leaving her men behind when she fell, and I had to save her neck, too! I may not be trained like you guys, but I have great instincts. I didn't place first in Nationals by being weak.

Sparring is all about strategy, and I'm effin fantastic at that!"

I saw all three men tense. "Why didn't you tell us about Jade and Natalie?"

"And have them accuse me of being jealous of them?" I scoffed. "Especially after I found out they were with you in the past. You guys already seemed to know what those girls were capable of doing. Did I really need to provide you with more evidence?" I ranted.

By then, we'd reached our destination, and I knew exactly who I needed to see. I began to jog, somewhat mindful of Isa, as I climbed the porch steps. It looked like they had just started dinner. Uncle Mitch was sitting at a table with Aunt Carol, Steph, Aunt Pam, Eddie, Axel, and Kingston.

I marched right up to the table and stopped in front of my uncle.

"Avery!" he cried out in delight before he carefully embraced me.

Uncle Mitch was a darker version of Wyatt. Wyatt may have inherited most of his mother's coloring, but he had his dad's good looks and green eyes.

"Hi, Uncle Mitch," I tried to enthuse, but I was still fighting mad. "Can I talk to you?"

"About what, honey?" he asked in concern.

"I want to go on the run tomorrow," I insisted. "I'm of more use out there than here. That is," I turned to look at Steph, "if you won't mind watching Isa for me?"

I felt somewhat ashamed that I hadn't thought of Isa first. I almost felt like changing my mind. Almost.

"No," Axel merely said with a shake of his head.

Steph looked warily between us. "I'll watch her anytime."

"Me too," Aunt Pam said with zero compunction. She

almost seemed peeved that the men were ordering me about.

"You're not going out with my team," Axel said, his jaw ticking in annoyance.

I smiled sweetly at him. "Good thing you're not the only team lead here,then." I turned on my heel in search of Joe.

I totally took a wild guess who else was going, and from Axel's clenching jaw, I knew I had guessed right.

I saw Joe several tables down sitting with Cal, Sylvia, Phil, Jenny, Josh, Amy, and Chad.

"Tell her no!" I heard Wyatt yell from behind me.

The dining room fell silent, but I didn't care. I continued marching over to Joe's table, and with zero preamble, braced my fist on it. "I want to go on the supply run tomorrow, can I go with you?"

As expected, Joe looked over at Axel, and I could tell he was going to capitulate to Axel's desires.

"You can go with Chad and me," Felix volunteered from the other table before he looked around the room. "Jade, you can stay and do your other assignment."

"I don't take orders from you," Jade sneered.

I blinked in shock as the joking, mild mannered Filipino then blew up.

"And I don't want you to watch my six." Felix stood up and glared at her. "Avery has already proven herself. She saved my ass, your ass, and Kingston's ass. I nearly died because you ran. You ran!"

I couldn't blame him—I'd react the same way, if not worse. I hadn't even realized Felix was in that predicament due to her. I'd never trust her again, either.

"Avery, supply teams, on me!" Uncle Mitch boomed out.

I turned and unstrapped Isa from my chest. It came as no surprise that Aunt Pam was already right behind me, ready to take her. Then, like good little soldiers, we all stood and left the dining hall.

⬚

"You're not going!" Wyatt boomed the moment he came into the room.

I looked away from him, pretending like I hadn't heard him and began to sing to myself instead. It was something that had always annoyed the boys growing up.

I chose Rachel Platten's *Fight Song*, finding it befitting for the situation.

"Big mistake," Corbin whispered rather loudly to Kingston. "Any time you tell Avery she can't do something, she'll go out of her way to prove you wrong."

"Is she singing *Fight Song*?" Kingston snickered.

I saw Wyatt, Axel, and Easton glare at him.

We waited as everyone else filed into the recreation center. The building had a movie room, a sizable gym, a kitchen, and a large meeting area. People came to play bingo and other games when it wasn't in use. Nana and Pop-pop had rented the space for guests who wanted to "go large" without the price tag the wedding hall had. They utilized it for baby showers, bridal showers, meetings, etc. Comfortably, the area could fit one hundred people.

I nearly scoffed aloud when I saw Trevor walk into the room. He had zero training, besides the target practice we did as kids and teens. With my martial arts, I was way more than a minor step above him.

I took a seat on one of the tables, not bothering to pull out a chair. Bane trotted over to my side immediately. I knew Axel had taken a tour after lunch today, and Bane was all too eager to accompany him. I smiled down at the big dog and stroked his head. He groaned and curled up at my feet. "Lazy boy," I teasingly chided. "Are you worn out, bud?"

"He's a great dog," Kingston praised as he took the spot next to me on the table. "We kicked up some deer when we were out. He took chase, but when we called, he came right back."

I knew Kingston had no issue with me accompanying them. Wyatt and Easton just wanted to protect me, and I understood that, but they didn't understand that I couldn't sit by idly waiting for their return.

I smiled. "Good boy, Bane."

"I'm kind of jealous we didn't come and get you. Now I want a dog," Kingston confessed. "I've always wanted one, but it wouldn't have been fair leaving them so often, so I never got one."

"Maybe we can find another local shelter," I said enthusiastically before I frowned. "It's been a few days. We should probably do that sooner than later, actually. Otherwise, there will be a lot of poor animals dying for no reason. A lot of them may have been abandoned."

A thoughtful look entered Kingston's eyes before a wide smile spread across his face. "I think I have a solution."

I didn't have the time to ask, because the last person filed into the room, followed by Uncle Mitch. He closed the door and looked at everyone slowly. His eyes landed on me in contemplation before swinging to Axel. "Why is it you don't want Avery to accompany us on the supply run?"

"She has no training," Axel clipped out, the nerve in his jaw still twitching.

"Maybe not the training you went to," I scoffed. "But neither has a handful of people in this room. I was a high contender for a spot on the USA Olympic Tae Kwon Do team. I've been trained in martial arts for the last eight years. I also held my own on my way here. I think helping three people out of sticky situations has more than proved my worth."

"You making it out here was just pure luck," Natalie sneered. "If you didn't have Axel, Felix, Chad, and Josh with you, you wouldn't have even made it here."

I turned, giving her a saccharine smile. "Is that why I had to help assist getting you out of a situation due to your ignorance? You risked not only your team, but the group as a whole when you decided to enter that mall without doing any reconnaissance first. And if I hadn't been there, Kingston probably would have been injured or worse."

Beside me, Kingston gnashed his teeth, and I gave him an apologetic smile. I guessed now I should've told him about that yesterday.

I turned back to Natalie. "You took down that infected and didn't even check to see if the threat was neutralized. You had no focus in the heat of battle and nearly caused your teammate his demise. So let's not pretend you're superior to me because you had a different type of training than I did."

"You have no proof of your accusations," Natalie derided. "I'm sorry if you found out about my previous involvement with Alpha Team," she scoffed. "Are you mad that you couldn't satisfy one man, when I could satisfy them all?" she pouted mockingly.

I tried not to let her words affect me, but I felt them.

"Shut up, Natalie," Corbin snapped. "Our arrangement was a short one, and you were found wanting. This discussion did not and should not have been taken there. If we're talking about competency in a professional aspect, you sadly lack in that area, too. There's a reason you got kicked off Delta Team and were about to be removed from Bravo. You're incompetent, and I no longer think you're capable of going out until you've had some type of retraining."

"I second that decision. Until Natalie and Jade are retrained, we don't need them out in the field. They can be used in a security aspect here at the camp," Kingston said coldly.

"I'm not staying behind because I threaten your new little plaything," Jade sneered.

"You're taking her word against mine?" Natalie screeched at the men. "She just wants my spot."

"Avery's speaking the truth," Felix said just as coldly. "You and Jade put us in danger and nearly cost me and Kingston our lives. I saw your inability to follow through with your kill, Natalie. Avery didn't leave my side as you did, Jade, and then she saved your neck as well. I much rather have her have my six, any day, than both of you."

"Is she putting out for you, too?" Jade scoffed. "Is she that manipulative you're willing to let an untrained girl take our spots? Poor Avery. I'm sorry we threaten you." Jade turned towards me with a glare.

"Why should she feel threatened by you?" Amy scoffed finally. "You both were only useful to them after nearly a year of no action. By then, anyone would've worked." At Kingston's scoff, she gave him an apologetic smile and shrug. "Sweetie, I know you all too well, don't forget that. You were merely a means to an end."

Amy was a pretty girl, in that girl-next-door sort of way, with short black hair cut in a sleek bob, fair skin, and large hazel eyes. She was average in height, but physically built, like she did Crossfit every day.

Amy turned back towards the girls. "You were intimidated by Avery before you even met her. I heard you ask Wyatt and Corbin to remove her pictures from their footlockers. You went as far as to remove them yourselves. How did that work for ya? That's right, you were both dropped."

I smiled at Amy. I hadn't had that much interaction with her, but she seemed really lovely, and I knew she was like a sister to the guys. She might be little for a badass, but she watched over them, and I knew they held an affection for her.

Uncle Mitch finally cleared his throat. "Okay... well, I'm not sure what rabbit trail we just went down, and I'm not sure I *want* to know." He was looking at the guys before his eyes fell back on me. I felt my cheeks redden. I didn't need my uncle speculating about my involvement with the guys. "Saying that, I for one am confident Avery can handle herself. She may not have a military background, but she didn't make the National Team by resting on her laurels."

He turned to Jade and Natalie. "Ladies, the distrust from your previous team members alarms me, so you can stay back on security here. Both of you will follow Eddie's commands, just as you followed your superiors' in the military."

Jade and Natalie began to protest, but Uncle Mitch held up a hand. "This is not up for debate. My brothers and I feared something like this might happen one day. We discussed the possibility of having to be responsible for a new community. We made plans, and we agreed on a lot of things. If there is any discord in the community, we won't be able to make it successful. I know war, ladies. I know what it's like to put your trust in your team. If you have people in this room not trusting you, then until you prove differently, I have to reassign you.'

Natalie and Jade looked pissed, but they remained silent.

"Follow the rules I set for you now," Uncle Mitch continued. "Help contribute to the community, and we keep you on. If not, then I'll put your removal up for a vote. As co-owner of these lands, I have the final say, but those who'd be voting alongside me are Corbin and Avery, since they're the eldest and the next in line for these lands."

I gaped at Uncle Mitch. That was all news to me. I had thought it odd when he had invited me up to the house earlier and not my twin. Did fourteen minutes really warrant a more significant say?

I looked over at Corbin, and it seemed like this was news to him, too.

"This is all a learning curve," Uncle Mitch explained, "and I'm sure things will change as we go, but there is no negotiation on this matter. Scott and Bryan made it abundantly clear that, in the event they weren't able to meet here, their firstborns would take their place."

"And if something were to happen to Corbin and Avery while they're out?" BJ frowned. "Is it even wise that they go on runs at all?"

Uncle Mitch smiled. "Then the next in line will be Trevor and you, BJ, but let's not worry about that now. Let's talk about this supply run so we can get back to dinner."

"Dad," Wyatt fumed. "If Avery is that important, she should stay behind."

"About supply... I think I have a solution that may work for everyone," Kingston spoke up. "We all know sustainability is important for us. We seem to have a lot in storage right now, but we can't grow flour from flour or plant beef and expect it to grow more beef. I saw the heritage seeds while we were reorganizing the storage buildings, but it's May, and no seeds have been planted except for the seeds in the greenhouses. If Josh is game, I think he could tell you where fields should be tilled, and things like where the wheat should be grown. His Grandpa did agriculture farming.

"I also notice that, except for the fish and wildlife, we don't have any other domesticated animals. People died— people who had farms. Chad's adoptive family had a livestock farm. They raised cattle, sheep, pigs, and chickens. If he's willing to switch teams, I think Chad, Avery, and I can drive around the local area and start collecting these animals. We don't know if the infected would show interest in them, and we don't know if their owners have fed or watered them in the last few days, so I think it's better if we go sooner rather than later."

I nearly smiled at my theory being proven correct; Kingston *did* hold his own kind of intelligence. An intelligence that he hid with big smiles, jokes, and a fake attitude of not caring about much.

"I can definitely share my knowledge," Chad said. "You have the land and most of the stuff you need in place. The horses don't need the west pasture, right?"

Uncle Mitch smiled. "We thought we could live off the land, but I do see the benefits of getting domesticated animals to raise and eat. Donny and his son Samuel can go with you. They know the area well and should be able to locate the farms rather easily. I'll have Eddie work on moving the horses out of the west pasture and move them to the east one."

He paused and looked around the room. I was sure he hadn't had time to meet everyone yet. "Josh?" he called. Josh raised his hand, already nodding before Uncle Mitch could say anything.

"I'm sure I can come up with a solid game plan," Josh said. "If someone can accompany me after dinner and show me what seeds are available, where you have fields, and what equipment you have on hand. I'd also like to look at your greenhouses. It's not too late to start our planting, but we should get on it really soon."

Uncle Mitch smiled again and clapped his hands. "Excellent! Axel, can you come up with a new schedule and rearrange the teams to reflect the changes tonight? If anyone else has any other helpful suggestions, please bring them to me. Oh, and also, if anyone else has any hidden talents or knowledge, it would be good to know. Now, let's go eat!"

I smiled at Kingston as Corbin squeezed my hand. I didn't need to look over at Wyatt, Axel, and Easton to know that they were still upset at me.

Sorry, not sorry, boys!

◊

Hours later, my victory felt hollow. Axel, Wyatt, and Easton weren't talking to me. Kingston and Corbin jumped into their own plans to improve our community.

Usually when I was this upset, I would run and hit the heavy bag, but that hadn't helped, so now I was in the kitchen. Mom had always found solace in there. She rarely ate what she made—being a model and all—but we always knew when she was upset or stressed, because we'd have treats galore for days on end.

Tonight at dinner, Aunt Carol had said something about having no bread and said she wanted to make some for lunches tomorrow. After a quick inventory of the pantry and fridges, I determined I could make some biscuits to freeze until we needed them tomorrow and make a few loaves of bread. I didn't think my aunts would mind. I even pulled out the ingredients for some double chocolate chip cookies.

The kitchens in the wedding lodge were beyond a dream. My mom would have been in...well, she would have been ecstatic. The number of appliances they had here was such a luxury to have on hand. They had four large industrial mixers, and in no time, I had them all going.

The mixtures would yield at least sixteen loaves of bread. Once they were done kneading, I'd divide them and let them rise individually.

I had my phone plugged in and charging. I might not be able to make calls on it or scroll through my social media, but at least it still had all my music. I had it connected to a bluetooth, and my 80s music poured from the speakers.

When I was around ten or so, Mom finally allowed me in the kitchen with her. She had a thing for 80s music. I could remember plenty a night that she would blast some Bryan

Adams, The Police, Eurythmics, and several other hit groups. She didn't like to talk, just sing. Loudly and off-key. It was in these moments I felt closest to her.

"There you are," Kingston's voice startled me from behind.

I yelped, and Bane barely moved. I looked at my dog. "What kind of guard dog are you?" I asked him. He lifted his head and sighed at me before laying back down next to Isa in her portable swing.

Unbeknownst to me, Easton had gone crazy in the baby department at the mall. He had picked up things like a crib, bassinet, playpen, swing, portable swing, high chair, booster seat, car seat, toys, books, playmats, baby bathtub, bouncer, activities saucer, and things called a jumperoo and mamaroo. Why a baby that small needed so many things was beyond me, but I was more than thankful for his efforts, because I'd only thought about diapers and clothing.

Kingston chuckled. "What'cha doing?" he asked as he jumped up on one of the prep tables.

I thought about glossing it over, but then I decided to tell him the truth. I wanted to get to know Easton, Kingston, and Axel more. Maybe if I opened up the lines of communication, they would too.

"My mom used to love to bake when she was stressed or wanted to contemplate on life. When she was in that mood, we knew not to disturb her. When I was about ten, she allowed me to come to help her," I explained. "She'd listen to 80s music and just bake and bake until whatever she was trying to work out...just did. I think that's why I've never been one to vocalize much when I'm stressed. I like peace and quiet. Sometimes, when I want to feel like I'm close to my mom again, I bake.

"I know the guys are upset with me. I understand why, but I can't change who I am. I tried for a little while before, and I was miserable. Trevor had always wanted me but in Emery's packaging. Emery loved her designer clothes. She cared about fashion, was a girly girl. I was a tomboy, still am, actually. For him, I changed for a little while. I made an effort to buy clothes he'd like to see on me. I bought the shoes with five-inch heels. I wore a ton of makeup and tried to portray the image he wanted me to have."

I shrugged. "It got old after a while," I continued. "I like dressing up from time to time, wearing heels and makeup on occasion, but it wasn't practical. I'm an athlete." I looked at him and smiled gently. "I never understood how calm my mom and Aunt Pam were every time they kissed their husbands' goodbye. I learned to cope with Dad gone so often, sure. But I can't just send you guys off with a kiss tomorrow, knowing I could be out there with you all, too."

Kingston looked at me in contemplation for a little while before cocking his head to the side. "So, this kiss you planned tomorrow, was it going to be like a kiss you give to your brother, or a quick peck on the lips? Or are we talking a duel of tongues?" he asked with a mischievous glint.

I laughed and pushed at his chest. He dramatically fell back and groaned.

"Since I'm going *with* you tomorrow, I guess you'll never know," I said smugly as I stopped the mixers.

I pulled the dough out and put it on my floured surface. I used a dough scraper to divide the mixture into four equal parts. Once that was done, I placed them in the large prepared bread pans and covered them with wet cloths to rise.

"What a tease." He sighed theatrically. "What's the chocolate chips for?" He eyed the ten-pound bag of chocolate chips.

"Cookies!" I smiled, rolling my eyes.

"Really?" he asked excitedly.

"Really. Soon as I get done with the loaves of bread and

biscuits, I plan to bake some cookies."

"What do we have to do to make this happen sooner than later?" he asked excitedly.

I handed him the empty mixing bowls. "Can you handwash these?" I asked. "I'll need them for the cookies." Even though we had a restaurant-style dishwasher, I hadn't had a chance to figure out how it worked yet. The deep, large sinks worked just as well.

"Okay," he said with a shrug as he walked over to the wash rack. "Although, if you can make me some of your chocolate cake with peanut butter frosting, that would be even better."

I laughed once more. I never thought when I sent those cakes-in-a-jars for Wyatt and Corbin's team that I would actually meet them all one day.

"That was one of my mom's recipes. Maybe one day, I can find some mini Reeses Peanut Butter cups and make her cupcakes. It's one of Dad's favorites," I said, yearning to talk to him. How was he?

Kingston moaned. "I'm going to make it my mission to find them now!"

I contemplated his words for a moment. "It's crazy to think that we can't just go to the store anymore and get them just like that," I snapped my fingers. "A lot of the things we took for granted aren't going to be there anymore."

"Some of the FOBs, or locations, we went to made me get accustomed to making do with what we can get," he said with a lift of his shoulder. "There were some locations that we went completely dark, but I still kept checking my phone for messages or Facebook or Instagram and then would realize, oh yeah."

"I just got back on Facebook and Instagram a few months ago," I said as I carried all the loaves of bread to a tall, rolling bakers rack with sheet pans. "I kind of got used to not having them."

"Wyatt and Corbin were pretty upset that you unfriended them," Kingston said with a serious expression. "Now I know why they were. You really are one of a kind, Avery. Don't let people like Emery, Natalie, and Jade tear you down, okay? Don't feed into their insecurities and lies. We may have had a relationship with one or two females in the past, but none of them hold a candle to you. With you, it's different, even if Easton or I haven't kissed you yet." Then he frowned. "Wait, did you kiss my brother yet?"

And just like that, his mask was back on. I savored the words of his confession, but I knew he was done revealing himself for now.

"Well," I teased with a severe tone. "He did get to see my breasts."

Kingston watched me with narrowed eyes. "Girl, don't make me spank you for lying."

An impish feeling took hold of me. "I have three nipples. I dyed my landing strip purple. I have my hood pierced. And I lick all the frosting off of cupcakes before I throw away the cake."

The mixing bowl clamored in the sink, and he started running towards me. I squealed.

"Sometimes, I read the last chapter of a book to see if I'll like the book!" I said as I ran from him. I tried to keep the table between us, and I was a fast runner, but his legs seemed to be eating up the distance between us. "I drink straight from the milk carton. I-" my next words were cut off as he wrapped his arms around my waist, and in one swift movement, he had both of my hands trapped in one of his.

He pushed his hips against my rear and tugged my hands up so that I was forced to bend over one of the prep tables. I barely had time to comprehend his intention when his palm was coming down on my bottom.

"My brother did *not* see your breasts." *Whack.* "I'm sure you have two rather normal nipples." *Whack.* "Your landing strip's jet black, like the drapes." *Whack.* "You would never get your hood pierced, your nipples maybe, but not your hood." *Whack.* "No one just eats the frosting off a cupcake after the age of two." *Whack.* "You like surprises. Reading the last chapter would ruin the whole story." *Whack.* "You are too considerate of others to drink straight from the carton."

His spankings hurt at first. I had yelped and tried to fight him with every motion. I stopped when I realized how excited he was when he spanked me. And quickly, the pain was replaced with pleasure. I found myself moaning and thrusting my hips towards him by the end.

He seemed to notice it and stilled. He cursed softly. "You liked that, didn't you?"

"No," I breathed out my denial.

Whack.

"You liked that, didn't you?" He ground his hips against me, his cock hard as steel.

"Yes," I admitted, biting my bottom lip.

He growled out and reached around my waist. "If I dip my fingers inside you, will you be wet?" he asked as he cupped my core.

I was so confused by my reaction. I never thought I would like spankings. From time to time, Trevor would lightly tap me when he was taking me from behind, but it was never hard enough to sting, let alone cause pleasure.

"No," I moaned out.

Whack.

"Should I check?" he asked, sliding his hands up the

wide leg of my shorts. I found myself eagerly nodding as the words escaped me. His fingers hooked onto the edge of my panties, and before I could even think, his fingers were rubbing my slit.

He silently cursed, and he rubbed himself against me. He leaned his forehead against my neck. "So wet," he muttered, stroking me. "I want to pull your shorts and panties down and fuck you right now. Would you like that?"

I had just been with Corbin and Wyatt that afternoon! I had been more than satisfied, but I would be lying to myself, and him, if I didn't admit that I wanted him, too. I still wanted to know him, Easton, and Axel on a more personal level, but I couldn't deny that, for once, my body wasn't being ruled by my thoughts.

"Yes," I gasped as his two fingers slipped inside me. I felt my inner walls stretch around him.

He groaned out once more. "So ready... for me."

I heard the slamming of the back screen door and tried to scramble away from him quickly. He jumped back and moved over to the other side of the prep table. My heart sped up. I couldn't believe I had nearly allowed him to take me in the kitchen, where anyone could have walked in!

"I thought I saw the lights on in here," Aunt Carol said with a smile. "What are you two getting into?"

"Bread!" I blurted out. "Biscuits. And cookies!"

She raised a brow at me. "Okay."

I silently cursed at myself. *Way to be obvious! Because you definitely don't sound like you have something to hide!*

Kingston chuckled. I looked over at him, and he was casually leaning over the prep table with his chin resting on one of his hands. "Avery was just telling me that her mother had an amazing recipe for a chocolate cupcakes stuffed with mini Reeses Peanut Buttercups and a peanut butter frosting.

Avery used to send us these cakes-in-a-jar things, and I always looked forward to the chocolate with the peanut butter frosting, as did Axel. Easton liked the red velvet cakes with the cream cheese frosting. Corbin was boring and liked the white cake with this chocolate frosting. And Wyatt–"

"Wyatt would have liked a lemon cake with lemon cream cheese frosting," my aunt finished with a smile. "It surprises me you remembered all that, Kingston. I'd be lucky if Mitch even remembered my favorite flower, and we've been married for over thirty years!"

Kingston looked around dramatically before he held a finger up to his mouth. "Don't let the guys know that. I have a reputation to maintain," he said with a smile, but I had a feeling he was serious. He really liked playing the role he created. "Those men are more than the guys I work with. As much as we're together, they're my best friends and brothers. I'd die for them, why shouldn't I know what makes them tick?"

"Aww," Aunt Carol cooed. "You are the sweetest. Every time you guys Facetimed or called, I got the impression that you were the one always trying to get them in trouble. Now I know you're like a two-sided coin."

Kingston seemed genuinely uncomfortable for a moment before he laughed. He ran a hand through the riot of his blond curls. "As I said, it has to remain our secret."

"Oh, it will be!" Aunt Carol giggled like a schoolgirl. "Now, how can I help?" she wandered over to the baker's rack.

When her back was turned, the Kingston I knew lifted his fingers and slowly sucked them in his mouth before he winked at me. I felt heat infuse my cheeks.

I turned around quickly and moved back to my bread, fully expecting to be mortified by almost getting caught. However, underneath the chagrin was an underlying feeling of thrill. The possibility of getting caught sent a weird sense of excitement in me. I groaned. No wonder Kingston was an exhibitionist; the feeling almost gave you a high.

"Have you ever made biscuits from scratch, Aunt Carol?" I asked, turning to see Kingston still watching me from the wash rack as he started washing the bowls. I gave him a slow smile and determined he was getting too much joy out of my discomfort. Maybe I should raise the bar a little, I thought.

Chapter 19

"Mom," I called out. "We're home!"

"Holy crap, can you be any louder?" Emery snapped. "Seriously, you're not on the basketball court."

I rolled my eyes. "I wasn't that loud."

"Mom!" Emery screamed directly next to my ear. "We're home!"

I winced and covered my ears. "I wasn't that loud, Em!" I seethed.

Seriously, she'd been so hateful since I'd decided I was never returning to modeling. I even confronted her about seeing Marlon and me together. I asked her why she thought I had been crying. It had been nearly three weeks, and she still denied she was even there. She claimed that she didn't walk in on my photoshoot, saying I made it all up to ruin her career.

Everything I did or said seemed to set her off lately. I asked her to walk with Trevor and me to our favorite ice cream shop, and she just rolled her eyes. She said I wanted her to be fatter than me. I wasn't overweight, and with her clavicles protruding from her top and her ribs prominently on display– when she's undressed– she could use a whole gallon of ice cream.

I asked her if she wanted to go to the mall, to play at the arcades since Corbin offered to take us for a ride. She was excited about that until she found out that Corbin wasn't staying. Then she proceeded to tell me that Trevor and I were lame and needed to grow up. Hanging out at the mall was "so last year."

"You were, too," she hissed. *"I'm going up to my room. Don't bother me tonight."* Her phone rang and she answered it immediately. *"Hey, girl! What's up? Yes, I'd love to go to the mall. Awesome! What are you wearing?"* She ran up the stairs, and I rolled my eyes once more.

I was becoming an expert at rolling my eyes.

So it was lame when I suggested it, but it was cool again when one of her new friends asked her? Where did my best friend go? Did I do something wrong?

I moved into the kitchen, realizing that Mom still hadn't answered me. That was strange. She usually had our snacks ready for us by now. Emery complained because she felt like it was too "babyish," especially when she made 'ants on a log' or something just as fun. I still enjoyed it.

I dropped my backpack onto the island. "Mom?" I called again.

Maybe she was outside...

I headed towards the back. Sometimes I'd find Mom and Aunt Pam on the back deck drinking wine or coffee. Coffee was for most days. The wine was for the days they needed to "decompress." It was beautiful outside, so the likelihood they were outdoors was high.

My phone rang, and I smiled when I noticed it was BJ. "Hey, buddy!" I exclaimed. *I'd really missed him. We just dropped him off at the academy last week, but it felt like forever already.*

"Hey, Ave," his voice sounded glum.

"What's wrong?" I asked in concern.

"I hate it here," he mumbled. *"There's this girl, Lisa, and she's just so mean."*

"What did she do?" I huffed out. *I felt my protective instincts kick in.*

"She..." he began to tell me, but I froze.

My mom was lying on the floor. There was a big gash on the side of her head, and blood was pooling out of it and onto the tile floor. Her whole body was twitching and jerking in stiff movements. Her eyes were rolled up into the back of her head.

Without a thought, I hung up the call, and with shaking fingers, I dialed 9-1-1. "Emery!" I screamed as the phone rang on the other end. I rushed over to the stove and grabbed the towel off the bar. I balled it up and tried to remember what they'd taught us about first aid in summer camp.

"Emery!" I screamed again, tears streaming down my face, hands shaking so badly I could barely hold the phone up to my ear.

"9-1-1, what's your emergency?" a calm female voice sounded in my ear.

"My mom," I sobbed. "I came home, and she's bleeding from her head, and she's…she's having a seizure."

"Okay, sweetie," the woman said in a soothing tone. "Can you tell me where you live?"

I tried to take in deep calming breaths so she could understand me as I rattled off my address.

"Okay, great, sweetie," she said. "I'm sending you someone right now. Can you find something to apply pressure to the bleeding?"

"I…I have a towel," I sobbed.

"Good job. Can you tell me your name?" she asked calmly.

"Avery," I answered, not knowing why she was asking me such an inane question.

"What a pretty name, I'm Alice. Avery, can you tell me if your mom takes any medications?" she inquired in the same dulcet tones.

"She takes her vitamins," I cried and then remembered how tired she was lately and how her head hurt her a lot. "She's been tired," I continued. "Her head hurts her all the time. She takes

Tylenol for it."

"Okay, good, thank you, Avery." I could faintly hear the clacking of keys on her end of the phone. "Do you know how old your mother is?"

I closed my eyes. She'd just had a birthday. She had Emery and me when she was twenty. "She just turned thirty-three, two weeks ago." I tried in vain to wipe the tears from my eyes. I could barely see. "The towel is all bloody," I told the lady. "Should I go get another one?"

"Can you keep it there, Avery?" she inquired. "We need to try and keep the pressure on it. Are you all alone?"

"No," I sobbed. "Emery's home, my sister. I'll yell for her again."

"Okay, you do that, sweetie. I'll be right here," she soothed.

"Emery!" I screamed once more after I set the phone down on the floor. "Emery, please come down here with some towels!" I sobbed my voice catching.

"A little spilled milk isn't anything to cry about, squirt." Corbin came laughing into the room moments later.

I saw his face fall, and the color leech out of it. "Oh shit! What happened?" he yelled as he tore the shirt off over his head and ran over.

Some part of my adolescent brain got a flash of broad shoulders, a narrow waist, and a full chest. Huh. When had that happened?

"I don't know," I sobbed. "Mom was lying on the floor, and she hasn't stopped twitching since I came home."

"It's okay, Ave." He pressed in close to me. "She'll be okay. Aunt Isabella, you're going to be okay," he murmured to mom next.

He was always so sweet to Mom. When Dad and Uncle Scott were away, he always cut our grass or helped Mom around the house. Dad said he was a good boy, because he never had to be asked or told to help out as he did.

"I hope so," I cried.

"Hey Ave?" Trevor came skipping into the room. His gray striped shirt was hanging off his tiny frame. "What..." he stopped and immediately threw up all over the entrance of the kitchen.

He'd always hated the sight of blood. I wanted to go hug him and tell him it was okay, but I couldn't leave my mom.

"Trev, call 9-1-1," Corbin said calmly, his hands already covered in blood.

"I already did," I said, remembering Alice was on the other line. "Alice? You still there?" I asked as I picked up the phone.

"Hi, Avery. Did your sister come and give you more towels?" Alice asked.

"Corbin's here." I sniffled. "He has his shirt on it."

"Okay, good." I heard the smile in her tone. "Is Corbin a friend?"

"Yes, no, sort of. He's my cousin, sort of. His dad and my dad were adopted around the same time," I began to ramble. "My mom and his mom are best friends. We're cousins but not by blood. We used to be friends, but he found girls a few years ago. Mom says boys get crazy when their balls drop."

Alice laughed. I had no clue why. It made no sense to me. "That's very true. My son just turned fourteen, and he won't even go to the mall with his mama no more."

The doorbell rang.

"I think they're here," I told Alice.

"Okay, Avery," she said. "I'm going to hang on until I'm sure. Is that okay with you?"

"Yes." I drew in a deep, shuddering breath.

"Trevor, go get the door," Corbin called over his shoulder.

"It's for me!" Emery came yelling down the stairs. "Oh,

hello," I heard as she opened the door, followed by a murmuring of voices. "No," she exclaimed. "I didn't call you."

"Em," I heard Trev call weakly. "She's back here, ma'am," he directed to the people at the door.

I vaguely noticed that he was still shaken and pale and that he had already cleaned up his mess. Emery walked in the room and smiled at Corbin as she batted her eyelashes at him. Then her eyes widened. Her mouth dropped. An ear-piercing scream left her mouth.

I looked up to see the paramedics walk into the room. It took me a second to realize that their gait was off, their mouths were foaming, and blood-like tears were falling from their eyes.

"Run!" I screamed at Trevor as the paramedic went to lunge for him. Trevor rushed passed me and out the back door.

"Come on, Ave, Emery, we have to go!" I heard Corbin yell.

"No!" I screamed. "I can't leave my mom!"

"She'll be okay," he murmured. "Run, Avery, run!"

My alarm went off forty-five minutes before we needed to leave. I rolled over to turn it off but found Axel on that side of the bed. I frowned. I didn't remember him coming in last night. When Kingston and I had returned to the cabin, Axel and Wyatt still hadn't returned.

Corbin and Easton had pulled out their hard drives that had thousands of movies and tv series on them. They put on *House*, and I got sucked into the drama. I'd never watched it before, and we were on the fourth or fifth episode when Easton insisted that we all go to bed.

I was surprised when Kingston walked me to my room and kissed my forehead before wishing me goodnight. I fully expected him to want to join me, but his sweet gesture and his thoughtfulness made me like him even more.

I leaned over to turn off the alarm. Had I been that tired,

that I didn't even feel Axel come to bed? I stopped to admire his body. He had no shirt on and only a pair of pajama bottoms clinging low on his hips. He had more than a six-pack, more like an eight-pack, and he had that delectable V. He was smooth all over, save for the little patch of black hair that stretched from his navel and slipping into his pants. I longed to trail my fingers down his happy trail and stroke what was at the end of it. I nearly snickered at my illogical thoughts.

I was going to give in to my impulses but thought better of it. After all, he was upset at me last night. Just as I was about to withdraw my arm, his own arms wrapped around me. He rolled me over, so that I was on my back.

"What were you staring at?" he asked smugly.

"Nothing." I smirked. Then frowned when I realized my voice was hoarse. My throat hurt. Had I tried to run again? I couldn't even remember whether I dreamed last night, let alone if I had run.

His eyes darkened for a moment, and he hummed in the back of his throat. Then he looked up and stared into my eyes, serious all of a sudden. "I never doubted your ability to watch our backs or hold your own," he murmured without preamble. "I just wanted you to stay here and be safe."

I gaped at Axel for a moment. My concern evaporated under his declaration. I figured this was his way of apologizing.

"I know." I sighed. "And I'm sorry if I challenged your decision. I know your heart was in the right place, but for years I saw my mother kiss my dad goodbye and worry about him. If—" my voice broke, "… if anything were to happen to you guys, I want to be there. I need to feel like I did everything in my power to help."

He nodded before he nuzzled my neck. "Were you okay finding me in your bed this morning?"

"I'll never complain," I said breathlessly without

hesitation as his lips trailed over my neck.

He continued to trail his lips over my neck, and his hand slid below my shirt, trailing over my ribs and up to cup my breast. His fingers found my bare nipple and rolled it between his thumb and forefinger.

"Mmm," I moaned, arching my chest up into his hands.

I heard a wailing right outside my door and stiffened. I groaned out from frustration as I realized Isa was awake. He surprised me by chuckling and rolling off of me in one fluid movement.

"Go hop in the shower," he murmured. "I'll go get her." He reached up and stretched momentarily. I admired the bunching and rippling of the muscles in his back. His movements were so smooth and fluid; he reminded me of a jungle cat.

I stopped my admiration of his perfectly tanned body when his words sank in.

My mouth gaped open in surprise. I wouldn't say he was adverse to children, but since we started our little journey here, he never made a move to touch or even go near one voluntarily. Did he even know how to hold a baby that young?

It took me a moment to realize he had closed the door behind him, and the light clicking sound snapped me from my shock. I hopped up and rushed to jump in the shower.

I washed my body and shaved all the essential areas. Now that my sex life had gone from zero to sixty, I wanted to make sure I was always at my best. I smiled to myself, thinking I was a lucky girl. The men in my life were all amazing, in their own way.

Our relationship was so new, and I knew I had yet to get to know Axel, Kingston, and Easton well enough, but I was excited to start. What little information I'd gleaned from them impressed me, and there was no denying our physical attraction.

With thoughts of them, I finished up and quickly brushed my teeth, then went into my room. The fact that they'd given me the master without any debate let me know they cared about my comfort. They had set up the alcove for Isa without a complaint, had unpacked my truck of all my belongings, and had set all my things out.

I walked over to my dresser, pulled out a razorback Ironman bra, and slipped it on. My hands hovered over a pair of panties, but I shook my head. I was going commando today. The pleather pants I was going to wear today were tight, and I hated thongs with a passion. Digging a piece of string out of my ass all day wasn't my idea of fun.

I slipped on the pants and was glad they fit, since I hadn't had a chance to try them on that day at the mall. I put on a simple black razorback top next. It was fitted and left a thin strip of my stomach showing. I grabbed my leather jacket at the last second. I was going to be hot, but I didn't know if we would run into the infected. I was really tired of washing their goop off of me.

I would suffer the heat if it meant I didn't have to wash their guts off of me.

When I exited the room, I found Corbin and Wyatt organizing weapons on the table, while Axel was walking around shirtless, feeding Isa against his hard chest. She was so tiny and small in his arms, and he was so big and gentle.

Wetness spread between my thighs. *I think I just felt my ovaries clench.*

"Quick, Ax," Kingston called out as he exited his room and tore off his shirt. "Hand me the baby, then take her back so Avery can club me over the head and drag me cavewoman style back to the room to fuck my brains out."

Four sets of eyes turned towards my bedroom door, and

I quickly ducked my head. I heard deep sounds of appreciation.

Corbin cleared his throat first. "Love your outfit, baby," he murmured.

"I'll like it better on my floor," Kingston leered at me.

Corbin chuckled. "You're such a dick, King."

"About wanting her clothing on my bedroom floor? Because we all want that. Or the fact that I called her out for eye-fucking Axel? Seriously, Ave," King teased. "What do I have to do to get that look in your eyes? Did no one else feel the temperature rise in here?"

Axel smirked. "Grow three inches, gain about fifty pounds, and get some more sun."

"Not fair, bro, you know I lack the melanin that you and Easton have," he grumbled.

"We should probably get going," I mumbled in embarrassment. "I'm meeting Aunt Pam at the kitchens to drop Isa off, and we still need to eat."

"She doesn't function until her second or third coffee," Corbin said as I turned. How he remembered that was beyond me. "Leave her be."

If I hadn't heard the laughter in his voice, I would've thought he was genuine in his attempt to stop Kingston from teasing me.

I sighed. If that was how the boys were going to play, not only was I going to have to learn the game, I would have to figure out a way to win.

I went over to the little alcove and to Isa's dresser. I knew this was just a temporary solution and that she'd quickly outgrow this situation. Eventually, we'd have to figure out how to fit seven people in a four-bedroom cabin.

I pulled out her diaper bag and placed some diapers in it, some wipes, extra clothing, and her empty bottles. Steph already told me to keep my milk in the fridge, and she would be pumping and bringing milk down for Isa. I then brought out another clean diaper and an outfit for her to wear right now. I impulsively grabbed a bow to put on her, even though she really did have a lot of hair.

"Does anyone else find it strange how Isa looks like a cross between Avery and Corbin?" Kingston said as he examined Isa's little fingers.

My heart stuttered to a stop. I remembered Isa's mother being fair, and her father could have been of Asian descent. Still, I never thought about the possibility of people actually mistaken her for mine. How was I supposed to handle that situation?

I wanted Isa to know about her family one day, and I always wanted her to feel like they had loved her. However, the older she got, the more she could understand. I never wanted her to feel unwanted by me either, though, if I immediately corrected people.

I stuffed all those thoughts away for now.

"All babies look the same," Wyatt scoffed.

He still hadn't looked up at me since Kingston's inappropriate comment. I didn't know how to fix it. Did I explain myself to him? I couldn't apologize for something I wasn't sorry for.

"Are we ready?" Easton asked as he breezed into the cabin.

I thought he was still getting ready? I hadn't realized he'd been outside.

He paused when he saw me. His eyes lighting with fire as he slowly perused my body down to the black boots I'd found. He took a few steps forward and cupped my cheek. "I'm sorry for being so..." he began.

I placed a finger over his lips. "I understand," I

whispered, then louder, so Wyatt could hear. "I understand that you guys are worried about me, but I don't want to be stuck here worrying about you when I can be out there *with* you."

"We don't want to worry about you either, Ave," Wyatt said as he pressed his chest to my back. "I understand your desire to be with us, but it doesn't make it easier for us to stop worrying about you. Promise me you'll listen to your instincts and Kingston while you're out there."

I nodded. "Just as long as you promise to look out for each other and come back to me."

I didn't recognize this woman. I had been nursing a broken heart less than a week ago, only to find that my heart wasn't broken at all, that it was able to expand, gladly accepting the caring and affection of five men. I wasn't going to say I loved them...yet. Not in the way a woman loved a man, but I cared for them deeply.

I loved Corbin and Wyatt like family, but had my love for them evolved? Attraction, yes, definitely.

With a sigh, I chose to put it all in my file to examine later. Right now, I had to focus on the mission at hand.

Wyatt brushed his lips against my temple, probably the closest to a promise I was going to get. I knew we were headed back out into danger, and sometimes we couldn't promise things out of our control.

"I will always pray that I return to you," Wyatt murmured. "After years of wanting you, I don't want this to end anytime soon."

I smiled at him feeling my heart lurch in my chest.

"And after finally meeting you," Easton added, "after hearing all the stories about you, I'm not ready to leave you before I find out what makes you smile, what makes your heart race, and everything else I can find out about you."

I brushed my lips against his cheek. His endearing words made me feel warm. I felt the exact same way about them.

"She'll be fine guys," Kingston said with his cocky grin in place. "She'll be with me, and you know I'll make sure she comes home. Especially since I haven't seen her wrapped around me yet."

Corbin reached out and smacked the back of Kingston's head. I hadn't even noticed that Axel had left the room, and now Corbin had Isa in his arms. She was still wide awake and alert, watching him as if she was dissecting him.

Kingston scowled at him. "You're lucky you're holding our princess."

I smiled secretly. Since when had Isa become...ours? I guess they'd known I had taken more than a personal responsibility for her, just as Easton had. I think it was natural for them to extend their affections towards her.

A week ago, I would have never thought any of this was possible. Yet here I stood, with five men who cared for an infant that depended on me.

▢

"Up here is a cattle farm. I know his heifers were dropping calves any day. He has a large herd of Angus," Donny said as we wound our way down a long gravel driveway.

Just in case the farmer was still alive, we had one hundred gallons of gas, two fifty-pound bags of rice, and seven cases of canned fruits and vegetables Nana had canned a couple of years ago.

I had been surprised to see the cellar in Nana's house nearly full of her canned fruits, vegetables, and jams. I couldn't resist the urge to swipe a few of her strawberry jams myself. She always made the best jams.

I heard Chad mutter a curse beside me and turned to see

what he was looking at. My stomach nearly revolted. There were at least fifteen Angus thrashing about on the ground. I couldn't tell if the infected or a wild animal had gotten to them. Were we too late? I silently cursed. If we had arrived a little bit earlier maybe we could have saved them.

True, we had planned to eat them and raise them ourselves, but what a horrible way to go.

"His barns and house are in the back," Donny said grimly. "And he has more pastures out that way too."

"What happened?" Samuel visibly gulped beside me.

Samuel was a fifteen-year-old teen that still seemed to be trying to figure out who he was. One moment he was trying to take on the mantle of a man, and the next, he was teasing his two younger brothers, reverting to his youthful ways.

He initially seemed excited and honored to be asked to come with us, but now I could see the scared teen he really was. Last week he was running track and texting his girlfriend every chance he got, and this morning he was witnessing our new world first hand.

Donny was one of campground's groundkeepers, and his wife was a line cook in the restaurant. Samuel worked weekends on the grounds with his dad or bused tables at the restaurant.

The whole Pitsch family were there when Uncle Mitch got the call. He asked them to stay on, and they ran home long enough to grab their essentials and returned a few hours later. There were a few other families that Uncle Mitch regarded as family, and they had stayed on as well.

They fully expected other employees and old guests to show up eventually, and already planned to do a vetting process before allowing them entrance. They didn't want to invite anyone that wasn't willing to contribute to the community nor take in any bad seeds.

"Stop the truck, man," Chad said gruffly.

Donny did but didn't question the big man any further. Kingston jumped out from the seat beside me, and I followed.

"Avery, you don't need to be here," Chad said grimly before he climbed between the barbed fence.

"I don't need to be. I want to be," I lied as I slid on a pair of gloves. I was serious about not getting blood on me.

I knew precisely what Chad wanted to do. I had been hunting enough with the guys to know what his intentions were. I walked over to the nearest cattle. He didn't want them to continue suffering in their state.

"I'm sorry," I murmured before slicing the female Angus' neck.

Kingston let out a loud expletive before jumping back from the cow he had been kneeling next to. "Come from behind, fast and quick!" he yelled as he began to move like a ninja through the bodies thrashing on the ground.

"They're turning!" Chad yelled over his shoulder to Donny and Samuel as they made their way under the fence too.

I saw a flash of blood-foamed mouths and bleeding eyes as I moved briskly. I was thankful for the sharpened hunting knife I got from Wyatt. Along with my sais, I now had two pistols, plenty of ammo, and a hunting knife.

With tunnel vision, I worked my way through the field. I looked around and noticed Chad and Kingston were slightly out of breath like I was.

"I think that's all of them," Donny said with slightly widened eyes, his chest heaving.

From what Uncle Mitch told us, they had been lucky enough to not run into any infected before or after the call from Uncle Scott. They all lived far enough away from civilization to be safe. We weren't delusional enough to believe it would last, but these people had been sheltered until now.

"Were the cows... infected?" Samuel looked whiter than the t-shirt he wore. His hands were trembling with nerves. "How?"

Chad and Kingston exchanged a look full of meaning before Kingston ran a hand through his curls. "So far, we know the infection is spread through saliva. If the infected attacked them and didn't kill them, they're now infected. We need to be alert, not only for the infected but animals, too. Let's go."

"Standby," Chad muttered. "We can't go into battle without praying first."

I noticed no one argued with him.

"Go ahead, Rev," Kingston murmured before taking my hand in his, squeezing it, and bowing his head.

⬚

"I have eyes on four," Chad stated as he peered out the front window.

We had pulled up to the old farmhouse. About two hundred yards away were the barns. The house looked like it was well-loved but had seen better days. The roof was missing a few shingles, and the siding was in desperate need of a paint job. Two older trucks sat in the driveway, and in the distance, I could see cattle trailers parked on the side of the barn.

"Rev," Kingston said as he placed his hand on the door. "Watch our backs." He tugged on my hand—he hadn't let go of it since we'd gotten back in the truck—and I realized he was talking about us. I slipped out behind him. Kingston pointed to the left, and I nodded, understanding his meaning. We both ran towards them just as they turned and noticed us.

It took us less than thirty seconds before they were dispatched.

"We're going to knock," Kingston stated to Chad as he wiped his kamas on one of the infected's clothing.

"I got your six," Chad called back as Donny and Samuel

exited the truck.

Both of them had experience hunting and seemed more than comfortable handling their rifles.

We climbed the old porch and made our way to the front door. "How did you become so good at the kamas?" I asked King, feeling the need to get out of my head.

"You're not the only martial artist in the group," he winked at me. "When we have some free time, you should ask Easton to pull out his nunchucks. He rivals Bruce Lee's skills."

I looked at him in surprise before I smiled. "I can't wait to see him in action. You're like a ninja with those things."

He chuckled. "Yet you make me look like an amateur."

"Whatever," I mumbled in embarrassment. I knew Kingston was serious and not teasing me, and that's what made me embarrassed. I could handle him teasing and joking. When he was thoughtful, it threw me off balance.

He chuckled once more. "And you don't know how to take compliments. You're like Easton, in that respect."

I didn't have time to ask what he meant, since we'd reached the front door. Kingston knocked. We waited for about twenty seconds, and he knocked once more.

"I guess no one's home," he said with a shrug.

We turned to walk away, when I saw a curtain twitch by the window. I saw tangled dark hair framed around a young face. The little girl looked like she was about six, and from the tomato stain shirt and snarled hair, I had a feeling she hadn't had any adult supervision for some time. The curtains closed once our eyes met. Her large brown eyes had looked like she was both happy to see me and frightened.

"There's a little girl in there." I pulled on Kingston's hand.

"Are you sure?" he was asking as I heard a dog going wild

inside, followed by the screams of children.

Kingston didn't hesitate as he went back and tried the door handle before kicking the door down. "Rev," he called on his radio. "We got children inside screaming up at the house. Might need back up."

We ran down a well worn but spotless wood floor in the direction of the barking and screaming. I skidded to a halt as I noticed a boy of about fourteen or so shoving a toddler and the disheveled little girl into a pantry. The dog was barking wildly at the back door, and a young boy of around eight was struggling to load a shotgun.

"Rev," Kingston barked into the radio. "Go around back. We have around twenty infected in the back yard."

I looked up and noticed a back yard surrounded by a white picket fence in desperate need of a coat of paint. There was a child's playset, a dilapidated trampoline, and about twenty infected all salivating to come inside.

The black German Sheperd's barks seemed to be deterring them from coming any closer, but it was still creepy the way they just stood there, watching, their bodies shifting side to side. I watched them for a moment. Some of them would look at each other before nudging or nodding at the other one beside them. Were they communicating? And how?

"Woah there, buddy," Kingston batted the shotgun out of the boy's hands. "We're here to help you. What's your name?"

The little boy's eyes were wide and haunted, but he nodded and mumbled with a lisp, "Wicky," he said, but I was pretty sure it was *Ricky.*

"Okay, Wicky." Kingston hadn't seemed to catch the lisp. "Why don't you go in there with your... brother and sister and my girlfriend, and I'll make all the bad guys go away?"

My head snapped up. *Girlfriend?*

The boy nodded numbly and ran into the pantry. The older boy turned, knife in hand.

"You can go in there too," I said gently.

The older boy had a square jaw, and a long narrow nose but was oddly beautiful with his shaggy, pale blond hair, large ice-blue eyes framed by long and surprisingly dark eyelashes. His features were delicate, and charming freckles dusted his golden skin.

"No," he shook his head resolutely with a slight southern accent. "This is my home now. They got some of the girls this mornin'. They took my pappy and my mamaw. They ain't gettin' my home too."

I looked at Kingston, and he nodded. "I'm going up top and see if I can pick them off from up there. You stay here and make sure none of them get inside."

Kingston might have been gone for less than a minute when I heard the gunshots begin, followed by the crashing of a window.

"I'm Avery," I said to the teenaged boy, noticing now that he was as tall as I was but lithe.

"Mike." He nodded, his eyes wide. I saw the fear in them, but more than that, I saw the strength there, too.

"It's nice to meet you, Mike," I murmured as I walked towards the sound I heard the crash come from. It didn't sound like it came from outside.

Goosebumps of awareness prickled across my skin, and a feeling of anxiety gripped my stomach. My instincts told me to be on alert. My instincts proved to be correct when, moments later, chaos erupted.

The dog realized that there was infected ambling down the hall from the direction of the side of the house. The moment the dog moved towards that threat, the French doors in the back shattered open.

"Can you tell him to stay there?" I called to Mike.

Mike nodded. "Roscoe, stay, stay!" he said firmly.

"Thanks," I cried out before the first infected began to fall through the broken door. I took advantage of the chokepoint and took them down as they tried to climb in.

One of the infected broke free from the pile, and Mike was right behind me, hacking away with repeated movements. Realizing he had a dull knife and no knowledge on how to take them down, I quickly bent down and withdrew my own knife, handing it to him.

"Just once to the temple, under their jaw and up to the brain, or in the ear," I commanded him as I continued taking the infected down.

"Thanks," he said in a high pitch voice before he lowered it. "Thanks," he repeated.

I didn't even look his way as I focused on taking the infected down. There were more than twenty of them and probably more on the side of the house.

I saw Donny and Chad in the backyard. The door was blocked entirely from the piles of bodies, so I moved towards the other threat. I turned and headed towards the hallway. My sais worked like an extension of my hands as I took the infected down one by one, with Mike working calmly by my side.

Roscoe's presence seemed to help us. None of the infected lunged towards us. I determined that I was going to train Bane, but how? If all the dogs could be trained to help us, it would make us safer.

When we finally reached the side bedroom, I noticed that there were only a few milling about in there. I was breathless when we finished.

"Avery!" I heard Kingston's panicked voice yell.

"Back here," I yelled in return as Mike stumbled to the

open window and promptly threw up.

I walked over to him and gently rubbed his back. He tensed at first and then nearly crumbled. I heard his silent sobs and felt terrible for him. In no world should it have been okay for a boy so young to have to see and do what he had just done.

"It's okay," I murmured soothingly. "You did outstanding, Mike. I've seen grownups not be able to do what you did today, nor as brave."

"I killed 'em," he sobbed. "Maybe they can be...fixed."

"Maybe one day," I said grimly. "But not today. Today they just want to hurt you and your siblings or worse."

He nodded numbly.

Kingston came running into the room, eyed me, and then I was caught up in an embrace. I was surprised by the sudden action until I realized he probably freaked when he saw all the infected but not me. I held him and kissed his jawline. "I'm okay," I murmured to him before I turned back to Mike.

"How long have you been by yourself?" I asked. "Was it just your grandparents, you, and the kids?"

Kingston turned me, so that my back was against his chest.

"Since Saturday," Mike mumbled. "Mom's an addict. None of us know our daddys. She just comes and drops us off when she realizes she cares about getting' high more than us. I haven't seen her in three years since she dropped off Carson. Mamaw was out feeding the chickens when the first monster came. Pappy tried to save her, but four of 'em came from nowhere and took him down. Ricky tried to go out there, but I wouldn't let him. He's still mad at me. Hasn't talked to me since." He shook his head.

With eyes wide, he continued. "The first night, it was only a few of them. They tried to get in, but Roscoe stopped them. The second night, more came. This morning, we saw them out at the pasture. I couldn't go out there, though. I couldn't help the girls."

Poor kids. They've been on their own for four days now! I couldn't imagine. I didn't want to imagine! I shuddered.

"You did the right thing," I reassured him. "How would you feel about coming with us? All of us. We have other children back at the campgrounds, food, and people to protect us. We came to see if your grandparents would do a trade with us," I admitted to him. "We were hoping to trade some gasoline, rice, and other stuff for cattle."

"This is my home," he said firmly.

"You're not safe here," Kingston said gently. "More infected will come. There's nothing to stop them from coming. You did a great job so far, but you look hungry and tired. Come with us and we'll protect you."

I saw Mike's internal battle and how easy it was to read his thoughts. This was the only home he'd ever known. He loved this place. His grandparents' memories were here, but he was tired and worried about his family.

"I'll have to tell Ricky and Molly. Carson's too young to understand," he said wearily, but I could hear the relief in his voice. "I think they got all the cattle in the pastures, but we have three dozen of 'em in the barns. I heard 'em this morning. I think they're still okay. Pappy's dogs were out there with him when he ran to help Mamaw. I still heard them barking this mornin'."

"We're clearing the infected now," Chad said softly from the doorway. "Do you think we can use those trailers out back to haul the cattle to the campgrounds?"

"Yeah." Mike nodded. He took a deep, shuddering breath before he straightened to his full height. "I can drive one of the trucks. But I don't know how to drive the tractor-trailer. We just got a new load of grain in." He cleared his throat. "The man who delivers our grains attacked my mamaw. He came in on Friday. She'd always had a kind heart, and had let him stay because he was all flushed-like. Saturday mornin' he attacked her." Bright tears glistened in his eyes.

"Are you old enough to drive?" Kingston inquired in surprise.

"Mister, I'm fifteen. I've been drivin' since I was ten. I live on a farm. We don't live the life of you city slickers," Mike bristled.

Chad chuckled. "Got 'em there, little brother."

Kingston laughed and held up his hands. "My apologies. Didn't mean to offend. If you say you can drive, then all means we'd love the help."

Mike ducked his head. Was he blushing?

"I'll go hook up the trucks," the boy said. "Molly and Ricky can pen up the chickens. They give us about two dozen eggs a day. They haven't left their coops since the monsters came."

"Do you want to wait until we do a little clean up first? The others are cleaning up the bodies now, and then we're burning them. Are you sure they should see that?" Kingston asked soothingly.

I was surprised by his thoughtfulness as he reached out to grip Mike's shoulders gently.

Mike was definitely blushing as he shook his head. Did he like...guys? I held no judgment, but I was curious. And Kingston being Kingston, well, I couldn't blame him.

"Yes," he said in a high pitched voice once more before he cleared his throat and shook his head resolutely. "They've already seen worse. Might as well tell 'em the monsters are goin' back to hell where they belong."

I gaped at his resolve as he marched out of the room without looking back.

◊

"That's thirty-eight cattle, twenty-two hens, one rooster, a few barn cats, and three dogs," Chad said with a mixture of satisfaction and sadness.

In true "Chad" fashion, he already had the youngest child, Carson, attached to his back in a baby carrier as he filled the trucks with everything we might need. He had just finished loading up the last trailer of all the cattle. He was determined to return to get some more farming equipment and other useful items we could use, but later on. Right now, our primary focus was on getting the animals back and settled in.

"Are we ready?" Kingston asked, eyeing the five vehicles we were leaving with.

Mike had been a font of knowledge, and we had been able to secure two more vehicles and trailers so we could get the livestock in one trip. He'd also identified their nearest neighbors among the infected, who had owned a pig farm. So we hoped to drop off the cattle and head straight back out for the pigs. They were already loaded and secured on their trailers so we could do a quick turn around.

Chad was going to lead the procession with the grain truck. I would be following with a trailer full of cattle and one of the children. Samuel was still on a permit, but Donny let him drive a flatbed with a tractor and chickens in the bed. Kingston was next in line, with a trailer of cattle and one of the children. Mike was going to drive a truck with a box trailer filled with many useful items. And Donny would bring up the rear with another cattle trailer and a child.

"As we'll ever be," Donny confirmed.

"Let's go, kids!" Kingston called.

They had all pitched in really well and seemed in decent spirits until I asked them to pack up their clothes and anything else they may want to bring with them. Reality hadn't set in until that moment. We had already loaded up their belongings, but they wanted a few moments to themselves.

"For a fifteen-year-old, Mike sure is an amazing kid," Kingston murmured to our small little circle. "I was such a shithead at that age, I wouldn't have cared for my younger siblings, let alone help run a farm this big."

I wanted to ask him if he had younger siblings, but his expression had turned shuttered.

"He really is a good kid," Chad agreed. "His grandparents raised him right."

Samuel snickered. "Mike isn't a boy."

Wait, *what?*

I saw Donny frown at his son while understanding dawned on me. I had just assumed Mike had an effeminate walk and features. I'd caught him—well, *her*—stealing glances at Kingston often but figured he—she!—liked guys. I wondered why she never corrected me and why she hid behind her baggy men's clothes, for that matter.

"Michaela's a freak." Samuel shook his head in exasperation. "She always came to school smelly and was always falling asleep in class a lot."

I saw the jealousy in Samuel's eyes. It was clear he hero-worshipped Kingston. He probably didn't like that Kingston had praised the girl.

"Ever wondered why, instead of ridiculing her?" Chad immediately bristled. "You ever work on a farm, boy? It's hard on a man. Imagine how tough it is on a girl. You realize she was probably up at four a.m., did three hours worth of chores before she went to school, then she had to do it all over again when she got home until the sun went down."

Samuel immediately blanched under the big man's glower.

Samuel had been a decent helper all day. Albeit, his father and Chad had to get on him several times for taking breaks, but I thought that was typical for a boy his age. Admittedly, Mike had run circles around him, though. Some people just weren't as driven as others.

"I'm disappointed in you, son." Donny frowned. "As much as your mother and I work, I thought you would have a little more empathy for those less fortunate than you. When we get back to the campground, I'm going to ask Mitch to give you a real job. Your mom and I weren't going to force the issue, but maybe we should."

"He can work by my side for a while." Chad gave Donny a respectful nod of his head. "We have a lot of work to do to secure the cattle, build their shelters, and figure out the placement and schematics of the rest of the animals. I hope you're ready to work."

Samuel ducked his head. "I didn't-" he started.

Donny cut him off. "He's all yours, Rev. Wake him up when you get up and send him home when you think the work is done for the day. Keep him out as long as you need him. If he gives you any problems, come see me."

"I can do that." Chad hid a satisfied smirk before he turned his back to me. "Can you secure this little one in his car seat, Avery?"

"Sure can." I smiled. The way they handled Samuel couldn't have been any better.

I didn't want to say anything aloud, but the baby was in desperate need of a bath, as were the other children. As I finished securing the baby, I wondered how long it had been since they'd had a bath. Out of curiosity, I wandered over to the house, wondering if my hunch was right. I turned on the faucet attached to the outdoor spigot, and nothing came out.

"What are you, doin'?" Mike asked, her younger siblings

in tow.

"How long have you been out of water?" I asked quietly.

"Why?" Mike bristled. "Did Samuel run his big fat mouth?"

I shook my head. She had her secrets. I'd let her keep them until she was ready to talk.

I was pretty sure I had figured it all out by the clues I had seen around and in the house. Her grandparents were barely making ends meet. They had four kids to feed, and it looked like they didn't get paid for their cattle until they were picked up. Feeding the cows, keeping them healthy, and all the other things associated with farm living added up. I imagined, at times, they had to determine what bills got paid and which didn't. I surmised the water and electrical bill had been a bill they sacrificed often.

Chapter 20

The sun was going down as we unloaded the last pig into a temporary corral. Easton's and Corbin's teams weren't back yet. I wasn't worried, though, until a few minutes ago. Easton's team was heading into the city an hour north of here, and no one had heard from them. Corbin's team had went "dark" about two hours ago, on the way back from a building supply company.

Kingston, Uncle Mitch, Wyatt, and Axel had gone up to the main house to strategize a possible recon mission for the missing teams. Their having a meeting made me feel ill at ease. Did they think something had happened to them?

"I think it's time we took a shower and get something to eat, Avery," Chad bade me. "There's no use worrying yet."

Everyone else in our team had already been sent to wash up and go to dinner. I had stayed behind to help Chad set up some old skids for a temporary enclosure for the sixty pigs we were able to procure.

I sighed. "Do you think they're okay?"

"I think knowing you're here waiting on them gives them every incentive to come home," Chad said diplomatically.

I nodded. I needed a distraction. "Hey, Chad, how do you know so much about farming?"

He smiled at my direction. "My eighth foster family took me in when I was around twelve. By then, I was an angry black boy who always wanted to pick fights. I knew I was stronger than most of the kids in my class, and I lived in Montana.

Know how many black kids live in Ennis, Montana?"

I shook my head. I had always grown up near military towns. I'd never known what it was like not to have a diverse group of ethnicities and colors of people. I knew statistically some cities and states would have less diversity than others, but I had never been to any of them.

"Zero." Chad chuckled darkly. "I was reminded of it almost daily. So the only way I knew how to cope with it was hitting. I moved in with Mama Jean and Papa George, and they... began to heal me. They were older and had one daughter I never met, but they went to church with my social worker. One day, Jill told them about me, and Mama Jean said she had a dream about me and knew God wanted me to live with them.

"Less than six months later, I was placed with them. They taught me how to love the land as much as they did. They taught me that I could be loved despite our physical differences."

"What happened to them?" I asked him. I knew a lot of them were here because they had no families to go home to.

His face revealed the pain he felt. "Gone. Killed. I was in my third year of school to become a pastor, and their estranged daughter returned. She sold the farm, and I no longer had a home. I joined the military, and I've never returned."

I rubbed his back, hoping it brought him comfort. By now, the sun had descended. The lights in the distance were our only illumination. "I'm sorry. I know words mean nothing, but...I'm sorry."

"What causes you to run?" he asked suddenly.

I cleared my throat. He'd shared his hurts. I figured I could give him some slight insight.

"It started soon after I left the modeling world. There was a photographer that showed a little too much...interest in me."

I felt him stiffen. "Marlon Gains."

Tensing, I let out a breath. "Yes," I whispered. "How did you know?"

"I watch the news...a lot," he muttered grimly. "One of my foster sisters in one of the homes I stayed in was a pretty little thing. She modeled for a bit. She had quit all of a sudden, and I always suspected that she had been molested. When the news broke, I called her. She admitted to me that he made her feel uncomfortable and was asking her to undress for him."

I nodded, unsure what to say as I saw headlights in the distance. "Easton, Corbin!" I nearly squealed as I grabbed Chad's hand and pulled him into a run.

Chad stifled his laugh as he began singing softly to himself. *"I'm a little more country than that..."*

"What?" I burst out in shocked laughter at his country twang.

"Easton Corbin..." his voice trailed off expectantly.

I looked at him blankly as I continued to jog up the hill. I saw Uncle Mitch, Wyatt, Kingston, and Axel was on their way down, too.

"I thought all white people listened to country music?" Chad teased.

I laughed as I vaguely remembered a country singer named Easton Corbin. I had never connected the dots until that moment.

"First off, I'm only fifty percent caucasian," I replied saucily. "Second of all, my knowledge of Country is limited to Florida Georgia Line, Rascal Flatts, Jana Kramer, and the old-school artists. You know, like Reba, Martina McBride, Alabama..."

"No Garth?" he asked aghast.

"Meh," I laughed, realizing I was talking about country music with a six-foot-four, two hundred and sixty pound-ish black man.

He held his chest as if he were physically hurt. I laughed, but then my sights alighted on Corbin. He hadn't seen me yet.

He barely caught me as I launched myself at him.

He gave out a surprised chuckle as I wrapped my arms around his shoulders and nuzzled his neck. "Hey there," he said in a sultry tone as he lifted me off my feet. "Someone's happy to see me."

I laughed, somewhat embarrassed at my show of affection. "I was worried," I confessed. "When you and Easton didn't show up before the sun went down, I got concerned."

The lead ball in my stomach wasn't alleviated when I realized that Easton wasn't among the vehicles that had returned. I looked over his shoulder and noticed Uncle Mitch, Kingston, Axel, and Wyatt were heading our way.

"Well, I'm here now, baby," Corbin murmured as he kissed the corner of my mouth. "We ran into a group of survivors. Amy will be here shortly with them. A pack surrounded them, and we couldn't just leave them. It's a good thing, too," he said as he turned to look at Uncle Mitch. "We found a plumber, an electrician, a contractor, and a cop among all the other people that may be able to help contribute. I already briefed them, and the people willing to help our community returned with us—" He cut off, turning with a frown. "East not back yet?"

"No," Axel shook his head. "We lost communication with them."

Corbin nodded, and I could tell they were all trying to act bravely in front of me. Corbin began to tell us about his day and why he'd lost contact– faulty radio. They had procured a bus and a large box truck to contain all their finds.

As he told us about our guests, a bus pulled up behind Corbin's truck. Amy came out of the bus first, and approximately sixty shell-shocked people exited behind her. The world may have turned to crap three days ago, but it might as well have been years, from their haggard appearance.

I saw a flash of khaki and black as Josh embraced Amy, much as I had Corbin. He had done his duty for some time now, but he had been lingering in wait. I knew it killed him to stay behind and work on our agricultural plan. He'd worked tirelessly and barely took a break, but it was clear he much rather be with her. Axel already reassured him that, once everyone got the hang of things around here, he would try to keep them both on the same mission.

Uncle Mitch was murmuring in his walkie talkie as we watched the people exit one by one. "Welcome, everyone," his booming voice enveloped the crowd. "I'm glad to see you have made it in relative safety. As my nephew has stated, we have food, water, and protection, but in order for us to continually prosper, we need everyone's help in making our community safe.

"I have my pals Eddie and one of our JOpS coming down to take you up to the showers. They will have to check you over to make sure you haven't been bitten or have any broken skin that may concern us. If you can't agree to a thorough search of your person, I'm going to have to ask you to leave," he paused, and I noticed a few people in the back begin to murmur among themselves.

When no one else said anything, he continued. "After you have had your showers, a late-night snack will be provided for you in the hall. I will have a list started in the there for your names, how many people are in your family unit, and your previous professions. Tonight, I'll be keeping you in the campers' cabins. Tomorrow, we can assign you jobs and provide you with your schedules and the vision for our future."

"I can take the guys up to the showers now," Chad murmured.

"Perfect." Uncle Mitch smiled. "Eddie will meet you up there. If you don't have any clothes, he has some scrubs they can change into for now," he said shrewdly as he looked at the ragtag bunch. Very few of them carried any possessions.

"We were able to acquire a lot of clothing from the store," Corbin stated. "I'm sure we can sort through it all and distribute it to them come morning."

"If all the men will follow my man Chad right now," Uncle Mitch commented to the crowd. "The women should be down shortly to gather the ladies."

The men separated from the women and started to make the trek up to the cabins with Chad.

"If I may?" A young man stepped forward with a beautiful little girl cradled in his arms and a baby strapped to his back. "Can I bring Elsa and Christopher with me? She won't go with anyone else."

"This is Officer Rhys Miller," Corbin introduced. "He was able to take down several of the infected when we stumbled upon the group in an Every-Mart. If you don't mind, Uncle Mitch, I'll escort him and his family to the smaller cabin next to Sylvia's family group and ours. I'll look them over and then head up to the showers as well. I don't think Chad should inspect them on his own. I have a feeling some of them will protest." He grimaced.

Uncle Mitch smiled and nodded. "Have at it, son."

"Are we taking one of the UTVs?" Kingston asked with a suggestive lift of his brows as he came back to our little group.

"Found them, did you?" Corbin grinned. He turned back to Uncle Mitch and pointed to the enclosed trailer behind his truck. "We found a dealership. We acquired four brand new

ATVs and four UTVs. Let's unload a few of them, King. I'm starving, and I'm sure Rhys and his family would appreciate a shower."

"Yes, that would be greatly appreciated," Rhys stated with a relieved look in his eyes.

From the haunted look I saw there, I imagined he had a story. There was no denying the likeness between him and his children. It made me wonder where the mom was.

"Do you know how to ride one of these?" Kingston asked Rhys, patting a UTV.

Rhys nodded and smirked slightly. "I grew up on them."

Kingston smiled. "We'll leave you one of these so you can come back down after you get settled in."

"Thanks, man." Rhys smiled once more.

"There's already some playpens in the hall, and we have some toys for the kids to play with," I told him as I gently pushed the tangle of curls off the little girl's face.

Aunt Pam, Steph, and Aunt Carol had used the dining hall as a daycare, of sorts, for the younger ones today. While the older kids were free to run and play under Gloria's care, the younger ones stayed with the women so they could be close by as they worked.

He gave me a grateful smile. "Thanks."

"We'll be right back." Corbin leaned down to bestow a quick kiss on my mouth. "I'm going to utilize the showers with the other men. Save me a seat at dinner?"

I gave him a bemused smile and nod.

"Me too?" Kingston asked with a mischievous glint, bestowing a kiss on my mouth as well.

I could see the confused looks on Uncle Mitch's face and that of Rhys'. I pushed Kingston, miffed at his mischievousness. "Get out of here and get a shower."

"Like you have room to talk," Kingston teased. "You smell like livestock."

"I'll take a quick shower before I go help in the kitchens," I said with an exaggerated eyeroll and stuck my tongue out at him. "And I smell like hard work. What have you been doing?"

I was merely teasing him. I knew he had been just as busy, if not more, since our return. Once we'd returned with all our loads, he had helped Josh plow some of the designated fields for planting in the morning. His work ethic, despite his jokes and laid-back behavior, was admirable. If anything, his ability to be fluid and go with the flow was much needed in our new environment.

Kingston chuckled before walking towards the back of the trailer. "Girl, quit playing. You know I've been busting my sexy tail around here."

I laughed and shook my head. I knew it was pointless to continue making my jibes at him. I had a feeling he would do or say something outrageous to top anything *I* could say and do. It was safer to quit while I could.

Uncle Mitch let out a long low whistle, and even Axel clapped, praising Amy and Corbin's loot. I rounded the moving truck and gaped. The team had not only found survivors but it looked like they had clothing, food, and other things crammed in, around, and on top of the other ATVs.

"The bus is packed with stuff, too," Amy said proudly. "After we hit up the building supply store, we found all this at the Every-Mart. Apparently, Officer Miller secured the building after he'd lost his wife and sister-in-law to a pack. They could have probably continued surviving on everything in the store, if it weren't for a few members of the group deciding to go out and smoke without securing the back door behind them."

"I hope they learned from their careless mistake," Aunt Pam said as she and Aunt Carol rounded the corner with Isa and Jenny sleeping soundly in a double stroller.

I walked over and bent down, bestowing a kiss on both little girls' warm foreheads. I had made sure to squeeze in some cuddles and feed Isa earlier. I wish I could have spent more time with her, but some sacrifices needed to be made to get our community where it needed to be, and she was in great hands with Aunt Pam, Aunt Carol, and Stephanie.

"I think a few of them did," Amy scoffed. "But there's a young, punk kid that wanted to place the blame on his friend."

"Is he here now?" Uncle Mitch frowned.

"Yes," Amy sneered. "I wanted to leave him, but Garth thought we should bring him back. Honestly, I think he's shady as shit. Him and his buddy seem to have an obsession with one of the younger girls. She's a pretty little thing, but she seems…strung out on something. The whole group feels off to me."

"Hmm," Axel murmured. "We should probably keep an eye on them. Point them out to me later."

"Okay," Amy said. "Are we unloading in the storage units?"

Uncle Mitch nodded. "Just drive on up there. Donny, Cal, Mike, and Sam are already up there unloading some of their finds."

Mike was another person that had impressed me. Once she had gotten her siblings settled in with Gloria and Aunt Pam, she had jumped in with helping settle, feed, and tend the cattle. Then she'd immediately went up to the storage building and began to help them organize, arrange, and catalog everything coming in.

"Copy that," Amy said with a smile.

"I'll follow you up," Joe said before heading towards Corbin's vehicle.

"If it's not too much trouble, can you take the clothes to the hall?" Aunt Carol asked. "After we figure out everyone's sizes, we should probably pass them out."

"No problem at all," Joe said with a smile.

Joe and Amy headed towards the supply building, and I stood by Axel, Wyatt, and Uncle Mitch, anxiously standing by. The sun was officially gone, and there still wasn't any sign of Easton yet. I worried on my bottom lip, and Axel seemed to pick up on my anxiety, because he placed an arm over my shoulder and pulled me in. My only consolation was Kingston seemed confident his brother would return. He was still in high spirits, so maybe I should take a page out of his book, I thought.

"You needed something?" Natalie appeared with a barely concealed sneer.

"Yes, ma' am," Uncle Mitch said, staring her down with a frosty glare. "I need you to take the girls and women to the shower houses up on the hill and inspect them for any signs of infection."

Natalie gritted her teeth. "I just got off watch."

"After you got to sleep-in this morning," Axel nearly growled. "Just do as you're told, Burns."

She stiffened but began to walk towards the hill. "Yes, sir," she gritted.

"Ladies?" Wyatt called out to the newcomers. "If you can follow JS Burns, she'll inspect you before your showers, show you your quarters, and then dinner will be awaiting you in the building behind me." He pointed towards the hall before turning back towards us.

"We can't continue letting attitudes like her's poison the community," Wyatt murmured. "We'll need to sit her down and talk to her. How did Jade do today?" he inquired of Uncle Mitch.

Uncle Mitch had decided to stay behind so he could direct people once they'd returned. A lot of progress had been made tonight, but we still had a long way to go.

Uncle Mitch's brows knitted. "The little Asian girl?"

Wyatt nodded. "That's her."

Uncle Mitch chuckled humorously. "After she pissed off some of the women by coming on to their husbands? Fine."

Wyatt and Axel snorted. "No surprise there," Wyatt sneered.

Uncle Mitch's walkie squawked to life once more. "Team Easton has returned," the jovial male voice said on the other end.

I couldn't help but squeak with happiness. Wyatt and Axel chuckled at me, but I could see the relief in their gazes as well.

"Told you he was fine," Kingston's smooth tones came over the radio.

I laughed in relief and looked at the guys.

"King swears that they know when the other's in danger," Wyatt scoffed an explanation to me and Uncle Mitch.

"Hey, I knew right when Emery had broken her leg on winter break with her friends," I protested. "And when she had phantom pains in her throat when I needed my tonsils removed, her pain didn't go away until mine did."

Wyatt hooted with laughter. "Horse crap!"

"According to Bryan, they did," Uncle Mitch said with a smirk and a shrug.

I could tell they both had trouble believing me. "Whatever," I grumbled, crossing my arms over my chest. "I believe Kingston. You have no clue what we twins are capable of."

Wyatt laughed and shook his head once more. "I'm going to go help at the supply building. I'll meet you guys at the debriefing meeting."

"Sure, run when you know you're wrong, Wy." I snorted teasingly.

He kissed my cheek. "Whatever you say, sweetheart."

"I'm going to say hi to Easton, shower, and then get to the kitchens. Are Trudy and Winnie already there?" I inquired.

Uncle Mitch nodded, looking at me, then his son, then back at me. "We had some leftovers from dinner, and I think they're just making a stew out of it, pulling out some fruits, and some of that leftover bread."

"Perfect." I nodded, and my stomach rumbled, reminding me of my lack of appetite today. Now that I knew all my guys were safe, it was returning with a vengeance.

I headed towards the vehicles rolling up, hoping to escape Uncle Mitch for a brief time. Easton jumped out of the vehicle and headed straight to me. I felt a flutter in my belly when Easton gave me a warm smile. He looked tired, and I couldn't miss the condition of his clothing. Uncaring, I embraced him.

I felt the slight tremor in his muscular frame. "That bad?" I asked as I held him tighter.

"Worse," he muttered reluctantly. "I expected the worst when I was overseas. To see it come here, it's...it's alarming."

"How'd you do?" Axel asked.

I started for a moment before Easton pulled away from me. He and Axel exchanged some bro-hug, hand-clapping thing before he pulled me in close once more.

I noticed Uncle Mitch looking at me inquisitively again. I ducked my head. I didn't want him to know the nature of my relationship with the guys, but on the other hand, I wasn't going to refrain from touching them or comforting them. It was evident that Easton had it the roughest today, and I was unwilling to curb my affectionate nature towards them.

Easton exhaled loudly. "It's bad out there, especially in

the city. We had to abandon our vehicle at our first stop. It was easier than trying to get it back," he said cryptically. I hadn't even noticed he was in a different vehicle than he'd left with. "Unfortunately, the radio was in that vehicle, but we were able to procure an ultrasound machine, antibiotics, pain-killers, and other vital medical supplies. I'm concerned about the number of medications we were able to locate, though."

"We can plan better next time, send more people," Axel said decisively.

Uncle Mitch nodded. "We're happy you returned safely. The vehicles and radios can be replaced." He reached out and squeezed Easton's shoulder. "I'll send someone down here to unload it all in the first-aid office. Why don't you get some grub and relax for now? We'll have a breakdown meeting once everyone's settled in."

Easton took a deep breath. "I'd like to ensure the medications are at least locked away properly first, if you don't mind. No offense, but I don't trust everyone enough with it all out in the open."

"This shit is like gold," Felix stumbled around the corner of the covered trailer carrying a large cardboard box.

He looked just as exhausted as Easton, and like Easton, he was covered in filth. Other than our first hoard, we had been lucky today. The rest of the teams reported back with similar stories. They had to take a few packs down but not a significant amount. We had already predicted Easton would have the most challenging task today. I imagined we weren't the only ones determined to take or procure medical supplies.

I shuddered at the thought of ever having to face non-infected enemies. I didn't think I could ever grievously harm anyone that wasn't infected. At least I could convince myself that the infected were no longer human and they wouldn't hesitate to end my life.

"I'll make sure everything gets secured," Axel reassured

Easton.

"Or," I suggested. "Why don't we take the medications back to our cabin, and tomorrow morning I'll help you put it all away? You really need to relax."

"That sounds like a great plan," Uncle Mitch agreed. "All of you need to rest. Tomorrow might be much like today."

Felix groaned but smiled. "Can I have kitchen duty? I make mean empanadas and chicken adobo."

Mitch, Easton, Axel, and I laughed at Felix's attempt at humor.

"We'll try not to send out any teams tomorrow," Uncle Mitch said placatingly.

Felix sighed in relief. "Can I sleep-in too?"

We all laughed once more.

"I'm sure we can give a few of ya'll a little more rest." Uncle Mitch smiled.

"I'll take it," Felix said with a relieved sigh.

"Why don't you put the box of medication on the golf cart over there," Axel stated. "I'll take it with me to the conference room, and we'll take it back to the cabin with us when we retire for the night."

I nodded at Easton before weaving my fingers through his. "Let's go get washed up. Uncle Mitch, can I take one of the four-wheelers?"

He tossed me a set of keys. "Go for it. Briefing in one hour."

I caught the keys and nodded at him. "Copy that."

I had planned to shower down here, but the idea of utilizing the bathroom with Easton sounded better. I had a feeling he would need a little extra human contact right now. I had no plans on becoming intimate with him, but I wanted to explore the attraction between us.

"Wanna drive?" I asked him when we reached the rows of ATVs and UTVs.

He shook his head with a faint smile. "No, that's all you. Honestly, I wouldn't know how to work one. Kingston and I grew up in the city. I didn't even get my driver's license until I was eighteen."

"Really?" I asked. "I can't imagine Kingston not seeking the freedom of driving until he was eighteen. A four-wheeler is much easier to learn to ride, though." I smiled at him. I started the vehicle. "This is the clutch," I reached for it with my left hand, "and this is the shifter," I explained to him as I patted my left leg and showed him the shift lever near my toes. "Just tap it up, and release," I told him as I released the clutch. We jolted forward, and he quickly embraced my waist.

I giggled as I sped up. I had to admit this machine was ten-times smoother and sweeter than the well-used one grandpa'd had. We learned how to ride at an early age. Mom and Aunt Pam had tried to scold Pop-pop, but it never stopped him from introducing us to some fun things.

"You'll have to show me how to ride when I can think clearer." Easton chuckled in my ear. "Kingston wasn't nearly as patient as I was. He was hotwiring and boosting cars by fourteen, and by fifteen, he had gained some notoriety on the drag strips."

I gaped at him over my shoulder. "You're pulling my leg!"

He shook his head and grimaced. "I wish I was. Our dad had four other children by the time we were born, leaving my mother to raise us on her own. He didn't pay child support, so she worked a lot to keep food on the table. It was too much freedom for a boy like Kingston. That, and he liked the finer things in life. Thrift store shopping was too beneath him, so he decided to try to make money on his own. He fell into the wrong crowd, and they began teaching him things he had no business ever knowing.

"When he was seventeen, he got caught boosting a car. The owner, surprisingly, wanted to talk to him once he was caught. When he was taken to court for judgment, the judge gave him two options; jail or the military. He chose the military, and we had no choice but to join."

He'd already told me why he himself had joined, that he wanted to be closer to his brother. "And did you ever just want to go back to medical school?" I asked as we entered our cabin.

"I figured I could always go back once he served his six years," he answered. "I didn't expect to like the culture. I didn't invision finding Axel, Wyatt, and Corbin along the way. They became like family, too, and the JOpS gave us something we could never have imagined, a place of belonging."

"And your mom? What did she think about it all?" I inquired.

He grimaced slightly. "She passed away when we were in boot camp."

I had a feeling there was more to the story, but I chose not to press it. Instead, I led us to the bathroom up in the loft. It had a more substantial walk-in shower that could fit us both comfortably.

I turned it on, so it could warm up and began to shed my clothing. He cleared his throat. I looked at him over my shoulder and grinned at him. "I want to take a shower with you, if that's okay."

He was biting his lower lip as his eyes hungrily scanned my body. "That's more than okay," he said huskily as he began to divulge his clothing.

I wasn't disappointed by what he had revealed. As I predicted, he wasn't stacked with muscles, but he was cut and toned. He worked out to stay in shape, not to beef up or become bulky.

I stepped in the shower to prevent myself from reaching out to him and feeling him up. I really did just want to spend some time with him. I knew it wasn't the most conventional way to do so, but with the others busy, I couldn't imagine that many private moments with Easton.

I took inventory of all the bottles lined up on the ledge in the shower. I smiled when I noticed one of them used a shampoo I could use.

"Let me," Easton said huskily as he plucked the bottle from my hands. "Maybe we should put some of your toiletries up here, hmm?" he hummed. "If Kingston notices you smell like him, we'll never hear the end of it."

I laughed as I felt his hands in my hair. I moaned and closed my eyes as he massaged my scalp. "Somehow, that doesn't surprise me," I groaned once more at his ministrations. "You know, I didn't want to share a shower with you just to have you wash my hair."

"I like to washing you," he gruffly muttered as he tilted my head into the streaming water.

"Oh, I'm not complaining." I sighed. "But you're going to have to let me return the favor."

He chuckled. "Deal."

He opened another bottle and pulled me gently out of the stream of water before putting the conditioner in my hair. He took his time, rubbing my scalp once more. It was heavenly and I enjoyed every second under his magical fingers. I wondered if his fingers were just as magical everywhere. I felt the warmth unfurl in my stomach and the wetness between my thighs.

"Did you do a rotation in Labor and Delivery?" I blurted out, hoping to divert my mind from dirty thoughts. No matter how right it felt, I feared I was going too fast with them.

"I did, and I've already talked to Stephanie." He chuckled

knowingly. "That was another reason why we decided to acquire an ultrasound machine. I plan to give her an ultrasound tomorrow. I'd like to see the baby's growth, see where we are. We were able to obtain Pitocin and Epidural anesthesia, just in case, too. I don't want to induce her, and she doesn't want an epidural, but I wanted to make sure we had the medication on hand in the event we needed it. I also obtained birth control for any of the females that wanted it. Did you..."

He seemed unsure how to proceed, and I appreciated him thinking about us females. In this zombie apocalypse, I believed everyone needed to be protected, in any way possible. The times were too perilous to have to worry about getting pregnant. The thought of being pregnant right now gave me the cold chills—not that that was a possibility right now. Wyatt had used a condom, and until I could get over my hang-ups, I planned to continue using them.

"I have an implant," I said, feeling my face warm. "I got if after I lost Bella. I had no intention of accepting Trevor back, but eventually, when I was in a relationship again, I wanted to have control of the situation. I got pregnant the first time because Trevor conveniently forgot to use a condom, and I hadn't known until it was too late."

We had always used condoms. I didn't trust the clinic on campus, and in order to see an OB, I needed my dad's insurance to visit one. I knew Dad wasn't dense, but I didn't want to make it so obvious that I was sexually active. In his eyes, Emery and I would always be his little girls, and I wanted him to continue seeing me as his little girl.

Easton made a sound between a growl and a hiss of anger as he wove his fingers through my conditioned hair, combing out my knots. "We'll have to make sure we record as much of everyone's medical information as possible. We'll need medical histories, list of allergies, etc. And you'll need to remove that IUD eventually, even if you choose to implant another one afterward."

He seemed to have flipped a switch mentally and become a doctor right before my eyes. I didn't know if it was because he didn't want to say something that might offend me, or if it was his way of coping with my truth.

"Maybe we should draw blood from everyone as well," he added thoughtfully.

I laughed. "Maybe we should finish our shower first, Dr. Rains, before we start sticking people. I'll help, though, when the time comes. Do we have enough supplies to collect samples from everyone?"

"We have enough to start," he confirmed with a chuckle. He placed me back into the stream of water.

I tilted my head back and let the water wash out the conditioner. I started when I felt him come back to me with a loofah. I opened my eyes and watched as he began to rub my arms down. He looked at me through dark eyelashes before he moved in closer. When his erection brushed across my stomach, I bit back a moan.

"May I kiss you?" he asked huskily, and just like that, the doctor had left the office.

"Yes," I hoarsely whispered.

I sighed as his lips brushed mine. His lips were so full, so soft, so supple. I didn't know what I expected from our first kiss. Maybe something reticent or reserved like him, but that's not what this was. It was passionate, sensual, and had my blood pumping within seconds. He took control of our kiss without being overbearing or suffocating.

I vaguely registered that he continued to wash me down at the same time his tongue flicked out to trace my lips. I opened my mouth and entangled my tongue with his. He made a noise of appreciation in the back of his throat, and it further enflamed me. I rubbed against him, restlessly wanting more and knowing I was quickly losing control.

He abruptly stepped back and resumed washing my body. I let out a sound of disappointment and frustration.

He smiled crookedly at me before placing a kiss between my breasts. "I want you," he softly explained. "But if it's okay with you, I want to take my time and savor this for a little longer but later. Is that okay?"

I wanted to tell him that I didn't want to wait, but at the same time, he was just echoing my earlier thoughts.

"Yes." I smiled at him before grabbing some shampoo. "I'm okay with that, more than okay with that." I threaded my hands through his curls and applied some pressure to my fingertips.

He groaned and tilted his head back. "Are you sure?"

I could hear the hint of vulnerability in his voice. I knew most guys would hop at any chance to get their dicks wet, but he struck me as someone that didn't have sex just to achieve physical gratification. He was an intellectual person, and I was sure he desired to connect with a woman on a mental level first.

A part of me wondered why he would have ever wanted Jade and Natalie, but I tamped those thoughts down. They were in the past. For all I knew, they had some desirable traits that I had yet to see.

He leaned in and kissed me. "I don't want to mess this up. I don't want to ruin what we could possibly have."

I sighed against his mouth before gently nipping at his full bottom lip. He groaned, and before I knew it, my back was against the wall, his hands were in my hair, and his erection was rubbing against my stomach.

I mewled and arched my back towards him. My mind told me I should respect his wishes, but my body wanted him desperately. I grasped his cock, and he hissed and groaned.

Shit! These guys were well above average, all of them. Well, at least I thought they were, even if I hadn't seen or felt Kingston up yet. I thought it was safe to assume, however, that Easton and Kingston were roughly packing the same length and girth, considering that they were practically identical.

I stroked down his warm, hard length before sliding back up. His mouth hungrily nipped, sucked, and ravaged mine.

"I can't resist you, but I need to," he moaned before trailing kisses down my neck.

His large hands caressed my spine, my hips, and finally, my thighs. In an unexpected move, he bent down slightly before lifting me. "Wrap your legs around me, honey," he bade before pushing me back against the shower.

I complied with no hesitancy. "I thought we were going to wait," I gently teased him before taking his lips with mine.

"We should." He looked down between our bodies.

I felt his hard cock graze against my clit and rock against me. I looked down and was mesmerized at his concentration as he continued to rub himself against my most sensitive area. The sensations he was evoking made every nerve end tingle with anticipation. I cried out and strived to lift my hips so I could feel him inside of me.

"Not yet, honey, not yet," he hoarsely muttered before increasing the movements of his hips. He sensually grinded into me.

"Please," I begged him, feeling so empty and knowing I needed him to make me fully.

I leaned over and took his lobe in my teeth. I nipped it before swirling my tongue around it.

He groaned aloud, and I watched his resistance snap before he lifted me with ease, and in one fluid moment, I was impaled on him. I cried out in completion and surprise, but then I froze when I noticed his stillness.

"I'm sorry," I muttered, breathless, before I attempted to unravel my legs from around him. "I know you wanted to wait. I shouldn't have pushed you."

"Oh, honey, you didn't push me," he breathed out. "I don't have a condom."

I moaned an unintelligible response. I didn't care that he didn't have a condom. I knew they were all clean, and plus, I was on the implant.

He groaned out as well. My eyes nearly rolled into the back of my head as he filled me with long, deep strokes. I began to make unintelligible noises as his pelvis rubbed against my clit. Every now and then between each thrust, he would rotate his hips in just a way to put more pressure and friction against me in the most delicious way.

"Easton," I breathed out in shock as I realized my body was heading towards the edge.

"Yes, honey?" he breathed back as he nibbled along my neck and collarbone.

"I think I'm going to come," I whispered in awe.

He chuckled softly. "Then come for me." He licked my lips before delving into my mouth once more.

He made that erotic motion with his hips once more, and I dug my fingers into his shoulders. He seemed to know how much I liked the way he thrust and grinded into me, because he continued to do it but picked up the intensity and speed of his strokes. My approach to the end was no longer a gentle jog; now it was a sprint, and when I arrived at the finish line, I catapulted over it in a mind-numbing, toe-curling, blissful scream.

He made a guttural groan, and I could feel myself contracting around him, but instead of slowing, his movements became more desperate. The erotic rocking of his hips increased. I gasped out when I felt *another* orgasm approaching. Crying out in astonishment, I shattered around him once again.

He cried out my name, pulled my head back against the stall, bit down on my collarbone as I felt his hot come fill me. I felt weightless as I came down from my high. I think I was even hearing taste and tasting sights! Nothing made sense to me, and I felt the tug of exhaustion on the edge of my consciousness.

I frowned when I remembered reality stood on the other side of the exterior door. Our night wasn't over yet. I was hungry. I had to help in the kitchens, and Easton needed to get something to eat. Then we had a debriefing. I didn't want to do any of it all of a sudden.

"So beautiful," Easton praised me as he gently kissed my lips. "I've never felt so...so..." For once, he was at a loss for words, and I giggled.

"Yeah, right there with you." I laughed before nuzzling his neck. "Better than good. It was mind-numbing and earth-shattering. Can we skip the meeting tonight, and you just take me to bed?"

He chuckled, withdrew entirely from me, and guided me down his body. "We can press pause and continue this later on." He kissed the tip of my nose.

I pouted. "No fun," I teased as I leaned into him.

I could see a thoughtful expression on his face as he looked at me.

"Everything okay?" I asked him hesitantly.

"I wanted us to end up here, but I needed you to get to know me first," he explained as he cupped my cheek and kissed my forhead. "I'm with you right now, but I have a tendency to obsess over things. Sometimes, I get so wrapped up in my work. I forget to eat, let alone give attention to others.

"Eventually, you'll realize I'm not giving you enough devotion, and one of two things will happen. The guys will provide you with more than enough, and you'll realize I'm not even needed in the equation, or you'll grow to resent me because, when I'm in a specific frame of mind, I can't snap out of it easily. With the apocalypse upon us, I know I'm going to spend plenty of time in the medical office and not enough time with you. The time you deserve."

Now it made sense why the others wouldn't have been interested in keeping them in their relationship. I could envision him getting like that. I could see him getting so wrapped up and lost in his head he would forget nearly everything around him.

Little did he know, I was okay with that. My father wasn't always there for us, and when he was, he was so lost in his work sometimes that we all faded away to the background. I overheard a handful of fights between my parents, and it all had to do with his preoccupation and obsessions. Eventually, he had learned to balance it all, and when he forgot, Mom was there to gently nudge him to the living.

Mom learned to devote herself to her career and us. She learned how to coax my father out and when to let him be.

I could figure out ways to make it work. I realized I had only known him a few short days, but something about him was endearing. His calming presence was like a balm to my soul, and there was no denying our chemistry and attraction.

"How about you let me decide that," I reassured him before leaning into him. "I know a bird needs to fly. It wouldn't be fair to clip their wings so I could keep it close. I know you're a brilliant man, and I will choose to watch you fly, and when I feel neglected or desire your company, I'll come fly with you, even if it's just to share a cup of coffee or a meal."

"Do you mean that?" he asked me, his gaze unwavering as he carressed my back.

"I more than mean it." I nodded. "I promise you, we can make it work. I know you all work better as a unit. I'm just touched and honored that you're allowing me into your tight-knit circle."

He gave me the sweetest smile and stepped back. It was then that I realized my legs still felt like jello. He chuckled and stepped forward. I was happy when he continued to hold me. When he felt like I had gained my footing, he finished washing me, and then I finished washing him. It was wonderfully intimate and sweet as we talked, kissed, and explored each other.

I may not have planned to become intimate with him so soon, but I didn't regret it. It just felt like another piece falling in place. There was no doubt in my mind that I was going to enjoy having him in my life.

Chapter 21

"What took you so long to get down here?" Kingston eyed us suspiciously as Easton and I both took a seat at the long conference table in the recreation hall.

All our guests had retired for the night, and the kitchens were closed by the time we'd made our way down. Trudy had left me a note commanding me to rest and reassured me that she could handle the bread tomorrow morning.

I reheated some stew and buttered hunks of bread for us before we made our way to the meeting.

"We took a brief nap." I smirked as I curled up in a chair with my food.

I was glad I chose to dress in comfortable boyfriend-sweats and a tank top. I hadn't even bothered with a bra. I was too tired even to pretend to care right now.

"Is that what you call having sex with all the men you live with?" Emery sneered nearby.

I hadn't even noticed that she was sitting in the corner beside Trevor. The whole room was nearly full, including Uncle Mitch, Aunt Carol, Aunt Pam, Trudy, Axel, Corbin, Wyatt, Kingston, Eddie, Josh, Amy, Chad, Trevor, Emery, BJ, and some guy I vaguely recognized as one of Uncle Mitch's employees.

My first instinct was to show embarrassment and look at Uncle Mitch, Aunt Carol, and Aunt Pam. They were the closest things to parents I had here, and I would die of mortification if my dad were here. I would much rather let him know in person that I was interested in all five of the men in my life before it was announced to a room full of people.

Then I realized that was her intention. Once again, the ugly green-eyed monster that resided in Emery was called forth. She wanted me to be embarrassed. She wanted to shame me for my ability to care for five men and their return of those feelings. If the situation were reversed, she would be basking in all the attention, flaunting it in everyone's face. She clearly despised me for not being as affected by her relationship with Trevor as she thought I'd be.

"Wouldn't you like to know?" I smirked at her before I made an exaggerated show of dipping my bread in my stew and taking a large bite of it. "In fact," I said around my food, not caring I was being uncouth and rude, "...it's none of your business."

"Simmer down, Em, no one cares for your theatrics right now," Corbin growled. "Unlike you, some of us actually did hard labor today. We just want to get this meeting rolling and get to bed."

"Emery worked today," Trevor protested half-heartedly once Emery shot Corbin a pointed look.

I tried not to look at Trevor. He had already tried to corner me before we'd left this morning, and I wasn't ready to talk to him. It was evident that he didn't like the fact that I was in a relationship with Corbin and Wyatt. He wanted to give me advice, like I was still his best friend, but he lost the right to have a say in my life when he became emotionally unavailable to me and cheated.

"More like she hid from work," Wyatt scoffed. "You showed up at the dining hall for five minutes, Emery, and then disappeared. When my mom found you, she sent you to the supply building, since you insisted you couldn't work in the kitchens. You lasted thirty minutes in there before you disappeared again."

"I was told we were going to all get jobs that played to our strengths," she protested vehemently. "I don't like cooking, and the supply building is disgusting."

"What exactly are your strengths?" Corbin said with a slight frown. "We all agreed yesterday that we needed to work together to make this community successful. In order to make things work, we're going to have to do things we don't necessarily enjoy."

"It's not like we need models or fashion designers, princess. You're going to have to adapt," Wyatt added. "It's not fair that people who have no family ties to the campgrounds are pulling more of their weight than you."

"Exactly," she nearly screeched. "*My* family. I shouldn't have to work nearly as hard as all these freeloaders."

I gaped at her audacity, then looked around the room and quickly saw the look of shock cross the faces of Eddie, Trudy, and Donny.

Uncle Mitch stood up, looking angry. "You've gone too far, Emery. You can leave the meeting right now. Your father would be so disappointed to hear the nonsense you're spewing. Some of these people have contributed above and beyond expectations. For you to treat them like quote un-quote 'freeloaders' is highly unacceptable. Especially since I haven't seen you do anything but complain and act entitled to something you never earned. In fact, you're going to have to earn your way back into our meetings. Tomorrow you'll be working by my side. I don't care if you think anything I assign you is below you, you *will* do it."

"Or what?" Emery almost sounded fearful for a moment before she looked over at Trevor. "Are you going to let them gang up on me? Are you going to kick me out, Uncle Mitch? Will you do that to *family*? You can't make me do anything I don't want to do."

"You brought this on yourself." Uncle Mitch scowled at her.

Trevor leaned down next to her ear and began to whisper to her urgently.

"I'm *not* saying sorry," I heard her screech out before she pushed away from the table. "This is total bullshit! I'm not a workhorse. I shouldn't have to work."

"Yes, you should!" Trevor stood up, showing a rare show of anger. "It's not fair to Uncle Mitch or our families to throw a temper tantrum. Please, Em, apologize."

Corbin snorted and shook his head. Trevor shot him a look of loathing before he tried to pull Emery close and comfort her.

"If you don't work, you don't eat, Emery Rose." Aunt Carol glared at her. "You're acting like a spoiled teenager, not a twenty-one-year-old woman."

Emery teared up dramatically and turned into Trevor's chest. "I can't believe you're treating me like this. I'm family. I'm scared, and I miss my daddy. Why can't you give me some more time?"

Corbin stood up and glared at her. "Not everything is about you, Em. You think we all want to be in this situation? Don't you think we all have someone we miss? You're going to have to get over yourself and suck it up."

She recoiled before she was on the defense once more. "This all started because I called your little whore out." She glared at me. "Are you happy that they're all ganging up on me?"

"Don't call her that again," Kingston said in a quiet, deadly tone. "You behave as if you didn't corner me last night in just your underwear. You propositioned me while your sister's ex-boyfriend was waiting for you at your cabin. Let's not throw stones from glasshouses. Your sister has more class in her pinky than you have in your entire body."

Trevor recoiled away from her. "What?" he inquired in a hurt tone. "Did you really do that?"

"No!" she cried out, looking panicked. "He's lying!"

Kingston began to laugh mirthlessly, crossed his arms over his chest, and shook his head. "Can we get on with this meeting? Your need for attention is comical."

"Why would he lie about something like that?" Trevor inquired with a deep frown. "You disappeared last night for a little while. Where did you go?"

A small part of me felt sympathy for Trevor. I knew how it felt to be betrayed. However, if Emery ever cheated on him, wasn't that karma coming back around?

I refused to acknowledge Emery and dug back into my soup like the whole conference room wasn't becoming privy to my private life. It hurt me and made me mystified by how we were sisters. More than sisters. We were identical twins. I couldn't understand how BJ and I could be so different. The same people raised us.

"She's having them lie about me now," Emery pouted. "She's mad that we're together and wants everyone to hate me."

"You're bringing this on yourself, Emery," BJ huffed out. "Stop lying. Stop trying to blame others for your behavior. Just leave. Some of us want to get some sleep tonight because we earned it. It's sad that you want to continue tearing Avery down and blame her for your actions. She's our sister. Why are you so jealous of her, Emery?"

"I'm not jealous of Avery. I just don't think it's fair she gets preferential treatment. Avery was late to our meeting. She disrupted it." Then her lips twisted grotesquely before she smirked. "Aunt Pam, Uncle Mitch, and Aunt Carol, what do *you* think about your sons sleeping with their cousin? You told some people tonight that they couldn't have a cabin because it needed to go to family units first. Yet you gave her a cabin with her boyfriends. Why do Trevor and I have to live in the big house with ya'll, and they get their own space? You've always favored her over me!"

Aunt Pam stood up and glared at Emery. She rarely got angry, and I cringed at the look in her eyes. "Emery, stop disrupting this meeting. There isn't enough room up at the house for all of them, and they are a team. They have more than pulled their weight around here, and in your father's absence, he appointed Avery a decision-maker. If she wants a cabin, she'll get one."

When Emery went to protest, Aunt Pam held up her hand. "Before you start throwing more of a pity party, it would behoove you to remember how irresponsible you've behaved in the past. You haven't shown any fiscal or personal responsibility, to the point where your father has had to pay for your expenses time and time again to bail you out. Avery has demonstrated her maturity for years now. She didn't blow through her grandparents' inheritance, her mother's inheritance, and modeling money as you have. She got scholarships on her own merit and has never had to call your father for a single dime.

"You're spreading lies about your sister. Don't think I haven't heard them. You are with Trevor now, and by your own accusations, he's your cousin, too, dear. You need to start doing some soul-searching and determine if you're the cause of most of your problems. Corbin is an adult. If he entered into an arrangement with Avery, then it's their business and no one else's. I, for one, love the fact that at least one of my sons will be happy."

Emery recoiled back, and for a split second, I believed Aunt Pam had truly hurt her. Real tears entered her eyes, and she appeared wounded by the inference that Trevor wouldn't be happy with her.

"I second that for Wyatt," Aunt Carol said with determination. "Avery has a huge heart, and I've seen how happy she's made Wyatt. At the end of the day, that's all that matters to his father and me."

I felt my heart expand at their approval as Aunt Pam smiled at me.

"Maybe you need a little time out," Uncle Mitch said. "Meet me at the dining hall at 0700. Tomorrow's a new day."

"Whatever. Are you coming with me?" Emery turned to Trevor.

He had sat back down and put his head in his hands. His eyes met mine for a moment, and for a split second, I was transported back in time to when I had opened the door of his bedroom. I had cried out like a wounded animal when I saw him lying beside Emery. He had woken up and looked at me in confusion before he looked over at a smiling Emery. When he had gazed back at me, I saw the horror, regret, and pain once he'd realized his mistake.

He had chased me out of his room, buck naked, as I called Sylvia to come pick me back up, hoping she hadn't gotten that far. He tried to beg me to forgive him, tried to convince me he hadn't realized what he'd done. Sobbing, I'd told him I couldn't be with him anymore, that I had needed him all day and he hadn't been there. I informed him about our lost Bella and told him I couldn't forgive him for his mistake. He had collapsed on the bottom of the stairs, amid red solo cups, beer bottles, female undergarments, and the rest of the party wreckage from the night before, begging me to return, revealing in every expression that he'd regretted his blunder.

Now as he looked at me, I wanted to feel sympathy, but he had brought this all on himself. I turned away.

"No, Em," he said finally. "I have a responsibility here,

and I'm going to take it seriously. We have no choice but to start acting like it."

I refused to look at her as she left the room. Wyatt came over and pulled me from the chair and back into his lap. He squeezed me close, and Easton reached over to grab my hand as the meeting finally began.

⬚

"Do you think if we were to procure campers and RVs that it would be a better long term solution?" Axel inquired as he jotted something down in his notebook. "If we continue finding more survivors, maybe the camper cabins can be used as transient facility until we can determine if the people will contribute as they should. You have all that space and hookups for campers and RVs, and they're not being utilized."

"I think that's a great idea," Aunt Carol enthused. "Young girls like Michaela shouldn't have to share a cabin with all the rest of the single females. She's determined to take care of her siblings, and she should have the space to do so."

"Should a girl of fifteen be given that amount of space?" Amy asked hesitantly. "Maybe it's best if we take care of her siblings and keep her in the single female cabin."

"We tried to offer it," Aunt Pam said with a slight frown. "She was opposed to the idea. She feels like her siblings are her responsibility. Plus, she's already more than proven herself. She deserves the space, but the hunter cabins may be too big."

"There's an RV dealership not too far from here," Eddie stated. "If we leave in the morning with enough people, we should be able to make one trip."

"Okay," Uncle Mitch said as he walked back over to me. "So, who do we have available to make the run?"

I had volunteered to take over the whiteboard, with the list of everyone's specialties. I had neat penmanship, and the project played to my strengths of organization. I had written out our primary focus areas: kitchen, clean up, contracting, gardens, livestock, security, recovery, and stocking. It was easy to slot some people into their "jobs," but there were others, like me, that would be considered a floater.

Out of necessity, people like Josh and Chad would have to lead the gardens and livestock occupations until everything was established and we had the right people allotted to those jobs. Both men were better utilized on security and recovery, but we couldn't move them just yet since they were the only ones with real experience when it came to farming and raising animals.

"These are the people that have no real spots yet," I stated as I began to list the people with no real "talents."

"I don't think it should be any of our newcomers," Axel stated firmly. "I don't like the idea of sending any of my men out with untrained civilians until I feel comfortable with their abilities." He eyed me warily as if he expected me to protest, but I wholeheartedly agreed.

"And people like Rhys Miller should never be required to do any recovery," Corbin added. "He has two young kids, and he can efficiently work security here without putting him in direct danger."

"How do we know when people can go with the recovery team?" Donny inquired. "Our list is long, and the longer we wait, the likelihood of danger of the undead kind arises."

"They can start on security," Uncle Mitch stated. "Between me, Axel, and Joe, we'll determine if they can be better utilized out there and decide what we absolutely need, from most important to least."

"We have to be realistic, though, and accept that most of them won't want the job or simply *can't* do the job," Axel stated bluntly. "From the sounds of it, Rhys and three other people could handle the stress and protect the super-mart they were holed up in. It's important anyone out there doesn't become a liability."

"It's a reasonable expectation," Uncle Mitch agreed. "How does our food supply look?"

"I'll go through the pantries tomorrow," Trudy stated. "Obviously, we hadn't planned on all the extra mouths to feed, so we have limited resources. Can I give you my list by lunch?"

"Sounds good." Axel nodded. "I'll need Eddie's and Donny's expertise for prime locations to acquire the goods. However, I am inclined to agree with Donny. I think we need to have a team or two dispatched every day. We already know there are just some items we need, regardless of a list."

"Okay." Uncle Mitch nodded. "Any other suggestions to make sure our community thrives?"

"Gas is not an infinite source. The equipment we have runs on gas, but we need to think about the long-term supply," Josh stated.

"We already have a few gas carts in the supply building," Wyatt stated. "We can go back to the mall and start siphoning the gas from the vehicles in the parking lot."

"Maybe we should hit up an automotive store, too, for fuel stabilizer, just in case the gas we get goes bad," Kingston suggested. "Plus, we'll need a mechanic for maintenance of the vehicles and campers we plan on getting. Felix has a basic understanding of engines and mechanics, but maybe we should approach Warren and find out how much he really knows about that stuff."

Warren was one of the guys that had arrived tonight. We were pleasantly surprised to find more than a handful of people with experience that would help our community in the long run.

"I'll approach him in the morning," Uncle Mitch agreed. "I already had the electrician and contractor approach me at dinner. They seem eager to jump into any projects. I know we need to finish installing those solar panels, just in case. And I'm hoping to have the contractor team up with Donny and have them start on sectioning off the camper cabins. Even if they are used as temporary living facilities, I want people to have some semblance of privacy. Anything else we should address right now?"

"I think we need to be mindful of how we handle our waste," Chad spoke up next. "We have pigs now. Our feed is limited, and pigs and chickens can be scavengers. Recycling and reusing waste will be important in the months ahead. I noticed a lot of people were quick to throw away uneaten food today, when the pigs and chickens will eat most of it if not all. We just need to be careful not to give the chickens garlic or onions. Scraps would cut back on some of their normal feed. I'll find some old trash cans, and we'll label them. It's not like we have trash collections coming by anymore."

"I didn't even think about the trash and recyling issue. I'll make sure to start recycling back in the kitchens, too," Trudy stated. "I forgot my grandma used to feed the chickens a lot of our food prep waste."

"Perfect," Chad said with a smile before looking at Donny. "I think I'll have Sam collect the food waste after every meal."

Donny smirked. "I'll let him know in the morning."

"Should we require someone that young to do that?" Eddie said with a slight frown. "Shouldn't we let the kids be kids? I don't want to put that much responsibility on their young shoulders."

"He has a learner's permit," Donny said with a shrug. "If society thinks he's old enough to be responsible behind the wheel, then he's old enough to help around the campground."

"We can even give some of the younger ones chores. It'll be good for them," Aunt Carol added. "I'll take a few of them down to the chickens tomorrow morning and we'll collect eggs."

"I'm sure some of them would love to feed the little ones," Wyatt said with a small smile.

Axel's team had taken Bane with them to a local farm and garden, center along with a small group of people. He said Bane did great, and the store wasn't even touched by the infected or any looters, surprisingly enough.

The team had been able to secure a couple tractor-trailers and nearly emptied the store of anything useful. They procured garden equipment, more fruit and nut trees, fruit bushes, seeds, and different kinds of feed. The store still had animals as well. The team had returned with over fourteen dozen different chickens, ducks, rabbits, and turkeys. They said it appeared like an employee had dumped bags of food in their enclosures and left gallons of water to keep them sustained.

The fowl were currently in the greenhouses, under heat lamps, until they were old enough to be slowly introduced to the other flock of chickens we were able to obtain. The kids had gone crazy over the tiny new additions.

Chad and Donny had a lot of work cut out for them tomorrow. The roosting boxes and perches would have to be built for the chickens. Some of the fencing needed repairing, and chicken wire would have to be erected around the fence as well, to prevent any predators from coming in.

"I'll take one of the older kids over to show them how to care for them," Aunt Carol volunteered.

"All good things. Okay, so let's finalize this list, and we'll leave shortly after breakfast," Uncle Mitch said. "We'll have another breakdown meeting tomorrow night, but earlier."

We all laughed. It wasn't even midnight yet, but we were all feeling today's activities. I was relieved when Stephanie had volunteered to watch Isa. I was so close to bringing her since I missed her, but Easton reasoned with me. She had been sleeping for hours, and it didn't make sense to wake her and disrupt her sleep.

"We'll have the list ready by breakfast," Corbin reassured Uncle Mitch before he walked over to where I was standing.

"I can stay back," Uncle Mitch blustered.

"Go to sleep, old man," Wyatt teased before coming over to the whiteboard as well.

"I'll show you *old man*," Uncle Mitch teased before putting Wyatt into a headlock. "Carol, keep the bed warm. I'll be up in a little bit." Uncle Mitch was built similar to his son and still in great shape. If they were serious, I had a feeling the wrestling would be a pretty even match.

"I'll more than keep it warm for you," Carol said suggestively with a bold wink.

"Mom!" Wyatt cried out in horror while making no real move to break his dad's hold. "I can't unhear these things!"

"Good, take some notes," Aunt Carol said saucily. "Ask your dad for some pointers. After nearly thirty years of marriage, your father still keeps me satisfied. I'm sure Avery would love to say the same in thirty years."

"Mom!"

"Aunt Carol!"

We cried out simultaneously as everyone laughed at our expense.

Everyone began to trickle out. Aunt Pam made a stop by Corbin first. He reached down and gave her a hug and a kiss on her cheek.

"You better treat her right," I heard her murmur to him.

Corbin looked over at me and gave me a warm smile that made butterflies take flight in my stomach. I didn't know I could feel so special and cherished by a mere smile. It was hard to imagine that my ex-fiancé's brother and childhood friend could ever garner the affection I felt for him now.

"Always, Ma, always." He kissed her forehead. "Night, see you in the morning."

Aunt Pam came over to me and took my hands in hers before standing on her tiptoes and kissing my cheek.

"I love you," I mumbled to her, still grateful for her acceptance of my relationship with Corbin and his friends.

"I love you, too, honey." She smiled. "It wasn't the way I planned it, but somehow I have a feeling your mother's looking down on us now, laughing. She always thought it was going to be Corbin, until you and Trevor became inseparable. One of the last conversations I had with her, she told me how she envisioned your brother's and sister's future mates *and* your wedding with Corbin. I thought the disease had made her more confused than normal. I never corrected her, but maybe even then, she knew."

It felt like a lead ball hit my stomach. Mom was very forgetful in the end. The disease had made her a shell of the person she once was. She nearly became unrecognizable. Some people couldn't handle seeing her that way or even visit her because of her mood swings and mental deterioration. Aunt Pam and Aunt Carol had rarely left her side, though, when Dad needed a break.

They had taken everything in stride and showed me the meaning of true friendship and love. I had admired them all my life and strived to be like them one day.

I never knew Mom had dreams of our partners or our marriages. One day, when I was mentally and emotionally prepared, I wanted to ask my aunt more about their conversation.

"I–" I paused, at a loss for words.

Aunt Pam smiled and patted my cheek once more. "We'll talk about it one day. I just wanted to let you know that I'm sure she would approve of your new arrangements, just as I do."

I was happy she understood my need to be emotionally and mentally prepared to hear more. I loved hearing stories about my mother and learning the other side I rarely caught a glimpse of. Now, however, wasn't the time, especially after Emery's theatrics tonight.

"Thanks, Aunt Pam." My voice came out shaky, and my eyes burned from unshed tears.

"Come on, Pam," Aunt Carol bade her. "I think our future daughter-in-law has been thrown enough feelings tonight."

I gasped and laughed at the same time, looking at Corbin and Wyatt for a little help. Nope! They both just laughed.

Corbin came up behind me and slipped his arms around my waist. "I like the sound of that," he murmured in my ear.

"Stop!" I protested, my maudlin thoughts dashed away at the mischievousness in his tone. "We're just starting to get to know each other again. We may grow sick of each other in a few weeks!"

"Not likely," Wyatt smirked as his dad let him go.

"Oh, I'm sure you'll get sick of M&M," Uncle Mitch roguishly said as he grinned at me. "These boys will never tire of your beauty and kindness, dear niece."

I gaped at him. M&M was my secret family nickname for them.

"M& M?" Kingston inquired with an evil grin.

"Uncle Mitch!" I protested loudly.

Uncle Mitch chuckled.

"I'm Mischief." Corbin smirked.

Wyatt grinned. "I'm Misfit."

"We teased her a lot growing up," Corbin said with zero shame.

"Sounds about right." Kingston smirked.

They all began to laugh at my expense, and I rolled my eyes. "Come on, let's figure out who's doing what so I can have it finalized and wheel this bad boy into the dining hall." I pointed to the presentation pad that Uncle Mitch had located for me. After I had finished transcribing our notes onto the whiteboard, I had to transfer it to the presentation pad. The idea was that, when everyone came down for breakfast, we'd all know who was going where. We had every intention of letting everyone know it was temporary and probational duty.

We realized not everyone was going to like where they were going or even be useful in that capacity we were provisionally placing them in. But we did want everyone to find their niche here. Some people might have multiple talents, while others might find a new one in the coming weeks and months. We were trying to navigate these unchartered territories to the best of our ability.

"Aww is someone getting embarrassed?" Kingston teased me before bopping my nose.

I snarled playfully at him. Honestly, I should be embarrassed. Even though I was emotionally wrung out tonight, I felt lighter than I had since our confrontation with Emery. Still, I was more relaxed now, knowing I had the support of my family in this unconventional relationship I had with the guys.

"Come on, boys," Axel said gruffly. "Let's get serious so that Avery can get her sleep."

Kingston sighed loudly. "Fine, let's-" he began before the clang and chime of a bell went off.

We all paused and looked at each other in confusion. From the distinct sound of the bell, I knew it came from the campers' cabins. My brows furrowed before a feeling of premonition grazed my stomach, into my heart, and up to my throat.

I didn't think, I just reacted. I grabbed my sais off the chair I had been sitting on. I don't think my feet hit the ground as adrenaline coursed through my veins. I vaguely registered Axel and Corbin falling into step beside me.

As we entered the chilly night air, my blood curdled in fear as I heard the screams of frightened people. It was closely followed by screams of infected. I witnessed people getting attacked as they tried to run away into the night and saw some infected dashing with inhuman speed towards Aunt Pam, Aunt Carol, and little James.

Chapter 22

"Everyone stay on me," Axel barked out as he began heading towards Aunt Pam, Aunt Carol, and James since they were the closest.

I never witnessed the infected at night. During the day, they scared me. At night, the paralyzingly fear petrified me.

"Get inside, now!" Uncle Mitch screamed at the women.

They had just closed the door when one of the infected reached them, tearing the screen door and ripping it clear off the door frame right where Aunt Pam stood. Axel's feet didn't even touch the stairs as he leaped onto the porch. The terrifying screams of Aunt Carol and James wasn't a sound I would ever forget.

Bane came from no where, snarling, his teeth pulled back, and if I hadn't known any better, I would have been terrified of him. He placed himself between Aunt Carol and James, and I was thankful he had seemed reluctant to leave Isa's side earlier tonight. I knew animals had a keen sense of danger, but had he known this?

The sounds of Axel's feet pounding on the wooden slats reverberated in my skull.

"Mom!" Corbin yelled, his voice breaking as the infected fell on top of Aunt Pam. The infected dragged her further out onto the porch as if he wanted to avoid Bane's viscous snaps.

I opened my mouth to scream in terror, but no sound came out. If Kingston hadn't nudged me as he ran past, I would have stayed frozen in fear. I didn't want to see if the infected had latched onto my beloved aunt.

Axel launched himself at the back of the infected hovering over Aunt Pam. Another infected was reaching for Axel just as Corbin hurled a knife into its eyes. He didn't stop moving as he slashed at the next person. A woman that I recognized as one of our new members bared her teeth at Corbin and launched herself towards his arm. I surged forward with my sai, connecting with her temple before turning towards the next infected. I turned just in time as another man went to grab me by my hair and yank me back into his gaping maw. I sliced out at him, grazing his cheek in my panic.

As he loomed even closer, I pulled my sai from the first infected's temple, and with both hands, struck out at the infected man. One of my sais landed in his neck, spraying his coagulated blood on my chest and chin. I closed my eyes and mouth just in time as I felt and smelled the metallic scent of blood striking me in the face. I tried to remember where the man was as I hit him with my other sai. The man fell, my hair still grasped in his meaty paws.

I really regret not putting my hair back, was my last thought as I stumbled back. The feeling of free-falling was alarming, and I hoped my aim had struck true. I was too afraid to open my eyes, too worried that his blood would enter them and infect me.

"I got you, goddess," I recognized one of the twin's voices. Without my sight, it was hard to tell which one of them it was. I never noticed how alike they sounded until that moment.

I was pulled into a chest before a cloth touched my face. "Don't open your eyes," he said in soothing tones.

"Was she bitten?" I heard his twin ask in panic, right as Corbin cried out in relief.

"I'm fine, I'm fine," I heard Aunt Pam laugh shakily.

"Phew, that was a close one!"

"Good boy, Bane," I heard Aunt Carol murmur. "I'm making you a steak for that one, buddy."

Ironically enough, Aunt Carol hadn't liked my dog upon meeting him, even though he was still a puppy. She wanted to believe that the media was correct when identifying dog breeds and their attacks. She was afraid that, since Bane had Pit Bull in him, he would turn one day. I had a feeling she'd be viewing him in a much different light in the future.

"Get inside and lock the door," Uncle Mitch said gruffly. "I'll come and let you know when everything's taken care of."

"Good job, Bane," I heard Axel praise the dog as well. "Now, stay."

I felt a wet cloth stroke my face. "Just a little more, goddess," the twin holding me murmured reassuringly.

I was shaking like a leaf. I felt like I was going to get sick. It felt like forever as my face was wiped down of the nasty bodily fluid.

"Okay, angel, open up," the other twin instructed me.

"Ave, why don't you stay with Aunt Pam and Mom?" Wyatt instructed as I blinked my eyes open.

I was beyond petrified as I looked up into Kingston's eyes. I should have recognized it was him, considering the fact he'd called me goddess. He had called me that once before.

"You're okay, none got in your eyes," he reassured me as he pulled me in close.

I melted into his embrace. I just wanted to break down and cry. I wanted to crawl into the house and hide. I looked over at Aunt Pam, Aunt Carol, and James hovering in the doorway as Uncle Mitch clutched them to his chest. He kissed all three of them tenderly, and I was reassured they would be okay as Aunt Carol insisted that Uncle Mitch figure out what was going on.

Another scream rent the air. Chills slid down my spine as I saw an infected chasing after Ricky, Mike's little brother. I knew then I couldn't break down or hide in fear. There were people out there that needed me.

I pulled away from Kingston and nuzzled his neck. "Thank you," I whispered before I grabbed the railing, jumped over it into the flower bed, and ran in the direction of the boathouse.

My determined gaze never left Ricky's as he slid into the boathouse. I watched in mortification as the three infected followed him in.

"Avery!" Wyatt yelled at me.

"No," I yelled back, not breaking stride. I didn't have time to stop and argue with him.

I reached the boathouse seconds before Kingston and Easton. The three infected were trying to push over a canoe, and I reached for the closest one, while Kingston struck out with his kamas. For the first time, I got to witness Easton in action with his nunchucks. I watched in awe and fascination as Easton's nunchucks whistled through the air and wrapped around an infected's throat. I blinked– it had happened that fast– and the infected was lying on the ground, his head twisted at an awkward angle. Easton whipped his nunchucks back to himself, his wrist turning fluidly as he swung the weapon back over his shoulder.

With a swiftness I was both shocked and impressed by, Kingston finished the kill.

"Ricky," I called out in fear.

"Hewe," he called out in a trembling voice.

I nearly sobbed at the sound of his sweet lisp.

A light was turned on behind us, and I saw Ricky illuminated in the bow of one of the canoes. He was curled into a tight little ball as far back as he could get.

390

"Are you okay, buddy?" Corbin asked as he stepped forward with the flashlight.

"Yes," he sobbed. "Mike wung the bell. She told me to wun with Molly, but I lost her. I lost her," he shrieked with his lisps. "Mike is going to be so mad at me."

"We'll go find her, come on, buddy, we got to take you somewhere safe," Corbin held out a hand.

"Mike will just be happy you're safe," Wyatt tried to reassure him.

Ricky didn't seem reassured as he eyed us with fear. It was apparent he was still frightened out of his mind.

"I'll go get him," Uncle Mitch rasped. "You help everyone else."

"You can't go alone," Wyatt insisted.

"I'll go with your dad," Easton reassured Wyatt grimly. "I'll take Ricky to the med clinic to inspect him."

I felt sick once more. The idea that a boy so young could get infected turned my stomach. If he was turned, then what? I didn't know what we would do in that situation.

"Avery, you should go with them, too," Wyatt said grimly.

"Not right now, Wy," I begged him. "I can be of greater help out there."

Another scream rent the air as if punctuating my point. Until the infected were cleared, we had no clue how many people were injured. Easton needed to return to get the clinic set up. Uncle Mitch had enough combat medical knowledge to be of help. My presence would just be overkill until the dust settled.

"Let's move out," Axel commanded, his eyes running over me as another inhuman shriek sounded nearby. "Eden, our girl comes with us."

I saw Wyatt open his mouth to protest, but his military training was deeply embedded in him, so he snapped his jaw closed and jerkily nodded. He knew he couldn't argue with his commanding officer, and even though they were no longer in the field, Axel still held power over him in times like these.

Axel turned to leave first, and we followed. We made our way up the hill. The following ten minutes, thirty minutes, hour–hell if I knew how much time had passed—went by in a blur. As a unit, Axel, Corbin, Wyatt, Kingston, and I worked together taking down infected.

My chest was heaving, and I didn't think I would ever be able to breathe again as we neared the campers' cabins. We met up with Chad, Joe, Cal, BJ, and Mike at the bathrooms. We turned to assess our surroundings. My eyes strained as I heard grunting off to the right. Wyatt and Kingston pulled out their flashlights, scanning the area.

I nearly cried out in warning as I saw Trevor approximately forty feet from us. He was taking shots at a couple of infected. It was clear his adrenaline was too high as he continued to miss. He didn't even hear the four other infected running up behind him. Axel and Corbin reached down to their hips, pulled out their guns- damn near in sync – and took careful aim, shooting the infected one by one and dispatching all of them in less than four seconds. Their ability to work together would never cease to impress me.

Trevor looked over at us in relief before he headed towards the lake. "Thanks," he mumbled as he ran shaking hands through his hair.

"Wait up. What are you even doing out here, Trev?" Corbin asked in a tight voice as he ran over to him. He embraced Trevor into a hug, then released him. I knew that, even though they may be at odds with each other, they still loved each other.

Trevor walked over to the deck boxes located near the

lake. It was usually full of beach toys and inflatables. He reached down, and when he stood, I nearly cried out in relief when I saw Molly's little arms wrapped around his neck.

"I was taking a walk around the lake when all hell broke loose," he explained. "That's when the bell began to ring. I saw a boy and this little one getting chased. She was nearly in the lake when I stuck her in there until it was safe."

"Molly!" Mike cried out as she ran towards the little girl. "Where's Ricky?"

"Ricky's safe," Corbin reassured her. "He's down at the med shack. Chad, would you mind taking them so we can do a final sweep and start the cleanup?"

"No problem," Chad nodded. "Come on, mini-warrior," he bade Mike before looking over at me with a tilt of his lips. "If you're a little warrior, this one here is a mini- warrior."

I smiled at his attempt to alleviate a stressful and scary situation.

Mike seemed to preen at his praise before muttering positively. "I did what I had to."

"And warned us all," BJ reminded her before swinging an arm around her shoulders and hugging her.

In the beam of the flashlight, I was pretty sure I saw her blushing under his attention.

"I gotta go get my brother," Mike murmured before stumbling back. She had her head down and wouldn't even look up at BJ.

That wasn't like the girl with grit I had come to know. She'd spent all afternoon working and had no problem telling people what should or shouldn't be done, in regards to the animals or farming in general. There was no doubt her grandparents had leaned on her and had her helping them from a very young age.

"Where's your other brother, uh... Carson, right?" I

asked her in concern, hoping to help her from her adolescent awkwardness.

"Mike rang the bell and started running some of the little ones towards the loft in the barn," Joe explained as he pointed in the direction of our cabins. "I ran into her as she was coming back out to fight off the infected. Felix, Josh, and Amy took the kids on the quads to Sylvia and Officer Miller in Sleepy Pines,"

Our cabin, Sylvia's cabin, Officer Rhys Miller's, and two other vacant cabins, shared a patch of land Nana named Sleepy Pines. Sleepy Pines was the closest set of cottages, but if you continued down the dirt road, other cabins were there. Not all of them were set up like ours, and some of them offered a lot more seclusion. We chose our cabin because of its vicinity to the central part of the camp and because it housed the smaller cottages. On one of the farthest points of Sanctuary Lakes' developed land, there was a cabin large enough to sleep thirty people.

"It's probably best if they stay there for now," Axel agreed with a nod. "Let's do our sweep and begin to burn the dead. Did anyone check them over for... bites?"

"Mike was able to get them to safety before they even encountered any infected," Cal reassured us.

"We should recheck them," Axel insisted.

We all stopped in the quiet of the now-still night and looked about us. It was dark, but the landscape lighting strategically placed on the paths was enough to illuminate some of the carnage.

Tonight at dinner, we had a little over a hundred people, with our new arrivals and those who had first taken refuge here. As I looked on, I recognized at least twenty of them among the dead.

I felt no shame as I stumbled towards my closest guy.

Wyatt pulled me in close and kissed my head tenderly.

He let me seek refuge in him despite the fact he hadn't wanted me out there. I understood his need to protect me, and I knew this wasn't the last time he would fight me with my decision to be in the thick of battle, but at least he was showing me he would be there for me no matter what.

"Let's get this little princess checked out," Trevor interrupted my thoughts, and I looked up in time to see him walk down the hill towards the first-aid building.

He threw one look over his shoulder, and I knew it bothered him to see me with Wyatt. His reason for being out here seemed to sink in as I watched him walk away. He never took long walks unless it was to clear his head. I knew he wasn't thrilled with Emery, but something must be keeping him with her.

He was a mama's boy, through and through, in fact, Corbin was too. Their mother's words held a lot of weight with them. Aunt Pam unwittingly admitting her belief that Emery would never make him happy must have affected him greatly.

Once again, a part of me felt sorry for him. His actions tonight demonstrated that, at his core, Trevor was still a nice guy. He'd put himself in danger to save a little girl.

"How did this happen?" Wyatt muttered in frustration. "Did the infected break our front gate?"

"No," Axel said grimly. "I don't think that was it at all." He made no further comment to that cryptic remark before he turned to begin our sweep and clean up.

⬚

Twenty-eight people. That's how many people we'd lost. By morning, it was possible we'd have five more to add to the list. Five people had been bitten, one clearly to the bone, but Easton had fought to keep them alive. Uncle Mitch, Borris the contractor, and a few other guys had made a makeshift quarantine area. They were contained separately and would be delivered food and meds, but we didn't think they would survive.

A little girl of six, who was now an orphan, broke my heart the most. I didn't want to think about what would happen if she turned. She had clearly been bitten, but the marks didn't seem to have broken the skin.

"I don't understand what happened. How did we miss an infected?" Corbin asked as he sat down next to me, taking a sip of his coffee. "Is it possible that they don't show signs before they turn?"

The sun was nearly coming up when we finished cleaning up and took our showers. We all made our way back to the dining hall, where almost everyone was now sleeping on the floor. Aunt Carol had erected a projector and put on children's movies for the scared children, and Trudy had put out some coffee and snacks for the cleanup crew.

Most of the survivors of tonight's wreckage were down here as well. Only two of the cabins had been cleaned and ready for "campers" before disaster had hit. Now with both cabins being aired out because of the strong bleach smell and a lot of items ruined for reuse, we had more items to add to the list of things we needed to do tomorrow– well, technically today. Our list of items had grown as well.

"Maybe they hid the symptoms," Kingston said as he took the seat on the other side of me.

Uncle Mitch, Borris, Axel, Corbin, Wyatt, Kingston, Trevor, BJ, Mike, and I were taking a brief break and decompressing after a harrowing night. Isa was safely tucked in my arms as I patted her back from the bottle she'd just had. Luckily, Stephanie, in her advanced pregnancy, was unaware of most of tonight's "excitement." It wasn't until she came down to start breakfast that she noticed us all together.

I took Isa from her immediately and just held the baby close for a long time. The guys had taken turns cuddling her as well. It was like she was a reminder of how tenuous life could be and made us appreciate the sign of new hope and beginnings.

"I think it's important we get walls erected in the cabins," Uncle Mitch said wearily. "We can't have what happened tonight happen again."

From the accounts of the survivors, most of them had woken to people screaming. They could tell that the infected had been in the cabin with them. Unfortunately, the turn rate at night seemed to be accelerated faster than during the day. People had gone down from infected to raring to attack moments later.

"I'll start working on it after a brief nap," Borris reassured him.

It had been clear early on that Borris was going to be an asset around here. He had jumped in with both feet and hadn't stopped when some of the others had– not that I blamed or faulted them. Regrettably, we had lost our plumber, and Donny's skill for maintenance only stretched so far.

"Hopefully by tonight, we'll have plenty of campers for people to sleep in," Axel murmured as he handed me another cup of coffee.

Even after the rest of the cabins were cleaned out and ready to go, we knew we couldn't force people to go back into the area that may bring back painful and horrible memories. As it was, Axel had determined we wouldn't burn the bodies immediately tonight. Instead, a funeral pyre was built, so some of the people could say goodbye to their friends and loved ones.

A few of the newbies volunteered to keep watch over them. We wanted to make sure nothing living came in too-close contact with them.

Aunt Pam came into the hall, her face red, and it was

clear she had been crying. Corbin hopped up and ran to her. I didn't need to ask to know that we had lost another person. As soon as Uncle Mitch gave the all-clear, she had immediately gone to the med clinic. A few people had some bumps and bruises, so she took care of them while Easton took care of the severe cases.

Mike sat down with another carafe of coffee and took a sip of her own.

"That'll stunt your growth," BJ gently teased her.

Mike tried to hide a blush. "I'm five-eight," she muttered. "I was already a giant compared to most girls in my class. A little bit of coffee won't make a difference."

The longer I spent with her, the more I realized her crush on Kingston had transferred to BJ. BJ seemed oblivious to it all and had teased her most of the night like a younger sister. It was also made clear that she wasn't like most of her peers, and the few that had helped tonight seemed to treat her like a pariah.

"Being tall isn't a bad thing," I gently reassured her. "I know how you feel, but eventually you'll realize most of your classmates were probably jealous of you."

"Says the model," she muttered.

I wasn't going to take her words to heart. I knew she was just lashing out after years of being teased and bullied.

"*She* hasn't modeled in years. That's her sister," Kingston joked before throwing a packet of sugar at her.

She picked it up and opened it with her teeth, shooting him a mock glare and poured it in her coffee with a smug grin.

Corbin came back as Aunt Carol ushered Aunt Pam away. He shook his head with apparent defeat. It hadn't been an easy night for any of us. I leaned into him and allowed Wyatt to take Isa away from me so I could wrap my arms around Corbin and give him further comfort. He seemed to appreciate it as he pulled me in closer.

"We need to make sure we inspect any new people more thoroughly in the future," Wyatt said with a deep sigh.

"Inspect 'em how?" Mike asked solemnly as she took another sip of coffee.

"Chad and I made sure no one was marked or showing any signs of infection before they took a shower," Corbin said in a weary tone.

"Who did it for the girls?" Mike asked as she leaned forward.

A sick feeling hit the pit of my stomach as suspicion entered my mind. Natalie had been directed to conduct the inspections. I knew how she loved to cut corners in the past and had no attention to detail, despite her military training.

I recalled Uncle Mitch asking Katie to help Natalie out, once Aunt Carol had called her out for her lack of performance earlier. According to Aunt Carol, Katie and Nico, her boyfriend, barely did anything yesterday. Katie, Nico, and Emery had tried to behave as if they shouldn't have to do anything, since manual labor was "beneath them."

Katie had been going to school to become a lawyer, and her boyfriend was studying to become a game designer. They still suffered under the illusion that things would be better soon, so they didn't see the need to improve our current surroundings.

"Burns and Katie conducted the inspections for them," Axel said as steel crept into his voice.

Mike shook her head. "No, they didn't. I was taking my shower when the new people began showin' up. When Katie arrived, Burns told her to show 'em to their cabin. She sat with her phone, listenin' to music the whole time the new arrivals took their shower. She never looked over any of them. I didn't even think about inspectin' them. I would have let you know."

"This isn't on you," Wyatt stated grimly as BJ put an arm around her shoulders and squeezed.

She reddened once more and ducked her head.

Axel tensed up, his eyes full of fury.

"One of the girls was in my cabin," Mike said with a horrified whisper. "Her boyfriend seemed really worried about her, but I thought she was goin' through, uh... withdrawals. She reminded me of my mom when she was detoxin', but maybe that wasn't it at all. When I woke up to the first scream, it was from her end of the cabin. Once I realized what was happenin', I opened the window next to my bed and began pushin' out who I could. Then I rang the bell."

I looked around. I hadn't seen Natalie all night. Come to think of it, I hadn't seen Jade or Garth, either. I knew they were assigned to the campers' cabins because they were single, and since it was the beginning of the season, very few cottages were ready to be moved into just yet.

"Where is she now?" Kingston stood up furiously.

"Let's find her," Axel bit out incensed. "Once I find her, I'm kicking her out."

"I'll get a vehicle ready for her and pack enough food and water to last her a week." Uncle Mitch stood and headed towards the kitchens.

"I saw her packin' up her bag with the another woman," Mike stated with a frown. "She said she found a better place for them to stay."

"Hey, Miguel?" Wyatt spoke into a walkie-talkie.

Miguel and three other people were manning the entrance. They hadn't even realized what had happened until we inspected out the only point of entry. Of course, it was all intact. That's when we knew for sure the infected had come in on the bus.

"Go," the walkie-talkie squawked back.

"Did anyone leave early this morning?" Wyatt asked.

"No, sir," Miguel responded immediately.

"Thanks," Wyatt said before looking up. "Well, she's here somewhere."

"Let's find her," Axel commanded.

When Wyatt handed Isa back to me, I didn't protest or even attempt to go with them. After the guys left, including BJ and Trevor, Mike came over to sit next to me.

"If she had just done her job, all those poor people wouldn't be dead," she said in a horrified whisper.

She surprised me when she allowed me to pull her in close for a hug. I had no words to comfort her with, though, because I carried the same guilt.

Chapter 23

I must have fallen asleep for a little while, despite the emotions running through me. It took me a moment to realize Isa was no longer sleeping on my chest and Mike was lying in my lap. I looked around, startled, afraid I had dropped the baby.

"She's in the playpen," Sylvia said soothingly as she handed me a cup of coffee.

"Thanks," I murmured, blinking the sleep away from my eyes. "How long have I been sleeping?"

"A little over an hour," Sylvia stated just as I heard raised voices outside. She grimaced. "They found Burns." Sylvia may not have returned to the hall, but she, Joe, Cal, and Chad had volunteered to open their cabin up to those who chose not to return down the hill. I knew she'd had a sleepless night like we'd had.

"It's all her fuckingfault," Mike murmured as she stretched, then she sat up and winced. "Sorry for my potty mouth and fallin' asleep on you."

"You're fine," I murmured as I patted her.

In a short amount of time, the girl had really grown on me. If I had a little sister, I would've wanted her to be exactly like Mike.

She stood up and shook her head as if she were shaking her tiredness away. "I'm gonna go check on the girls."

She was talking about the cows. I knew she was

exhausted, but it didn't seem to stop her drive and hard work ethics. I admired her, but I didn't want her to burn herself out or think she needed to work herself ragged. She needed to be just a fifteen year old at times. I could see that we would have to monitor her to prevent her from over-working herself.

"You should eat first," I told her as I noticed Trudy, Winnie, and Aunt Carol loading the steam tables.

"Chad and Sam are already taking care of them," Sylvia quickly reassured Mike.

Another scream was heard from outdoors, and I couldn't resist standing up to look out the window. I could see my guys, Uncle Mitch, Eddie, and quite a few people outside, with Natalie in the middle of the crowd.

Isa startled awake, and I scooped her up. "Shh, shh, shh," I cradled her to my chest and gently rocked her.

It had been nearly two hours since she'd last eaten. Unlike formula, I found out, breastmilk didn't seem to keep her full as long. I frowned when I realized I had left all her milk up at the cabin.

"Is Stephanie still in the back?" I asked Sylvia.

"No." Sylvia shook her head. "Easton and Aunt Pam took her to the clinic to do an ultrasound. She doesn't think she's going to last another week, let alone two. She told me if you needed more milk, she has some in the fridge up at the main house."

I nodded, relieved that Isa didn't seem overly hungry yet as she settled back onto my chest.

"I guess I'll go get some more milk," I murmured.

"I can go get it," Mike volunteered.

"No, thanks, hon. You eat." I smiled at her as I headed towards the door.

I stopped short when I realized I would have to weave

through the people still sleeping if I headed towards the side door. After their night, I expected them to want to get a little bit more sleep.

So I had no choice but to exit the front, and quite frankly, I wanted to avoid the latest drama.

Natalie needed to leave. Natalie had proven to be a liability to our community. Because of her carelessness and blatant disregard for a direct order, she caused a lot of people their lives.

I stepped outside, pausing at the sound of Natalie's desperate cry.

"I did inspect them!" Natalie was crying as she fought against Kingston's and Corbin's hold. "They didn't have anything on them."

Natalie, Jade, Garth, and Nico looked like they had been woken up and dragged out as they were. I had a suspicion they had found one of the cottages to crash in. Just not any of the ones near us.

I knew they'd had an issue with where they were placed the other day, but they had lived in harsher conditions when they were overseas. I figured that after years in the military, they would have become accustomed to less than ideal conditions, especially if it was a temporary situation.

"What's going on?" Katie came around the corner, slipping on her hoodie. She stopped short when she saw Nico shirtless and only wearing a pair of sweatpants. "I thought you had front gate duty." She looked at him inquisitively.

Wyatt laughed humorously as he looked over at his sister. "Did you really believe that line? When has he ever done more work than he had to?"

It was no secret that Wyatt didn't like Nico. Apparently, Katie and Nico had been dating for a year, and he had accompanied her to the 4th of July family get together last year. I had heard Wyatt make disparaging remarks against Nico, and admittedly he rubbed me the wrong way as well. He behaved entitled, vain, and arrogant.

"Did you inspect the new arrivals yesterday?" Axel crossed his arms over his chest, looking intimidating, drawn up to his full height.

Katie looked further confused. "No, Dad told me to go help Natalie, and she asked me to show the girls the cabins when they came out of the showers. Why are you in your pajamas?" she looked at Nico.

Nico refused to look at her or respond as he glared at Wyatt.

"Because of your carelessness and desire to do as little as necessary, thirty-one people lost their lives," Wyatt snapped. "Because of you two, some people lost their mothers, fathers, sons, daughters, brothers, sisters, aunts, uncles, parents. Are you going to explain to that three-year-old boy inside that you were the cause of his mom and dad dying and possibly his six-year-old sister as well?"

I cringed and tensed up as I realized the death toll had risen. Thank God for Mike's quick thinking, because she had been able to grab the three-year-old in question, tossing him out the window when she realized what was going down. Who knew how many other people would have suffered had it not been for her?

"Wyatt," Uncle Mitch warned him softly. I knew he wasn't trying to excuse his daughter's behavior, more like he was trying to calm Wyatt down.

Katie looked crestfallen, and her eyes immediately filled with tears. "What are you talking about, Wyatt?"

"Did you really think we only wanted you to show people to their cabins? Didn't you think it was odd that Burns was only sent to sit and watch people take showers? You're going to school to become a damn lawyer, Katie! You graduated with a 4.0 average. How could you have been so dense, or was it just another way for you to demonstrate that you think you are too good to do any work?" Wyatt said with deadly calmness.

"I didn't know!" Katie sobbed. "I just did what she told me to do."

I wanted to feel bad for Katie. A part of me did, but Wyatt was right. She was ridiculously smart and should have realized she wasn't there just to hang out.

"I did my job," Natalie snarled as tears and snot ran down her face. "This virus is unpredictable, and you know that."

"You didn't inspect everyone," Officer Rhys spoke up at the back of the crowd.

He stepped forward with another man I didn't recognize. Between them, they carried a slip of a woman. I assumed she was the one Mike thought was detoxing, because she was almost frighteningly thin. She was covered in blood, and I had to force myself to look at her despite the roiling sickness in my stomach.

Officer Rhys leaned forward and lifted her shirt slightly. There was no denying the evidence of a bite mark on her stomach. I didn't study forensic science or was an expert on wounds, by any means, but there was no doubt that the teeth indentations were old. Judging by the bruising and deterioration of the skin around the mark, it wasn't recently acquired. It reminded me of the bruising I received in tournaments. I had sported quite a few of them, even with the protective equipment. By my guess, she received the wound approximately three or four days ago.

"That wasn't there." Natalie still insisted on sticking to her lie.

"It's been there for at least three days," Officer Rhys confirmed my suspicions as his jaw clenched in something akin to anger.

"Well, with the evidence presented before us, who thinks she should remain here?" Uncle Mitch stated as he stepped forward.

I hadn't realized Uncle Mitch was pretty much putting Natalie's fate in the hands of those gathered around.

Natalie looked over at Garth and Jade. "Really? None of you are going to have my back, after I've had yours time and time again?" Then she smirked towards Katie and Nico. "Maybe I rushed things because Nico was waiting on me, but I shouldn't be punished for a mistake."

Jade looked away.

Garth shook his head. "You messed up, Nat. Big time." He looked shaken and truly horrified by his friend's actions. His head hung down in shame, as if his association with her made him culpable.

"Don't place the blame on me," Nico scoffed. "You told me when and where to meet you. I didn't orchestrate any of this." He looked over at Katie. I think he was silently trying to beg her for forgiveness, but his eyes showed no remorse. It was evident by his cocky stance this wasn't the first time he had cheated on her, and if she remained with him, I doubt it would be the last.

"We will be driving you to the road," Corbin told Natalie. "Your Jeep is waiting for you there. It's already stocked with a week's worth of food. You are no longer welcome here, Burns."

Natalie began to lash out and kick with everything she had. I could tell the men were struggling to keep their hold on her and their tempers, and knowing them, they would never hit a woman. I moved forward, hoping to help them out a smidge. I passed Isa off to Wyatt and walked over to Natalie. Then I pulled back my fist and smashed it into her jaw. She immediately stopped thrashing about, and her eyes rolled back. She was dazed but not knocked out entirely.

I wasn't generally a violent person. I took my frustrations and aggressive energy out in the ring and never got in fights outside of it. Hitting her was way more satisfying than I'd anticipated. She deserved far more for her transgressions.

"That should make her more compliant," I said coldly as I stepped back.

Wyatt chuckled maliciously before placing an arm around my shoulders and squeezed me close. I watched as Kingston and Corbin dragged her to a running, waiting vehicle.

"Be lucky they're... holding me back, you... bitch," Natalie slurred as she was hauled away.

"Nico, you can go with her," Katie said tearfully. "I don't want you here anymore, and since you were cheating on me with her, you belong with her."

"What about you?" a woman sobbed out. "I lost my son and husband because of you, too."

Everyone went deathly silent.

"Does anyone else feel that she's guilty?"

It seemed to pain Uncle Mitch to ask the question. He was a fair man. If he determined to take it to a vote and they found her guilty, I knew he would do what he had to do, blood or not. He hadn't heard from his son MJ in days, and we had no clue if he was safe or where he was, but my uncle would still do what was best for the community, even if it meant losing another child.

"She may have acted with naivety, but she never knew she was supposed to inspect everyone," Axel spoke up first.

Natalie began yelling once more, but the guys had her hands zipped-tied behind her back and sitting on the tailgate of the truck.

"We're sorry for you loss, Tara, but Katie can't be held accountable for what she didn't know," Officer Rhys spoke up quietly. "I lost my wife and sister-in-law because of someone else's carelessness as well. I understand your need to blame someone. Katie may have been clueless, but she shouldn't be held responsible for last night."

I could see the relief in Uncle Mitch's eyes before he carefully masked it. "Does anyone else find her blameworthy?" I knew he was just trying to be cautious.

No one else spoke up, and Katie stepped into her father's arms. "I'm sorry. I'm so, so sorry! I didn't know. I promise I'll do better."

Uncle Mitch held her close and patted her back.

"Let's go, Nico," Natalie said with jagged tears.

"Nah." Nico shook his head with a smirk. "You weren't that good of a lay."

His audacity knew no bounds, and I hated him even more.

"Leave!" Katie sobbed. "I don't want you here anymore."

Corbin and Kingston stepped forward to grab Nico next, but Uncle Mitch held his hand up. "We can't throw him out because he has reprehensible morals. As much as I despise the guy, he hasn't committed any crime against the community. Did you want to stay or go with her?"

"I'm staying," Nico said haughtily. "I came with Katie instead of going home to my own family."

"You don't even like your family," Katie protested. "You wanted to come here."

"Sorry, honey, but we can't put him out because you're upset at him. However," Uncle Mitch quickly added as Nico smirked. "You, Nico, are on probation. Not because of how you treated my daughter, but because you've been hiding and trying to avoid working."

He looked around the gathering crowd and addressed them, too. "Life isn't like we once knew it. It isn't going to be easy, and we're going to have to work for our comfort. We will be holding a funeral for the lives we lost last night, but beginning tomorrow, no one is exempt from working. You will work in your assigned sections. Your workgroup leaders will report to me. If you don't work, you don't eat. If you continue not to work, we'll be putting you out. No one gets a free ride here. I'll explain more after breakfast.

"For all our newcomers, I'm sorry, truly sorry for your introduction to our community. If you want to leave, I'll understand. I also don't expect any of you to work today, and my wife and sister-in-law will be coming around to visit some of you later."

There was silence after his announcement. I saw a few people whispering to each other, probably contemplating their next move. Even with what had occurred last night, I was positive our community was the safest place to be in our new world.

It wasn't long before the whispering stopped, and Aunt Carol announced from behind us that breakfast was ready.

Chapter 24

I closed my eyes and sighed as I leaned back into Axel's chest. I had crawled into his open legs, seeking comfort. He pulled me in closer and wrapped his arms around my middle. I tried to let the stress of the day go as I absorbed the warmth of the fire and relaxed to the sound of Wyatt playing his guitar.

"Want one?" Rhys asked as he held out two beers.

I smiled and took one. "Thanks."

"Thanks, man," Axel said as he tapped his bottle against the other man's.

At first, when Corbin and Kingston suggested a bonfire at the RV lot, my first reaction was to decline, but now I was glad I had ignored my initial reservations. I thought it was what most of us needed after another physically and emotionally draining day.

We were able to acquire a substantial amount of RVs. The older couples and families with younger kids ended up taking the spots in the front half. The younger guys and girls like BJ, Mike, and Felix chose to take the back half.

The back half also boasted a large bonfire pit. Sylvia, Rhys, and I had temporarily commandeered Mike's new camper to put all the children down for the night while we relaxed by the bonfire. Easton made sure to put a baby monitor in the camper so we could hear if any of the children woke up.

I took a sip of my beer and barely contained my wince. It was a local brew that was a little on the hoppy side. I never was a big beer drinker unless pizza or crab was involved, but when in Rome....

Wyatt started to strum a tune I recognized as *Stay With Me* by Sam Smith. He looked over at me and winked before he began singing the lyrics. I felt the goosebumps erupt across my skin as his smooth tone caressed me. When he changed the notes to make his voice break out into a high falsetto, I smiled at him.

Someone next to him began to play the guitar, and I still couldn't tear my gaze away from Wyatt. He kept eye contact with me the entire time, and when he was finished, I grinned like a fool.

He bent down and whispered into one of the younger newcomer's ears before he stood, put his guitar down, and held his hands out to me. I didn't want to dance in front of everyone, but it was hard to resist his smile. That and Axel had placed a kiss on my shoulder before grasping my waist and hoisting me up.

I took Wyatt's hands and let him pull me close. The new guy began to play *Kiss Me* by Ed Sheeran, and this time, Wyatt sang to me as he danced with me around the bonfire.

"I wanna dance too," I heard Emery whine somewhere to my left.

When Kingston and Corbin suggested the bonfire, they had left an open invitation to everyone. Most of the older people chose not to join us, but I was surprised by the number of people who had shown up. Wyatt had procured some beer, wine, and liquor for us from the restaurant, and Uncle Mitch had given us his blessings to "let off a little steam."

I ignored Emery as she continued to whine. I tried to shut her out. At dinner tonight, she looked like she was still angry about having to work all day. True to his word, Uncle Mitch had kept her by his side all day. He hadn't shown her any mercy. When he delivered building material to Borris, Emery had to do it. When he helped in the supply building, she had to assist as well. When he helped Chad and Samuel in the poultry house, she was required to pitch in, too. She did a lot of whining, according to Aunt Carol, but she had no other choice but to stay by his side.

Katie, apparently, had learned a lot from last night's nightmare. She had jumped into helping in the greenhouses with both feet. When she was done with that, she had gone up to the campers' cabins and began emptying them so Borris could get in there and erect walls. By the time the project was done, they were hoping to have four decent sized rooms for the transients and people on a probationary stay.

"I need to hold you tonight," Wyatt murmured in my ear as the song ended.

"If you don't mind sharing me with Easton," I whispered back to him.

When I had visited Easton earlier tonight to make him come to dinner, I could tell the day had emotionally drained him. Only the six-year-old girl remained from all our critically injured. Eddie had offered to "take care" of the others that had turned, but Easton almost wore his responsibility like a heavy mantle. He chose to do it, and I knew it weighed heavily on him.

If Aunt Pam hadn't forced him from the clinic and reassured him that she was going to remain there- in addition to a couple of guards- he would have stayed there all night. I already told him he was sleeping with me tonight. I may have only known him for a few days, but I knew he took comfort from physical touch.

I wanted to just hold him and allow him to take comfort and strength from me.

"I'm okay with that." Wyatt smirked.

"My turn," Kingston insisted, pushing Wy out of the way and twirling me around.

The music changed to a faster number, and I found myself laughing and smiling as Kingston danced eccentrically with and around me. Kingston was seriously a great dancer. He gyrated his hips and moved his body like a practiced dancer, and I would have to be blind to not notice his passionate moves. I began to wonder if those hips moved just as well in the bedroom. In no time, I was getting all hot and bothered by his seductive moves.

Sylvia jumped up and pulled her men up with her. Soon she was sandwiched between Joe, Cal, and Chad. My eyes widened slightly when I noticed the touches between Chad and Sylvia. I hadn't realized they had started gravitating towards each other as well.

Other people joined us, and I just let the atmosphere carry me away from the pain, fear, and hurt. One song blended into another, and all the guys took their turn dancing with me, save Axel. Wyatt couldn't do anything but slow dance, but I was okay with that. Corbin was comical when he danced, but he had some moves. Some. Easton and Kingston were the most skilled, by far.

Axel didn't seem to want to join the festivities. He casually sipped his beer and talked to Rhys most of the night. I wouldn't say he was having a horrible time, but I knew he wasn't losing any of his careful control. He remained alert and watchful. I could tell the big man was still feeling responsible for last night, but unlike Easton, there were no cuddles or coaxing to get him out of his somber mood.

I was out of breath and ready to take a break when I went back over to him and curled up into his arms once more. I took in the group and the conversations and general camaraderie around the fire. Even in these trying times, people were opening themselves up to new beginnings. They were meeting new people and bonding over shared experiences.

I noticed BJ had met a girl today. She was pretty and

seemed nice, but I could tell it had bothered Mike.

Mike refused to go near him or talk to him despite their closeness the night before. I felt terrible for her, but she was young, and I was sure someone would recognize her worth someday.

Besides, I hoped she realized my brother was eighteen, and at fifteen, he wouldn't look at her the way she wanted him to.

"Having fun?" Axel asked with a gentle, teasing tone.

"It was exactly what I needed," I admitted to him before stealing his beer from his hand and taking a long pull from it.

He raised a brow at me as his lips twisted up slightly. "Thirsty?"

"Just a little bit," I said saucily.

He chuckled and pulled me in close. He lowered his head to my bare shoulder and kissed it, then buried his head in my hair and inhaled. "Has someone already claimed your bed tonight?" he asked.

I nodded. "Wy and Easton," I told him and wished we had a bed big enough for all of us.

"Good," he murmured. Always the martyr. The one that always put his team's desires above his own. "They seem to need you tonight."

"What about you, JS Tacka," I teased him. "Will you ever tell me when you need me?"

He grinned, and once again, my breath was taken away at the beautiful sight. "Yes, but my team's needs will always supersede mine."

I rolled my eyes and grasped his face in my hands before placing a kiss on the corner of his mouth. "One day, I'll figure out a way to break you of that habit," I taunted him.

"Oh yeah?" he flirted.

"Yeah," I answered with conviction.

He captured my lips with his own. I melted into him and took comfort in his open display of affection for me. For someone who didn't like kissing and had used sex as a release and not an emotion, he had no reservations in showing me how much I had come to mean to him.

He put his hands through my hair and tilted my head back, taking more command of our kiss. I slid my tongue along his and moaned. My turned-on state only heightened under his passionate demonstrations.

"I need new tennis shoes." Emery planted herself in front of us.

I sighed at her rude interruption.

"So?" I asked her with a raised brow.

Why was she always so determined to engage me in her drama? I was having a great night, and all she wanted to do was ruin it. I knew she was upset that Trevor wouldn't dance with her. She behaved as if she hadn't grown up with him, too.

Trevor hated dancing, and unless you fed him a lot of alcohol, he wouldn't ever be caught on a dance floor, even a makeshift one.

"I was talking to him," she sneered at me.

"So?" Axel asked her with a deadpan look.

"Em, I told you I'd figure it out," Trevor stated as he tried to pull her back to their seat on the other side of the fire. "We're here to enjoy the night."

"Well, I'm not enjoying myself, and you say a lot of things. You fail to come through with most of your statements," Emery snarled. "I need new shoes. I don't have enough underwear. My flat-iron broke, and I need new Armani Beauty Silk Foundation."

"And you're telling Axel this, why?" Kingston asked as he

took a seat on the other side of Axel and me.

"If you're out running around, I need those items," Emery explained as if Kingston was dense.

I blinked at her. Seriously, what did she not understand about our new situation? We weren't making a run to the local department store for our enjoyment. We weren't running out for a gallon of milk and driving by a store she wanted stuff from.

Kingston began to laugh uproariously as the baby monitor started emitting a baby's cry.

"I got her," Easton reassured me as he headed towards the camper.

How he had recognized Isa's cry impressed me beyond belief.

"How does that work?" a younger woman in her mid to late twenties crept over.

I recognized her as one of the women who had helped Aunt Carol, Trudy, and Winnie in the kitchens for most of the day.

"I mean, I need... lady stuff," she explained.

"I have some of that up at my cabin," I reassured her. "Do you need it now? If not, I'll bring some to the dining hall in the morning. If you don't feel comfortable with that, I can drop it off in the med clinic."

"The dining hall will work." She grinned. "Thanks."

"Have you been hoarding stuff?" Emery protested out in anger. "I saw you with a cold Starbucks Frappuccino earlier. Where did you get it from? I looked in the fridges, I couldn't find any."

"Emery, relax, I told you I'd figure it out." Trevor attempted to pull her back once more.

"First off," Wyatt stepped up into Emery's space.

"Anything Avery has, she has gotten on her own. She's been risking her life to obtain those items. Second off, you had a chance to fill a vehicle with all the items that you may want or need before we got here. If you were too stupid to think about your necessities over your wants, that's on you. Third off," he looked around the now silent campfire, "Avery may have held back some stuff for herself, but the majority of the items have gone to the supply shed. She worked to get those items and barely held any items back."

"Then give me a key so that I can get some." Emery held out her palm.

Her sense of entitlement baffled me. She behaved as if we were all her slaves, here to do her bidding and satisfy her wants. She still had this convoluted notion that she could do and say anything she wanted without giving anything in return.

Corbin, Wyatt, and Kingston began to laugh mirthlessly again. "There's a reason you don't have a key, princess," Corbin scoffed. "Those items are for the community, not for your own personal use to use at will."

"Seriously, Em, we were having a good night, why must you always start stuff?" BJ huffed. "We aren't going to hand you over the keys so you can treat it as your own personal stores. We need to stock the building before we hand out everything all willy nilly. Until then, we are only handing out what is necessary. And," he interrupted her when she opened her mouth, "what we think is necessary, not what you think is. You have already proven your priorities."

"I ruined my shoes in the fields today," another guy piped up. "Do you have a pair of size twelve boots?"

"I only have two pairs of socks," another man added. "Do you have any extras?"

"If the items are for the community–" Another man who instantly rubbed me the wrong way, came swaggering forward

—"when can we look and grab what we need?"

Axel tapped my shoulder, and I leaned forward, understanding his need to stand. He took a few steps forward as if he was asserting dominance over the man, just as Chad and Corbin flanked the man's sides.

"Let's get one thing clear," Axel said quietly, but his voice carried around the clearing. "I know some of you are struggling." He looked over at Emery. "I understand some of you may not realize what's truly going on here, but let me make it clear to you all, as I will tomorrow morning if there are any other misconceptions.

"My recovery team volunteered to put themselves in danger, time and time again to acquire goods for the community. Just because it's there doesn't mean we'll hand it out like candy." He looked over at the first two men. "I'll make sure you get your socks and shoes. You need them, and according to Josh and Chad, you've worked hard to earn that and then some. You put in the work, you get the rewards. We might not have what you want or need at the time, but we'll try to do our best. Even then," he looked at Emery, "I highly doubt we'll be getting a specific makeup brand because you're high maintenance enough to believe you're entitled to it."

"We'll start a list tomorrow," Easton promised as he cradled Isa to his chest, feeding her. "It'll be at the table near the door. As Axel said, we may not have what you want, and we might not be able to ever get it, but we'll try. And just because it's on the list doesn't mean we'll ever even try to get it, to be honest. Food and clothes are our priority, so if your... hairdryer broke, sorry, see if someone else has one. We won't put ourselves in harm's way for it."

"*I* need it," Emery snarled out.

"Trev?" Corbin said in warning.

Trevor nodded and bodily began to move Emery away as she screamed curses at us. Corbin and Trevor had a heart to heart earlier today. I didn't know what was said, but it seemed like they were working on their relationship again. I was okay with that; in fact, I was more than pleased about it. Aunt Pam seemed so happy to see her sons talking again, too. Mine and Trevor's past shouldn't affect their present.

Corbin might be angry or disappointed by the treatment Trev had put me through, but he was still his brother. Nearly losing Trevor last night was a huge wake-up call for him. They may have grown apart over time, but they had talked at least weekly for a while there. I knew Corbin wanted to mend their relationship. He loved his brother, flaws and all.

"How does one get on the recovery team?" A big beefy man stepped up. "I was a correctional officer before. I don't mind manning the gates, but I'll go crazy if I have to be locked down all the time."

Axel looked over at Rhys, and he gave him a subtle nod. I knew Rhys and Axel began to have a friendship, of sorts. I even thought Rhys had become the unofficial work captain for the security in the community. Uncle Mitch seemed just as impressed with him. Since Rhys had been out there with the other man, I assumed Axel was deferring to his judgment.

"Two days from now, once we get into a rhythm, my team and I will begin our morning workouts," Axel stated. "It begins there. If we see something in you, we'll be glad to take you on."

"Is it open to anyone?" Nico strutted forward.

"Yes and no," Wyatt spoke up immediately. "Your work captains will have to approve, for right now, there's no way in hell we'll trust you out there."

"I need to run out and get stuff, too," Nico barely concealed his sneer.

"That right there is why I doubt you'll ever make it," Axel pronounced. "My team doesn't go out for their selfish needs or wants. They have the community in mind first and foremost. I don't think you could ever get your head out of your ass long enough to recognize that, Nico."

Almost everyone laughed at his assertion. Nico nearly growled as he stomped away. At least he had the intelligence to walk away when he should.

"What are the parameters for approval?" Mike spoke up next.

Samuel and three other teens began to laugh. "You're just a kid. They ain't letting you leave."

I immediately bristled at his smug tone and began to speak.

But Chad beat me to the punch. "Where were *you* last night?" he asked Samuel.

Samuel immediately stopped laughing. "I was with my friends down at the docks." He visibly gulped. He may be a bit of a bully and had teen brashness about him, but he wasn't completely oblivious. He knew he'd screwed up.

"And what did you do when you realized what was going down?" Cal asked next.

"I ran to safety," Samuel said sullenly.

"You've been out before, right?" Kingston asked next.

Samuel nodded. I could see he never expected the guys to stand up for Mike.

"Everyone that is armed, drop your weapons," Kingston called out.

I dropped my sais and two knives at my feet. All the recovery teams dropped most of their weapons as well. Mike, followed by the burly correctional officer, Rhys, another woman, and a man I wasn't familiar with, dropped their weapons as well.

"Where's yours, Sam?" Chad asked calmly.

"I don't have any with me, sir." Sam looked highly embarrassed now.

"But you have some?" Kingston inquired. "I heard you're a great hunter. I know you have shotguns and hunting knives."

Sam nodded once more.

"Yet this girl, who you want to scoff and mock, has hers." Corbin frowned. "Do you know where she was last night when the infected began to attack? While you were running?"

Sam hung his head and shook it, along with his friends.

"She rang that bell last night," the woman who had dropped a knife said with a trembling lip. "If I hadn't woken up, they would have gotten my children. She helped hide my sons and me until we could reach safety."

"These are different times," Axel added softly. "We can't take everything we once had for granted anymore."

"Does that mean I can go on runs?" Mike asked, hopefully.

"Mike," BJ started to say, shaking his head, before Corbin interrupted him.

Mike shot him a rebellious look and seemed to brace herself for rejection.

"It's something I will discuss with my uncle," Corbin stated gently. "You're not an adult yet, and, technically, you don't have anyone to make those decisions on your behalf. You are responsible, and I like your instincts and strength, but it's something we need to discuss."

It was such a slippery slope. I would want someone like her at my back, but I couldn't ignore her age. She deserved to contribute the way she wanted to; on the other hand, we would never forgive ourselves if something happened to her while we were out there.

Mike opened her mouth mutinously but then snapped it

shut as she realized arguing wouldn't help her case.

There was a stillness in the air, and I looked over at Wyatt. I understood why he fiercely tried to protect me, but Mike and I were worlds apart in some aspects. I was an adult. I was trained to defend myself. Mike worked on pure instincts, which were fantastic, but she was still a teenager with zero additional training.

A beep and a sound of static filled the silent clearing moments before a man's voice came from Axel's hip. "Alpha One," it called.

Alpha One was the call-sign delegated to Axel. Uncle Mitch was assigned to Papa One. It was important that someone had contact with the gates at all times, and right now that was Axel.

"Go ahead," Axel spoke into the walkie talkie that seemed to be permanently attached to his waist.

"We have visitors," the voice called back. "And they're not alone. I'm going to need your help."

Through the transmission, I could hear the unnerving yells and grunting of the infected.

And just like that, our normal night turned to chaos again.

Sylvia immediately took Isa away from Easton.

"Recovery team and security, on me!" Axel barked out.

With no hesitation, the security and recovery team took off running towards the quad barn. I didn't have to look over my shoulder to know Mike wasn't too far behind us.

As I ran towards a four-wheeler, reality sank in. This was our new life. We were going to face situations beyond our wildest dreams—or nightmares, really. We had to be prepared to defend and fight for our new community.

Axel pulled me up on the back of the quad, and one by

one, Easton, Wyatt, Kingston, and Corbin dropped reassuring kisses on my face and lips before climbing on their quads. Their need to comfort me and draw comfort in return warmed my heart. I knew they were an intricate part of me now. They were my future.

I didn't know what tomorrow held, but at least I had them. With them by my side, we could and *would* face it together.

Author's Note

I want to take the time to thank everyone that continues to encourage and assist me with my writing endeavors. To my wonderful readers who continue to support me and give me the confidence to continue reading, thank you for your patience, humbling praise, and for cheering me on.

Thank you to my husband, children, and family for their understanding when I'm not "here" mentally with them. Or understanding when I'm lost in the stories locked in my head. Or lost into my laptop as the words spill from my fingertips.

Thank you, Jenifer, for being there with me, nearly from the beginning, guiding me, advising me, and assisting me! You are amazing. Thank you for imparting your knowledge and wisdom. And thank you for introducing me to more wonderful ladies willing to provide me with honest feedback, suggestions.

Books By This Author

Gifted Connections Series

Peyton's Path Series

Printed in Great Britain
by Amazon

36169329R00248